PENGUIN BO

# I Am Missing

Tim Weaver is the bestselling author of eight books, all of which feature missing persons investigator David Raker. His novels have been selected for the Richard and Judy Book Club, nominated for a National Book Award, and shortlisted for the Crime Writers' Association Dagger in the Library, which considers an author's entire body of work. He also writes and presents the chart-topping podcast *Missing*, about why people disappear and how investigators track them down. A former journalist and magazine editor, he lives near Bath with his wife and daughter. Find out more about Tim Weaver and his writing at TimWeaverBooks.com

# I Am Missing

## TIM WEAVER

PENGUIN BOOKS

PENGUIN BOOKS

UK | USA | Canada | Ireland | Australia
India | New Zealand | South Africa

Penguin Books is part of the Penguin Random House group of companies
whose addresses can be found at global.penguinrandomhouse.com.

Published in Penguin Books 2017
001

Copyright © Tim Weaver, 2017

The moral right of the author has been asserted

Set in 12.5/14.75 pt Garamond MT Std
Typeset by Jouve (UK), Milton Keynes
Printed in Great Britain by Clays Ltd, St Ives plc

A CIP catalogue record for this book is available from the British Library

ISBN: 978–1–405–91784–1

www.greenpenguin.co.uk

MIX
Paper from
responsible sources
FSC® C018179

Penguin Random House is committed to a
sustainable future for our business, our readers
and our planet. This book is made from Forest
Stewardship Council® certified paper.

*For Erin*

# PART ONE

# I

The church was on the coast, perched on the edge of a limestone bluff like a limpet clinging to a rock.

I pulled up outside and turned the engine off.

The wind and the rain shifted the Audi on its axle, the skies slate grey, the sea fierce and choppy. The building was three miles outside of Christchurch and, across the water, lost in a fine gossamer mist, the Needles drifted in and out of view like rudderless ships. As I grabbed my notepad from the back seat, I remembered the time my wife and I had taken a ferry over to the Isle of Wight, bumping across the Channel in a winter storm, and felt a twinge of regret that it could only ever be a memory.

I locked the car and headed to the church.

The door was open. Inside, I found ten wooden benches, a stone altar at the front, and a stained-glass window above that. Despite the weather outside, the image in the glass was leaking a coloured reflection across the nave. Against the cracks in the stone floor, a scene from the Last Supper moved like a puddle of oily water.

He was sitting in the second row on the left, his body pressed tightly against the end of the pew, his hands loosely together on the bench in front, as if he were about to say a prayer, or had just finished one. He wore a blue raincoat and grey beanie, and I could see one of his boots, poking out from under the bench. It was spattered in mud and badly scuffed.

I was almost level with him by the time he seemed to realize I'd arrived. He turned on the pew, dropped his hands to his lap and looked at me with an expression half-way between worry and relief.

'Mr Kite?' I said.

'Yes.' He got to his feet. 'Yes, that's me.'

'I'm David Raker.'

We shook hands. They were small, just like him, and bone dry. I could feel scratch marks on his fingertips – cuts, maybe, or callouses – and there were marks on his face too: new scars, the biggest in a fat arc from his chin to his lip.

'Thank you for coming, Mr Raker.'

'David's fine,' I said. 'Sorry I'm a bit late. I know we said ten o'clock.'

'Don't worry.'

I looked back up to the window, to the vaulted ceiling. 'I've worked a lot of cases, but I can't remember any of them starting inside a church.'

He smiled briefly. 'Do they ever end up here?'

I studied him, his eyes shifting from me, along the nave, to the front of the church. Two wooden funeral biers – the stands upon which a coffin was placed – had been collapsed and were leaning against the wall. His gaze lingered on them.

I replied, 'I try to prevent that from happening if I can.'

He attempted another smile, but it got lost halfway to being formed, and it made me think he'd probably glimpsed the truth already: that I could only try to affect a person's fate once I knew they were alive. When someone was already dead, and all you were returning to the families was bones and earth, it became a different job. You became a sort of artist, painting a picture of motivation and reason; someone who constructed narratives from the things people left behind.

'You didn't say much on the phone, Mr Kite.'

'Richard,' he said quietly. 'I know I didn't say much. I'm sorry. I don't like talking about this sort of thing over the phone. I'm not good on phones. I prefer talking to people face-to-face.'

'Okay,' I said, and watched him for a moment.

He looked sad, weighed down. That wasn't unusual. In my line of work, I saw that all the time. But there was something else, hidden behind his anguish. He seemed confused somehow, as if uncertain of himself, the expression strangely out of place on a guy who didn't look older than thirty-five. He forced a smile again, seemingly aware of it, but it didn't go away. It was anchored in his eyes, in the crescent of his mouth, and it had spread and thrived like the roots of a weed. I'd tried to find evidence of him online after his call, of a life lived out on social media like everyone else his age. But there was nothing. I couldn't find any trace of Richard Kite anywhere.

'I work here on Tuesdays and Thursdays,' he said, gesturing to his surroundings. 'I help the vicar keep the garden up together – the grounds, that sort of thing. I'm not a gardener, really, but I do my best.' He stopped, his eyes back on the funeral biers. 'Anyway, Reverend Parsons said we could use the room at the back – if you wanted.'

There was an open door at the rear of the church, leading through to a corridor. A yellow bucket was on the floor partway down, catching a leak.

'I'm happy to talk,' I said to him, 'but maybe you should just tell me who it is you want me to find first.'

'Yes, of course.'

He held up an apologetic hand but didn't continue. He looked away again instead, searching the shadows for the words he wanted, his face thin and pale, black stubble lining his jaw, his eyes oddly colourless. And as he did, something struck me: *I've seen him before. I know him from somewhere.*

Had the two of us met at some point?

'I called you,' he said, 'because I know that you find missing people. That's what you do, and that's . . . well, that's what I need.' He stopped, swallowed hard. 'Someone's missing, and I need you to find them.'

'So who is it that's missing?'

I was still thrown by the familiarity I felt. As I waited, I tried to wheel back, to figure out where our paths may have crossed, but I couldn't think. If I'd met him, it wasn't on any case.

'Richard,' I said again, 'who is it that's missing?'

It was like he hadn't heard me, his eyes still probing the corners of the church where the light from the windows didn't reach. But then, just as I was about to repeat myself a third time, he turned to face me.

'I am,' he said.

I frowned. 'You are what?'

'I'm the person that's missing.'

## 2

'I have dissociative amnesia,' he said quietly.

I'd heard of it, although didn't know much about it – but something made sense now. When he'd called me the day before, I'd tried to get information out of him and he'd told me he would prefer to meet in person. He'd referred to the case as *unusual* and *difficult to explain*, and those were enough to get me interested. It had been the sadness in his tone too, his voice carrying the echo of loss that I heard in all the families I helped. I just thought the loss he felt would be for a wife, or a parent, a brother, a sister, a child. But it wasn't any of those.

It was for a life he couldn't remember.

We moved through to the back room. A salt-misted window looked out over a small but well-maintained garden, and then the cliff dropped away and there were just the frills of the copper-coloured shingle and miles of sea and cloud. In front of me, a table had been pushed up against one of the walls. Richard brought two chairs across from a stack in the far corner, and asked if I wanted something to drink. There was a kitchen area – little more than a shelf with a jar of instant coffee and some milk on it – but I'd driven ninety-six miles to get here, so however the coffee came, it was welcome.

After a couple of minutes, he returned to the table, set my coffee down and perched himself on the edge of the chair opposite. He looked nervous and unsettled. Steam curled out of a mug in front of him, his fingers half covering four lines of thick black lettering that read: HOW DOES JESUS MAKE THIS TEA? HEBREWS IT. As I watched him, his head bowed, I thought again about how familiar he was to me.

'Have we met before, Richard?'

He looked up, frowning. Of all the questions he'd expected me to ask first, I doubted that would have been one of them.

'No,' he said. 'I don't think so.'

I couldn't yet see a reason for him to lie, so I let it go and picked up my pen. 'Okay,' I said softly, attempting to put him at ease again, 'why don't you explain what dissociative amnesia is?'

He nodded and cleared his throat, like the words were already sticking to the back of his mouth.

'It's a condition where you forget important information,' he said. 'It's like the brain erases these huge tracts of who you are. It's not the same as the amnesia most people have heard of. With that, you lose these vertical pieces of memory – they're gone and not coming back – but you can remember everything else either side of that: what you did before, what you've done since. Your name, your age, who your family are, where you work – all that sort of thing. With me . . . it's different. I don't have any of that. Vertically and horizontally, everything important to me is gone. I have no memory of who I am.'

'At all?'

'Very little.'

'Is Richard even your name?'

'I *think* so.' He paused. 'When I was first asked what my name was, that was what I remembered it being. It was just there, in my head.' He took one hand away from his mug and began rubbing at an eye. 'With this type of amnesia, the memories aren't always gone for ever – but most of them are buried so deep I might never find them. I've had therapy sessions, I've even had hypnosis, and I've been able to remember a few things. I think I'm called Richard. I think I grew up by the sea. But if you asked me whether I had a girlfriend somewhere, or who my parents were – if my parents are even *alive* – I wouldn't know. I honestly wouldn't know.' His words fell away, and he turned his head and looked out through the rain-smeared window. 'I gave myself the surname "Kite" because I sit here sometimes and watch kids flying kites on the beach down there. I watch them with their parents. I feel sad when I do – jealous, I guess – which makes me think I *must* have had someone who loved me, because why would I feel jealous of those kids otherwise? But I can't remember, so maybe I didn't. I don't know.'

He may only have been in his thirties, but he spoke like someone a lot older. The loss of such important memories – the idea of there being people who may have loved him, and who he may have loved back – had altered him.

'You said you think you grew up by the sea?'

'Yes,' he said.

'Because I'm trying to place your accent.'

His mouth flattened into a half-smile. 'Yes.'

'Other people have mentioned that already?'

He nodded. 'The police spent a lot of time trying to figure out if it was a West Country accent – or whether I was born into royalty. It's a mix of the two.'

9

He was clearly joking about the royalty part, but it was a pretty accurate assessment of how he spoke: most of the time, his accent maintained a kind of elegance, almost what might be termed 'posh', but then he'd hit words like *are* or *there* and he'd start rolling his *R*'s. *Alive* came out more like *aloive*, *gone* as *gahn*. It was a strange symmetry, a line walked between two competing dialects.

'You don't remember anything else about where you're from?'

He shook his head. 'No. I just have this one clear memory of the sea, this strong feeling of being young, and of looking out of a window and on to a beach.'

I finished making some notes and spent a moment going back over my shorthand account of what Richard had just told me.

'I woke up near a lifeboat station.'

I looked up at him.

'That's where they found me. That's where my memory begins. I woke up on the Hampshire coast at the start of the year, right outside a lifeboat station.'

'You woke up on the . . .'

But then I stopped.

'You're the Lost Man,' I said, almost to myself.

He didn't like the name he'd been given. The second I said it, his nose wrinkled and his lip curled and he looked out of the window again, as if wounded by what I'd said. But that was what he'd become known as in the regional press. That was how I knew him: the case had been covered by the media along the south coast, in an effort to try and find out who he was. I hadn't met him, I'd just read about him in the Devon newspapers when I'd been down there visiting my daughter: the young man who'd been found unconscious at the mouth of Southampton Water, with no memory of who he was.

*The Lost Man.*

I'd seen his story at the time, had read about how he couldn't remember anything, even his full name or his family, but the publicity, such as it was – his plea to anyone who knew him to come forward – faded quickly when he got no response. That was why I hadn't instantly made the connection. He looked different now, which was another reason it hadn't clicked: older, more beaten down, even though, in January, he'd had plasters on his face and blood in his eye. Now he just had the scars.

'I'm sorry,' I said.

He shrugged. 'There's no need to apologize. That's what they called me. When all that was happening, I thought, "There's no way they won't find out where I came from. All this coverage, all these newspapers writing about me, someone I know will see it and will come forward and I'll have somewhere to start." But no one came forward. Not a single person.'

'There were no leads at all?'

'None.'

I gave him a moment.

'So you woke up next to that lifeboat station.'

He nodded.

'That's the first thing you remember?'

'Yes.'

'Nothing that happened before then?'

'You mean, do I remember how I ended up there? No, I don't remember anything.'

'What date was it in January again?'

'They found me on Wednesday the twentieth.'

'The people from the lifeboat station?'

'Yes.'

Today was 25 October – over nine months on. It felt like even longer since I'd read about him, since his plight was pushed aside by a million other stories. I'd been a part of that machine once, a journalist consigning people's lives to a footnote before they'd ever really found a voice. That was what the media did. To them, to me back then, nine months was like nine years.

'What was the place called where they found you?' I asked.

'Coldwell Point.'

'Can you remind me where that is?'

'It's a sandbank about a mile and a half long, just where the River Hamble meets Southampton Water. There's not much there. A little car park and a small shingle shore. A slipway. The RNLI station is right on the end of it, as far out along the peninsula as you can get. That's where the guys from the station found me.'

'What were their names?'

'Rory found me first. Rory Yarkley. He was one of the mechanics there. He called another guy over – Simon Griffin. He was one of the shore crew.'

'And you were injured, right?'

He gestured to the scars on his face. There were five, all on his left side – two small ones dotted along the ridge of his cheekbone, two more at the angle of his jaw. The fifth and biggest was much harder to miss. I'd not seen it at the time he was found because, in the photos, it had been covered up with bandaging. But I saw it as soon as I met him, and I looked at it more closely now: a white, worm-like blemish stretching from the cleft of his chin to the corner of his lip. Police thought he might have been attacked, or had fallen very heavily on that side of his face, or both, and as he began to roll up his left sleeve, I saw that his elbow was marked with more scarring, his forearm too, the back of his hand.

'It looks like you fell,' I said.

'Or collapsed. Or was attacked.'

'Do you *think* you were attacked?'

He shrugged. 'I don't know.'

It was said with a bleakness that was difficult to ignore. I glanced outside – the rain was getting harder, the mist thickening – and tried to gather my thoughts.

'Did you have any broken bones?'

'No.'

'Just cuts and bruising?'

'Yes. The smaller ones had already healed by the time I was found, but this one . . .' He placed a finger against his chin. I could see star-shaped stitch marks tracing the line of the scar. 'This one became pretty badly infected. The middle of my face was swollen and there was pus coming out of the wound. I got some sort of bone infection off the back of it as well. It was bad.'

'Were you dressed when the RNLI guys found you?'

'Yes. I had trousers on, a T-shirt, a fleece. One of my shoes was missing.'

'What happened after that?'

'They took me back to the lifeboat station, put a blanket around me, got me something hot to drink, and called the police. While we were waiting, they started asking me questions – who I was, where I was from, if there was anyone they could call for me, that sort of thing – and I couldn't answer most of them. All I could really give them was my name.'

'Are you still in touch with them?'

'No,' he said. 'Rory called me for a while, to see how I was getting on – if there was anything new, an update. I think, in a weird way, him and Simon felt this sense of responsibility for me, because they were the ones that found me.'

'But they don't call you any more?'

'No. I still don't know who I am and I still don't know where I came from. What else is there left for them to ask?'

It was difficult to know how to reply to that.

'Where did you go from there?'

'A local charity paid for a bed in a hostel for me. I was very appreciative, don't get me wrong, but I hated it. I had to share a room with three other people, they were all coming and going the whole time, it was noisy and disruptive, and I felt like some sort of alien there. I couldn't talk to any of them about anything, because I knew nothing. I mean, imagine someone asking you what your full name is, or where you're from, and all you can say to them is, "I don't know." The people I roomed with, they just ended up staring at me, like I was some car accident at the side of the road. The best thing that ever happened was when the newspaper coverage started, because Reverend Parsons saw it and that was when he asked to meet me.'

'He helped set you up in this area?'

'Yes. He's been good to me.'

I looked down at my notes.

'Do you know if there are CCTV cameras at Coldwell Point?'

'One, apparently. It was on the side of the RNLI station, but it didn't work. Police told me it was due to be repaired the following week. So even if someone came into the car park in a vehicle and left me there, or they approached by boat, or I swam all the way to shore from wherever it was I went overboard, none of it makes much difference. I can't remember and there's no CCTV to help me.'

'You have absolutely no recollection of the lead-up to being found out there? You said you have these slivers of memory – like growing up by a beach.'

'*Probably* growing up by a beach.'

I just looked at him as he shook his head.

'Nothing,' he said. 'I remember nothing about what happened to me and I have no idea how I ended up where I did. No one came to claim me after I was found. I was discovered out there, on that river, alone – and I'm still alone now.'

# 3

I made us some fresh coffee, even though he'd hardly touched his first cup, and after giving him a moment to recover some composure, I said, 'That memory you have of growing up by a beach – why is it you feel it's from your childhood?'

'I'm not sure.' He paused, trying to articulate his thoughts. 'It's difficult to explain. I guess that's just how memory works, right? You remember something, an image or a feeling or whatever, and you attach some sort of time-line to it. You know *when* it was, automatically, without having to process it. I know it's a memory from when I was growing up. I just know it. But I couldn't tell you why.'

'What else do you recall about it?'

He drew the mug of coffee towards him. 'I'm standing at a window, looking out, and I can see a beach. The way I see it now, in my head, it goes on for ever, stretching as far in each direction as it's possible to go. That makes it sound exotic, but it's not like that at all. It's not some tropical island paradise. It's typically British. It's like looking out of the window today. The skies are grey. It's really miserable, it's drizzling.'

He stopped, gazing into space, the light from the window dancing in his eyes as he tried to draw more details out of the black. Attempting to coax memories out of Richard Kite would be dangerous. I wasn't a psychiatrist or a psychologist, and I had no training, so anything I tried would be rudimentary at best – and I'd interviewed enough people in my life to know that pressurizing them into remembering fine details generally didn't lead anywhere useful. Interviewees like Richard, desperate for answers and keen to progress a search, would try their hardest to fill in blanks, and that was how witness statements became mangled. Recall got overstretched, memories got unintentionally tweaked, and then you spent the days and weeks afterwards chasing down bogus leads.

'Okay,' I said. 'Anything else apart from that memory?'

'Just one other thing. I have this memory of a TV programme. It was animated and there was this television mast on top of a hill, and it was sending out all these signals into the sky. It could have been a kids' TV show, I guess. It had that sort of feel about it.'

'So you think it could have been part of an intro sequence?'

'Like the opening credits or something? I don't know. Maybe.'

'Do you think you could draw it for me?'

'Draw it?'

'Don't worry,' I assured him. I turned my pad around and handed him my pen. 'It doesn't have to be a work of art. Just put down what you can remember.'

When he was done, I took the sketch from him. It showed a triangular TV mast, criss-crossed with studded iron girders, projecting crescent-shaped signals from its apex. The higher the signals got, the wider they became. It was like the universal symbol for Wi-Fi. He'd also drawn a few flowers at the foot of the mast.

I tried to think if I'd ever seen anything like it before, but if it was a kids' show, I hadn't come across it, and if Richard had watched it as a child, it could be a couple of decades old by now. I'd have to dig around some more.

'Anything else?' I asked. 'Anything at all?'

His brow furrowed, the smaller scars whitening as the skin creased at his eyes. 'I know how to swim. I'm actually a pretty good swimmer.' He shrugged, and the rest of the sentence was there, in his face: *Like that makes any difference any more.* 'I'm good with my hands,' he went on, quieter now. 'I can fix things. That comes naturally to me. When I do stuff around here, when I do stuff at the caravan park up the road, it's easy. Mike, the policeman who was looking after my case, he says he thinks I might have been a mechanic or a tradesman or something like that.'

I nodded. 'What's Mike's surname?'

'Barton. Detective Constable Mike Barton.'

'From Hampshire Police?'

'Yes. He's based in Southampton.'

'When was the last time you heard from him?'

'Two, maybe three months ago.' He sounded disappointed. 'He called to give me an update, to say he's still trying to piece everything together. Maybe he is, I don't know. I want to give him the benefit of the doubt. But, the truth is, I think I'm probably in a filing cabinet somewhere. I mean, why *wouldn't* I be? I'm not in danger. I'm not a danger to anyone else. I understand why it's happened.'

He spoke of acceptance, of understanding why his case had been relegated to a drawer, but his face told a different story. He was hurt, frustrated.

'You work here,' I said, trying to keep things moving,

'and you talked about working at a caravan park up the road too.'

'Yes. It's about a mile away.'

'So you're working two jobs?'

'Kind of. The job at the caravan park is just a basic park-assistant role – it's everything from mowing the lawns to making repairs to cleaning out the toilet block. But it's seasonal. April through to the end of September, it's five days a week; October to March, it's only twice a week. That's why – over the winter – I'm helping out here a couple of days a week. I'm trying to make ends meet however I can, but I can only do it when the people I'm working for are kind enough to accept my situation.'

'Your situation?'

'They have to bend the rules.'

'In what way?'

'I haven't got a National Insurance number, and I can't get one. I'm a non-person. The government won't issue me a new number because no one's allowed to have two, and they must have already given me one before at some point. I've spent hours on the phone to them, trying to explain my situation. I've told them over and over that I don't remember my name. I've sent them letters from the doctors who treated me, from Reverend Parsons, I've sent them cuttings from the newspaper coverage, but it's hopeless. My applications get lost in layers of bureaucracy.'

'Can't they issue you a temporary number?'

'I asked. They stopped doing that in 2001.'

'So by "bending the rules", you mean you're being paid cash?'

'Or I'm not being paid at all. I live at the caravan park,

on-site. They let me live in one of the static vans for nothing – water, electric, gas, it's all included. In exchange, I work the rental cost off in hours. Here at the church, it's just a small job. Forty pounds a day. No one's going to miss that. But the caravan park's part of a chain. They've got sites all along the coast. They can't get caught trying to avoid paying their taxes.'

Again, his words were even-handed on the surface, but it was clear that he'd been wounded by all of this. It flickered in his face the whole time, like a fire that didn't go out. It made me think of someone learning lines by rote – sometimes, hearing Richard, it was possible to think that he had accepted his fate, the intransigence of government, the knowledge that he'd been cast adrift as some sort of refugee; but then you looked at him and the mask slipped. Without an NI number, he was a ghost in the system. He may have been flesh and bone, a living, breathing person sitting across the table from me, but because he wasn't on a hard drive in Whitehall, he was just a mimic, an echo of someone who had existed at some point in history. Employers couldn't hire him because he couldn't pay tax. He wasn't able to sign on, or claim housing benefit. If he walked into a hospital, if he got sick or broke a bone, he wouldn't be seen as an NHS patient. It didn't take much to imagine how traumatic that would become; a build-up of emotion and enmity and heartache, collecting on him like bruises.

'If you're worried about how I'm going to be able to afford to pay you,' he said, a sudden panic in his voice, 'I made some money from all the publicity at the start of the year. I've saved a bit. The church are sponsoring me too. I'll be fine.'

'I wasn't worried,' I said, holding up a hand to him, playing it down, but I had started to wonder how and where the money would come from. I watched him take a long drink of his coffee, and then continued: 'So you have no form of ID at all?'

'No, none.' He shook his head. 'I can't get a passport because I don't know what my name is, or where I was born, or what my birthday is. I don't know who my parents are. I can't get a driving licence because you need another form of ID – like a passport – and an NI number.'

'Which means you have no bank account either?'

'No.'

I didn't press him any further on it, but it underlined how desperate his situation was. Storing banknotes in a drawer in a caravan was his new reality. He needed ID in order to do anything, but he couldn't apply for ID because he didn't know who he was.

'Would you mind me taking a look at your caravan?'

'Not at all,' he said. 'Anything that will help.'

'Do you have a mobile phone?'

'Yes. I bought it in a supermarket – a Pay-As-You-Go plan. That was all I could get.'

'Email? Social media?'

'I have an email account, and the people here at the church set some social media things up for me after I was found – Facebook and Twitter and all of that stuff – to help try and spread the word. But I don't use any social media myself.'

'So you have a computer?'

'A laptop. But not a very good one.'

'I'll need access to that as well. Is that okay?'

'Yes, of course.'

Everything was back to front. Normally, financial trails, emails, texts and phone calls were how I began building a picture of a missing person – who orbited their life, where that person may have gone, the decisions they made along the way, contacts they forged. With Richard Kite, the person I was trying to locate was sitting two feet in front of me. I wasn't exactly sure what I expected to find on his laptop, but if I didn't go through it I risked missing something.

'You mentioned you'd undergone hypnosis earlier.'

He nodded. 'Yes. With Naomi, my therapist.'

'Is she a psychiatrist or a psychologist?'

'I'm not sure I know what the difference is.'

'Has she ever prescribed you medicine?'

'No.'

'Has she ever talked about doing so?'

'Not that I can remember.'

'Psychiatry's a medical specialism, so she could prescribe you medicine if she wanted to. It sounds more like she's a psychologist. What's her surname?'

'Russum.'

I wrote it down. 'How often do you see her?'

'Twice a month now.'

'But it was more often to start with?'

'Yes. To start with, I was seeing her twice a week. We did long sessions in an effort to help me try and remember. Like I said, she put me under hypnosis, but I didn't really respond to that. We also go through photographs of people – figures from recent history, politicians, landmarks, that sort of thing – to see what I remember, who

I'm aware of, and who I'm not. She does it to try and narrow down my exact age, where I'm from, where I was brought up.'

'But she hasn't got anywhere?'

He shrugged. 'No.'

'Where's Naomi based?'

'London. But she comes here. I can give you her address.'

I definitely needed to speak to her, and her being based in London made it convenient to where I lived in Ealing, but she wasn't going to release records of their sessions to me, and I seriously doubted that she would be prepared to give me an overview of them either.

'How do you afford to pay for the sessions with her?' I asked.

'She does them for free.'

'She doesn't charge you anything?'

'No.'

'So she instigated contact with you?'

'Yes. She called me about five weeks after I was found.'

'Did she say why she got in touch?'

A fleeting smile. 'I think she sees me as a challenge.'

*Or she sees you as a meal ticket.* I wasn't necessarily saying I blamed her – a case as extreme as Richard Kite's was big news within the sphere in which she operated. With his permission, she could probably write papers, columns, maybe even go on TV. But her charging him nothing for her time instantly made me want to talk to her. I didn't doubt that she wanted to help him, and I didn't doubt that she was doing the best possible job. But, these days, people rarely did something for nothing.

'So the sessions haven't really got you anywhere?' I asked.

His head dropped, his fingers opening and closing around the mug. 'No. Naomi tells me they're worth it, but what good is it when all I have to fall back on are vague recollections of things that don't even matter? How is my memory of that beach going to help? Or that show with the TV mast? What difference does being a good swimmer make?' He stopped again. 'It's worthless.'

'It might not be.'

'But it probably is.'

'Don't lose heart before we've even started.'

He smiled at me, as if grateful for the words of support, for the fact that I'd agreed to help him in the first place. But, soon, the smile was gone again, and all that was left behind was the sound of the rain.

# 4

Richard said he still had some jobs he needed to finish up at the church, so he gave me the key to his caravan and suggested he meet me there. I headed out to the car and then sat there for a moment, listening to the rain, trying to clear my head. I'd been sucked in by his story, by the things he'd been through, and I was already committed to helping him. But I felt discomfited too, not only because his experience was a complete inversion of a missing persons case, but because, in truth, I felt uncertainty about where to start. I couldn't begin with him, with his family, with his job. I couldn't start with any relationship he'd ever held with anyone. Basically, the only things I had to work with for now were where he'd been found, the condition he'd been found in, the few memories he held on to, and the people that he'd interacted with.

I pushed down the doubts, started up the car and headed for the caravan park. It was about a mile inland, wedged between a couple of farms on the southern corner of the New Forest. The surrounding countryside was pretty, even in the rain: fields rolled off either side of the road, and were divided by high walls of ivy and ash trees that had begun to bronze as autumn set in. From the road, the campsite was hardly visible, but when I followed signs along a tarmacked lane, I discovered six fields of roughly half an acre each. Five of them were for touring caravans, and this time of the year all that meant was a relentless parade of empty pitches. The sixth was for static vans – they were lined up like white cargo containers in eight rows of ten.

I found Richard's a couple of minutes later, tucked away in a far corner, big trees hemming it in. As I got out, I looked to see if he had any neighbours, but the units immediately adjacent to his were dark and empty and looked as if they might have been that way for a while. Further out, a few vans were occupied, likely privately owned and lived in permanently: there were hanging baskets outside, satellite dishes, washing lines and gas barbecues. Most of them, though, clearly hadn't been used since the summer holidays. It gave the place a weird feeling, as if it were at the ends of the earth, and as I opened up Richard's caravan I wondered if this was the best place for him – being here would surely only feed his sense of isolation.

The inside of the van was pretty standard – a tiny kitchen in front of me, a living room with a wraparound sofa, a table and a television, and then a series of cupboards at head height. A narrow hallway steered off right, down to where two bedrooms and the bathroom were. On the table, his laptop was plugged in, recharging, and next to the TV there were piles of DVDs, books and magazines.

The rain sounded like gravel against the roof as I walked towards the two bedrooms. In the first, the bed was unmade, the sheets crumpled, a glass of half-drunk water on the bedside cabinet beside a packet of ibuprofen. Across the hall, in the other room, two single beds had been stripped of their sheets and there was a box sitting on top of one of them.

I pulled it towards me, looked inside and found it was full of cuttings, photocopies and printouts. Richard had collected the media stories that had followed his discovery. I removed a front page from the *Daily Echo*. The headline read THE LOST MAN, and there was a picture of him, staring into the camera, a few days after he was found at Coldwell Point. He looked frightened and confused.

I took the box through to the living area, set it down on the table next to the laptop, and then returned to the bedrooms and started going through his wardrobes. Normally, in the search for a missing person, I felt no compunction about going through the clothes they'd worn and the belongings they'd once held dear. Looking at photos of them alongside the families that were mourning them, at private emails intended only for the recipient – it never bothered me, because if I didn't do it, there was always the risk that something important would be overlooked.

Here, though, it felt different: these clothes were being worn every day, these drawers were being opened; any photographs he had, any notes he'd made or emails he'd sent, it was all part of a life happening now. It felt intrusive even going through the pockets of his jeans – an invasion of the limited existence he'd managed to carve out for himself.

I found nothing in his wardrobes, in his clothes, and there were no photos anywhere. That wasn't so surprising, given he didn't know who he was, where he was from or who his family were, but that also meant the search had immediately begun to contract, and that was unhelpful at the start of a case. I returned to the living area and sat at the table with the box.

At first glance, the media coverage looked limited and most of it seemed to have trod the same path. Even so, I arranged everything into chronological order and then went back through it, trying to plot a course from the moment he was found on 20 January. He'd chosen to do his talking in a controlled environment, where people sympathetic to him – Barton from Hampshire Police; members of the charity Starting Again; Reverend Parsons – were always at his side. He came across as he had at the church: quiet, eloquent, oddly old-fashioned in the way he spoke; timid, sometimes disconcerted and anxious.

I wondered whether his timidity was simply because of what he'd gone through, a reaction to the disorientating nature of memory loss, or whether it was a carry-over from whoever he'd been before. If he'd been timid before he woke up outside that lifeboat station, *why* was he timid? There were other questions too. Had he always spoken as elegantly? What did that say about his education, his family, about the area he was brought up in? I kept coming back to his accent, the strange amalgam of dialects. Surprisingly few of the media outlets had picked up on it, perhaps because it wasn't the most compelling part of the story.

In all, there had been three separate attempts to use the press: one on 21 January, one on 29 January and then a third on 12 February. It was possible to chart the increasing futility of them directly from the decline in the coverage. Off the back of the first push, I found three front pages – one each in the Southampton and Bournemouth *Echo*s, and one in the Plymouth *Herald*. The next week, with no break-through to report, just another plea for information, there were none. Tens of thousands of words about the Lost Man became thousands of words by 29 January, and then – the third time Richard was wheeled out – the story migrated to 'Local' sections, or sidebars, or easily missed pages deep inside the papers. I felt for him, for Parsons too, who had clearly worked hard trying to rejuvenate interest in the case, but less than a month after he'd been found, the Lost Man was already forgotten again.

There was an unintentional side issue too. Enlisting the local press meant the case became something it may not even have been: the story of a local man found at the edge of a Hampshire river. In fact, Richard might not have been from Hampshire at all, or Dorset, or Devon, or anywhere on the south coast, but because he didn't know *where* he was from, the assumption just got made and, understandably for the media based in those areas, that became the heart of the story. Pretty soon after that, it became an accepted truth that Richard Kite was from the local area and the problem with that was that it had a bleed effect. If anyone else in the country was even paying attention to the story in the first place, they would have soon stopped once it looked like the person in question was from the south coast.

Of course, that didn't mean Richard *wasn't* from there. The hard *R*'s that seeded his accent were certainly consistent with the type of dialect you'd find in parts of Dorset, in Devon too. But, so far, nothing I'd heard from him – or read about him in the newspapers – confirmed it for sure one way or the other.

I pushed the box aside and turned to his laptop.

It was an old HP, scuffed along its sides, the keys shaded with grime, the screen specked with dirt. Next to the track pad was a blue sticker saying it had been reconditioned by a local computer repair shop. I punched in the password he'd given me and found a clean, well-organized desktop, with a series of folders and documents on the right-hand side. In one of the folders there were scans of more newspaper articles, some of which were repeats of cuttings I'd already been through. In the next one, I found images he'd sourced from the Internet, hundreds of them: photograph after photograph of different coastlines, cliff faces and lagoons, different-coloured seas and different beaches – sand, shingle, pebble, some shores as white as chalk, others as grey as ash. It was obvious what it was: an effort to try and find the beach he could remember in his head, something that would spark off another memory, a lead, an idea, anything. It had proved every bit as futile as the newspaper coverage.

In one file, composite.jpg, he'd even used an editing program to crudely cut out segments of the other photos he'd collected, then attempted to stitch them all together into one picture that most closely represented what he remembered. It was messy, but I wondered if it might prove useful, not least because what he'd described to me earlier was *almost* like this, but not quite. He'd only talked about a beach, but in the picture he'd included grass in the foreground, before the sand even started – so was this the lawn of the property he was in, or just beach grass?

I moved on in my search, but the only other thing that really grabbed my attention was a Word document. It contained a list of all the things he thought he knew about himself.

> My name is Richard.
> I know how to swim.
> I know how to drive.
> I spent part of my childhood next to a beach.
> I remember a TV show where the

But then the list stopped.

The memory of the TV show wasn't something he could be certain about, and neither really was his recollection of being at the beach as a kid. He knew how to swim because he'd been in a pool or out in the sea, and he knew how to drive because he'd sat behind the wheel of a car at some point and, even if he hadn't taken it out on the road, something had clicked. It was reflex, instinct, knowledge buried deep that had shuddered to the surface. It was possible the TV show was the same, his recollection of the beach as well, but he couldn't be absolutely certain because he couldn't prove them. He remembered the beach, but hadn't been able to locate it. He recalled a TV show, but it could just as easily have been a web video, an advert, even a static image in a comic or magazine that his memory had brought to life. Even his name was a feeling, not a proven fact. That was what made memories so dangerous.

The mind invented things.

As I looked at the list again, rereading the first three lines, I felt profoundly sorry for Richard Kite. In a strange way, his list may have been one of the most distressing things I'd ever read; a short, meagre testament to what his life had become, nine months after he woke up in a world he didn't recognize. He was a man without an anchor to his history. He was a story that couldn't be finished because his story hadn't even been started. He was five incomplete lines on a page – and maybe not even that much.

In the end, the press had been right about something. This was a man that was lost.

# 5

Before Richard arrived back at the caravan, I went through his emails and calls.

His inbox only held one thing of any interest: an information breakdown that Reverend Parsons had written, which he'd then emailed to Richard. It was compiled from various sources: DC Barton, things that had run in the media and been printed or put online, and material that Starting Again, the charity, had been able to get hold of. It wasn't a case file in the traditional sense, but it wasn't far off. I emailed it to myself, and then turned my attention to Richard's phone account.

He'd given me the username and password for it and I'd logged in online and been back through his texts and calls, from 2 February – when he first got a mobile phone – to 24 October, which was yesterday. He made few calls and sent even fewer texts. There were no names attached to the numbers, but it didn't take long to run them down. The numbers that appeared most often were for the warden at the caravan park, the office of his psychologist, Naomi Russum, and Reverend Parsons's landline and mobile. Other numbers turned out to be just as innocuous. Richard had repeatedly phoned an 0345 number during the first few months, which turned out to be a National Insurance helpline. He'd also made calls to a journalist at the *Daily Echo*, Barton at Hampshire Police, and the local doctor's surgery, where he'd gone for check-ups in the weeks after being found. Mostly, though, it was the same people on repeat.

I picked out Naomi Russum's number and tried calling her, hoping to arrange a time to meet, but the line was engaged, and when I tried again ten minutes later it was still engaged. Impatient about getting a better handle on dissociative amnesia, I went online and found some other clinics. After being rebuffed pretty much everywhere, I finally got some success when I called a place in London specializing in dissociative conditions, and spoke to a psychotherapist called Matthew Wilson, who was fascinated by Richard's story.

'I can't talk about Richard specifically,' Wilson said, 'because I don't know him and haven't treated him, but typically dissociative amnesia is categorized as the loss of personal information that would not ordinarily be lost in the process of forgetting something. So it's that autobiographical memory. Some patients can lose everything, even down to well-learned skills and known information about the world, although that's much rarer. What's more common is that the forgotten information – who they are, where they come from, family, history, et cetera – is no longer accessible to the conscious memory, but still influences behaviour.'

'In what way?' I asked.

'You could have a child, say, who was locked in a cellar by an abusive parent, over and over again for years. With this kind of generalized amnesia, that person may have a fear of being in cellars or basements, or may outright refuse to go into them, but they will have no memory of the abuse they suffered, so will have no understanding of why they feel that way. They just do.'

34

'Do the lost memories ever come back?'

'They might.'

'But they might not?'

'It's different for everyone. Some memories could return, or all of them, or none of them. Unfortunately, it's hard to say with any kind of certainty. The only thing I see with any regularity is the impact. Patients can have difficulty forming relationships. They can become depressed very easily. They can sometimes be suicidal. As you can imagine, this kind of amnesia is a huge mental adjustment.'

That much seemed obvious already.

After I finished with Wilson, I glanced at the cardboard box, at the laptop, at the emptiness of the caravan, and thought about how little I still knew of Richard Kite – and, again, felt a murmur of disquiet. I tried to ignore it as I downloaded his texts, calls and Internet activity using an option on his account page, but, by the time I was done, the feeling still hadn't gone away and, as I sat there in silence and waited for Richard to return, I started to wonder for the first time whether taking this case may have been a mistake.

# 6

Richard Kite arrived back at four-fifteen, soaked through to the skin. From the front of the caravan, I was able to watch him approach, free-wheeling a pushbike across the empty car park and then down towards me. He had a backpack on, and the same blue raincoat and grey beanie he'd been wearing at the church.

Once he was inside, he looked across the room at me, rolled his eyes and lowered his hood. 'These are the days when I wish I could get a driving licence.'

I smiled. 'Shall I stick the kettle on?'

'That would be great.'

As Richard went to the bedroom for a change of clothes, I checked my phone and saw that I'd missed a text. It was from my daughter, Annabel. I messaged her back and told her I'd give her a shout when I got home, and then Richard returned in tracksuit trousers and a green T-shirt with the name of the caravan park on it. Without the beanie on, it was the first time I'd seen his actual hair. It was long on top, swept back from his face, but shaved at the sides. Where it was still wet, it had darkened slightly, a mix of red and brown depending on where the light caught it.

'How was the rest of your day?' I asked him.

He shrugged and held out his hands, turning them over. There were fresh cuts on his fingers, raw scratches all over his skin, criss-crossing like wire mesh.

'Pyracantha thorns,' he said.

I nodded and handed him a tea. 'I've been through the box, through your computer. I saw that picture you'd created – the composite of the beach scene.'

'I'm not very good at using that editing software.'

'It wasn't a criticism. I emailed a copy to myself because I think it's quite interesting. There's also something I wanted to ask you about.' I brought up the picture. 'This grass area at the front. Is it supposed to be lawn or beach grass?'

He leaned back on the sofa, eyes fixed on the picture.

'I'm not sure,' he said.

'But you think this might be where you grew up?'

His eyes were on the laptop again, his face strained, as if he were trying to pull old bones out of a deep hole. Eventually, he shook his head, and his breath caught in his throat. He'd been holding it in, trying to force an answer out, but all he managed was, 'I don't know.'

It had become a familiar refrain, but I felt reluctant to push him too much, because I still worried that he would fish some memory out of the darkness that wasn't entirely accurate. The more he felt like I was turning the screw, the more he would feel like he had to give me something. I didn't want that but, at the same time, these were small things that might build into something important; individual brush strokes in a bigger painting.

'You know something weird?' he said.

I looked at him.

'I never dream.'

The change of direction surprised me for a second.

'What do you mean?'

'I mean, I never have them. Ever.'

'You haven't had a single dream in nine months?'

'Nothing. Or nothing I remember, anyway. It's like . . .' He exhaled, his body shrinking, as if punctured. 'It's like that part of me is gone.'

A heavy silence settled around us. I searched for something to say, something that might comfort him, but I couldn't think of anything. Eventually, I looked at my watch.

Four thirty.

It was an hour and a half until sunset and probably another thirty minutes after that until it was dark. I finished the rest of my tea and then put my coat on.

Richard looked up at me.

'Do you fancy a drive?' I asked him.

'Uh, okay. Where?'

'I'd like you to show me where you woke up.'

# 7

We cut up through the New Forest and then hit traffic on the motorway, looping around Southampton in a slow arc. Richard talked on the way about work, and sport, and shows he'd seen on TV over the past nine months. I quickly realized that those things had become important to him, not because he was genuinely passionate about them, although he may have been, but because they'd become a way into discussions that ordinary people had. So much of his life was a blank, so many of his cultural references had gone the same way too, so talking about sporting events that had taken place over the last nine months, films and TV shows he'd watched, even politics he'd seen on the news, no longer made him the Lost Man. He was a part of the conversation again, not the subject of it.

Seventy-five minutes later, we arrived at Coldwell Point, a long rectangle of paved parking spaces, hemmed in by the River Hamble to the right and Southampton Water to the front. The RNLI station lay on a spit of land at the very edge of the river mouth as it fed into the estuary, and had a slipway at the front.

From the car park, the mouth of the Hamble was hardly visible. Mostly all I could see was the vast sweep of Southampton Water, opening out in a gradual V shape as it moved from the city all the way down to the Solent. On its far bank, about a mile and a quarter across from where we were, there was a pancake-flat expanse of land that housed the chimneys and turrets of factories, and the hulking carcasses of container boats. The rain had finally gone and the skies had cleared, so even the mediocre view looked better with some light on it, the sun bleeding red across the clouds that still remained. But if I'd been hoping to find something – some steer on how and why Richard Kite woke up on the edge of the water here – I already knew that the trip was going to end in disappointment.

We got out of the car.

I watched him for a moment, standing next to the door of the vehicle, his eyes on a spot about twenty feet away. His gaze travelled from there to the end of the peninsula, where the RNLI station was, and then out to the opposite end, where a camper van had parked up. A couple were out at the front, taking pictures of the estuary and boiling water on a portable stove.

I pushed my door shut and came around to the front of the car. Richard was still breathing the place in, his eyes back on the spot that he'd zeroed in on at the start. I figured this was where he'd woken up nine months ago. The car park, and everything up to the station, was fenced in, although it was easy enough to get beyond the barrier and out into the water: the fence was more for show than safety. On the other side, I could see that the peninsula was surrounded by a frill of shingle, like a pale outline.

'There,' he said. 'That's where they found me.'

He was pointing to the place he'd been looking at, about halfway between us and the RNLI station. I started moving across the tarmac and, gingerly at first, he followed. Around us, the light was changing quickly, the sun a disc melting into the horizon. When I got to the fence, I looked down, the sea glinting in the embers of evening. There was nothing to mark out the particular patch of land that he'd been found on – it was the same mix of shingle, stones and sand that existed everywhere else along this unremarkable finger of land.

There were no lights on inside the RNLI station either and no cars parked in the spaces outside. I thought about whether it was worth me staying in the area, so I could speak to the men who'd found Richard, whether it might be worth doing the same with Reverend Parsons, who'd been away for the day as well. But I figured I'd take a look at the report that Parsons had put together first and, if I needed to return to the area, I'd just have to come back again.

I tried to see if I'd missed anything – any kinks in the car park's layout, things that looked out of place, anything that might give me an idea of how Richard had ended up here – but there was nothing. As he'd already told me, there was no working CCTV camera here at the time of his discovery. So where might the next nearest camera be located? A mile back on the main road? Across the other side of the estuary from where we were? Again, those answers could have been in the report that Parsons had compiled, but even if there *were* other cameras, they'd clearly been of no use in answering questions about how Richard Kite came to be discovered out here.

I turned and looked back at him.

He was standing right in front of the fence, his knees almost touching it, looking down at the shingle. Beyond him, vessels carved out trails on the water – huge tankers slowly making their way south, speedboats, yachts – their wakes interconnected, the chop and rhythm of the sea eventually washing all the way back to us. When he finally looked up, the sun was gone and the sky had started to bruise, and it seemed to perfectly reflect the expression in his face.

This place held no answers for him now, just as it had held no answers for him when he'd woken up on the edge of the water, bloodied and forgotten.

# 8

I got home just before 9 p.m. The house was quiet, something that had become familiar in the years since my wife had died, but it felt cold and abandoned as well, and that was harder to adjust to. I could put the fire on in the living room, put the lights on everywhere else, and they'd brighten the house and warm it up, but I knew neither of those things would alter the way it felt.

I showered and changed and then called Annabel.

Although she was twenty-eight, we'd only known each other for four years. All that came before that was a lie, first told to me, then told to her. We were making up for lost time, but – with her on the edges of Dartmoor – it was hard living so far apart. Once or twice we'd talked about her moving to London to join me, or me moving back to Devon – where I'd grown up – to be closer to her. But things were complicated, with my work, with the fact that Annabel had a twelve-year-old sister, Olivia, for whom Annabel was the most important thing in the world, and the idea always drifted. We were both adults and we were rooted to lives we knew long before we knew one another.

'Hey,' she said, after picking up.

'Hey, sweetheart. How are you?'

'Pretty good,' she replied, although it didn't sound convincing. 'I mean, Liv's being a nightmare – but then you knew that already.'

'What's up with her now?'

'The usual crap. She's twelve. You tell her one thing, she does the total opposite. I'd have more luck trying to reason with a tree.'

Biologically, Annabel and Olivia weren't sisters, but they'd been brought up thinking they were. Olivia's mum and dad – and the couple who Annabel had always believed were her parents – were gone now, and Annabel had a fractious relationship with her real mother, so in these moments I knew I should offer to help, but never really knew how to. It felt awkward offering advice to Annabel. I had no experience in bringing up a twelve-year-old girl. I had no experience of raising a child at all.

Despite that, I did what I could to act as a sounding board, and then Annabel started chatting about her work as a dance and drama teacher, and asked me about my day, about what case I was working. I told her about Richard Kite.

'I think I vaguely remember him,' she said.

'Yeah, he was on the front page of the *Herald* back in January. That's where I recognized him from. I must have been down with you that week because his case wasn't really covered much beyond the south coast.'

'So he can't remember anything?'

'Some small things, but nothing useful.'

'Not even his name?'

'His name, his age, family, friends – nothing.'

'Shit,' she said softly. 'Poor bloke.'

'Yeah,' was all I could think to say in response.

'How do you even end up with something like that?'

'Deep trauma, an accident, abuse, the impact of a war

44

or some disaster. The thing is, the memories aren't gone, they're buried. Some might come back by themselves, or they might not. That's why he's in therapy, why he's been put under hypnosis as well: they're trying to draw his memories out.'

'But it hasn't worked.'

'Not yet, no.'

'Imagine not even being able to remember your own name or your family,' Annabel said, and then we both fell silent for our own reasons. I looked up at the walls of my living room, at the photographs of my daughter, of Olivia, and of my wife, Derryn, whose pictures I'd gradually got out again over the past six months. I'd unwrapped and hung them after my last relationship had collapsed, and in returning to these same, small biographies of a life, I found some comfort.

Derryn was a woman I'd connected with better than anyone I'd ever met, who I understood and who understood me – all my faults, all the ways in which she could make me better. I'd trusted her, and I'd loved her, and even eight years after I buried her, sometimes I missed her so much it hurt.

But at least, however lonely I got, I had her photographs.

I had my memories of her.

Richard Kite had nothing.

# 9

I woke early, went for a run, and got back before the sun was up. By the time I'd showered and had breakfast, the forty-page document that Reverend Parsons had put together for Richard Kite was sitting in the printer tray.

I took it through to the living room and started with the information that DC Barton had provided to Parsons and Richard, trying to see what I had to work with. It wouldn't be everything Barton had come up with, but – given that the case had already hit a wall, and there was no victim as such, and therefore no traditional parameters for keeping the information, evidence and any potential leads secret – it would be enough for now. If I needed to get hold of the actual case file, I had old newspaper sources who could organize that for me.

Pretty quickly, it was obvious how difficult Richard's case was to categorize. It wasn't a criminal investigation, because there was no testimony to confirm that a crime had taken place. Barton talked to Parsons about where Richard had been found and about *how* he had been found – his clothes, the shoe that was missing – and then spent a while detailing all the cuts and bruises on the left side of his face. He also included an overview of the forensic investigation, which stated that the bruising around Richard's left eye, and his cheek and chin on that same side, disguised subcutaneous lacerations – or tissue tears beneath the skin – consistent with blunt force trauma. That suggested Richard was the victim of an attack, but because he couldn't remember anything, and because there was no definitive way of confirming what weapon may have been used, it was hard for forensics to reach a definitive verdict.

I carried on reading. In testing, forensics had found faint traces of calcium hypochlorite on Richard's hands. That was the main ingredient in swimming-pool chlorine tablets. It was also used in granular form to disinfect drinking water. Richard had described himself as a strong swimmer, but what was likely to be more relevant – if Barton's theory was correct – was that it was used in polishes and waxes, in solvents, in oils and hydraulic fluids. Those were substances and solutions, if Richard *had* been some sort of mechanic or tradesman, that could easily show up on his hands. The same test had looked for other chemicals, and combinations of chemicals, with a view to narrowing down where the calcium hypochlorite had come from – a particular type of oil, for example – but the results were inconclusive. Forensics blamed the introduction of seawater. Richard could have been lying at Coldwell Point for hours and, depending on tidal patterns, parts of his body may have been fully submerged at various times. The seawater would then act as a contaminant, skewing or fully obscuring potential results. I made a note of it and moved on.

Hampshire Police had come to the conclusion that there were really only three possible reasons for Richard to have been found where he was. The first was that he'd gone to Coldwell Point, whatever his motivation for doing so, and been attacked there. The second was that he'd been attacked somewhere else, perhaps knocked unconscious, and driven to Coldwell Point and dumped. The third was that he'd washed up there.

The first two made most sense, and not just because of his injuries. When I checked notes from his medical — trying to find reasons to support the third — I saw that he'd swallowed no great amount of water, and there was no evidence of damage to his body consistent with a struggle to stay afloat. That either discounted him being carried to the river's edge by the tide, or it meant he'd swum. The idea of him doing that wasn't impossible, again because Richard had referred to himself as a proficient swimmer, but Southampton Water was over a mile wide at the place he was found, so it would have made for a hell of a swim. There were other, related questions too. If he'd been on a boat, why had he gone overboard? Was he being taken somewhere against his will? Had it been an escape attempt? If it was, why hadn't his abductors come after him as soon as he hit the estuary? On the assumption that he'd gone overboard, and that *hadn't* been the plan, I struggled to see why someone would abduct him and then just let him go. And even if they hadn't realized he was gone until much later, why didn't they return for him at some point? It seemed much more likely that Richard was the victim of an attack.

Two other, smaller things stuck with me.

One was a tattoo that Richard had. I referred back to his personal information — height, weight, eye colour, hair colour, basically areas of his life that weren't intangible or impossible to prove — and found a more detailed reference to it under DISTINGUISHING MARKS. It was on his upper left arm, about an inch from the shoulder blade, five centimetres high by four centimetres wide. There was an over-saturated picture of it, on his arm, in the report. I leaned in closer, lightly tracing the outline of the design with my finger.

It was the silhouette of a bird in flight.

Was it just a coincidence that he had this tattoo and that 'kite' was also a type of bird? No one had picked up on it in the report, and Richard himself had said nothing to me about the tattoo or his reasons for getting it, so I just made a note of it and moved on again.

The other thing I noticed was that, in all the reports, he was referred to as Richard, rather than Mr Kite, Richard Kite, or just Kite, because this was before he'd ever come up with a surname for himself. It seemed to add to the sense that this was a man lost in the system, isolated and detached. I'd never given a lot of thought as to how important a surname was, but it seemed obvious now: it was a way to normalize yourself, to fit into a structure. People fought against structure all the time, about the idea of being a cog in a machine and a name on a database. But it was easier to fight the system when you were already part of it, when you'd been assigned an identity and a number, when your wallet was full of ATM cards, and people didn't look at you sideways if you told them that you couldn't remember what your name was, or that you knew how to drive but weren't allowed to, or that you couldn't open a bank account like everyone else.

A surname was nothing until it was everything – and economically, bureaucratically and socially, it was everything to Richard Kite.

# 10

After failing to speak to her the day before, I tried Richard Kite's psychologist again. This time I got through to Naomi Russum's secretary. She told me her boss had back-to-back appointments and would struggle to find time for me today, but then I told her I was looking into the case of Richard Kite, got put on hold, transferred, and put on hold again – and finally Russum herself picked up.

'Mr Raker?'

Her voice was soft, well spoken. I'd found a photograph of her online and had been through her website. She was in her mid forties, slim, had brown eyes, olive skin, and dark hair styled into a bob. Her practice was called the Aldgate Clinic and was at the western end of Aldgate High Street, and Russum employed three people – one other psychologist, and two consultant psychiatrists. In her bio, it said she was a research fellow at King's College London and worked and taught in both the NHS and the private sector.

'Thanks for taking my call, Dr Russum.'

'You're phoning about Richard?'

I told her that he had come to me, asking for my help. 'I suppose what he's asking me to do is recover his identity,' I said, and then paused, seeing how that sat with her. She didn't reply. 'I want to assure you, I'm not here to step on your toes. I'm just hoping there might be a way we can help each other.'

'I'm not sure I see how.'

She wasn't being obtuse – at least, it didn't come across that way – but she was making it clear she didn't believe there was any common ground between us. She was approaching Richard's life from a clinical standpoint; my approach was emotional, intuitional. There was method to my work, but not the kind of method she applied to her sessions. I sensed she was heading off any request I might have been thinking about making in terms of sharing information as well. I hadn't expected her to reveal her conclusions, data she'd gathered, the content of her time with Richard, but she was making absolutely sure I knew that, just in case.

'Would it be possible to meet in person?' I asked.

'What would be the point of that?'

'It might be useful.'

'For whom?'

I didn't respond, and there was a long pause.

'Okay,' she sighed, 'although I doubt it'll be of any use.'

'I appreciate it.'

She gave me a time of five o'clock and I hung up before she could change her mind. In truth, I wasn't even sure what I hoped to get from her, but as one of the people who'd spent the most amount of time with Richard Kite, she was someone I needed to see.

There were others too.

After being passed around for a while, I managed to locate Simon Griffin and Rory Yarkley, the two men from the lifeboat station who first found Richard on the shores of Southampton Water. Separately, they both expressed guilt about not having kept in touch with him, and sounded genuine as they asked how he was doing, but neither could add much to what I already knew.

Finally, there was Reverend Colin Parsons, who I hadn't been able to chat to the previous day. He had a delicacy to his tone, a compassion, that put me in mind of a concerned parent, and maybe – in lieu of a mother, or father, or any family coming forward at all – that was what he'd become to Richard. I tried to focus his attention on the things that Richard could remember, rather than the things that he struggled to, because ultimately that was going to be the only way forward.

'Some days he seems so confused,' Parsons said to me. 'Did he mention that he has this very strong memory of growing up close to a beach, to the sea?'

'He did, yes.'

'That's been pretty consistent since the start. I wasn't around right at the beginning, when they first found him; he was in the custody of the police and the authorities. It was only later I decided to pick up the phone. I saw an article in one of the local newspapers, and I really felt for him. "The Lost Man" they called him. Anyway, he seemed so alone, so I got in contact with Hampshire Police and told them that, if he was inclined, he could give me a call at the church and I'd do what I could to help him. He called about two hours later.'

I returned to something he'd said a second ago. 'You mentioned that he seems confused some days. Do you mean confused about something in particular, or confused as a by-product of the condition he's suffering from?'

'I would say both,' Parsons said, 'but then those two things are related. I mean, dissociative amnesia, by its very nature, is confusing. But there *have* been times over the months I've got to know him when he's said things that are at odds with something else.' He paused. 'I'm not explaining this very well, am I? I suppose what I mean is, that memory he has of looking out at the beach, the sea, as a child – that's been pretty consistent all the way through. But then, occasionally, when he's been talking about that same memory of the beach, he remembers it slightly differently.'

'Differently how?'

'He can suddenly picture other houses there, or see crowds of people out on the beach. Once he said to me that he thought it was a "popular seaside town". The time I remember most clearly, though, is when he said the sea wasn't sea at all, but a river, and on the other side of the river was a city. He said he could picture big buildings, and long roads, and cars, and traffic – all that sort of stuff.'

I frowned. 'What did you say to that?'

'I replied, "But you've never mentioned a city to me before, Richard," and he just seemed kind of bewildered by it, and said, "I could never see it until now."'

'But suddenly he could?'

'Suddenly he could.'

'When was this?'

'I don't know. Four, five months ago.'

'He never talked about that when I spoke to him.'

Parsons sighed. 'In the end, that whole thing just slipped away again.'

'So his recollection of the city didn't last?'

'No. A week or so later I said to him, "Do you remember anything else about the city?" and he shook his head and said, "I'm not sure there even *was* a city." That's kind of what it's been like. He has these moments where the story changes – and then it changes back.'

'You think he's lying?'

'Oh, no. No, no, absolutely not. I don't believe for one minute he's ever told me, or anyone else, a lie. But I *do* think he's deeply confused. I think there's a kind of . . . I don't know, I'm not a doctor, so I don't know what you'd call it. Maybe emotional "interference". He thinks of things, then tries to make them the truth.'

'He makes things up?'

'No. Or maybe, yes – but not deliberately or vindictively. I mean, just put yourself in his position. If you became convinced that you grew up by a beach, in view of the sea, or you possibly remembered the introduction to a children's TV show, but *no one else* in the entire world knew what part of the country you were describing, or which TV show you were talking about, what would you do next?'

'Try harder to remember.'

'Exactly. Try harder, and then harder, and then harder. And then, one day, you'd start thinking, "What if there actually *were* people on that beach but I just don't remember them?" And the longer you spend thinking about that, the more the idea grips, the more your mind starts moving on: "What *sort* of people would there be? How *many* people?" You'd start to think, "If there are people, there are houses. If there are houses, there's a village. Or maybe a town. Or maybe a city." It just goes on and on until one day you have this clear view of what you think *might* have been there.'

'Except it might not have been there at all.'

'Right. But by that stage, it's too late already because it's not some flight of imagination any more. It feels real, because you want to *believe* it's real.'

'So, are you saying you don't think any of his memories can be trusted?'

'I wouldn't necessarily go that far,' Parsons replied. 'I guess what I'm saying is, if he's suddenly uncertain about his memory of the beach, it does tend to shake one's belief in what might be true, or . . . you know . . .'

'What might not be.'

'Yes,' Parsons said glumly. 'Yes, exactly.'

There was a delay on the Tube heading out of Ealing Broadway, so I found a bench halfway down the platform and got out my notes and my phone. I wanted to ensure I was prepared for Naomi Russum – partly because I doubted she'd make it easy for me, but mostly because I wanted to make certain that I hadn't missed anything.

I opened up the PDF I'd emailed myself from Richard's mobile phone account online – a complete breakdown of calls, texts and data usage over the course of the entire time he'd owned the phone – and soon discovered something. While I'd chased down all the calls and texts and found them to be dead ends, I hadn't looked as closely at his data. Now I did, I noticed an anomaly.

His mobile was a Huawei Y3. It was an entry-level phone, running on the Android OS. There were plenty of apps available for it, so Richard could have used social media and, in theory, watched something like iPlayer on it too. But the truth was, if he was going to do that, he probably would have wanted something higher spec. The phone was for people who only really wanted to text and make calls, or who wanted to keep payments down through low-cost monthly plans. It was why the Huawei Y3 should have suited Richard Kite down to the ground: he didn't do social media, he wasn't registered with the Android store, he hadn't downloaded any apps, and he used his laptop and the caravan park's Wi-Fi to get on to the Internet, not his phone.

And yet there was something weird here: the amount of data he was using every month was high. Not ridiculously high, but higher than it should have been. He'd bought no apps from the store, hardly used the phone at all for day-to-day surfing, never used it as a GPS, or to check the news, or to stream TV shows or movies. And yet, each month, he burned through about 500MB of data.

*How was he using that much?*

It was the equivalent of sending about 17,000 emails, except he didn't email anyone; it was twenty-five hours on Facebook, but he had no social media accounts in his own name, and didn't ever check the ones that were set up to publicize his case. He didn't google anything, didn't use streaming services of any kind, and didn't do much more than watch a few YouTube videos; and he'd have had to watch thirty-five or forty before he got anywhere near 500MB of data.

Returning to my laptop, I logged back into his mobile phone account and retraced my steps through to the section of the website dealing with his Internet use. There, I found a series of pie charts, breaking down each of the eight months. I looked at September: of the 500MB he'd used, 42MB was web activity, 61MB were emails, and

398MB was apps – and yet he didn't ever use or download apps. It made no sense. Either it was an admin error at the network, or there was some kind of a technical issue with the phone.

Or it was something much worse than both.

Richard Kite was lying to me.

# Penny

*Penny's dad disappeared when she was three. She was too young to remember much about him, although she kept photographs of the two of them together, faded colour portraits taken in the back garden of their old home. In one, she was running away from her father – arms out, laughing – as he chased her across the lawn. In another, she was on his knee, the two of them in a deckchair with a barbecue smoking in the background. The picture always made her smile because she and her father were both dressed in winter coats and the sky was like granite. 'Proper British barbecuing weather,' her mum would always say.*

*Her mum never liked talking about what had happened to Penny's dad. Some of Penny's earliest memories were of her mum bursting into tears as they walked home from school, or hearing sobs through the kitchen window as she played outside with the other kids. After a while, the sobbing stopped, but Fiona seemed to carry her grief around like a weight; like pounds she couldn't shed. Penny would hear people talking about her mum at the shops, in the playground at pick-up time, in the changing rooms at swimming lessons when they didn't realize Penny was in the next cubicle. They said her mum brought the mood down.*

*When she turned eight, Penny was supposed to have a birthday party in the church hall, but it got cancelled when a leg bone was found in the hills surrounding their town. She didn't understand what all the fuss was about until her mum sat her down the same evening and told her that Ray Sankle, whose dog had found the bone, thought it might be human; and, if it was human, there was the possibility it might belong to her dad. 'Doctors are testing it,' was all her mum said.*

*That night, after Penny went to bed, she heard her mum sobbing again. She crept down the staircase and stopped halfway, looking at her through the banisters. A man was sitting next to her on the sofa.*

*He was hugging her.*

*The man was called Jack. Eventually he became Penny's stepfather. Penny liked him, but she liked her new stepsister even more. Beth was two years younger than Penny, but the two girls got on almost immediately. They'd play together in the garden and build dens from old sheets of tin and corrugated iron. On warm summer days, they'd go swimming together at the lido on the edge of town, an art deco relic with a main building that looked like a flying saucer from a black and white sci-fi film. The two girls even looked vaguely similar, so they started to refer to themselves as sisters, rather than stepsisters, whenever people asked.*

*The human bone turned out not to be Penny's father. Her mum sat her down again and told her, trying to comfort Penny by pressing her face to her chest, by enclosing her daughter's hands inside hers. Penny just listened, not saying anything, and when her mum started crying again, her father's name like a switch that still set her off, Penny repeatedly told her that everything would be fine, because Mrs Hardew, her teacher, had read them a story in class one day and that was something a woman had said to a man who'd lost his cat.*

*The next day, before school, when her mum was upstairs showering, Penny saw the front page of the local newspaper. It said the bone belonged to a woman and that tests had revealed that it was a tourist who'd gone missing during a hike in the hills years before. So, as they walked to school together that morning, Penny told Beth about what she'd read, expecting her to be fascinated and frightened. But Beth just shrugged her shoulders and said matter-of-factly, 'Dad reckons Ray Sankle was an idiot. He says Mr Sankle and his dog could have been killed.'*

Penny looked at her. 'What are you talking about?'

'Mr Sankle. His dog was the one that found the bone.'

'Yeah, I know that. But why would they have got killed?'

'Because Dad says there's something up in the hills.'

Penny frowned. 'What do you mean?'

'Like a monster or something.'

Unlike a lot of girls in her class who preferred writing and art, Penny loved things like science and history. She loved watching wildlife documentaries when her mum could get hold of them from the library, or when, very rarely, they appeared on TV, and she loved seeing how people lived in the olden days. Old black and white films. Old fashions. Her mum said she knew a lot about history for a girl her age, but Penny knew even more about animals and science.

'There's no such thing as monsters,' she told Beth.

Beth didn't seem particularly bothered either way. 'Well, Dad says it's the real reason they put the fence up.'

'What fence?'

'Up in the hills.'

Beth pointed to the peaks north of the town. Penny had never been up there before. They told the kids to steer clear of the area because it was dangerous. Penny had always thought they meant dangerous because kids could get lost out there, just like that tourist had.

But maybe they meant something else.

'Ages and ages ago,' Beth went on, 'Dad says we put bombs up there to stop the baddies invading us.'

'Are you talking about the Second World War?'

Beth didn't seem to know what that was, but it must have been what she was referring to. Penny had borrowed a book from the library once and it had talked about how some places in Britain had put landmines down to protect against a Nazi sea invasion.

'So is Jack saying there aren't really any bombs up there?'

'I don't know,' Beth said.

'He reckons that's not the real reason they put the fence up?'

'I don't know,' she said again. 'I guess.'

'Have you ever been up there?'

'Yeah.'

'Really?' Penny couldn't hide her surprise. 'How many times?'

'Only once.'

'With Jack?'

'Yeah. Dad went to check on the fence after Mr Sankle's dog found that bone.' Beth broke into a smile and started pretending her hands were paws; that she was a dog digging in the earth. 'It found a gap in the fence and then dug, dug, dug until it squeezed through. Have you ever seen Mr Sankle's dog?'

'No.'

'Her name's Jessie. She's so cute.'

Penny just nodded. 'What was it like?'

'What?'

'The fence?'

'It was boring. It's just a big fence.'

Beth clamped her hands on to the straps of a backpack way too big for her, and neither of them said much for a while. But eventually, Penny noticed Beth looking sideways at her, hesitating, as if unsure whether to say what she was thinking.

'What's the matter?' Penny said.

'Nothing.' Beth cleared her throat. 'It's just, after him and my mum split up, Dad got drunk one night and started telling me loads of things that he shouldn't have. Mum would have called it "gossip".' She stopped, cleared her throat a second time. 'Did you know that your mum has got absolutely loads of money?'

Penny glanced at her. 'No, she hasn't.'

'She has. Your dad was rich.'

'No, he wasn't.'

'He was. He kept all his money in bags.'

'No, he didn't.'

Beth shrugged.

'He wasn't rich, Beth,' Penny said. 'Rich people live in huge mansions like in Beverly Hills 90210. If Mum has loads of money, why doesn't she have a Ferrari and a butler? Or a pool. Wouldn't it be cool if we had a heart-shaped swimming pool?'

'Very cool.'

'And a waterslide.'

'No, a death slide!' Beth shrieked. 'It would be, like, fifty storeys high and — by the time you got to the bottom — your costume would be right up your bum!'

They began giggling, and then the giggling descended into laughter, and pretty soon after that Penny had forgotten about the idea of her mum being rich.

But she didn't forget about the bombs in the hills.

A couple of weeks later, after Jack and Beth had officially moved in with Fiona and Penny, Penny was walking through the town, the air damp with fog, and found her attention drifting to the slopes beyond the rooftops. The mist was so thick on the high ground, it was impossible to see anything more than the vaguest hint of three worm-like trails working their way up the side of the mountain. She began thinking about what Beth had said, about the fence, about the idea of there being something up there, a monster of some kind, and then about the bone that had been found by Mr Sankle's dog. What if that tourist hadn't died because she'd got lost on a hike? What if she was attacked? What if there really was something up there and the bombs were just a story invented to keep people out?

What if her father was out there somewhere too?

What if the monster was the reason he disappeared?

## 11

By the time I emerged from Aldgate station, the rain had become a mist. It cast a petrol-blue tint across everything, from the clouds to the roads, as if all the light had escaped. When I looked right, I could see the giants of the City – the Gherkin, the Cheesegrater, the Walkie Talkie – but almost as soon as they appeared they were gone again, blinking in and out of existence like wraiths.

I crossed the street, jumping puddles that had settled on uneven tarmac, and looked for the door to the Aldgate Clinic. Eventually I found it, halfway along a short alleyway. I pushed the buzzer and waited.

'Can I help you?'

I leaned in towards the intercom. 'David Raker for Dr Russum.'

The door whirred and bumped away from its frame, and I found myself in a tiny foyer with a lift and a staircase. I took the lift up to the top floor. Behind another door, a woman at the front desk buzzed me into a small reception area with walls of frosted glass on either side.

'Mr Raker?'

'Yes.'

'Dr Russum won't be long.'

A couple of minutes later, I saw a flicker of movement in the glass on the left side of the room, a shadow forming behind the frost. When the door clinked open, Russum appeared. She came across, attempting a smile. It wasn't exactly effervescent, but she'd agreed to see me, and that was all that mattered.

'Thanks for sparing me some time,' I said, shaking hands with her.

She nodded and led me back through the door into a modern office with views west along Fenchurch Street. Two expensive leather chairs sat facing one another to my left, and there was a sofa, a spare seat and filing cabinets on my right. In the middle was her desk – fastidiously tidy, even down to pens being lined up in a row beside her keyboard – and another cabinet with a bonsai on it.

She brought the spare seat across for me.

We both sat down and I started to fill her in on what I'd found out about Richard's case so far. She spent the whole time sitting forward in her chair, arms folded, not saying anything. In the moments when I would pause to check my notes, the silence was filled with the low rumble of vehicles passing and the whine of construction cranes at Bishopsgate.

'I was wondering if you could talk about the kinds of areas you explore with Richard,' I said, 'perhaps where you hope to get to.'

'I hope to get to a complete recovery,' she replied tartly.

'To a point where he remembers everything?'

'Yes.'

'Is that likely?'

She shrugged. 'It's difficult to say. I've always believed that brains are like fingerprints. They're unique.'

'So it might happen – or it might not?'

Her expression remained neutral, but her lips thinned.

'This is a complex psychological condition,' she said slowly, as if she were dealing with a moron. 'In localized amnesia, a person is unable to recall a specific event, or a period of time. In systemized amnesia, they forget one particular area – like one person, or one place. In generalized amnesia, which is what Richard is suffering from, the patient forgets their entire history and all sense of their identity. He has lost the fundamental building blocks of his life, the things that made him who he is. He almost certainly still has those memories, but the issue is finding them.'

'So it could take years?'

'It might.'

'Or he could remember everything tomorrow?'

'That's possible too.' Again, she shrugged. 'All sorts of things could trigger those forgotten memories and return them to the surface. He might watch a film and suddenly remember seeing it in a cinema in a certain town, in a certain year. Or he might see a building in a magazine feature and recognize it as somewhere he went on a school trip. Those are just examples, but you get what I'm driving at. As I said to you before, the brain is a very particular and peculiar animal, and it's hard to say with precision when memories will re-emerge – if they do at all.'

'So, equally, he might never remember?'

'That's something he has to accept, yes.'

She leaned back in her chair, the leather wheezing against her weight. If I didn't know before, I knew for certain now: she wasn't going to discuss the actual content of their sessions, and not only because she was bound by the ethics of her profession. I could see it in her face, in the way she chose not to say anything: she didn't approve of Richard's decision to employ me, but if she raised an objection, she endangered her own work with him. If he thought she was going against his interests, getting in the way of what he wanted, he'd walk away from her, and all her ambitions – the commissions she hoped to get, the lectures she hoped to give – crumbled to dust. She'd agreed to meet me because it maintained the equilibrium.

'I see you're a qualified hypnotherapist.'

She eyed me. 'Correct.'

'Richard says you've used hypnosis before.'

'There's a lot of misconceptions about hypnosis,' she said, firing back at an accusation I'd never even made. Her fingers were on the edge of the desk. It was clear she didn't want to talk about this either, but at the same time wasn't prepared to let me leave with the wrong impression. 'Hypnosis isn't a circus act,' she went on. 'It's not making people dance around on stage, thinking they're chimpanzees. If used in the right way, it can be an extremely powerful tool. Sadly, a lot of clinicians remain unconvinced by hypnotherapy – and not without reason. I spent two years doing a masters and three years studying for a PhD, both times in Psychology. My thesis was *on* hypnotherapy. I both run, and attend, training courses most months of the year, I lecture at King's College, I like to think I know what I'm talking about. But it's still a constant learning process. You learn all the time. You're under an *obligation* to learn, as far as I'm concerned. Yet, here in the UK, you don't actually need to learn a thing. You can practise hypnotherapy with little training, and you don't have to join a professional association. The result is that a lot of people claim to be hypnotherapists, but they simply aren't fit for purpose. I'm sure I don't need to spell out the reasons why that is a potential area of concern.'

'So how many times did you use it with Richard?'

'Twice.'

'Why only twice?'

'Because you have to ascertain whether it's the right tool for the job – and, after two sessions, I didn't believe it was the correct fit for Richard. The bottom line is, you don't use hypnotherapy like a map. You don't just dive into someone's head, find the things that have become lost in there and bring them back with you. You can't pause and rewind and fast-forward, until you get to the bit you want. People are forgetting things all the time. As humans, I'd argue that we *need* to forget. If we remembered every single thing we'd ever done in our lives, we'd be unable to function. So, primarily, I used hypnosis to relax Richard. As you might imagine, when he first came to me, he was fractious, disorientated, scared. I did some initial work on trying to explore memories, feelings and thoughts that he might have hidden from his conscious mind, but it unsettled him.'

'Which is why you stopped after two sessions?'

'Correct.'

'So is that what you're trying to do with him currently?' I asked. 'You're trying to drill down to events he may be hiding in his unconscious mind?'

'In essence, yes – although it's slightly different with Richard. There aren't the traditional pegs on which to hang the therapy. You can't ask him to talk about his family, or upbringing, or whether he went to university, because he doesn't recall any of it. And *my* approach has to be even more delicate as a result. Anything erroneous – any lapse on my part – could be problematic.'

'What do you mean, "lapse"?'

'I mean, it's why training is so important,' she said. 'Memory is a minefield. It's full of potential hazards – and not just for the person affected.'

I waited for her to expand on her point but, instead, it looked like she was assessing how much she'd given me already, and whether I might be manipulating her some-how. I couldn't deny that I was interested in what they discussed, but I'd long since accepted that she wasn't going to tell me. And the truth was, I was starting to think there might not be that much worth discovering, anyway. Richard had been seeing her for eight months and he had nothing to show for it: his memories of the beach and the TV intro sequence were there from the start, before he ever set foot in Russum's office.

She began rolling a pen back and forth across the desk, her reticence still obvious. 'Have you heard of the Ameri-can psychologist Elizabeth Loftus?'

'No.'

'She's an expert on human memory and misinformation. One of her most famous studies, back in the seventies, was into whether eyewitness memory could be altered by apply-ing information *after* the event. As an example, she had participants in the study watch footage of a car crash, and then a week later, she and her research team asked them about their memories of it. She found that the participants were more likely to describe having seen broken glass during the accident if researchers asked about the car "smash", rather than using words like "collision". This was despite the fact that there was no broken glass visible anywhere in the film the participants watched.' She rolled the pen back into place at the side of her keyboard. 'So that's what I mean. With someone like Richard, it's important that the right questions are asked in the right way. It's things as apparently trivial as language that can lead to problems.'

I wheeled back to what Reverend Parsons had told me over the phone, about the moments of confusion Richard had experienced over the last nine months; the time when his memories of the beach became the recollection of an entire city.

'I talked to Reverend Colin Parsons earlier on,' I said to her, 'and he seemed to suggest Richard had become a little . . . confused.'

'Of course he's confused.'

'No, I mean about his memories.'

She frowned. 'In what sense?'

I explained about Richard remembering the beach as a city.

'He never mentioned that,' she said coolly.

'Richard didn't talk about those memories with you?'

There was a long pause.

'Dr Russum?'

Her eyes returned to me and she straightened in her seat. 'I'd suggest that Reverend Parsons misunderstood Richard.'

'I don't think he misunderstood.'

'I'm sure Richard would have mentioned something to me.'

'Or maybe he wouldn't have.'

She prickled again. 'I think we're done, Mr Raker.'

She got to her feet, not attempting to disguise the fact that she'd taken offence, and when I stood she immediately began to lead me out to the lift.

But then something odd happened: she forced a smile and started chatting about the evenings closing in, about how she hated it when the clocks went back, and about how soon Christmas would be with us. It was so jarring, such a sudden change, it was impossible not to notice it. She was being too casual now, her conversation too forced, and it was totally out of sync with how she'd been in the office. There, she'd been stoic and expressionless, her face starched and hard; here, she was something else – awkward and unconvincing, as if she were trying to put on some sort of act.

I watched her closely as we shook hands at the lift, the doors sliding open behind me, and then kept my eyes on her as the doors bumped shut again.

I wasn't sure what had just happened.

But I was going to find out.

Russum left work just after seven. Rain was still in the air, although it had eased slightly, the mist drifting away. In its place were slick pavements, gutters full of water and leaves, and puddles reflecting back the colours of the city.

I followed her, keeping my distance, weaving between crowds of people coming the other way. She was on her phone, one side of her face illuminated by it. Great Tower Street became Eastcheap, Eastcheap became Cannon Street, and she just kept walking. After a while, she pocketed her phone and appeared to be more aware of her surroundings, so I dropped back, in case she glanced over her shoulder, but almost as soon as I did she took another left, this time into a small road called River Hill. I slowed, stopping at a deli on the corner, its lights spilling across the pavement in pale blocks of cream. She was about eighty feet down from me, heading south, her long jacket swinging behind her. There was a bag over her shoulder, black like her coat, one I hadn't noticed before because she'd had it tucked between the inside of her arm and her ribcage. She pulled it around to her front and began to go through it, her pace decreasing. Eventually, she came to a complete halt.

Next to her was an archway that looked like it might lead to some sort of courtyard, but then I realized she wasn't going in there, she was going into a glass door adjacent to it. She took out a swipe card, ran it through a reader on the wall, and then pushed through the door into whatever lay beyond.

I headed after her. At the door, I could see a coat of arms etched into the glass and a corridor inside – oak floors, cream walls – that ran for about ten feet to another door and a second card reader. I stepped back and took in the whole building. It was big: three floors, eight windows on each floor, closed wooden shutters behind each pane of glass. On closer inspection, I saw that the courtyard adjacent to it was actually a small car park. Above the entrance to the courtyard was a wooden sign: RED TREE EMPLOYEES ONLY.

Thinking there must be a main entrance to the building somewhere, I walked to the bottom of River Hill, where the road dog-legged into a small cul-de-sac. Beyond that was a paved, pedestrianized area full of benches and raised flower beds, a sculpture – a tree made from iron, with red metal leaves – on a plinth at its centre. To my right, beyond the flower beds and benches, were the noise, lights and traffic of Upper Thames Street. To my left was the front of the building, an elegant Georgian façade with restored sash windows and marble pillars, and a set of steps leading up to four opaque glass doors, all imprinted with the same coat of arms I'd seen on the side door. In front of those – all of which were locked, the interior semi-lit by pale yellow night lights – were four huge advertising flags. Each one showed staged shots of school kids in uniform, focused and engaged in lessons, or out on the sports field with hockey sticks or rugby balls. Words like *Respect*, *Responsibility* and *Innovation* were printed on the flags, as was the same coat of arms. So was the name of the school.

The Red Tree City of London School.

As I tried to think whether any of this even mattered, whether Russum, or her behaviour, or her reasons for coming to the school, held any importance in the case, my phone burst into life.

It was Richard Kite.

'David,' he said after I answered. 'You left a message for me.'

I'd called him about the unexplained data on his phone. He listened in silence as I told him about the anomalies I'd found in his app usage.

'But I never use apps,' he said.

'I know. That's what makes it odd.'

'Do you think there's something wrong with the phone?'

'I don't know,' I said. 'Has it been acting up?'

'Not really. Nothing major, anyway.'

'But it *has* been acting up?'

'Sometimes it just switches itself off, that's all.'

I paused. 'It just shuts down for no reason?'

'Yes.'

'It does that even when the battery isn't flat?'

'Yes,' he said. 'It can do it at any time. It did it to me yesterday, and I'd only just recharged it.'

I felt a stir of unease.

'Anything else like that?'

'I don't know,' he said, giving it some more thought. 'Not really. I guess it depends on how far back you want to go.'

'As far back as you can remember.'

'Well, for a while, when I first got the phone, there would sometimes be weird noises during calls.'

'Weird how?'

'Like, echoes and buzzes. Interference.'

'All the time?'

'No,' he said. 'Just for a short period.'

The stir of unease became something worse.

'Richard, you're breaking up a bit.'

'Am I? Oh. You sound okay.'

'Yeah, I'm really struggling to hear you properly. Is there a phone at the caravan park you can use?'

'You mean a landline?'

'Yeah.'

'Yes, there's one in the clubhouse.'

'Could you call me back on that?'

'Uh, okay.'

I told him I'd wait, and five minutes later my phone started buzzing again. It was a Christchurch number.

'Richard?'

'Yes, I'm here.'

'I don't want you calling me on your mobile phone again, okay?'

'What?' A confused pause. 'Why?'

'Because it's been compromised.'

A hesitation. 'What are you talking about?'

'I'm pretty sure there's spyware installed on it. All of these things – the data usage, the weird behaviour – they're spyware warning signs. I mean, it's not *sophisticated* spyware, but it's spyware. Someone's watching you, monitoring your calls and texts, what you look at on the Internet. The static, the interference; whoever it is, they're using the handset like a conference call. They're listening.'

He was silent.

'Richard?'

'I can't . . . I don't . . .' He faded out. 'How did it even get on there?'

'Probably through an email or a text. It's like phishing. You click on a link you think is legitimate, but what you're really doing is opening your phone up.'

'So whoever it is can see and hear everything I do?'

'I think we have to assume they can. We have to assume your phone calls, your texts, your emails – they're being watched and monitored. Until I figure out why, I need to change how you and I communicate.'

He went silent again.

'Richard?'

'I . . . I don't understand.'

If he didn't know what spyware was he could probably take a pretty good guess. What he didn't understand was why he was being watched.

'Have you got any idea who might have done this?' I asked.

'No,' he said, a little breathless. 'No.'

'I know you probably don't believe me at this point, but you're not in any danger.' I paused. *Was that even true?* 'This has been going on since you first got the phone, and no one has made any kind of move. To me, that suggests that – whoever it is – they're happy watching for the moment. So I want you to continue to use the mobile to speak to the people you normally would – the caravan park, Reverend Parsons . . .' I stopped, glancing at the front of the school. 'Naomi Russum too.'

'Okay.'

'And then first thing tomorrow, go and buy the cheapest

phone and SIM card you can find and call me on that.' My
eyes returned to the school. 'One thing, though: I need you
to keep this whole spyware stuff just between the two of us.
I don't want you mentioning it to anybody.'

'Okay,' he said again.

'That means anybody. Dr Russum too.'

*Especially Dr Russum.*

'Is that all right?'

'Yes,' he said.

For a moment, neither of us spoke.

'I don't understand who would do this to me.'

'I don't know either,' I said to him.

But as my gaze shifted back to the school, and I thought
of Naomi Russum and how she'd been at her office, I
wasn't really sure if I believed that or not.

# 13

I spent the next few hours trying to trace the origins of the spyware using old contacts of mine from my newspaper days. All I got was dead ends. The spyware might not have been sophisticated but its origins were well masked. After that, I left the pub I'd set up in, returned to Russum's office building and watched it for an hour, trying to establish its rhythms and behaviour.

The lights remained off pretty much the entire time, on every floor except the first: through the windows on that one, a security guard sat at a desk playing games on a handheld console. Every thirty minutes, he'd get up, do the same route on each floor, the lights flickering into life as he passed under them, before returning to the same desk. A minute or so later, all the lights snapped off again.

I made my way along the alleyway, checking for any signs of life from adjacent buildings, and then, picks in hand, started working on the clinic door. It took a couple of minutes of frustration before I felt the familiar click, before the door bumped out from its frame and into the darkness of the foyer. Once it did, I waited, crouched, listening for an alarm, movement, footsteps.

It was silent.

I took the stairs, drifting past the door for the first floor. When I checked my watch, I saw that I had about twenty-five minutes before the security guard started doing his rounds again. That meant I'd have to work fast and be ready to leave inside twenty minutes if I didn't want to meet him on the stairs.

Once I'd picked the door into the reception area, I grabbed a fire extinguisher off the wall and used it to keep the door propped ajar. Lights flicked on above me. I kept low, trying to prevent myself from being seen from the street. In Russum's office, more lights popped into life, so I dropped both sets of window blinds and turned to face the room.

Going to her computer first, I slid in at the desk and powered it on. While it was booting up, I checked the drawers and started going through a cabinet behind me. I didn't find anything relevant. Pushing it closed, I returned to the PC.

As quickly as possible, I searched through the computer. She was using the default mail client, but I couldn't get into it because, although I knew what her email address was, I had no password. I didn't waste time trying to find a workaround and pushed on, opening up a folder full of scans – medical reports, patient information – and then another one covering sessions she took and presentations she was giving: transcripts, notes, papers she'd written and essays she was planning.

I couldn't find anything on Richard Kite.

I kept going, but there wasn't a single mention of him in any of the folders I clicked on. I did a system search, thinking I must have been looking in the wrong place, but the search came back with zero results. It seemed to confirm what my gut had been telling me: something was going on. She'd been treating him for eight months, she'd actively gone out of her way to help him, she'd made journeys back and forth to Dorset, but there was no mention of him anywhere.

Then something else caught my eye.

On the right-hand side of the screen was a .m4a audio file. I'd looked at it a couple of times without its filename registering with me because Russum's desktop was so packed full of other folders and documents. But I noticed it now: 261016.

The filename was today's date.

I double-clicked on it and it started playing. There was a faint hiss and the sound of a door opening. Voices, too dull to make out at first, and then gradually becoming clearer as they got closer. It was Russum and me talking. We were coming back from the front desk, getting louder as we returned to her office. I heard her shuffle in at her chair and then I heard myself chatting politely.

*She'd recorded our conversation.*

As the audio file continued to play, I tried to figure out why. For whose benefit? Hers? Someone else's? I couldn't check her email to see if she'd forwarded it on to anyone, but that seemed the most likely endgame.

Switching off the computer, I headed for the filing cabinets on the far side of the room. They were locked and the keys weren't anywhere obvious, so I had to get the picks out for a third time. As I slid the top drawer of the first one open, I found reams of patient files inside and felt a pang of guilt – not for Russum, but for the patients whose privacy I was about to shatter. I checked my watch again, saw I had ten minutes, and returned my attention to the drawer – but the sense of guilt didn't disappear. These were people's lives. Their vulnerabilities, their fears, their secrets. I could feel the betrayal, every bit of it, because in the years after Derryn died, it could easily have been me in here.

Every person's notes were in a grey suspension file, each one fixed to a runner, a tab on top listing their name and a number. They were in alphabetical order, this cabinet covering *M* through to *Z*, so I immediately sprung the lock to the second cabinet and found files covering surnames from *A* to *L*.

I found Richard about halfway in.

Pulling the folder out, I took it across to the desk. Even before I'd looked at it, something didn't feel right, but I didn't realize what until I had the file open.

It was virtually empty.

It contained a top sheet where Russum had listed everything that Richard Kite could remember about himself. It included all the things he'd told me, from the few memories he maintained, to him remembering how to swim. Where there should have been things like age, date of birth, medical history and employment, the boxes had been left blank. I'd expected that, but not what I found next. Beneath the top sheet, where I expected to find copious notes about their sessions, the hypnotherapy he'd been given, there was absolutely nothing.

No notes at all; just a series of photos.

I flicked through them. They were of renowned historical figures, celebrities, world monuments and famous buildings. I remembered what Richard had told me about his sessions with Russum: *We go through photographs to see what I remember, who I'm aware of, and who I'm not.* She'd been doing it in an effort to narrow down his age, where he was from and brought up. So where were her conclusions? Where were all the notes?

I went back to the cabinets and picked out another patient at random. The file was thick. I put it back and tried another. *Exactly the same.* In all the others, Russum had done her job – she'd asked questions and tried to dig away at answers; she'd written up conclusions, whole transcripts in some cases. It didn't take much effort to see the difference between Richard's file and the rest of the files in the cabinets. Those were all maps of the human experience; his was an incongruent parade of celebrities. Yet he'd been deliberately sought out by Russum. She'd called him up and offered to help him. She'd worked for free. I thought she'd seen him as a meal ticket – but, given that Richard's phone was being monitored, I started to wonder if it was more calculated than that. Was the treatment she'd been giving him an elaborate cover for something else?

I paused there for a moment, looking down at what constituted Richard's file – a single piece of paper and a gallery of faces and locations – and then checked my watch and saw that I had three minutes before I needed to get out. I started gathering up the photos from the file and placing them back inside.

But one of them made me stop.

It was of a woman in her early thirties, blonde hair, green eyes, sitting on the edge of a park bench somewhere. The photograph had been closely cropped, so that only her face, her shoulders and the tops of both arms were visible – but I could see the slats of the bench behind her, trees a few feet further out, and then the blurred figures of families and couples beyond that. Right on the edge of the shot there was something else too: a sliver of grey, breaking above the treeline.

*The BT Tower.*

It was Regent's Park.

Setting the picture aside, I went through the others again, looking for any that seemed similarly out of place, and I found a second photograph of the woman, exactly matching the other one. Same bench in Regent's Park, same pose, same angle on the BT Tower in the background. Why would Russum have two identical photographs of the same person?

I put the two pictures side by side and then kept searching the others, but all I found were figures from history and pop culture, and landmarks I instantly recognized; and not only that, they were all *professional* photographs, either cut out of magazines or newspapers and photocopied on to thin sheets of card, or printed directly off the Internet using a high-quality laser printer. The celebrity pictures all had that high-level sheen; the landmarks were picturesque, perfectly lit.

The matching photographs weren't.

It wasn't that the picture was bad necessarily, it just clearly wasn't taken by a pro: the colours were slightly washed out and there was a minor movement blur on her left side. When I looked at her more closely, trying to work out if she was someone I just hadn't seen or heard of before – a YouTube star, a pop singer – I figured she was probably too old to be making walk-throughs of videogames on the Internet, even in her early thirties, and despite a pair of silver hoop earrings she was quite plain, a little coy, which made me doubt that she was a singer or an actress either. So who was she? And what was she doing in Richard's file?

I grabbed my phone, took a series of shots of the two photographs side by side, and then returned everything to the filing cabinets.

I was running ninety seconds late.

Checking that everything was exactly as I left it, I headed out of the office, on to the landing and paused. Four floors below me, I could hear movement: the dulled sound of footsteps; a door opening. I grabbed the fire extinguisher, placed it back where I'd found it and gently pushed the clinic door shut until it clicked.

I headed down a floor and then stopped.

Backing into the shadows of the stairwell, I looked down through the centre, banisters circling back and forth, and watched the security guard emerge on to the first floor, one hand on the railing.

He was coming up.

I stayed where I was, watching his hand move, his wedding ring chiming against the metal railing. When he got to the office on the second floor, he ran a card through a reader and the door fanned out towards him. I waited for him to go inside, waited for the door to suck shut, and then I moved, taking two steps at a time. I crouched as I passed the door he'd gone through and, by the time I got to the foyer, I could hear him above me again – the door, the railing, his footsteps.

I didn't move until he entered the third floor.

Once he did, I exited the building for good.

# The Brink

The first time the girls went up into the hills together was two months before Penny turned nine. It took them a while to pluck up the courage, but then their curiosity got the better of them and they crept out of the house after dark, when their parents thought the two of them were asleep, and they followed one of the trails up to the top. It turned out that Beth wasn't making it up: at the end of one of the routes, there actually was a fence. Penny wasn't good at measuring heights, didn't really understand feet and inches, but it was at least as tall as her stepdad, Jack, maybe taller. But about a minute after they arrived, they heard a weird noise coming from the other side of it, and it was enough to send them running all the way home again.

Eventually, though, they went back, and because the second time wasn't as scary as the first, they decided to go a third time, and a fourth, and each time they stayed a little longer, until five minutes became thirty, and thirty became an hour.

Every time they went back, they heard and saw a little more. Sometimes, they swore they could actually spot something moving out there. The wind would still, the clouds would drift apart, and moonlight would blanket the headland like a pale gauze, revealing the sea of long grass that surrounded them, and the fence that marked the boundary between where they were and the marshland beyond it. From the inside of a hideout they'd found — an old concrete pillbox — the movement on the other side of the fence only ever appeared as flickers, as brief flashes, and always way off into the distance, in an *area that Jack — and, as time went on, pretty much everyone else in town — referred to as the Brink.*

*And that was the thing: they could have made sure that there was something out there — or not — if they'd gone further than the pillbox, if they'd gone up to the fence, or even, in a feat of bravery, over it and on to the other side. Yet, if Penny had become more fearless every time they'd crept out of the house after dark to return here, if all the science books she'd read had argued that there could be nothing in the grass and the bogs beyond the fence — no monsters, or ghosts, or giant animals — the more time that went on, the more often they returned, the more doubts would continue to nag at her.*

*'Si Rickles reckons they found an arm near the fence once,' Beth said on their eighteenth visit. Si Rickles was an annoying kid from their school whose dad was a sergeant in the police force. When Penny — ten by that time, mature for her age, independent — argued against it, questioning why it wasn't in the newspapers, or why no one in town was talking about it, her sister said, 'Dad reckons all the people would stop wanting to come here if they found out, so no one talks about it.'*

*If that seemed unlikely to Penny, other things were more difficult to dispute. One time, when they finally lost count of how often they'd been up there, the two of them were hunkered down inside the shelter, looking out at the grass that ringed their hideout, when they heard the soft suck of something out in the marshland.*

*They glanced at each other, skin glazed white in the spill from the torch, uncertain about what they'd heard. They stared out at the bogs, talking in hushed whispers to one another. They told each other that, if the sound came from anywhere, it came from the Brink; they were safe on this side of the fence, it wasn't anything to worry about. Yet, their sense of unease lingered. It didn't help that it was ten o'clock at night, the entire headland pitch black, so even as they shone their* torch out through the embrasure on the pillbox – the window – they couldn't see very far. They couldn't see what part of the bog the noise came from.

And then it came again.

This time it sounded exactly like a foot pressing into the peat and lifting out again. Or a paw. Or a claw. And whoever – or whatever – it was, it was close, much closer than before. They whispered to each other that if it was as close as it sounded, it should have been right on top of them, on this side of the fence. They should have been able to see it. But it didn't help. When you were children, the blindness of the night held no logic.

'I'm scared,' Beth muttered, her voice cracking in the silence.

'Me too,' Penny replied, taking her sister's hand.

'I mean it. I'm really scared, Pen. I want to go home.'

'I know. I know you're scared.' She looked at her sister. 'So am I.'

That night, they ran faster than they'd ever run. They burst through the rear door of the pillbox and carved a path down the hill, back towards the dots of light that marked out the town. By the time they got home, breathless, terrified, their hearts thumping like fists on a door, they could see their parents through the windows at the front of the house, getting ready to go to bed. The two girls scrambled up the trellising and in through the bedroom window they'd left ajar, and then they lay under the covers, chests still beating out a rhythm, and pretended they were asleep. As the silence pressed hard against their ears, they whispered to one another that they would never go back.

They'd never go back to the Brink.

But then they did.

It took three months. By then, time had repaired some of their anxieties. Penny spent twelve weeks walking to and from school, talking them both around, and the more they talked, the braver they became. They were going to go back. There was nothing up there. There was nothing stalking the grassland. There was nothing beyond the fence but landmines buried deep in the earth — and maybe not even that if Penny's stepdad was to be believed.

Even so, the first time they returned, they were scared. The night they ran, the night they heard movement out in the bogs, trailed their thoughts as they went back to the pillbox. It stayed with them on the second visit too, on the third, on the tenth night they returned, on the twentieth. In truth, it never really went away.

Sometimes the fear made them see shapes out there in the long grass: what could have been the flick of hair, or the curve of a leg or an arm; what could have been fingers, bone white under the moon, or eyes, tiny pinpricks of light dancing in them. On those occasions, they'd hold each other's hands, Penny trying to be courageous, trying not to show how frightened she was even though her muscles were as rigid as iron. Frequently, they were terrified, but they were fascinated by the Brink too, by the idea there might be something out there. They were drawn to it, obsessed by it.

They never talked to their friends at school about going out after dark, because they didn't want it getting back to their parents. There didn't seem to be any actual rules to say that you couldn't go up to the perimeter fence, to the place where the pillbox was located. You just weren't allowed to go beyond it. But, gradually, over time, Penny and Beth heard the people in the town talk about the Brink more and more. It became a subject of discussion in shops, in the school playground, out in the streets when people passed each other. Jack would go with other men up into the hills to make sure the fence was still secure, that no one could accidentally wander into the minefield, or that an animal couldn't squeeze through again like Mr Sankle's dog had. Penny and Beth would ask Jack about what was out there,

*about the bombs and the idea of there being something else —*
*something worse — living in the Brink, but Jack told them as long as*
*they never went up there, they wouldn't ever have to worry about it.*
*He'd cuddle them and tell them he loved them, and that there were*
*some things in this world that children shouldn't have to think about.*
*Penny asked him what he meant by that and he just laughed, but she*
*thought she saw something else too. The same thing she saw in Beth's*
*face when they were out at the pillbox sometimes; the same thing Beth*
*saw in her.*

*Fear.*

*Sometime after that, the police declared the Brink officially out of*
*bounds to everyone in town, citing the unexploded bombs. It became a*
*hinterland that existed in the tall grass and steep slopes of the hills*
*beyond their homes, where no one would stray. To the kids, to the*
*adults too, the area beyond the fence became a place of whispers and*
*shadows, a place they didn't mention to outsiders, a repository for*
*secrets they were too scared or too embarrassed to talk about. The fence*
*was checked over and strengthened, and — halfway along one of the*
*three trails that snaked from the town into the hills — the town council*
*built an eight-foot gate in an effort to stop hikers and tourists — or*
*drunken rubberneckers from the town who had nothing better to do —*
*unwittingly ending up at the Brink.*

*But it didn't stop Penny and Beth.*

*Four months after the gate went up, the girls returned to the hill*
*again. They said goodnight to their parents, waited an hour, placed*
*pillows under their duvets, and then climbed down the trellising on*
*the outside of the house.*

*Breath gathering in the darkness above them, they headed out*
*through the northern edges of the town — avoiding shops, the pub, the*
*community hall — and picked up the trail. They didn't switch their*
*torches on until they were out of sight, and when they did, they*

quickened their pace, tracing the twisting path that would eventually take them to the gate. It was much scarier on the trail after dark, the hills bigger and more frightening, but it was easier to go out at night. They wouldn't risk running into anyone, and no one would suspect a couple of girls — one of them now twelve, the other ten — of having the guts to go out like this. They weren't exactly sure what they were going to do when they got to the gate, how they were going to get past it or over it — they'd just work it out once they were there. But that was when they discovered something.

A gate had never been built.

The adults were lying.

# 14

I woke early the next morning.

Padding through to the kitchen, I filled the kettle and looked again at the photos I'd taken of the woman in Richard Kite's file. I'd studied her face on the journey back the previous night, trying to see if I recognized anything else in the picture, but I'd slowly tired as my adrenalin fizzled out.

Off the back of a night's rest, I still struggled to find anything new in the picture and also didn't understand why Russum would have two copies of the same shot. Even if I was willing to believe that she'd selected the image to see if Richard recognized Regent's Park, there were a thousand other pictures she could have chosen, all of which would have provided a clearer view. So why was this woman in the file twice? Who was she?

I couldn't find any obvious answers.

Making myself a coffee, I grabbed my laptop and switched my attention to the school I'd followed Russum to instead. I'd never heard of the Red Tree before, but I'd done a cursory search on my mobile the previous evening and found out pretty quickly that it was one of London's most prestigious private schools. As I went back to their website again, I now saw that, under *Fees*, it was almost seven grand a term for day pupils and over eleven for boarders. It wasn't quite Harrow, Malvern or Eton, but it wasn't far off.

In *History*, I discovered that the school was named after a copper beech that had grown in the yard at the front of the building – its leaves a distinctive purple-red – until it was struck by lightning in 1962. I found out that the current building was constructed on the site of a church burned down during the Great Fire of London and, before it became a school, it had been a government office, a home, a museum and a bank. I also came across an *Our Staff* page, with photographs of the headmaster – a man in his late forties called Roland Dell, handsome and well groomed – as well as his deputies and the various heads of department.

Again, I started to wonder if any of this really mattered. The only vaguely relevant question was why Naomi Russum had visited the school, and why she had a swipe card for the security door, but even that was beginning to seem more obvious in the cold light of day: the bio on the Aldgate Clinic's website said that Russum taught in both the NHS and the private sector. This whole thread had come about not from a direct connection to Richard Kite, but because – certain that she'd been keeping something back from me at her office – I'd followed her.

*So why would she record our conversation?*

Unable to come up with anything, I went back to the shot of the woman, sitting on a bench in a sun-dappled Regent's Park. I studied her face, trying to work out who the woman might be, why Russum might be showing Richard her picture, and why Russum kept two identical photographs of her. I looked at the two pictures individually and then together, and then individually again, and as I did, I found my gaze drifting to the woman's neck, her collar, her shoulders.

I stopped.

Scooping the phone up off the table, I pinch-zoomed into an area at the top of her left arm. Her blouse was opaque on the chest and shoulders, but at the arms it switched from a silky material to a kind of thick gauze. It was still hard to make out the skin beneath, but I could see the outline of something now, under the material of her blouse and poking out, just fractionally, below the hem of the short sleeve. I swiped right, going to the second, identical photograph of the woman.

*They're not the same.*

I leaned closer to the screen, swiping back and forth between the two photos. In the first, the woman had a small black mark beneath her blouse. But in the second picture, there was no mark. It was gone. The two shots were identical except for a single tiny thing: in one of them, the woman had a tattoo on her arm; in the other, it had been digitally removed.

The tattoo was a silhouette of a bird in flight.

It was exactly the same as the one Richard Kite had.

# 15

I called the landline at the church. It was a Thursday morning, which was when Richard helped out there, but the church secretary said he'd called in sick.

I put the phone down and thought of the conversation he and I had had the previous evening about his phone being tapped. I wouldn't have blamed him if he was spooked and didn't want to go into work. I called his mobile this time: once I got hold of him, I'd have him find a landline at the caravan park – or, even better, if he'd already gone out and got himself a replacement phone, we'd just use that.

But all I got was his voicemail.

I hung up without leaving a message and tried to think laterally. Maybe he genuinely was sick. Maybe he was asleep. Maybe he'd already headed out to get a new handset and left the old one at home in the caravan. If any of those were true, he'd either return, or wake up and find out he'd missed a call from me.

Except something else happened instead.

Forty minutes later, as I stood at the kitchen counter making more coffee, I watched a man appear at the gates of my drive, study the house and its number, and then move gingerly, almost timidly, to the front door.

I opened it before he'd even rung the bell.

'Richard?'

He had a rucksack on his back and a brand-new mobile phone clutched in his hands.

'Sorry to surprise you like this,' he said.

'What are you doing here?'

'I, uh . . .' He swallowed. 'I'm sorry, I just got a bit . . .' *Scared*.

I invited him in, then made him a drink. When I took it through to the living room, he still looked panicked, shorn of his maturity, smaller somehow as he leaned over the table and took in what amounted to his case so far. He pointed to the paperwork as I approached him.

'Have you found out who I am yet?'

He said it with a smile on his face, but his eyes betrayed him: deep down, a part of him was clinging on to the hope that the answer might be yes.

'I've been thinking a lot about the phone,' he continued softly.

I looked at the new handset he was holding.

'I got the replacement like you said, but I can't stop thinking about the old one.'

He glanced at the table again. It was an untidy mix of papers and partially hidden photographs and would have meant about as much to him as if there had been nothing on the table at all. His eyes were red, ringed with the evidence of a sleepless night; a night when every noise he heard outside the caravan had sounded like whispers and footsteps. He seemed even more confused, and was probably a little angry too, but mostly he was frightened. I hadn't really seen it the day I'd met him, but I saw it now – the child in him, the echoes of who he'd once been.

'Why would someone be trying to track me?' he said. 'I just don't get it.'

'Neither do I yet, but I'm going to find out.'

He nodded.

'I mean it.'

I went to the table, pushed aside some paperwork and picked up one of two printouts I'd made of the woman in Regent's Park. This was the photograph with the tattoo removed. I looked at her for a second, at the BT Tower behind her, at her face, at her arm, and then handed it to Richard.

'Do you recognize her?'

He frowned, taking the printout. In all the years I'd worked missing persons, in all the years I'd been a journalist before that, I never thought there was much subtlety to confusion: you were either confused or you weren't. But every time I looked at Richard Kite, I realized how wrong I was. He was in a perpetual state of turbulence, disorientated to the point where every new question he had, every answer he didn't expect or understand, knocked him a little further off course.

'Yes,' he said, and looked up at me. 'I recognize her.'

'Where from?'

'She's one of the women Naomi shows me.'

'Does she show you this woman's picture often?'

'I don't know about often. But sometimes.'

'Does she say why?'

He shrugged. 'Trying to jog my memory, I guess. She shows me all sorts of pictures of people, landmarks and events. This woman ... I think Naomi said she's some sort of singer.'

'Right. What did she say her name was?'

'She doesn't really tell me their names. She says it's better for me long term if I can try and remember them using visual cues.'

That sounded like bullshit even to a layman like me.

Richard eyed me. 'Don't you know her then?'

This was where I had to be careful. I needed him to act normally the next time he sat down with Russum – otherwise she'd instantly know something was up – and I was already asking him to keep from her the idea that his phone was being tracked. Making him question the veracity of the things she was showing him would make him question the treatment she was giving him, and that would only lead us into deeper water.

'No,' I said to him, trying to make light of the situation, 'but then I've always been more of an Elvis man.'

He smiled, studying the picture again, while I went hunting for musicians on my laptop, using the woman's physical description as a way to try and narrow the search. I didn't get very far but I remained pretty convinced that she wasn't a famous singer.

Taking the printout back from him, I slid it beneath a stack of other papers and said, 'Have you ever heard of the Red Tree before?'

He looked at me. 'The Red Tree? No.'

'It's a school. You've never come across that name? Maybe it's somewhere that Naomi might have mentioned in your sessions?'

'No,' he said again. 'Never.'

I moved on.

'I read in the paperwork that you've got a tattoo on your arm.'

'Yes.'

'Can I take a look?'

He removed his thin anorak and put it on the back of the chair. Underneath, he had on an army-green fleece. He unzipped that too but only took one arm out. Even before he'd turned his shoulder to me, I could see it.

He took a step closer, holding the sleeve of his T-shirt in place at the top of his arm. The tattoo was simplistic and not particularly detailed – exactly as it had looked in the file I'd read. I'd been hoping I might have been able to tell what bird it was up close.

'Any memory of getting this at all?'

He shook his head. 'No.'

'No idea where or when?'

'No, none.' He looked down at his arm, his red hair falling forward. 'I wish I could remember,' he added quietly.

But when he looked up at me again, there was something else in his face – and whatever it was, I couldn't read it as clearly this time.

'Are you okay, Richard?'

'Yes,' he said.

'Is there anything else you want to tell me?'

He shook his head.

'Are you sure?'

'It's just so frustrating,' he said, and then started readjusting his T-shirt and fleece until the tattoo was covered up again. 'It's just so frustrating not being able to remember.'

I nodded, watching him closely.

As I did, I felt suspicion start to surface again, forming

like a ball at the back of my throat. I just wasn't sure if it was for what I'd found out about Naomi Russum, about the lies she'd been telling me — or whether, much worse than that, I was genuinely starting to doubt Richard Kite himself.

# 16

I offered Richard the sofa bed in my spare room, left him to sleep off the effects of a night without rest, and tried to get my thinking straight. If he was lying to me, or keeping something back, it wouldn't be the first time that some-one had hired me and sat on a secret. But, equally, I knew there was an easy explanation for his hesitancy and general sense of confusion.

The truth was, I didn't see him as a liar, certainly not a vindictive and deliberate one, and so far couldn't see how he would benefit from having me chase my tail for weeks on end, searching for answers he already had. And because suspicion tended to dismantle a case quickly – especially if it was cast in the wrong direction – for now I chose to believe he wasn't playing me and returned to the casework.

The first thing I did was call an old friend of mine, Ewan Tasker, who was a semi-retired ex-detective doing consulting work for the National Crime Agency. I'd known him since my days as a journalist, when I'd used him as a source and, in return, he'd used me to help push stories out into the wild that aided his cause.

He picked up after a couple of rings.

'Raker, you old dog.'

'Hey, Task,' I said, smiling. 'How's things?'

We chatted for a while – about his wife, who hadn't

been well; his golf swing; people we knew inside and outside the Met – and then I gently steered the conversation around again and told him I was hoping for a bit of help.

'What are you after?'

'A database search,' I said. 'I'm trying to ID someone. A white female in her early to mid thirties. I don't know anything about her – name, DOB, address, history, anything. She's basically a blank. To be honest, she may not even be *in* the database, but if she is, I think it might be a tattoo she has that could narrow the search down. It's a silhouette of a bird on her upper left arm. You can just about make it out in the photo I'm sending you.'

Tasker whistled. 'Okay.'

'I know it's super vague.'

'So you think she's in the database because she hasn't been ID'd yet?'

He meant, did I think she was dead.

'I don't know,' I said. 'I don't know what to think about her.'

As I pondered that, a second thought came to me: if she *was* in the database, her tattoo would have been entered as a distinguishing mark – so why hadn't Richard been linked to her already? After all, they had the same mark in exactly the same place. It meant that either DC Barton had done a half-arsed job during his initial investigation – which I doubted – or the woman definitely wasn't in the database. The more I thought about it, the more likely it seemed that I'd end up with nothing from Tasker's search, but nothing was pretty much what I had on her at the moment, so I wasn't sacrificing anything by getting him to look.

'All right,' Tasker said. 'Leave it with me.'

'Thanks, old man. Could you also run the name Naomi Russum?'

'You got a DOB there?'

'Nineteen seventy-two is as good as it gets,' I said, looking down at my notes. I'd found the date in a biography at the end of a paper she'd written.

Task said he would do that as well and rang off.

I returned to my laptop and went searching for Russum myself. There was plenty to find: she was widely published in academic circles, she'd been frequently featured as an expert on news channels and radio phone-ins, and in an image search I stumbled across a series of pictures of her at social functions, charity events and minor celebrity junkets. The photos were mostly from magazine websites like *Hello!* and *OK!*, the sort of high-polish, stage-managed shots that showed people with rigid smiles and champagne glasses in hand. In accompanying captions, Russum was variously referred to as a *renowned psychologist*, a *writer and broadcaster*, a *successful city businesswoman*, and *MD of the exclusive Aldgate Clinic*. In all the photographs of her, she was immaculately dressed and styled, but the awkward smile and the lack of light in her eyes immediately put me in mind of when I was at her office.

I went back and forth through the pictures, taking a closer look at the people surrounding her. I was looking for faces I recognized, things that might start to connect her, and other people she knew, to Richard Kite, but after a while it just became the same faces in the same sort of locations with the same cut-and-paste captions.

Then, on another run-through, a two-year-old magazine

scan of her at a charity event made me stop. It was some-where on the Southbank, a fundraiser for displaced children in the Middle East and Africa, and Russum was standing next to a fireplace, flanked by five other people: three men I'd never seen or heard of before, a woman I vaguely recog-nized from a morning TV show about antiques, and a fourth man in a fawn blazer. He was in his thirties, tall, a little awkward. I didn't know him either, but I could see something in a repeated pattern on his tie.

A coat of arms.

*The same one I'd seen on the doors of the Red Tree.*

I dragged the picture on to my desktop and zoomed into it. The man was to the right of Russum, a good four or five inches taller, clean-shaven with brown hair that was starting to thin on top. In the caption beneath the picture, it said his name was Jacob Howson, a *published author and head of department at the exclusive Red Tree School.*

Was he what connected Russum to the school?

I did a search for Howson. He had a Facebook page, but his wall and all the photos were locked. Instead, I found a picture of him on the Red Tree website, among the staff photos. His book, the *published author* part of the magazine caption, turned out to be a biography of Joseph Conrad.

I returned to the photograph of him and Russum and started to get the feeling that there was something else in it too; something I hadn't seen yet.

I magnified it a couple of times more before inching back out again, unsure of what I'd glimpsed. It was subtle, but it was there. I cropped in on Russum and Howson, trying to look for tells in their expressions, and then moved on to the other people in the picture, double-checking that I definitely hadn't seen them anywhere since starting Richard's case. I hadn't. I was sure of it.

So what had I glimpsed?

I returned to Howson and Russum. Their stances mirrored one another, presumably at the behest of the photographer: they were facing inwards, their elbows up on the mantelpiece behind them, striking the kind of artificial pose you only ever saw in photo shoots. My eyes moved left, to the other men and woman, then back to Howson and Russum. Was it something to do with how they were positioned?

Or was it *where* they were positioned?

Above the fireplace behind them, above the mantelpiece that they were both resting against, was a large, golden-framed mirror. The glass was reflecting back the room they were in. I could see crowds of people in the mirror, milling around off camera – expensive suits, colourful dresses, champagne glasses.

I zoomed in a little more, in towards the rectangle of mirror between Howson and Russum, so that – by the time I was done – most of what I was looking at in the photograph was glass, except for the edges, which were taken up by the fawn of Howson's suit and the blue of Russum's dress. The mirror's reflection showed a group of four people talking off camera, and then a fifth – a woman, across to the side – her head slightly bowed as she looked down at her mobile phone screen.

I recognized her straight away.

It was the woman on the Regent's Park bench.

# 17

The more I looked at the image of the woman, reflected in the mirror, the more convinced I became by the idea that she was there *with* Jacob Howson and Naomi Russum; that this wasn't coincidence, a quirk of fate that had put her at the same party, in the same London venue, at exactly the same time. I'd already established a connection between Russum and the woman by virtue of the fact that Russum was showing Richard Kite a photograph of her, but this confirmed a knowledge of each other, a relationship of some kind.

The woman may have been off camera, may not have been an official part of the picture that had run in *British Society* magazine, but it looked like she was waiting for the two of them. There was something in her stance – it was comfortable, relaxed, as if she was easy being part of the group – and in her proximity to them too, the way she was on her mobile phone, filling dead time while photographs were being taken.

They knew who she was and she knew them.

A few minutes later, Richard came through, his face pale and fatigued. I took a break from the photograph and made us both some seafood linguine for lunch, and then we sat at the counter in the kitchen and ate.

'Sometimes,' he said after a while, bent over his bowl of pasta, the steam rising past his face in white strands, 'I taste things and they feel familiar to me.'

I looked at him. 'You remember eating them?'

'No.' He shook his head. 'No, it's not that. It's not like I get a clear memory of eating them, it's more like a general sense that I like them, and always have.'

'Like an echo?'

'Right.' He nodded, more vigorously a second time when he thought about it. 'An echo, right. Food, *taste* – I call them "connectors". I'm eating this and I'm thinking, "This tastes really good because I love seafood," but I don't have any memory of eating seafood, I just know I like it.' He paused for a moment, furrows forming in his brow, and then speared a prawn with his fork. 'This is a connector. This connects me back to who I was before, because I know I really like prawns.'

'Like you know how to swim?'

'Right.'

'Is it just food that does that?'

'Food definitely does,' he said, chewing. 'I like steak too. I love bananas – they're my favourite fruit; I could eat them all day – and I knew I'd like them even before I tasted them. But I hate cauliflower. I've never eaten cauliflower since they found me, I just know I don't like it. It's the smell it has when it's being boiled.' He waved a hand in front of his face. 'My stomach turns the minute I catch a whiff of it. That's another connector – but a more negative one.'

'So it's like an instinct that kicks in?'

He nodded. 'Yes.'

'What else do you feel that instinct about?'

His fork hovered over the linguine. 'I don't know really,' he said softly.

'Nothing comes to mind?'

He shrugged. 'I mean, I like books.'

'What type of books?'

'I really like science-fiction novels. I'm reading *This Perfect Day* at the moment by a guy called Ira Levin. Have you heard of him?'

'I have. He's a great writer.'

'I'm really enjoying it.'

'Do you think you might have read him before?'

'I don't know. I don't think so.'

'You don't feel that connection?'

He shook his head. 'No. Just a blank.'

He became quieter after that, and although he was polite and asked me questions about the house, about the people in the photos I had on display in the living room, about my work and my life in London, eventually we arrived at the question he really wanted answered.

'Do you think you'll ever find out?'

I looked at him. 'Find out what?'

'Who I am.'

'Yes,' I said. 'I do.'

I meant it, even if there were moments when I had doubts, but – as he looked at me – I got the sense that he didn't believe me, or at least wasn't allowing himself to believe it just yet. He'd been burned once, when he thought the media coverage would bring him an answer, a biography of who he was, a family. This time, there was something else to unnerve him as well: not only the fear that I would fail to find anything, but that someone was watching his phone – his calls, texts, his activity.

'Do you want to crash here tonight?' I asked him.

He looked embarrassed. 'I don't know,' he said. 'I'm sorry for just turning up like this. I didn't know what else to do this morning. Reverend Parsons is away . . .' His voice tailed off.

'It's fine,' I said.

'I don't expect you to –'

'Honestly, Richard, it's fine. You can stay.'

He seemed so grateful at such a small act.

'Thank you,' he said. 'Thank you so much.'

I told him I needed to get back to work and he offered to wash up, so I left him in the kitchen and headed back to the living room.

As I did, my phone started buzzing.

It had only been a couple of hours since I'd called Ewan Tasker, and usually – if he was phoning back so quickly – it was because the police database had an answer for me. That didn't mean the answers were going to be good. In fact, it probably meant the woman in the photograph wasn't on the system at all, or was simply impossible to find.

I heard movement and background noise as Tasker found somewhere quiet, and then he said, 'Let's start with Naomi Russum. There's not much on her, really. Or nothing exciting, anyway. Born 13 January 1972 in Oxford, hasn't had any cautions or arrests, hasn't been convicted of anything. She's the owner of a Porsche 718 and her home address is listed as Belmont Road in Clapham.'

'What about the woman with the tattoo?'

'Nothing you can use,' Task said. 'The tattoo leads nowhere – or, rather, the only place it leads is your guy, Richard Kite. There's people with similar tats on the database, but – other than Kite – not the exact same one, and not a female who looks like the woman in the picture you sent me.'

A dead end. But, despite that, the woman had existed, had a name, a history, a family – and all of those things left trails, however well hidden.

I just had to find hers.

## 18

Returning to the photograph in Regent's Park, I placed the two colour printouts side by side on the table. Did the woman work with Russum at the clinic? Did she work at the school with Jacob Howson? Could Russum and Howson have had a professional relationship as well as a social one? What did Russum do at the school?

I considered the idea that Russum and Howson might be going out, but I couldn't find any evidence that Russum had a partner, much less that it was Howson. Although Howson's Facebook page was inaccessible, in his profile picture and in the photo of him at the charity event, he wasn't wearing a wedding ring. That didn't necessarily mean anything, but there was no mention of a wife or a partner in the biography he had for his book on Conrad either.

Frustrated, I returned to the woman on the bench, to the two pictures of her, one where the bird's wings extended across the flesh at the top of her arm, the other where there was no bird and no proof that it had ever existed. Russum herself, or someone she knew or worked with, must have removed the tattoo on a computer.

As I thought of that, I thought of something else: what if a surgeon had actually removed it from the woman's skin in real life, sometime after the picture was taken? That would explain the lack of a trail back to her in the police database, *if* she was even in it in the first place and *if* the police had had some cause to add her to the system.

Even if the removal was successful, though, and the woman in the picture hadn't been left with scarring or changes in the pigment of her skin, it should have been obvious to investigators – if she subsequently turned up as a suspect or a victim – that, at some point, she'd had a tattoo. The fact that there was so much black in the bird, and in such a concentrated area, made it likely there would be ghosting or textural changes to the skin, however subtle. I found it hard to swallow the idea that it would get missed – or would fail to be noted.

*Unless the police never realized it was there at all.*

Instantly, another idea started to form.

I pulled my laptop towards me. The more the idea grew, the more I could sense something bad, a certainty built on years of following this same path into the dark. Tasker had already done a search for women reported missing using the tattoo as an identifier, but this time I took the tattoo out of the equation entirely and went searching based on physical description and approximate age only.

And not for missing women, but for unidentified remains.

It took me a while, applying and reapplying different search parameters on the Missing Persons Bureau website – but then finally I found something.

My stomach dropped.

I went back to Google, using the basic information on the MPB to search for media coverage. The first link was to a story in the *Guardian*, but I discovered different versions of the same event covered in other nationals as well. All of them were short, and all of them had been published on the same date two years ago: Thursday 6 November 2014.

I looked at a headline in the *Mail*.

### GRISLY FIND AT LONDON HOUSING ESTATE

The housing estate in the headline was the Armbury in Abbey Wood, south-east London. It ran parallel to a set of train tracks which had been closed since 2014 due to the Crossrail excavation, so there was a half-mile stretch of line which no one ever used. The papers described it as a dumping ground and said that a local man, Alan Havenger, had got over the fence and on to the tracks. Witnesses told reporters that Havenger was always over there, and that, if he ever saw something he liked, he'd take it back to his flat and try to fix it up – broken lawn-mowers, TVs, bicycles.

On 5 November 2014, he found a body.

I felt myself tense as I read through the rest of the article. So soon after the body was found, there wasn't much more than basic information in the newspapers, including a vague physical description: a white female in her early to mid thirties with blonde hair. I skipped forward, trying to find the follow-up pieces that surely had to have appeared in the days afterwards – but all I got was a small piece in the *Evening Standard* five days on.

From that, it was clear that investigators still had no idea who the woman was. That was the reason the nationals had lost interest: with no name, there was no story. Forensics believed the victim had been there a fortnight, and the reason Havenger didn't find her until then was because her body had been pushed into a pile of railway sleepers. And not just pushed either: shoved, crammed, squeezed until her bones snapped.

It was hard to tell what the worst bit of the story was: that, or what else was found on her body. I knew now why Tasker had failed to find a match for the tattoo on the database: because when the woman was found, she didn't have one.

The tattoo had been cut out of her.

It had been flayed from her arm, along with similar chunks from her legs and her right arm too. It seemed obvious why: to throw detectives off the scent. Deliberately flay one piece of skin and the cops would ask why. Why that part of the body? What had been cut out? Flay three and it began to look like something else: a work of frenzy and chaos; the work of a murderer spiralling out of control.

But that wasn't the reality.

This wasn't someone out of control. It was a deliberate act – and it was a killer who knew exactly what he was doing.

I called Ewan Tasker back and told him what I'd discovered, and then he went to the database and found her. The case hadn't come up in his results because the woman had never been reported missing, or as being in any kind of danger, and she had no tattoo. Because of the flayed skin, investigators had come at the injuries from the wrong direction, with the wrong type of killer in mind, and the file had been constructed from there.

'What about the victim's DNA?' I asked. 'Teeth? Fingerprints?'

'It leads nowhere.'

'Nothing at all?'

Tasker took a long breath. 'Look, Raker, you know I can't pretend I haven't found this now. If there's a chance we can try and find out who she is, and why she was killed – if there's a chance to find the prick who did this – we need to take it. I can give you three or four days, a week maybe, but after that I'm going to have to pass it up the chain. I can't in all good conscience sit on this.'

'I understand.'

'I'm sorry, old friend.'

'You don't have to apologize, Task.'

Tasker was giving me a week.

I had to make it count.

# PART TWO

# Extract from *No Ordinary Route: The Hidden Corners of Britain* by Andrew Reece

This book started out as a travelogue, a cele-
bration of Britain, Britons and the far corners
of our country we still don't know about, but
my meeting with my friend the journalist and
broadcaster Tomas Cassell changes all that.

'Have you ever been to the place before?'
Tomas asks me.

'No. Never. What's it like?'

He seems confused, which is very unlike Tomas.

'My dad was a pilot and the RAF station was
a few miles out of the town back then.' He stops
again. 'That was how I ended up going there as
a kid.'

'What do you remember about it?'

'Rain.'

'Rain?'

'It rains a lot there. Like, a *lot*.'

'Well, that's British weather for you.'

Tomas smiles. 'Yes, I suppose.'

But then the smile fades again.

'The people,' he says.

'What about them?'

'I never warmed to them.'

'Why?'

'They were just very, very strange.'

Seven weeks later, I think of what Tomas said to me as the town comes into view. The approach – especially at night – feels like it goes on for ever, a journey to the edge of the world. You'll see twinkles of light in the darkness first, stardust scattered in the folds of Mount Strathyde, and if you choose to come across the suspension bridge, built in 1985 and funded by the Thatcher government to the tune of a cool £25 million, you'll be greeted by a Union Jack standee made from red, blue and white plastic sheep. It's a nod to the community's farming roots, but also an attempt to show the town as welcoming, with a knowing sense of humour.

Except, once I park up and check in at the only B&B around, there seems to be a total lack of playfulness among the people who inhabit this place. Perhaps it's the perpetual feeling that things are on the verge of breaking down here. The small and compact centre is a good example of this. It's very easy to navigate, really just a square with some shops, a pub, a community hall and a school around it. But every-thing feels dilapidated. Paint is peeling. The awnings on shopfronts are faded and discol-oured. The school looks more like a prison than a place of education. Even the lido, further out, an odd and – in its own way – beautiful building, a sort of cross between a castle and a spaceship, has gone the same way. It's still open but its walls are cracked and there are weeds everywhere.

Ultimately, there seems to be only one reason to visit, and that's for the hiking. But that's where things get weird again. Routes aren't marked on local maps, and there's a strange lack of cooperation from locals when you ask for advice on where the best trails are located. Basically, I have to work it all out for myself as I make my way up to Steep Fell, a road that runs along the northern edge of the town. Here, I find a set of steps that takes me up to a scree path, which in turn splits into three.

Two of the routes coil around the eastern flanks of Mount Strathyde as it rises eleven hundred metres, and they end up in almost the same place, at a lookout with breathtaking views across the Wallace Strait. The other route is less challenging but also less rewarding. It heads west, in a shallow diagonal along a straightforward path, until it reaches a kind of plateau. After that, the path disappears and I find myself in a mix of thick grassland and peat bogs, and on the wrong side of a six-foot-high security fence. If the locals show a lack of cooperation in helping me plan a hike on the way up, on the way down they're pretty effusive about the reasons the security fence has been erected: the marshland is dangerous and incredibly easy to get lost in, and with no local mountain rescue force, it's safer if everyone just steers clear.

But not everyone is singing from the same hymn sheet. Afterwards, most people tell me the area is shut off because it's full of explosives left over from when – to protect against German invasion – the coast was landmined during the Second World War. But the man mowing the grass banks of the empty lido says it's to do with an outbreak of brucellosis in the sheep and someone else tells me it's due to a rockfall. When I talk to the lady running my B&B, she says she isn't sure what the reasons are and then hurries out of the room to make me a fried breakfast I never asked for.

It sums up the weirdness of this town perfectly.

In a lot of ways, it's like a living museum, a place that exists on the periphery of Britain, in a bubble of time forty years old. The Union Jacks, the red telephone boxes, the scones, pots of tea on the village green, it's like riding a wormhole back to the 1950s. The fact that there's not much in the way of ethnic diversity might, if you don't happen to be white, make you think that the way the townsfolk respond to you is down to skin colour. It's not. White, black, Asian, mixed race, it doesn't really matter that much: locals will talk to you if you talk to them, but you get the impression they're watching their words. In fact, if you were to let your imagination run away with you, you might start to think that they're all hiding something.

*They're all hiding something.*

I first wrote that sentence, in shorthand, on the day I arrived in town, as a joke; the idea that the folk here are harbouring some dark and terrible secret was meant to have been a light-hearted comment. But, the thing is, by the time you leave, you're not so sure any more.

Because it actually feels like they might be.

# 19

The Armbury estate was a compact series of three-storey flats about half a mile east of Abbey Wood station. It was shaped like an insect on its side, eight cul-de-sacs, each two hundred yards long, sprouting north out of a long horizontal road called Skylark Avenue. Once I arrived, I could see the name didn't really fit the place: the approach from the station was bleak and depressing.

On the train journey across London, I'd spent the time familiarizing myself with the case file in the unsolved murder of the woman. Richard Kite had come with me, sitting on the opposite side of a near-empty end carriage, reading his copy of *This Perfect Day*. I'd shown him one of the pictures that Ewan Tasker had sent me, taken at the scene: a wide-angled shot of the railway line and the pile of sleepers in which the body had been found.

'Do you recognize this place?' I'd asked him.

He'd laid the book down on his lap and taken my phone from me. As I'd waited, I'd gone through some of the other photographs Tasker had sent over that I wouldn't be showing him. If I'd held any doubts that the victim might not be the woman in the Regent's Park photograph, they'd soon been dispelled. In situ crime scene pictures were more ambiguous, but a shot from the autopsy was definitely her.

'No,' he'd said finally, shaking his head. 'Where is that place?'

'I'll show you when we get there.'

Once we did, I went back to the casework and saw that the body had been found on the railway line, level with the three-quarter mark of Skylark Avenue. An old chain-link fence was all that separated the road from the tracks, although the line was in a dip – about twenty feet below the level of the housing estate – and the bank that led to it ran away sharply and was littered with debris. When I stopped and looked through, trying to trace an easy path down, I saw that someone had dumped a TV in the grass immediately in front of me. Beyond that were tyres, a bookcase, mulched cardboard. I caught sight of something else too, blue, still knotted around the trunk of a tree on the far side of the tracks.

Police tape.

Richard had shadowed me all the way along the road, saying nothing, his book in one hand, his new mobile phone in the other. He looked nervous. As I grabbed hold of the fence, lacing my fingers through it, I pointed down the slope. 'This is the place in the photograph that I showed you on the train,' I said.

He stepped up to the fence and looked through.

'It definitely doesn't ring any bells?' I asked.

'No.' He looked more frustrated this time, his eyes sweeping across the bank as it slid away towards the railway tracks. 'I don't remember any of it.'

'You might not have ever been here.'

He realized I was trying to help – reassuring him that it didn't matter – but it mattered to him because it was another blank; another question mark he couldn't find an answer to. His eyes lingered on the items that were dumped in the grass.

'Something was found down there,' I said.

I tried to work out what I lost by telling him the truth. I'd brought him here based on our conversation at lunch, hoping for that one second of clarity – that moment of connection – when his deep-rooted instinct kicked in. Telling him about the woman's murder didn't concern me: what concerned me was the relationship he'd built – or thought he'd built – with Naomi Russum. I needed all of this kept away from her for as long as possible, and I worried that Richard would unwittingly let it slip, even if I asked him not to talk to Russum about it.

'When do you next see Naomi?' I asked.

He frowned, not understanding the change of direction, and – not for the first time – I saw an intelligence behind his eyes; a smart man trying to work out where this was heading as he felt his way through the disorder of memory loss.

'Next week,' he said. 'Friday.'

So either I had eight days where I couldn't tell him anything, or I had eight days to wrap this case up. If I wrapped it up, it wouldn't matter what he told Russum.

'A body was found down there,' I said.

His face blanched. 'A body?'

'A woman. I'm trying to figure out who she is.' I stopped, looked at him. 'I think there's a chance you might have known her before you lost your memory.'

He looked even more unsettled now, his eyes moving beyond the fence to the pile of sleepers in which she'd been found, and then down to the phone he held in his left hand. This wasn't the phone that had been tapped, but he was making the same connections I had: his phone had been compromised; now a woman he may have known was dead.

'Who was she?' he asked.

'I don't know her name.'

'So how would I have known her?'

'I don't know that either. But she had the same tattoo as you.'

'What?'

He seemed almost punch-drunk now.

I glanced behind me at the bank of flats, searching for signs we were being watched. When I turned back to him, he looked like he'd lost even more colour.

'Do you want to come with me?' I asked him.

He swallowed, eyes on the sleepers again.

'You can stay here if you want.'

But he was already shaking his head.

'No,' he said. 'No, I'll come.'

## 20

We landed on the other side.

As quickly as possible, I weaved a path down the bank between bits of old furniture and appliances, black dustbin bags that had split and showered their contents across the grass. The whole place stank of rotten food and the long grass was slick with rainwater, the mud slimy underneath. The closer we got to the line, the less light there seemed to be: the drop was twenty feet, but it was like abseiling into a cave.

At the bottom, I looked back at Richard and saw that he was ten feet behind me, his left hand gripping his book. While I waited, I removed a torch I'd brought with me and shone it in the direction of the railway sleepers. Shadows danced across the space in between, junk embedded in the line like old teeth. Mostly, though, it was just grass and weeds, braided around the tracks.

I was facing east: to my right was a high breezeblock wall; much further down, visible in the deteriorating light, was an enclosed railway footbridge. It ran between two platforms, and its entrances – the stairs up and back down the other side – were boarded up. The bridge was covered in graffiti, a vivid wall of colour so vast it was hard to see any of the original wood panels underneath. When I checked behind me, I saw that the line carried on for about sixty yards in the other direction before hitting a tunnel. The tunnel had been bricked up. It meant this whole stretch of line had been completely severed from the network.

As my eyes adjusted further it became slightly easier to see, but I kept the torch on all the same.

'You okay?' I said to Richard.

He moved in beside me and told me he was, then his eyes began shifting up and down the line, taking it in just as I had. I watched him, his reaction to everything, looking for some spark of recognition.

'I don't remember this place at all,' he said.

I let him have a moment more and then started to move, hearing him fall in behind me. Grass and weeds moved around my knees and ankles, and a couple of times I lost track of where the railway lines were and stumbled as my boots skimmed against them. A skeletal tree sat against the breezeblock wall, an arm breaking out of the earth. The police tape I'd seen from the top was wrapped around its trunk, but where it had been tied at the other end it had come loose, and now it lay across the tracks and grass, coiled like a worm.

I stopped at the railway sleepers.

There were eighteen, maybe twenty of them, stacked in a vague rectangle, each one about ten feet long and probably fifty kilos apiece. Originally they must have been part of the track that ran through here, but now they were just dormant chunks of lumber that wouldn't be going anywhere without a crane.

As I stood there, the torn police tape whipping against my legs, I went to my phone, bringing up the casework I'd been looking at on the train. Alan Havenger had told police that it was the smell that had drawn him in – 'this terrible, terrible smell' – and that, when he'd got to the sleepers, he'd been able to see 'something white'.

HAVENGER: I thought it was a piece of broken plate or china or something. There's tons of that sort of stuff down there. Some of the kids toss things like that over to see how far it'll go. But the closer I got, the worse the smell became. And then I got down on to my knees and looked through a gap in the side of the pile, and that was when I saw her.

I backed up and went to the crime scene photos. Even on a small screen, with some of the finer detail dialled down, it was pretty hard to stomach. A pale half-face had been visible. An eye, glazed and misty. Strands of dirty blonde hair, matted to her cheek.

Other photographs showed the pile of sleepers from different angles, but although hints of her body were evident in milky slivers – the knotty bump of an elbow through the torn fabric of her blouse; the flaky remains of blue nail varnish at the ends of her fingers – most of the woman remained hidden from view. That was the point: whoever killed her had forced her inside a gap in the sleepers, thinking she would never get found. Because of that, she'd been bent double, one knee touching her face, the bones in her arms and legs and neck all broken as she was folded and manipulated into the tiny space.

'How did she end up here?'

I looked at Richard. I'd been thinking the same thing: how did the killer get her down the bank? It would have been almost impossible to get her over the fence and all the way down here – at least, if the killer was alone – and, even if that was the case, the whole thing would have been an insane risk given how many windows looked out at the fence.

'Do you think she was carried down the bank?'

I shook my head. 'I doubt it.'

'Why?'

'Too hard and too much risk.'

He nodded, as if that made sense.

'She was brought in somewhere else,' I said.

He nodded again, and his eyes followed mine in the direction of the footbridge.

'Do you want me to go and look?'

He was standing about six feet from me, a V-shaped fan of grass between us, the hood up on his anorak now. The top of his book poked out of one of his pockets, the pages darkening as they were dampened by the rain.

'I can use the torch on my phone.'

'Okay,' I said. 'Give me a shout if you find anything.'

He started moving off in the direction of the foot-bridge. I watched him for a while, his head down, a cone of dusty light in the grass ahead of him – and then I returned my attention to the sleepers.

Swiping through the rest of the crime scene photog-raphy, I paused for a second time on the autopsy picture of the woman's face. She'd been cleaned up, her hair swept back from her forehead. There were cuts everywhere, small ones dotting her chin and cheeks, where the rough edges of the sleepers had snipped at the skin. There was bruising too – not so much on her face, but all around her neck like a scarf. In the pathologist's notes, he referred to breaks in, or severe damage to, the epiglottis, thyroid and cricoid cartilage, as well as the trachea, all of which were at the front of the neck. It seemed to confirm the force with which the body was manoeuvred into the space. The pathologist suggested the injuries the woman had suffered in those areas were almost certainly down to the way her head was bent forward, the way it was pressed with such ferocity to her throat. She'd suffered more injuries at the back too – vertebrae had snapped, so had the ligaments in her jaw. As I read the clinical description of her suffering, all I could cling on to was the hope that she'd been dead before she ever arrived here.

'David!'

Richard was trying to get my attention.

'I've found something,' he said.

I headed towards the footbridge.

The closer I got, the worse the weather became. It was fifteen minutes until the sun went down, the light was almost gone, and in the torch's glow the rain looked like thick lines of silver thread. For the first time, I realized something else too: the footbridge wasn't actually the shape I thought it was. I thought it had simply connected one platform to the other, and allowed passengers to cross from the westbound to the eastbound track. But on the eastbound side, the right as I looked at it, I realized now that it was split at the top, and that a second enclosed walkway continued into a housing estate on the other side of the breezeblock wall. I hadn't been able to see it until now because one walkway was obscured behind the other.

'Here,' Richard said.

He was standing at the top of the slope on the east-bound platform. Rain drifted off the roof of the footbridge, down the walls of graffiti, across the track and the platform, dotting my face, my jacket, my hands. I could smell old wood and oil, rotten food, urine, rust. But it hardly registered with me: I was too busy looking at the footbridge, at Richard on his haunches in front of the boarding that was supposed to have prevented anyone accessing the stairs.

Someone had cut a hole in it.

I instinctively looked up and down the line, as if answers might be hidden somewhere out there, buried in the shadows. When I turned back to the boarding, dropping to my knees next to Richard, I saw that a square about three feet high and roughly the same wide had been removed. I went to the casework on my phone and did a keyword search for *footbridge*. Buried in the middle of the investigation was something I'd missed: a one-line confirmation that the police believed this was how the body had arrived at the scene.

We returned to the sleepers, darkness settling like a blanket now. Moving left, around to the far side, I found thicker weeds and taller grass, everything more dense, the torchlight glinting off the undergrowth and the oil-stained wood.

And something else.

It was inside the sleepers, hidden deep within the shadows.

As I approached, I shone my torch into the interior. The sleepers had been shifted slightly to allow investigators to retrieve the body, but it was still untidy here like everywhere else, overrun, nature growing unchecked.

I moved even closer.

This time, I could see what had reflected back at me from inside the pile: a thin sheet of cellophane, rain-dotted and crinkled. As I angled the light into the space, I caught sight of more, and then more, and then saw that there was a whole collection: twenty, maybe thirty sheets. I realized too that the sheets of cellophane weren't flat, but conical in shape, and that each one had a label attached to it.

On each of the labels something had been handwritten.

'David?' Richard called from behind me. 'What can you see in there?'

I dropped to my haunches at the sleepers.

'Bouquets of flowers,' I said.

I reached in, my fingers brushing the cellophane of the one nearest to me, and pulled at it. The plastic snapped as I yanked it out through the gap. Inside was a bunch of yellow, red and pink carnations, but they'd just begun to turn: the petals had drooped, the edges fraying and fringed with the faint brown of decay.

The label, originally attached to the plastic with a staple, gently fell away, fluttering into my lap. When I picked it up and turned it over, I found a handwritten message smudged with damp and earth.

*I miss you x*

My eyes lingered on it for a moment and then I set it down and reached inside again, face pressed against one of the railway sleepers, trying to go further in than before. I managed to grab two bunches this time, one after the other. They were both carnations too – but one was in an advanced stage of decay, the flowers almost black, and the other was well on its way, with only a single red flower yet to rot.

Both had handwritten labels.

One said the same thing as the first flowers I'd grabbed – *I miss you x* – and was written in the same hand, with the same pen. The other was different.

*Please forgive me.*

My chest tightened. Tearing the card away from the cellophane, I held it out for Richard to take a look at and then kept going, pulling more and more flowers out of the sleepers until I had a pile of fifteen in a circle around me. There were still at least as many trapped inside. As I looked around at the ones I'd got out, I saw most of the flowers were long gone – reduced to stems, or gooey slop – but almost all the messages remained pinned to the plastic, and most were variations on the same theme. *I miss you. Please forgive me. I'm so sorry.*

'Do you recognize that handwriting?' I asked him.

He shook his head. 'No.'

'What about these flowers?'

He stepped closer.

'Do they ring any bells with you?'

'No,' he said again, and he looked to me for meaning, for an explanation of what was going on. I tried again to see if I could grab any more of the flowers, but the rest of them had been pushed too far out of my reach and getting to them meant moving one of the sleepers. It wouldn't be impossible with Richard's help, but it would be hard and I wasn't sure it really mattered: given what was written on the cards, and the fact the flowers were there in the first place – hidden inside the spot the woman's body had been dumped – it already felt like I had enough.

'Do you think the person who killed her left these?'

I glanced at Richard. It was an obvious question, but I wasn't sure if he really wanted the answer or not. He looked knocked off balance, and I wondered if I'd made the right decision in bringing him with me. Nothing had jogged his memory, and instead I'd filled the spaces in his head with new images that no one deserved to carry with them.

'I'm not sure,' I said.

It wasn't a lie, I didn't know for certain that her killer had left the flowers – but they'd clearly been left by someone battling with their conscience.

I picked up a couple of the cards.

They were all the same design – plain on the front except for a faint grey border, and then the logo of the florist on the back. Haggerty's. It was just one name in an ornate font – no address, email, phone or website – but, when I returned to my mobile and googled the business, I found it in less than five seconds.

It was based on Upper Thames Street.

Directly across the road from the Red Tree School.

# Born Ready

*The girls didn't go up to the Brink the night they discovered there was no gate. Instead, they turned around and ran home, worried that it might be a game one of the adults was playing; a trick to catch them out, an effort to prove that they'd both been disobeying the town rules. In fact, they became so invested in the idea, so paranoid about being found out, that they didn't return to the hills for another seven months.*

*Because they knew that if they were caught up there, they'd have to tell the adults everything: that they'd been going up to the Brink for four years, on and off; that they thought there might be something in the marshland – a monster, or a ghost, or an animal; and that, ultimately, what they'd always wanted more than anything else – the real reason they kept returning – was to find the courage to climb the fence and find out the truth for themselves.*

*Eventually, though, Penny grew tired of waiting.*

*'What if we actually did it?' she said as the girls walked to school one morning. 'What if we actually climbed over?'*

*Beth looked at her. 'Over the fence?'*

*'Sssshhhh,' Penny said, glancing around at the other kids walking to school, at some of the parents who were with them. 'Keep your voice down.'*

*They walked in silence for a while and then, quietly, Beth said: 'Are you serious, Pen? You really want to go back?'*

*'Yes. Don't you?'*

*'Yeah. I mean, I guess. But actually climb the fence?'*

Beth's voice was a little shaky: excited, anxious, frightened. Deep down, Penny felt the same, her heart racing at the idea of actually going out into the Brink; not just watching it and talking about it, but actually going out there. What if there really were bombs buried under the earth? What if there really was something even scarier than that?

'Pen?'

'I think we should do it,' Penny said, but although she sounded confident, she didn't feel it. 'First, though, I think we should start gathering evidence. Like, when we go up there and we think we see something in the Brink, we make a note of it. If we hear a weird noise, we do the same. We should write everything down and then we might start to see a pattern. It might show us the best time to climb over.'

Penny could see her sister relax a little when she realized they weren't going out any time soon. She didn't admit that she felt the same way as Beth.

'We should write down what the adults say too.'

Beth frowned. 'Why?'

'Because most people seem to believe there are bombs out there, right? But a few people like Jack, like that farmer who comes to the house sometimes, I don't think they believe that there are just bombs out there. I reckon that's the reason they're the ones that go up to check on the fence. Maybe they saw stuff when they were up there — the sort of stuff we've been seeing. Maybe they've seen more than we have. Maybe they've actually been over the fence and that's the reason Jack doesn't want to talk about it.'

'So you think Dad's scared?'

'Yeah,' Penny said, but became less certain the more she thought about it. 'I don't know. Maybe. If he isn't scared, what else could he be?'

'What do you mean?'

'I mean, if it's not fear, what is it?'

They were at the school gates now.

'I don't understand,' Beth said.

'Maybe he's lying.' Penny leaned in a little closer to her sister so no one could hear them. 'There was supposed to be a gate up on the trail, to stop people even going up to the Brink, but there's no gate. So what if the fence is just for show too?'

'Why would Dad lie to us?'

'I don't know,' Penny said. 'That's what we need to find out.'

They waited another month, just to be sure, and then started going back again.

They'd take notebooks with them and record everything – every movement, every sound – and, several months later, when spring came, when summer followed and the evenings got longer, they started taking more risks, heading out before the sun was down in order to see the Brink in the last vestiges of light. They'd never witnessed the marshland in anything other than darkness, but despite being able to get a better sense of how vast it was – the immenseness of what lay beyond the fence – they didn't ever spot anything.

Towards the end of summer, they were almost caught coming off the trail by some men stumbling out of the pub, so Penny said they should delay their next visit until the autumn. The wait was excruciating. After a month, as the evenings began drawing in again, Penny was tempted to go back up, but she told Beth they should wait an extra month, just to be sure.

The night they returned there was rain in the air. Penny was wearing a new windbreaker that Fiona and Jack had bought her for hockey, and Beth was dressed in a thick red coat, frayed at the sleeves, and thick woollen leggings. She also had a pair of mud-spattered, fur-lined boots on, hand-me-downs from Penny. At twelve now, Beth was of an age where she hated wearing Penny's old clothes, not because she disliked them but because she objected to having to wear second-hand skirts and jumpers. But she loved the boots. She wore them all the time, even inside the house, and Penny's mum had to make running repairs to them the whole time.

Penny looked out of the pillbox towards the fence. In the blackness of the marshland, she thought she could see movement, a brief flash of colour, but then it was gone again and she wasn't sure she'd actually seen anything at all. Even so, she reached into her pocket, took out her notebook, opened it to the right date and made a note of the sighting.

After she was done, she started going back through the notebook, back over a year's worth of entries, of glimpses and non-sightings and things the adults said that might have been important but probably weren't. The longer they'd been doing this, the more she'd begun to believe that there really wasn't anything out in the Brink at all, and if there wasn't, it made her wonder why people would say that there was. The two of them had looked out at the same swathe of grass, heard the same noises at night, seen the same hints of movement. Once or twice, they'd still got spooked, but most of the time they'd begun to outgrow any fear. She'd begun to outgrow the story of the landmines too. She'd read up on the Second World War at lunchtimes and after school and she couldn't find a single account of bombs being laid in this part of the country.

As a result, she'd talked about her suspicions to Beth, and her sister had started to see the logic in it. They spent long hours thinking about the movements and noises they'd heard over the years, about the stories they'd been told, and the explanations began to seem so obvious: the noises were the wind and the rain and the snow, beating against the hillside, against the grass, against the peat of the bogs; the movement was sheep, grazing in the crags, in the pockets of tussock grass, disguised by the colour of night. There were sheep farms everywhere, animals dotted in the fields that encircled the town for miles and miles in every direction, whichever road you took. They wandered. They found gaps in the boundary line, breaks in the fence, and they escaped to the other side, which was why the two of them had sometimes seen hints of something out in the Brink, low to the ground, a head below the level of the grass. And if there were sheep grazing out there, they should have set off the landmines, but the landmines never detonated. Nothing had ever exploded out there.

*Because there aren't any bombs,* Penny thought.

'I've met someone.'

Beth's voice made her flinch. It was the first sound – other than the beating rain – that either of them had heard since leaving the house. Penny turned to look at her. In the corner of the pillbox, swallowed by shadows, Beth's face formed a perfect oval inside the line of her hood. The darkness made her face look like it was detached from her body, a porcelain mask floating in time and space.

Beth was still physically small for her age, so Penny would sometimes forget that her sister was almost a teenager now – at least, until she spoke. That was when it would hit home again, because there had always been this weird contrast between the way Beth looked and the way she spoke. She appeared young but she spoke with such maturity that, sometimes, even knowing her so well, almost better than anyone else, it took Penny a moment to adjust.

'You've met someone?' Penny said. 'What are you talking about?'

'I've met someone.'

'A boy?'

'His name's Jason.'

Penny frowned, trying to think about whether she'd heard of a kid *in the town called Jason. But then she looked at Beth again and realized what she meant.*

'He's from somewhere else?'

Beth nodded. 'Yes.'

'How did you meet him?'

'He came here on holiday.'

'Does anyone know?'

'No. Of course not. Dad would have a shit-fit.'

*Penny looked out through the window in the pillbox, out through the grey tint of the rain to where the long grass swirled like an ocean on the other side of the fence. She studied it for a while, but there was nothing out there.*

'Penny?'

*She glanced at Beth.* 'What?'

'That's it? I thought you'd lecture me.'

'Why didn't you tell me before?'

'Because I thought you'd lecture me,' *Beth repeated.*

*Penny scanned the spaces beyond the boundary fence, half concentrating on what Beth had told her, half concentrating on hints of movement out in the grass.*

*Finally, she said,* 'Is he still here?'

'No, he went back last week.'

*Penny didn't say anything.*

*Beth rolled her eyes, as if she saw some accusation in her sister's silence.* 'Come on, Pen. Have you ever thought about what sort of future you have here? Because I have, and there isn't one. I'm not staying here for the rest of my life, dating some drone from the school whose idea of a great life is working for sixty years in a cow shed a mile from his front door. No way.'

*Penny smiled, despite herself.*

'What are you smiling at?'

'Sometimes it's hard to believe you're only twelve.'

Beth seemed unsure whether to take that as a compliment or an insult. She came forward on the piece of concrete she was perched on and said, 'So, do you?'

'Do I what?'

'Do you want to stay in this shithole for the rest of your life?'

'It's not that bad.'

'It's the most boring place on earth, Pen.'

'It's not.'

'How do you know? Have you ever been anywhere else?'

Penny shrugged. 'Neither of us has been anywhere.'

'Exactly my point.'

Beth hadn't meant it as a put-down but, for some reason, it felt like one. Maybe it was because Penny had thought these same things herself: even at fourteen she'd dreamed of escaping. But every time her thoughts got away from her, every time she wondered what it would be like to be somewhere else, to be someone different, she'd think of how sad her mum would be, and then of moving miles away without ever finding out where her dad had gone.

'If you want to get anywhere, you've got to take risks, Pen.'

Penny stifled a laugh. 'Where did you learn that from?'

'It's true, though, isn't it? I mean, it's like this,' Beth said, waving a hand around the pillbox. 'How long have we been sitting in here for? Five years? Six? It's been so long I can't even remember. There's nothing out there, Pen. You said it yourself. We should have climbed over that fence ages ago.'

Penny looked at Beth, then down at her notebook, then out into the night, into the mist that still swirled like a pale curtain in front of the pillbox. Beyond it, the fence drifted in and out of the dark, as if it were a boat lost at sea, rolling and pitching on the waves.

Quietly, Penny said, 'You want to go out there?'

'What?' Beth replied from behind her.

'I said, do you want go out there?'

Beth frowned. 'Are you serious?'

'Yes.'

It was hard to tell whether Beth was frightened or exhilarated by the idea, and after a while Penny thought it might be a mix of both. She moved off her concrete seat, still swamped by the thickness of her coat, shuffled into the space next to Penny, and the two girls watched the darkness, the rain, the grass, the fence. After a time, Penny looked at her watch. It was nine forty-three.

'Are we really going to do this?' Beth said.

Penny nodded. 'If anyone finds out that we've been coming up here all this time, we're in trouble. If anyone catches us out there, we're in deeper trouble. But if we have something we can fight back with, if we can prove there are no bombs out there, no monsters, no ghosts — which there aren't, I guarantee it — if we can find out the real reason they put up the fence, they won't be able to punish us.' Penny shrugged, turning her attention back to the window. 'I mean, how can you be punished for finding out the truth about something?'

Beth seemed to grow in confidence. 'Okay.'

'Yeah?'

'Yeah, let's do this.'

Penny grabbed the rucksack, put the notebook inside and zipped up her windbreaker, all the way to her chin. Her hood was still wet from the walk up, and as she pulled it over her head again, it clung to one side of her face like a wet flannel. In her bag were the two torches she'd packed for them. She got one out, the most powerful, and handed the other one to Beth.

Beams of light criss-crossed in the centre of the room, creating flat circles of phosphorous white on the concrete. It was so bright inside the enclosed space that the light seemed to leak out through the door,

*into the long grass, like a path showing their way. Penny slipped on
the rucksack.*

*'Are you ready?' she said to Beth.*

*Beth smiled bravely. 'I was born ready.'*

*They headed out into the night.*

# 22

Unable to sleep, I got out of bed before the sun was even up, put on some coffee and made myself breakfast. As I was finishing up, Richard wandered through.

'Morning,' I said. 'How'd you sleep?'

'Good, thank you.'

I dumped my plate in the sink.

'Listen, Richard, I need to run out and do a couple of things this morning, so make yourself at home here. There's food in the cupboard, Netflix on the TV, and if you finish *This Perfect Day*, there's some more Ira Levin in the spare room.'

'Oh. Right. Do you need a hand with anything?'

'If I do, I'll phone you.'

He paused. 'Okay.'

He seemed disappointed, or maybe offended, or maybe both. Or perhaps he was worried about being alone again. Whichever it was I'd have to accept it for now. I'd made some calls on the way home the previous evening and tried to set up a meeting with Jacob Howson, the Red Tree department head I'd seen pictured with Naomi Russum in the society magazine. I'd been told he would be out on a trip, so I'd made do with the school's headmaster instead, and I wasn't about to take Richard Kite along with me until I figured out if he had a connection to the school, where the murdered woman fitted in – and how all of it connected back to Russum.

When the doors of the Tube eased open at Cannon Street, it was like a bough breaking, a sea of suits washing towards the exits. I held back a while, letting the crowd thin, remembering why I'd always hated the rush hour, and then rode the escalators up, the pale autumn sunshine winking in the glass panels at the station entrance.

Haggerty's, the florist's, was in a building at the corner of Upper Thames Street and Queen Street Place. When I got there, a woman in her forties with a green apron on was arranging a display out front.

'Good morning,' I said.

The florist wiped her hands clean on her apron front.

'Good morning,' she said, smiling.

I went to my pocket and passed her a business card.

'My name's David Raker,' I said. 'I'm hoping you might be able to help me. I'm trying to find someone who may have a connection to your shop.'

She studied the card for a second, a frown forming, and then mild panic set in. I could see it in her eyes. But it wasn't the panic of the guilty, a liar trying to devise another half-truth, it was the opposite: it was the reaction of someone worrying about what she may have done wrong. Good people got anxious about things like that when investigators turned up out of nowhere, asking questions.

'Don't worry, you're not in any trouble, I promise.'

She relaxed instantly. I felt a moment of guilt, as I always did, at how easy it was to convince people – without having to even say anything – that, because you were an

146

investigator, you were part of the police, and they were duty-bound to help you in the same way, but then I moved on: 'Can I ask your name, madam?'

'Lorie.'

'Hi, Lorie.' I smiled. 'I'm trying to trace someone who I *think* comes in here relatively regularly to buy flowers. Their usual choice is twelve carnations.'

She frowned again.

'That doesn't sound familiar?'

'No,' she said, shaking her head. She wiped her hands on the front of her apron again and gestured inside the shop. 'Thing is, I usually work weekends – I've got young kids – but I'm helping out this week because my manager's just had a shoulder op.'

'Okay.' I glanced beyond her to the door. I could see a counter with a cash register on top. There was an old PC sitting next to it and some kind of ledger adjacent to that. 'Do you think it's something that might be on the system you have in there? I mean, if this person's a regular, maybe your boss has their name written down somewhere – or maybe they're in the diary so she knows what day to prepare the carnations for.' I thought back to what I'd found on the railway line the previous night: a lot of the flowers had died, or were going that way, but two or three bunches looked newer, fresher. That meant whoever kept returning to the scene had been to Haggerty's in the last few weeks.

'I can check for you,' she said.

'That would be fantastic – thank you.'

I followed her into the shop and waited while she began looking. After a minute or so, she looked up. 'I might have something.'

Onscreen I could see what looked like a spreadsheet. It was full of words and numbers that I was too far away to read, but I could make out a title in bold at the top: REGU- LAR ORDERS. She placed a finger against the screen.

'Monday 17 October,' she said. 'Twelve carnations.'

'Does it say what colour the carnations were?'

'Red, pink and yellow.'

I felt a shot of adrenalin.

'That's the person I'm after.' I took a step closer to her. 'Would you have a name there, Lorie? An address?'

But she was already shaking her head.

'I've only got a first name, I'm afraid.'

'Okay. What name have you got?'

'Jacob,' she said.

# 23

Sunlight streamed into the foyer at the Red Tree, the glass doors casting pale rectangles across the marble floor. It was a large room with high ceilings and oak-panelled walls, trophy cabinets, paintings of the school as it once had been – no cars, no surrounding buildings – and artistic photographs of the building as it was now. A staircase wound up to a mezzanine level where older students were working on laptops, and the reception desk was tucked into the space beneath it. There were also three doors, all of them open, each one with signs pointing the way to various departments.

I made a beeline for the front desk, told the receptionist I had a meeting with the headmaster, and she smiled robotically in return and asked me to take a seat. The truth was, I wasn't really interested in the headmaster, I was interested in Jacob Howson – even more so now – but Roland Dell would have to do for the time being. If nothing else, he might be able to fill in some background on Howson. As the head, he'd also be able to help me understand what Naomi Russum's relationship was to the school, and why it was she had access to the building. If I got really lucky, he might even recognize Richard Kite.

As I waited, I watched people pass the school, the trees outside shivering in the wind, and realized I didn't have much of a plan for the next fifteen minutes, thirty minutes, hour, however long it took. I wanted to get inside, to have a look around if I could, or something more surreptitious if not, but mostly I wanted to talk to Jacob Howson. Whether I did that here or cornered him somewhere else would depend on how the morning went. But plan or no plan, it wouldn't have quite allayed the sense of unease I felt. What I'd found at the railway line, what I'd found written on the cards, the fate of the woman in the photograph, the spyware on Richard's phone, the fact that three days after our first meeting I still knew next to nothing about him – it was all building like a pressure behind my eyes.

'Mr Raker?'

I looked up. A good-looking man in his late thirties was standing next to me, dressed in a charcoal-grey suit and a mauve tie. I stood, we shook hands, and he introduced himself as Alexander. He told me he ran security at the school and handed me a visitors' log to fill in and sign.

'Sorry,' he said. 'I know it's boring.'

'No problem.'

Once I was done, he tore part of the form away, folded it in half and slid it into a plastic wallet on the end of a lanyard.

'Just pop that around your neck,' he said.

I did as he asked.

'Great,' he said. 'Follow me.'

As we walked, he started filling the space between us with polite conversation about the cold weather, about how he loved autumn days like these. The more he talked, the more I could hear a slight accent – central European; German or Austrian, or possibly Czech – but it was faint and, at times, hard to even detect. He led me along a central corridor that fed into other hallways, a maze of classrooms and libraries and labs and IT suites, talking about what wonderful opportunities the kids had here, how the sports facilities were amazing, and how one of their alumni had won gold in Rio. And then he told me why it was necessary to have security on-site: because they had kids at the school who were the daughters of oligarchs, the sons of Saudi billionaires, the children of celebrities and Premier League footballers and high-ranking politicians. 'We don't want to be paranoid,' he said, 'and we don't want to scare the students, but our number-one priority is their safety.'

I spent the journey only partly listening, especially as we headed past a couple of classrooms that were clearly being used to teach English. Subtly, I tried to look inside, to see if Howson – as head of department – was in either of them, but I couldn't see him, and I remembered he was supposed to be out on a trip. The next minute we'd reached a door marked HEADMASTER.

Alexander knocked twice.

'Come in.'

He pushed the door open and Roland Dell looked up.

'Ah,' Dell said, coming out from behind his desk. He looked pretty much exactly as he did on the school website: late forties but good on it, an athletic build, blue eyes, a full head of black hair slicked back from his face in a wave. The only difference now was that he'd begun to grow a beard.

He held out a hand.

'Mr Raker, is it?'

'David. Thanks for seeing me.'

Dell waved it away. 'Not a problem. Would you like some coffee, David?'

'That would be great.'

He looked to Alexander. 'Can you get Sandra to bring some in, please?'

After Alexander was gone, Dell directed me to a chair and returned to his. The leather breathed as he sat, and – with his eyes still on the door – he said, 'I hope you didn't mind Alexander coming to meet you.' He paused, seemed embarrassed about it. 'He's very good at his job and feels it's important to know who's on school premises at all times, and I admit that *is* important. But I'm old-fashioned, I suppose. I'm not a great fan of visitors being met by security staff. It makes it feel like you're about to enter the Pentagon.'

I smiled. 'Honestly, it's not a problem.'

'Okay, thank you. So, to be doubly rude, would you mind if I just finish the rest of this email I was writing?' He rolled his eyes. 'School governors.'

'No, that's fine.'

As I waited, I took in the room: filing cabinets, books, a window looking out over a small but attractive court-yard, and on one of the walls closest to me, a framed article from an education supplement. There was a big photo of Dell and the headline RED TREE SCHOOL TOPS A-LEVEL TABLES FOR THE FIRST TIME. I leaned in a little closer to it, starting at a paragraph midway in.

Everyone in the independent schools sector knows the story: after working in state education for four years, and gaining a reputation as a progressive and innovative thinker, Dell was hired by the Red Tree City of London School in 1995 to head up their history department. In 2000, aged just thirty-two, and after the retirement of long-time head Bryan Austin-Smith, he was the surprise choice of school governors for headmaster. So began Dell's sometimes controversial but ultimately hugely successful re-imagining of the Red Tree as a co-ed school, with a focus on core subjects and sporting excellence. In just three years, Dell improved GCSE and A-level performance by almost a third, with over 70 per cent of all results either an A or A\*. By 2008 the Red Tree had taken its place as the top independent school in London, and this year it had the best A-level performance of any school in the country.

'Sorry about that,' Dell said, and when I turned to face him again I could see he wasn't referring to the email he'd had to send, but to the article in the frame. 'I generally find people who frame articles about themselves to be bores, so it took a lot of soul-searching before I could bring myself to put that up.'

'It sounds like you have plenty to be proud of.'

'Thank you,' he said.

I reached across the desk and handed him a business card, told him what I did, and then started talking to him about Richard Kite. The more I watched him, the more I could see what was coming: he didn't know Richard – or, at least, he didn't know the name – but he was fascinated by his condition. I didn't blame him necessarily, but it showed the difficulty in getting people to focus on less interesting elements of the case when all they really wanted to know was how a man could forget everything about himself.

'So he recalls nothing?' Dell asked.

'Small things, but it's difficult to say if they're directly relevant.'

'How awful.'

'Yeah, it's tough on him.'

'And you think he may have a connection to the school?'

'It's possible,' I said, unwilling to give too much away until I figured out how the Red Tree fitted into Richard's life. 'But, equally, I've got no evidence that that's the case. I think he may have been associated with, or involved in, education in some way, possibly in this part of London, which is why I'm visiting as many schools in the area as I can. *Or* all of this could just be a dead end.'

There was some element of truth in that, though not much, but it seemed to satisfy Dell, so I shuffled forward, removed a photo of Richard and set it down on the desk in front of him.

He picked up some glasses, slid them on and studied the photograph.

'Could he have been a teacher here?' I asked.

Dell immediately shook his head. 'Not one I've employed.'

'Maybe he was a student at one time, then?'

'Well, you said he's – what? – in his mid thirties?' He took a long breath. 'If that's the case, and he *was* a student here, he would have attended the school somewhere between '93 and, say, 2000, 2001. I started here in '95, but it's a long, long time ago.' He paused again for a moment, thinking to himself, and then set the photograph down and went to one of the filing cabinets. Pulling one of the drawers out, he started going through a few of the files. 'Just give me a second.'

As he was standing at the cabinet, his PA walked in, carrying a tray with two mugs of coffee on it. She placed them on the desk without saying anything and, soon after she was gone, Dell slid the drawer shut and seated himself.

'That's a shame,' he said, taking a long, frustrated breath. 'I'm not a Luddite, I promise, but I'm a big believer in paperwork, so I tend to keep hard copies of old documents – but I don't have anything that goes back that far. We don't keep records of all the students that ever attended the school for obvious reasons – not only is it inappropriate and borderline illegal, it would also be an administrative nightmare. I'd need much bigger cabinets than these.'

He picked up the photo of Richard again.

'But I don't recognize him at all,' he said. 'I've had a lot of students pass through these doors during my time here, but as we're an independent school – and a small independent school at that – I'd at least like to *think* I would remember most of them. Or their faces, anyway.'

I took the picture back from him and got out a second one: the photo of the woman on the bench in Regent's Park.

'What about her?' I asked. 'Do you recognize her?'

He took the picture from me.

'Yes,' he said, but just as I started to feel a charge of electricity, a moment of hope, a concerned frown formed on his face. 'That's Corrine.'

'Corrine?'

'Corrine Wilson. She was a teacher here.'

'When was this?'

'She joined us in September 2009 and she resigned . . .' He was trying to remember. 'It must have been end of October or beginning of November 2014.'

*The month her body was found on the railway line.*

He looked up from the picture, the same expression on his face: puzzled, surprised. 'Have you spoken to her, then? I'd love to know how she's doing.'

'No,' I said, 'I haven't spoken to her.' I felt bad for not telling him the truth, but I pushed on all the same. 'I found a photograph of her among Richard's things.'

'So does he know Corrine?'

'If he does, he doesn't remember.'

Dell nodded, his eyes returning to the picture of the woman.

'You haven't been in contact with her since 2014?'

He shook his head. 'No. Not a peep. I mean, it was all a bit strange, really. She was one of our best teachers: the kids loved her, were totally engaged with her, the staff here all thought the world of her. It's so rare to find that natural talent, that ability to just switch kids on immediately. I told her loads of times that she had a very bright future at the school, and then I came into work one day and found a letter – here.'

He tapped a finger against the desk.

'It was a resignation letter?'

'Yes.' He frowned again. 'I never got a hint from her that she was even remotely unhappy, that was the weird thing. I tried calling her, I sent her a few emails, seeing if it was something that we'd done – that *I'd* done – but she never picked up the phone and never responded to any of my emails. Normally, we ask our teachers to give us a term's notice if they intend to resign, but I couldn't get hold of Corrine to argue the point. Even Jacob didn't know where she'd gone.'

I stopped. 'Jacob?'

'Sorry. Jacob Howson. Her boyfriend.'

I felt another stab of electricity.

'He's the department head in English,' Dell went on. 'Corrine was an English teacher too. That's how the two of them met. Anyway, after I found the letter, I asked Jacob to come and see me to find out what was going on, and he told me he had no idea. He said he would talk to her that evening, but the next day he came in and said he'd got home and *also* found a letter. Like a "Dear John" kind of thing.' Dell grimaced. 'He said Corrine told him not to try to contact her.'

*Or maybe she didn't.*

Maybe she never wrote him a letter. Maybe Howson lied about that, and he lied about not knowing where she was going, and he wrote her resignation letter himself.

'Is Jacob coming in at all today?' I asked.

'No. He's with a group of A-level students at the Museum of London. They're studying *Great Expectations* and he thought the exhibitions might bring it to life.' Dell glanced at his watch. 'He should be done by four, although I'm not sure if he'll come back here or go straight home. He does tend to work into the evenings a lot these days.' Dell stopped again, shrugged, the inference clear: *ever since Corrine left.* 'Would you like his number?'

'That would be good,' I said, and thought about my next move as Dell wrote it down. I wasn't sure what Howson's story was, and what part he may have played in the murder, but he surely would have foreseen this day coming. Someone turning up. Someone asking questions. Someone trying to understand what had really happened to Corrine Wilson. The issue now was whether, if I turned up at his home, he gave me the truth, he lied, or he bolted. He had ties here, a good job that was hard to walk away from, but that didn't mean he wouldn't run. People ran all the time when they were desperate.

'There we go,' Dell said.

I took the number and gathered the photos together.

'Can I ask you one last question?' I said.

'Please.'

'Richard is seeing a psychologist called Naomi Russum. Have you heard of her before?'

'Naomi? Yes, of course. She works here. Well, part-time. She does four days a month as a counsellor.'

'Right,' I said, noting it down.

'There are things some kids can't tell their parents,' Dell went on, 'or their teachers – or sometimes even their friends. Naomi gives them an opportunity to do that. She's highly qualified in her field, and we thought it would be a great tool for the kids, and the feedback we get from them seems to suggest it's been worth every penny.'

It made sense: it explained how she had access to the building, how she knew Howson and why they were pictured together in the photo at the charity event; and if all three of them – Howson, Russum and Corrine Wilson – worked in the same place, I now knew what bound them together.

But two questions remained unanswered: why Russum was showing Richard Kite photographs of Corrine Wilson – and why Corrine and Richard had exactly the same tattoo.

# 24

After making a couple of calls, I found out that Jacob Howson's mobile phone number was registered to an address in Kennington. It was a townhouse halfway along a short, quiet road with a rank of hire bikes on an island in the centre. I waited for him there and, at five thirty, he finally turned up, looking like I remembered him in the magazine: tall, thin, a little ungainly. He was dressed in a black suit and a pale green raincoat, and his brown hair had thinned to the point where his scalp shone under the street lights. He seemed tired, his eyes carrying dark smears.

I shifted forward a couple of steps, in behind the bulk of a Range Rover, and watched through its windows as he removed some keys and then looked out at his surroundings – the other cars, the other buildings – before letting himself in. I'd called him as soon as I'd left the school, and left a message, telling him very briefly who I was and what I wanted to talk to him about. I wanted to see what his next move would be.

Three minutes later, I found out.

When he reappeared he had an A4 plastic sleeve in his hands. Before he started to lock up properly, sliding the sleeve between his ribs and the inside of his arm, I was able to get a glimpse of what it contained: paperwork of some sort, printouts, maybe photocopies, maybe pictures.

Something else too: smaller, blacker, about the size of a credit card.

He finished at the house, looked both ways along the street again, and took off in the opposite direction to me, hurrying, glancing over his shoulder.

I held back for a moment and then followed.

I trailed him for about a mile to the bottom of Waterloo Road, where he entered a shabby-looking hotel called The Tudor. It was squeezed between a kebab shop and a newsagent and had a sign at one of the ground-floor windows promising low rates for bed and breakfast. It wasn't hard to see why.

As I hovered at the main door, looking in along a worn hallway, I could see Howson at the reception desk. He was paying in cash, taking money from a roll of notes. It was hard to tell from where I was standing, but it looked like there was a lot in his hands. He hadn't stopped at an ATM on the way, and even if he had, he wouldn't have been able to get that much out in one go. Which meant he must have kept the roll of money alongside the plastic sleeve at home. In turn, that meant he'd definitely seen this day coming. The roll of notes, going home to retrieve the sleeve, lying low in a crappy hotel while he presumably figured out his next move – he'd been planning this for a while.

He took the key from the receptionist and headed for some stairs on the other side of the dingy lobby. Once he was out of sight, I entered the hotel, striding through the reception area as if I was already a guest and knew exactly where I was going. I needn't have worried: the woman behind the desk didn't even look up, her eyes fixed on a small TV in the corner.

The hotel had three floors, and signs in the lobby suggested there were six rooms on the ground and eight on the others. I headed up. At a door leading to the second floor, I looked through the glass to the corridor on the other side. There was no sign of Howson. Almost on cue, I heard the stairs creak above me and the soft jangle of keys, so I kept going, along the thinning carpets.

I held back as I got to the top floor, allowing the door into the corridor to snap shut. Once it did, I stepped up to the glass and looked through. Howson was at the end, half hidden by more dingy lighting, letting himself into a room.

I waited, thinking about my next move. There weren't many choices. If I knocked on his door and told him it was me, even if I reassured him that I was no threat to him, his guard would be up. If I waited, I lost time. If I didn't take the chance at all, I might never find out about Corrine Wilson and how she was connected to Naomi Russum and Richard Kite.

Heading into the corridor, I listened for sounds of activity in the adjacent rooms, but mostly all I could hear was the hum of traffic from Waterloo Road and the chatter of a broken air-conditioning unit on the wall. The whole hotel smelled musty, as if a window had never once been opened in the entire time it had been standing.

At his door, I knocked twice.

Immediately, I heard movement: the squeak of mattress springs, the dull clunk of drawers, soft footsteps coming towards me. There was no peephole in the door, so he had to either pretend he wasn't in or open up. A couple of seconds later, I heard the metallic scrape of a chain sliding into place.

'Who is it?' he said.

'Jacob, it's David Raker. I tried calling you earlier.'

A pause.

I bent down and slid a card beneath the door.

'I just want to talk,' I said. I heard movement as he picked it up; the muted moan of a floorboard. 'I want to talk to you about Corrine Wilson.'

An even longer pause.

'How did you know I was here?'

'I followed you,' I said. There was no point in lying to him. 'I went down to the railway line at Abbey Wood. I saw the flowers you left there. I saw what you wrote on those cards.' I stopped again, letting him process that. 'I think Corrine might have known someone I'm trying to help. Maybe you did too.'

More movement. He was right next to the door now.

'His name's Richard Kite.'

Nothing.

'Do you know who Richard is, Jacob?'

'No, I don't. Now go away.'

'Why don't you open up?'

'Leave me alone.'

'Look,' I said, 'I'm giving you the chance to tell me your side of the story. I'll sit here and listen to you and I won't judge what you've done.' That wasn't true, but he didn't need to know that. '*Or* I can give the police your name and they'll come and arrest you. Either way, you're going to tell one of us the truth.'

Again, there was no reaction. I looked along the corridor, one of the light bulbs flickering, and then returned my gaze to the door.

'Jacob?'

It opened a crack but remained on the chain. He'd removed his tie, his coat, his suit jacket. He'd rolled up the sleeves on his shirt. I could only see one half of his face but it was enough: he looked distressed, his eye bloodshot.

I held up a hand. 'I'm not here to hurt you, Jacob.'

'So what are you here to do?'

'To help you.'

He wiped the back of his hand under his nose, his gaze shifting over my shoulder into the corridor beyond. When his attention fixed on me again, it was like his thoughts were written across his face: he was frightened about letting me in, but desperate to accept my help. He looked like so many people I'd met over the years, shrinking under their burden.

'Why should I trust you?' he said.

'Because I don't think you have anyone else.'

He swallowed, saying nothing.

'I know Corrine was your girlfriend, Jacob.'

He stared at me and a tear broke free from his eye, tracing the ridge of his cheekbone. He wiped at it, but didn't look away. For a second I wasn't sure if he was going to respond again, but eventually, and very quietly, he said, 'Yes.'

'How did she end up at the railway tracks?'

He just looked at me, his skin as pale as milk.

'Did you kill Corrine, Jacob?'

'That was just what she told everyone.'

I frowned. 'What?'

'Her name. She told everyone her name was Corrine.'

I watched him for a moment.

'That wasn't her real name?'

More tears began to form.

'Jacob, what was her real name?'

'Penny,' he said softly. 'Her name was Penny Beck.'

# The Monster

*The girls headed out of the pillbox.*

*Immediately, the driving rain knocked Penny off balance. She gripped her torch more tightly, its beam cutting across the bogs into the darkness, and made sure Beth was close. Penny asked if she was okay, but she didn't hear the reply — her hood was up and Beth's voice was suppressed by the roar of the storm. Within the arc of Penny's beam, the rain looked like needles, jagging from left to right, and when they hit her exposed skin, they felt like them too. Penny shouted to her sister again and this time Beth gave a thumbs up.*

*They moved out across the soggy ground, towards the boundary fence. Under foot, the bog squelched and moved, as if they were crossing the spine of some great, dormant creature, and when the wind came, it came hard, the long grass whipping back and forth against their hands until their fingers were raw. Everything above the level of the grass was black, except for the fence itself; their torchlight glinted off the wire as they approached, and when they came to a stop in front of it, the boundary seemed to run for ever either side of them, greying and blurring as it disappeared into the darkness.*

*The Brink awaited them.*

*Penny watched as Beth drew level with her. They were both soaked through already, thick strands of Beth's hair escaping out of her hood and visible at the side of her face. Breath formed in front of them like balls of spun sugar and, the closer Penny inched to the fence, the more she could feel her pulse quicken. It was six feet high, with enough foot holds to make it a relatively easy climb. Going* beyond it was as simple as climbing up and dropping down on to the other side. But everyone knew you didn't do that.

Not unless you didn't want to come back.

But that was bullshit, Penny reminded herself. That was a story invented by the people in the town and, sooner or later, it was always going to come to this. Penny was always going to have to stand at the fence and demand answers about why the story was created.

Why keep everyone in the town away from here?

Even so, she still spent a moment watching the grass on the other side of the mesh, instinctively looking for signs of movement. It was habit. Routine. Muscle memory. The problem was, the whole hillside was moving, the long grass swaying and bowing in a synchronized dance. It shivered so rhythmically that, for a while, Penny was trans-fixed by it. But then Beth, who seemed to have grown in confidence on the walk across, said, 'What's the matter?'

Penny looked at her. 'Nothing.'

'Don't you want to go any more?'

Penny wondered if Beth might have preferred it if she'd said no. No, we're not going. No, we're not climbing over the fence. I'm too scared, Beth.

I'm way too scared.

But, after taking a long breath, Penny answered her sister by lacing her fingers through the mesh and starting to climb. At the top, she paused, one foot on either side of the fence, and waited for Beth, and then they both looked out into the darkness. Finally, they swung their other legs over and dropped down.

Penny felt her feet slip slightly in the mud, and then the bog suck at the heels of her boots. She looked across the hillside in front of them, watching as it sloped away into a wall of absolute black. If she hadn't known what the terrain was like out here, if she hadn't seen it from the town, and from the pillbox on late summer evenings as *the sun went down, she'd never have been able to work it out. All she could see around her — within the confines of the torch — was grass and mud. No landmarks. No signs of life.*

*They began moving further into the Brink.*

*After a while, Penny's flashlight picked up a vague trail, a path that followed the slant of the hill and snaked between clumps of tussock grass. She looked for evidence that the path had been made by feet, by animals, by anything, and then the further down they got, the less certain she was that it was actually a path at all. She started to think it might have been the rain, or the wind, or maybe the flurries of snow they'd already had, flattening grass, compacting it for the winter.*

*Sometime after, she looked back to check on Beth and saw that she was a few yards behind her, and that they'd travelled much further than Penny had thought — four hundred feet maybe; possibly even more. She watched Beth for a second, the rain crackling against the fabric of their jackets, and then Penny realized that the fence was now above their eyeline.*

*'Is everything okay?' Beth asked, shouting over the rain.*

*Penny nodded.*

*'So why have we stopped?'*

*This time she didn't reply. Instead, she looked harder at the boundary fence, running across the hillside, vaguely backlit by the lights from the town. Something had changed. Something was different.*

*'Pen?'*

*What was different?*

*'Penny?'*

*Penny stepped closer, past Beth, eyes still fixed on the fence, trying to figure out what it was that had altered. What had she seen? What had changed up there?*

*'Pen?' Beth said from behind her. 'What's going on?'*

The rain was really heavy now; a wall of sound. Penny turned to her sister and shouted, 'I'm not sure.'

'Can you see something?'

'I don't know.'

Beth didn't hear the response, must have thought that Penny hadn't replied at all, because she stepped closer and repeated herself: 'Can you see something?'

Penny shrugged. 'I don't know.'

Beth squinted into the storm as it continued to lash across the slopes of the hillside. 'I can't see anything,' she said.

Penny kept her eyes on the fence.

'Pen, what can you see?'

'I'm not sure,' Penny said. 'I thought maybe I saw a . . .'

She stopped. One of the fence posts was moving.

'Shit,' she said softly.

'What?'

'Someone's up here with us.'

Beth spun on her heel, slipping on the wet ground, and they both looked up the hill. A shape was standing behind the wire, watching them, its silhouette half obscured by a fence post. That was why it had taken Penny a moment to figure out what she was seeing. Suddenly panicked, she glanced at Beth again: Beth looked exactly like a twelve-year-old now – unnerved, scared. For a moment, they just stood there frozen to the spot, shoulder to shoulder, the two of them staring at the shape, the shape staring back.

'What should we do?' Beth said.

Penny was trying to think.

'Pen?' Beth said, more desperately. 'What are we going to do?'

'I don't know. Give me a second to thin–'

Out of nowhere, a sound tore across the night.

It was so unexpected, so loud, it seemed to reverberate through the

168

ground like an earthquake. It sounded like some sort of animal call; a screech.

'What's happening?' Beth said, frantic now.

Penny looked at her, was about to say she didn't know, when she saw something move out of the corner of her eye. She turned, looking across the slopes to her right, off into the darkness.

'Pen?'

Beth's voice was tremoring. She grabbed hold of Penny's hand, squeezed it, her fingers slick with rainwater and sweat. Penny squeezed back.

'I'm scared, Pen.'

'I know.'

'I'm really scared.'

'I know you are.'

Penny looked hard into the night, down the hillside, in the direction they'd been heading. She couldn't see anything. A sudden hush seemed to have settled across the valley, the wind dropping away, the rain easing off. The only other sound was Beth: she'd started to sob. Penny put her arm around her shoulders, and raised the torch, aiming it out into the dark. The tussock grass shone wet with rain, the clumps weird and disconcerting – like heads of hair; like hundreds of people were face down in the earth, lined up in shallow graves for as far as the eye could see.

Beth moaned, her voice muffled against Penny's chest. She squeezed Beth even harder, grabbed her hand and said, 'We need to go.'

They looked to the fence.

There was no one up there now.

'We need to get back up to the top.'

'Okay,' Beth said. 'Are we going home?'

'Yes. We need to get back up to the top and we –'

*More movement to their right.*

*Beth didn't see it — but Penny did. It was about a hundred feet away, on the fringes of the torchlight. She swallowed, tensed, and as she did Beth felt the shift, the stiffening of her sister's muscles, and followed her gaze, out into the blackness of the downward slope. The rain gradually became harder again, pounding at them, at their jackets, the sound like waves crashing on a pebble beach. Every time Penny swallowed, it felt like she had chips of glass in her throat. She'd come out here convinced it was all a myth, lies made up by the people in the town.*

*But it didn't feel like a lie any more.*

*'Let's go,' she said, and tugged at Beth's hand.*

*They began running up the hillside, beating a retreat. Penny could feel Beth struggle, her legs dragging, her breath coarse and ragged. She looked back at her, pulling at her arm, and, as she did, glimpsed something in the long grass, forty feet to their right.*

*Penny's heart hit her throat.*

*Whatever it was, it was following them, crouched slightly, the arch of its back, its arms, visible above the apex of the grass. Penny wanted to say something, to tell Beth, to warn her, but the words got lost. Instead, she made a low, soft whine which instantly vanished in the rain, and then pulled at Beth's hand again — trying to draw her closer in — half concentrating on where they were heading, half focused on the grass to their right. For the first time, Penny could see breath hissing out of the bog, like the ground itself was panting.*

*'Quickly!' Penny shouted.*

*This time, Beth heard the terror in her sister's voice and looked back over her shoulder. She spotted the shape instantly, trailing them. Beth screamed and started to sob even harder, and Penny yanked at her again, almost dragging her up the hillside.*

*Thirty feet to the wire fence.*

'Come on!' Penny screamed, pulling so hard at Beth's arm it felt like she might tear it from its socket. Beth shrieked in pain but didn't let go of her hand.

Twenty feet.

'Come on!' she shouted again and felt Beth move, accelerating, as if she realized they were close to the boundary fence. Penny glanced back over her shoulder, searching for it in the grass behind them – but now she couldn't see it.

Ten feet.

She looked again and glimpsed something.

They let go of each other's hand and leaped for the fence, Penny hitting it a fraction later than Beth. Scrambling up, the toes of Penny's boots slipped on the wire mesh, and at the top she slipped again, her torch falling from her grasp. It hit the wet ground beneath her with a dull thunk at the same time as Beth landed on the other side.

'Penny!' Beth shouted. 'Quickly!'

Penny, at the top, one foot on either side of the boundary line, looked down at the torch, hesitating, wondering whether to go back for it. Jack would notice if it wasn't in the cupboard tomorrow. But then she saw movement beyond the range of the prone torch.

I can't go back for it, she thought.

She dropped down, into the long grass, and landed awkwardly, rolling on to her backside and scrambling away on her hands, like a crab heading for shelter. From where they were, they could only see a few feet into the Brink now.

But that was enough.

Something stayed there on the edge of the torchlight for a moment, as if deliberately trying to prevent itself from being seen, an obscure mass in the thick swirl of the darkness. They watched it moving back and forth, Beth barely able to look at all, her eyes on the ground, her *head tilted away. Penny reached out for her sister again and squeezed her hand, telling her they were safe now, telling her everything would be all right.*

*And then she looked back through to the other side of the fence.*

*Whatever had been out there was gone.*

# 25

The room was lit by a single lamp in the corner. After Howson let me in, he checked the corridor before pushing the door shut and reattaching the chain. I made my way around to the other side of the bed, its sheets crumpled. The lights of the city leaked in through the half-open curtains, spilling across the bed like a pot of paint.

I pulled a chair out from the wall. Sitting opposite the bed, I watched Howson perch himself on its edge, trying to summon some strength by taking a series of long breaths while wiping his eyes and cheeks with his sleeve. I texted Richard Kite, gave him the address of the hotel and the room number, and told him to come immediately. I wanted to see if they knew one another. When I tuned back in, Howson had gathered himself a little but it had made no difference at all: the tears had stopped, but he still looked rinsed.

'I'm sorry,' he said softly.

I wasn't sure if he was talking about his tears or his crimes, so I remained silent. He took another long breath, his eyes flicking across to a dark wardrobe, its doors so warped they failed to align. I looked around at the rest of the room, searching for the plastic sleeve he'd been carrying. It was probably in the wardrobe.

'Why don't you tell me about Penny, Jacob?'

'I didn't kill her,' he said immediately.

His voice was uneven. He was from somewhere in the Home Counties but it was hard to be more specific than that because the heaviness of his words seemed to weigh on his diction.

'I would never have hurt her.'

'So who killed her?'

'I don't know.'

'Really?'

'I don't. Not for sure.' He looked up, still tearful. 'But it's got something to do with the school.'

'In what way?'

'I think Corrine – Penny – she found something there.'

'What did she find?'

'I don't know,' he said.

I watched him for a moment, uncertain whether to trust him or not. His grief looked and sounded genuine, but with his head angled towards the floor, it was hard to see his eyes, and the eyes were always the best way to pick a liar.

'Is that why she changed her name?'

He shrugged. 'She was Corrine before she arrived at the school. No one knew her real name was Penny Beck. I only found out after she was dead.'

'How?'

I wasn't even sure if he was listening.

'How, Jacob?'

'I eventually found an old passport hidden in our flat. Her real name was on that.'

'Okay.' I watched him. 'What else?'

He swallowed, sniffed.

'Maybe we should just start at the beginning,' he said.

I tried to keep the impatience out of my voice. 'Fine. Let's start at the beginning – but don't leave anything out.'

Slowly, he started talking about Penny. He said he'd met her at the Red Tree when he first joined the school as Head of English in July 2012. A year after he started, they were dating. A year on from that, her body was found on the railway tracks beside the Armbury estate.

'I found the messages you left for her,' I said. 'The flowers.'

He nodded.

'She's never been identified by the police.' I got out my notepad and opened the front. 'So how did you know the woman on the railway tracks was Penny?'

Again, he didn't reply, but not because he didn't want to – because he was summoning the courage. After a while, he looked from the pad to me and across to the window. The light of the city was scorched against the dark.

'Jacob?'

A hint of a smile on his face. 'When I asked her out, she said no to start with. So I just kept asking her, over and over again. Eventually, she caved in.' He smiled again, but after a while it became a sort of grimace. 'Whatever's going on, it's got something to do with Marek.'

'Who the hell is Marek?'

'He's responsible for school security,' Howson said.

*Alexander.*

He was the man who'd come to meet me in reception, who'd walked me to Roland Dell's office.

'He's a psycho,' Howson said. 'Everyone at the Red Tree is scared of him. Or, if they're not, they think he's weird and remote. Even Roland's frightened of him. I mean,

Marek just does what he wants. He doesn't give a fuck what Roland thinks, and Roland's too weak to do anything about it.'

I thought of Dell apologizing after Marek had gone. Dell had told me he was uncomfortable with the idea of security meeting guests in reception, even if he understood the reasoning, but it was something Marek had insisted upon. Maybe now I knew why.

'So you think Marek killed Penny?'

'I don't know for sure, but . . .'

'Why would he kill her?'

A flicker of something in Howson's face.

'Jacob?'

'I think she found out something about him.'

'Like what?'

I'd paused, my pen hovering above my pad. For the first time, Howson's face hardened.

'I don't know exactly,' he said. 'Thing is, I've seen what Marek's like. You get on the wrong side of him and he'll make your life an absolute fucking misery. And he seems to get a kick out of it, that's the thing. Once you're in his sights, he'll just keep pushing.' Howson swallowed. 'But he was never like that with Penny. In fact, it was the opposite with her.'

He glanced at me again; a flash of jealousy.

'You're saying he had a soft spot for her?'

He shrugged. 'I mean . . . yeah. I guess.'

'Did anything ever happen between them?'

'No,' he said, vociferous now. 'No way. She didn't like Marek. She was like the rest of us. But I think Corrine – *Penny* – was using him, or trying to use him, to get at

176

something. Something he knew. So she played the game. She batted off his flirting, his comments, but stayed just close enough to the right side of him to get what she needed.' He frowned, as if he hadn't liked how that last part had come out. 'Marek had a blind spot when it came to Penny.'

'A blind spot?'

'He thought he knew her.'

It was only five words, but there was a density to them that seemed to thicken the atmosphere in the room. Howson moved position on the bed again, the springs wheezing beneath his weight.

'But he *didn't* know her?' I said.

'I think the reason she got close to him was so she could gain access to the security suite – or, at least, the computers in there. Marek's files. The camera footage he collects. What goes on in the school when we're not around; what's been going on at the school since before I ever arrived. Marek's been there years. He guards that place like it's Fort Knox. I think Corr– Penny . . . I think she knew that.'

'So what did she find?'

'A pattern.'

'What sort of pattern?'

Howson's eyes drifted to the wardrobe, and then he shifted off the bed and walked across to it. The doors juddered stiffly, filling the room with the smell of mothballs.

It was empty – except for the plastic sleeve.

He took it out and brought it back to the bed. As he moved, pictures at the front shifted around, glimpses of a face briefly visible. Printouts that looked like timesheets, although a lot of the type was too small, the room too badly lit, for me to be one hundred per cent sure.

He set the sleeve down beside him and looked at me; it was clear he was having doubts about sharing its contents. I'd got him to let me in, I'd got him to talk to me about Penny, but the printouts were what he was really trying to protect.

'Is what she found out on those printouts?' I asked him.

His eyes fell to the plastic sleeve.

'Is that evidence against Marek?'

'Evidence,' he repeated, not looking up at me. 'I don't know if it's evidence. I've been over and over it, collecting together everything that she left behind, and I still don't know. But there's something in here.' Howson removed the contents of the plastic sleeve. 'Somewhere in here is the reason why Penny was killed.'

# 26

Immediately, I saw that the photos in the sleeve were all of Penny. The printouts, they were evidence, or they were a way to get at answers. But these portraits of a woman's life, these brief snapshots of who she'd been, were more than that.

They were Howson's memories of her.

His eyes lingered on them as he pulled them out, handling them so delicately it was like he was frightened they'd blow away. There were three in all. I waited and eventually he looked across the room at me, as if remembering he wasn't alone, and held them out. Two were of Penny on her own; one was of her and Howson together. None of them was the same picture I already knew, of her on the Regent's Park bench.

'Did you take these?' I asked.

'Yes.'

I looked up at him. 'You know Naomi Russum, right?'

'Yes,' he said, puzzled by the question. 'She works at the school.'

'You know her well?'

He shrugged. 'Well enough, I guess. I've ended up at a few events with her. I've talked to her in the staffroom, that sort of thing.'

'Because she also had a picture of Penny. A different one.'

His frown deepened, the confusion evident. But there was something else in his face too. I just couldn't work out what.

'Why would she have a picture of Penny?' he asked.

I watched him for a second, trying to see whether he was playing me.

'I don't know,' I said. 'Why do *you* think she would?'

'I don't know,' he replied.

I let it go for now, and focused on the immediate questions. How did Russum end up with the photograph? Why was she showing it to Richard?

'Do you ever remember taking a picture of Penny at Regent's Park?'

'Yes,' he said. 'I took that picture the week before she went missing; a month before she was discovered. It was the last photograph I ever took of her.'

'Do you still have a copy of it?'

'I have a digital copy at home on my computer somewhere. But the one physical copy I made of it . . .' He glanced at me.

'What?'

'I had it stuck to the inside of a notebook I used for lesson planning. After she went missing, I printed it out and put it in there because I wanted to be able to see her. I missed her. I was confused. I had no idea where she'd gone, or what she was doing, or *why* she was doing it. All I had was this.'

He selected one of the printouts from the sleeve. It was a photocopy of a typewritten letter.

*Dear Jacob,*

*I love you so much, but I need to go. I can't begin to explain to you why. It isn't you. Please don't try to look for me.*

*Corrine*

He looked at me. 'You know what's wrong with this letter?'

'What?'

'She never called me Jacob. She called me Jake.'

'So you think it was written by someone else?'

'Yes.'

'Marek?'

He nodded. 'Yes. I mean, I don't know for sure, but . . .' His words fell away.

'So Penny just disappeared one day?'

'Pretty much,' he said. 'She left home on a Tuesday morning in October, just like every other day, because she had to be at school early – and that was the last time I ever saw her. I didn't start to look for her until morning break. At lunch, I still couldn't find her anywhere, so started asking around – and then Roland called me up to his office. He showed me her resignation letter. It didn't sound like her either, but it was enough to convince Roland; enough to convince everyone else. I mean, Roland was annoyed because it's pretty standard to give a term's worth of notice – but the actual resignation letter? He believed it.'

'But you didn't?'

He drew a long breath. 'I just felt like something was wrong, so I called the police and they said people disappear all the time, and that they couldn't go out and look for her, or file a report or whatever else, until there was evidence that she was actually in some sort of danger. I said, "I really think she *might* be in danger," because I knew the letter that she left for me wasn't written by her, I *knew* it even if I couldn't prove it. But they said, "A person has the right to disappear," and after that, I became angry, irrational. For a while, I started to believe that she *had* left on purpose, that what we'd had together, all the time we'd spent as a couple, was a sham and she'd run off with someone else. And then, in the two weeks before her body was found, the anger went away and it became this clear sense that something was wrong; that she *was* in trouble, that something awful had happened. Penny didn't have any family to look out for her – her parents were gone; she was an only child – so I was all she had. I think that was another reason I stuck that photograph of her in my notebook. I needed a reminder not to let up, not to forget her. When I put it inside those pages . . .' He faded out again, his voice replaced by the gurgle of water pipes behind the walls and the soft drone of the traffic. 'When I put it there,' he said again, much quieter this time, 'honestly, I had every intention of going back to see the police.'

'So why didn't you?'

Remorse clung to his face. 'If I'd gone back to the police after three weeks and said, "She's *still* missing," they would have taken me seriously. It was so out of character for her. But I didn't. I never went back, so they had no official record of her disappearance. That's why they never matched her to that body.'

'Why didn't you go back?' I asked again.

He turned his head towards the window. I could see a shaving rash at his jaw, red skin and dots of dried blood still visible above his shirt collar.

'I used the computers in the school library to try and look for her one day,' he said, distant now, as if he wasn't talking to me but to the ghost of the woman he'd loved and lost. 'I went looking for people who'd been reported missing, for anyone who might be her. I didn't know what I was doing or looking for, but I just wanted some answers. When I couldn't find anything, I decided I was going to go back to the police the next day. I trawled websites looking for the best way to report a missing person; the best way to get the police to sit up and take notice. I printed some things out, and then I went and got a sandwich from down the street, and after that I went back to my classroom. I remember it so clearly. I decided to work late, do some marking, try to keep my mind on other things.' A long pause. 'It wasn't there.'

'What wasn't?'

'The photograph of Penny I put in the notebook. It had been removed.'

'Someone had taken it?'

He nodded again.

'Do you think it was Marek?'

'Yes.'

'Did you look around for the picture?'

'I searched everywhere, but it was gone. I couldn't understand it. I was so upset. Then I saw there was a Post-it note at the back of the notebook, poking out of the top of it like a bookmark.'

He shuffled another printout out of the pack and held it up for me. The yellow Post-it note had been taped to it.

*Go to the police and you're dead*

It was hard to rip my eyes away from it, and when I did, I immediately thought of the flowers Howson had left on the railway line, and the messages he'd written on the cards. *I miss you. Please forgive me. I'm so sorry.* I looked at him, wondering for a minute whether this could all be some elaborate lie he was spinning. But it didn't feel like it. It felt like he'd written those cards to her because, by failing to go back to the police, he'd utterly betrayed the woman he'd loved.

I moved my thinking on to Naomi Russum. She must have been passed the photograph by Marek. But why would he give it to her to show to Richard Kite? What did that make their relationship? Professional? Personal? Both? It was why Howson had seemed like he was hiding something earlier when I told him Russum had a picture of Penny: he knew I must have been talking about the one he'd had stolen. He must have been trying to work out why Naomi Russum had ended up with a copy of it.

However it had arrived in her possession, I now knew why Penny had never been identified: Howson didn't go back to the police, so she was never registered as missing, and everyone else just believed she'd resigned. And the things she had in common with the body on the railway line – her DNA, her features, her hair and eye colour – were never brought to light. But there were still questions. Penny was killed over a year before Richard Kite ever came on to the scene, so what – apart from the tattoo they shared – connected them? Was that why Richard's phone was being tracked? Was it because there was something damaging about Marek – perhaps about Naomi Russum too – buried in his head and if he remembered it, they'd need to do something about it quickly, before it caused them too much harm?

If that was true, he was in more danger than I thought.

I looked at Howson.

'I read about Penny in the papers a couple of days after she was found,' he said. He'd become emotional again. 'It wasn't big news because the media had no pictures of her. I mean, it's not like they could show crime scene photos. The way they described her, some of the injuries she had . . .' He ground to a halt, his chin against his chest. 'The police didn't know who she was, so they couldn't go to friends, to me, and get a photograph of her for the media to print. That was why no one at work, no one she spent any time with – anyone but me, really – ever made the connection. But I knew. I knew it was her.'

'Whoever killed her cut out her tattoo.'

He looked at me, fresh tears in his eyes; nodded once. He'd read about the skin flayed from her body. He was smart enough to have put two and two together.

'Did she ever talk about that?' I asked.

'About the tattoo?' Howson shook his head. 'Not much. I asked her about it, but she just said it was something she'd got when she was a teenager.'

Howson had mentioned that Penny was an only child, so she and Richard weren't brother and sister – but what if they'd been part of the same social circle or lived in the same place? Could the tattoo have been a regional symbol of some kind?

'Did Penny ever say much about her childhood?'

'She didn't like to talk about it.'

'How come?'

'She just didn't.' He frowned, as if trying to draw his memories to the surface. 'She'd talk about her dad sometimes. That was the main thing. He went missing when she was really young. I think she was three.'

I looked at him. 'Her dad disappeared?'

'That's what she told me.'

'What else did she say about him?'

'That was it. Just that it happened when she was young.'

'Did he ever turn up?'

'I don't think so, no.'

'Anything else you remember her saying?'

As he gave it some thought, I tried to work out if the disappearance of Penny Beck's father might be connected to this. I couldn't see anything obvious, but that didn't give me much comfort: her dad had vanished – and so had she.

'She was born in London,' Howson said.

I noted it down. 'So did she grow up here too?'

'No. Her family moved when she was a couple of months old to some tiny farming town called Sophia. I think it's up north somewhere, because she said it always rained there.' I thought of Richard Kite's memory of the beach, and something he'd said to me the first time we met, when describing it: *The skies are grey. It's really miserable, it's drizzling.*

'She was never specific about where this place was?'

'No,' Howson said. 'I tried to bring it up once, to ask her where exactly it was, and she said, "Why are you even interested? It's the most boring place on earth." But I was interested because I could never find that place on any map.'

'Are you serious?'

'See for yourself.'

I went to my phone and put in a search for towns in northern England and Scotland called Sophia. It took all of five seconds to find out that Howson was right.

When I looked at him again, he shrugged. 'It always felt like I was on the outside looking in when it came to her childhood. I'd spend the entire time trying to piece things together from the tiny fragments she gave me. Like, the town was called Sophia. That was one thing. And her father used to work here in London in some boring office job, but quit to go and farm sheep up north – that's another. Her father disappeared, that's a third, and her mum remarried some guy called Jack. Four. And the fifth thing was that she had a stepsister called Beth, but they ended up having a big falling-out.'

'About what?'

'Penny never said. She just said they didn't speak any more.'

A disappearance of someone close to her, a falling-out, a town that wasn't on any map – the last one in particular rang alarm bells. To me, it suggested that, at best, Penny had been sidestepping the truth, at worst lying about her background. The only question that remained was whether the lie had a direct relevance to her murder, or to the case of Richard Kite.

I chewed on it for a while and then returned to the idea that Richard and Penny knew each other, had moved in the same social circles, had perhaps even been in a relationship. If Howson was right and Penny had moved north with her family when she was still a baby, then that could easily have been where she and Richard met: in the town, whatever its real name, in which Penny's father was a sheep farmer. Maybe I could locate Penny's stepsister there too. Except some things still didn't sit *quite* right. If Richard had family up north, why hadn't they come forward in the time since he was found? They surely would have picked up on the media coverage if they were looking for him. Also, why would Penny even lie about the name of the town in the first place? And if Richard was from up north, why didn't he have a northern accent?

That made me think of something.

'How did Penny speak?'

Howson frowned at me. 'What do you mean?'

'I mean, what sort of accent did she have?'

'Oh.' He nodded. 'She worked hard to hide it but, occasionally, it would slip. It was weird, actually. I'd never heard anything like it before. She was well spoken mostly, but –'

'Sometimes her *R*'s would come out hard?'

'Yes.'

'Like she might be from the West Country?'

'Yes,' he said, his frown deepening. 'Yes, that's it.'

Now I knew for sure: Penny was from the same place as Richard.

## 27

Richard Kite and Penny Beck came from the same part of the country.

*But which part?*

I looked at Howson's three photographs of her.

In one, Penny was a little younger, maybe late twenties, and was sitting on some steps with the Millennium Bridge in the background, her skin shining in the sunlight. She seemed different. Dressed in a cream blouse with a ruffled neck and a tan skirt, she had none of the weariness of the Regent's Park photograph; in that one, she was two or three years older and looked plainer, more fatigued. Something had disturbed her. From all that Howson had said so far, it sounded like she'd never told him what.

In the shot taken by the Thames, she was immaculate, a cord of blonde hair formed into a French braid that traced the arc of her forehead. Her smile was so broad and full and bright, it was like an internal lamp had snapped on: it lit the green of her eyes, it brought colour to her cheeks; in a way, it changed her entire physical appearance. It was the same in the others, one of her in a rose garden, and the other – a selfie – taken by Howson himself, his arm visible at the very edge of the shot.

'What's that?'

He followed my gaze to the thin pile of papers he'd separated out from the others and placed beside him.

'Accounts,' he said.

'That's what Penny found in the school's security suite?'

'Yes,' Howson said again. 'She discovered that there were seventeen years of Red Tree business on Marek's computer. He'd kept it all without anyone even knowing. All the money the school raised, all the fees they were being paid, all the donations they received. It was all on his hard drive.'

'Why?'

'So he knew everything that was going on. Because he thought it might be useful, or a bargaining tool, or a way to exert pressure.' He shrugged. 'I don't know. But what I *do* know is that there's something hidden in it.'

'In what?'

'In the records he kept. There's a pattern – or was – and Penny found it.'

'What's the pattern?'

'Between September 2000 and January 2003, the Red Tree was paying money into three offshore bank accounts.'

'Why would they do that?'

'Exactly,' Howson said. 'Independent schools like us, we're registered as charities, right? So we already receive an eighty per cent cut in business rates. What would be the point in setting up offshore bank accounts – which are there to help you *avoid* tax – when we're hardly paying any tax anyway?'

I thought about it – but not for long.

'Because the offshore bank accounts don't belong to the school.'

Howson nodded. 'Right. It wasn't the school that was

trying to be opaque with its money. It was Marek. He used the Red Tree as cover to shift his *own* cash around.'

'Why?'

'I don't know. Not fully.'

'And no one at the Red Tree is aware of this?'

'No,' Howson said. 'Marek's careful. Everything was done from the security suite that only he has access to. Anything that reaches Roland's desk, Marek will have checked over first. You saw how he was at the school. You saw how Roland was around him. When even the head-master is scared of him, who's going to ask questions about Marek? And even if anyone *did* look closer, he'd soon know. He has access to all the logins, to all the email accounts, all the data, everything. No one can catch him out.'

'But Penny did.'

'I don't have the whole picture,' he said, talking faster now. 'These' – he held up the printouts to me – 'they're just fragments. Scraps. Pieces of the puzzle that Penny was putting together, but they're as much as I've been able to glean from the things she left behind. What I *do* know is that Penny found out about the payments that were being made from the school to those offshore accounts, and she discovered that they were always made at the same time: the tenth of the month, every month, for twenty-nine months.'

'How much are we talking?'

'About twelve thousand pounds a month, split into three chunks of four grand – so three hundred and fifty thousand pounds in total.'

'Was Marek stealing money from the school?'

'No, that's the thing. The same amounts were coming

*into* the school the day before they were transferred out again. What I mean is, on the ninth of every month between September 2000 and January 2003, twelve thousand pounds would be paid *into* the Red Tree, and the very next day, it would be split up into four-grand chunks and then fired off into the three offshore bank accounts.'

'Who was paying the money *into* the Red Tree?'

'I don't know. It's impossible to say because it was physically being paid into a bank by someone, at a branch, not transferred from another account. All I have to go on is a name written on one of the financial statements: Caleb.'

'That's what Penny wrote down?'

'Yes,' Howson said. 'I tried to look around for who this "Caleb" might be but I'm afraid I didn't get very far.'

He handed me all the papers he'd collected, including the accounts. It was a mess of handwritten notes, sheets full of numbers, and printouts that made no sense. If Howson, one of the people who'd known Penny the best, had struggled to grasp the complexities of what was written here, it would be even harder for me. I didn't know how Penny Beck thought. The fact was, I didn't know her at all.

I spent a couple more minutes flicking through the papers, reading notes she'd made in margins, entries she'd underlined.

'Where did she leave all of this?' I asked.

'She hid everything by spreading it out, but then, by chance, six months after she was killed, I found some notes in a novel she loved. Just left there, obviously in an attempt to hide them. A couple of months after that, I went to open a chest of drawers in my bedroom and the runner got stuck. So I loosened it and managed to lever the drawer out. Taped to the underside of the drawer were some bank statements' – he gestured to a photocopy I was holding of the Red Tree's accounts from May 2002 – 'with Penny's writing in the margins. After that, I tore the house apart looking for other things, and what you have in your hands is the sum total of what I found. There could be more, but I've no idea where.'

She'd gone to the effort of hiding what she was finding – not just to protect Howson, but to protect herself too. As I continued to leaf through the paperwork, I eventually ended up back at the sheet with *Caleb* written at the top. Did all of this come back to that name?

'This is absolutely everything you found in the house?'

He nodded. 'Everything.'

'And you've no idea where the rest of it is?'

'Maybe there isn't a rest of it.' He shrugged. 'If there is, she's hidden it too well. Or it's shredded, or thrown away, or lost.' He pointed to the printouts again. 'This is as much as I've managed to collect together in the two years since she died. This is as good as it gets – and I've had to work so hard even for this much.'

'She never told you about what she was doing, even once?'

'No.'

'Why wouldn't she tell you?'

He looked into his lap. 'I'm not sure she trusted me.'

'Why not?'

'I think she worried that I'd accidentally drop her in it at work. I would never have done that knowingly, but I wasn't as smart as her; not as discreet or cautious. Ultimately, I think she was protecting me against myself – if I didn't know anything, I couldn't place myself in trouble, or jeopardize her search.'

'But a search for what?'

'That's the thing,' he said. 'I just don't know.'

*The search for wherever the name Caleb led.*

We fell into silence, Howson staring off into space, me going through the paperwork, trying to find things that might mean something: a hint, a tip, a lead.

Then there was a knock at the door.

# 28

Howson's eyes widened, a sudden panic in his face.

I held up a hand to him, trying to calm him down, and then moved to the door, inched it open and looked through the gap.

Richard Kite smiled at me.

'Phew,' he said, clearly relieved that he'd got the right place. 'Sorry it took me so long. I got confused on the Tube. I changed at Bond Street – but I took the northbound Jubilee line instead of the southbound one.'

'Don't worry,' I said, and let him in.

He and Howson stared at each other, and I knew instantly that inviting Richard here was of little or no value: he didn't know Howson, and Howson didn't know him.

'Richard, this is Jacob,' I said, pushing the door shut.

He nodded at Howson. 'Hello.'

'Who the hell is this?' Howson responded.

Richard looked rattled, intimidated by the welcome he'd been given, uncertain of who Howson was and why I'd asked him to meet us here.

'You remember that I asked you about a man called Richard Kite?' I said to Howson. His eyes shifted between me and Richard. 'Well, this is him. Richard suffers from dissociative amnesia. He can't remember who he is or where he came from.'

Howson looked at me like I might be joking.

'I'm pretty sure that Richard came from the same place as Penny,' I said, and handed Richard one of Howson's photographs.

He took the picture from me.

'She's not a singer, Richard. She was a teacher.'

I said it softly, trying to lessen the blow, but another pillar in his life had just collapsed. He looked from the photo of Penny on the edge of the Thames to me, then to Howson, and then back to the photo, and in that second he put it together: if she wasn't a singer, then Naomi Russum had lied to him; and if Russum had lied to him about that, what else had she lied about?

I offered him the chair I'd been using. For a second, it was like he didn't hear me, and it took all I had not to look away, his expression so lucid, so full of betrayal, it was an almost childlike mix of rejection and grief.

'Penny and him knew each other?' Howson said.

I watched Richard, his eyes still on the photograph of Penny.

'Penny and him were both from Sophia?'

This time I turned to Howson and said, 'There *is* no Sophia. I think you have to accept that Penny lied to you about where she came from.' I watched his face dissolve, and he and Richard took on a similar look: conned, misled. 'But, wherever it is she's from, I think it's the same place that Richard came from. If I can find this town, I can find out who Richard is.'

The two men glanced at each other.

There were no physical similarities between them – Richard was stockier and better-looking; Howson was plain, taller, skinnier – but they were still two sides of the same coin: Richard had no memory of who he was, of relationships he'd had, of where he came from; Howson remembered everything, but had come to realize that what he remembered, what he'd been told by Penny, was a lie.

'Has anyone ever mentioned a town called Sophia to you, Richard?'

'No,' he said, his expression blank.

'The name Penny Beck doesn't ring any bells either?'

'No,' he said again, his voice cracking.

'Penny, the woman in that picture, had a stepsister called Beth.' I waited for a reaction. 'Do you recall hearing that name?'

'No.'

'What about the name Alexander Marek?'

'No.'

'Caleb?'

'No,' he said again.

Howson was starting to get it now: the pain in Richard's face, the inability to remember anything, the sense of being shackled to nothing. He shuffled forward on the bed and said to Richard, 'You don't remember anything at all?'

Richard tore his gaze away from the picture of Penny Beck. Tears glimmered in his eyes.

'No,' he said. 'Nothing.'

Howson was about to ask him something else, but I held up a hand. He looked from Richard to the photograph of Penny and, for the first time, I saw questions in his face, questions I'd thought about myself too. *What if this guy had been Penny's boyfriend before? What if Penny had loved this man first? What if he was the reason she didn't talk about her past?*

I retraced my steps to the conversation Howson and I were having before Richard arrived. 'Did Penny show anyone else what she had found out?'

'No, I don't think so.'

'We need more than you've got,' I said. 'We need more if you want to pin her murder on Marek.'

At the mention of *murder*, Richard looked up from the picture.

As a silence hung in the air, Howson went back to the sleeve and picked something out. It was the item I'd spotted earlier that looked like a credit card, the one I remembered glimpsing as Howson had left his home.

Except it wasn't a credit card at all.

There were no numbers on it, no bank name, no logos or security chip. But on the back, I could see a magnetic strip and a tiny blood-red symbol.

A red tree.

'Is that a keycard?'

Howson looked at the card and then back to me. 'Yes.'

'Is it yours?'

'No. I think Penny must have stolen it. I found it hidden at home.'

'Stolen it? Are you saying it's for the security suite?'

'Yes.'

'Have you used it?'

The answer surfaced in his face: he hadn't. He was too scared, too worried about Marek catching him in the act.

'I think Penny got into that room and went looking for answers,' Howson said, his eyes flashing in the half-light. 'She got in there, and she stole all of this' – he held up the paperwork – 'and, sometime after that, Marek found out.'

'And that was when he came after her.'

'Yes,' he said. 'I think that was when he killed her.'

I glanced at Richard and saw that he was already staring at me, his face pale, his eyes coloured by fear. He didn't understand everything that Howson and I were talking about, but he understood enough. He already knew that his phone had been tapped. He'd been to the place where a woman's body had been dumped. Now it looked like the woman was from the same town as him. Maybe they'd known each other, been friends, perhaps even more than that.

More than ever, Richard was the key to everything.

That meant I needed to get him somewhere safe.

## 29

We waited until the early hours of the morning and then left the hotel, heading north along Waterloo Road in the direction of the station. The city had quietened, the pavements slick with the rain that had fallen in the hours before.

Both Richard and Howson were silent, their heads bowed. At the hotel, we'd spent another hour talking, trying to jog some distant recollection in Richard's head, a glimpse of Penny, or of the secrets she'd unravelled, but I ended the discussion when I started seeing the effect on him: with every question that didn't find an answer, he spiralled a little further down. After that, I told them both to rest and, once Howson had fallen asleep on the bed and Richard in the armchair, I went through everything Penny had collated.

I didn't find anything new.

Now, as we made our way north, Howson was clutching the plastic sleeve to his chest, but I had the keycard for the security suite. When we'd left the hotel he'd offered it to me – a tacit acknowledgement that he would never find the courage to use it himself – his voice meagre, his eyes pitched somewhere between guilt and fear.

I understood the conflict playing out in him. He'd never told the police that the woman on the railway line was Penny, even though he knew it was; he'd never shown the world what he'd found hidden at home, the printouts he'd discovered, the hints and clues that Penny had left behind in books and in drawers. He'd never told anyone about the pattern she'd uncovered – one that, ultimately, probably got her killed.

Because of that, the guilt was like a disease eating him up from the inside, and the fear he carried only made it worse: if he told the police what he knew, if he showed his hand, he'd have to admit he'd spent two years concealing his knowledge of Penny's death, and in turn defy the warning from whoever had left the message for him in his notebook. But doing nothing meant the killer got away with their crime.

Tell, don't tell: it was torture for him.

I didn't doubt that he saw me as a conduit, a way to act on the things he'd not had the guts to do himself, but it didn't have the air of a calculated move. He was too much of a mess for that, too emotional, his perspective too skewed by the fallout from Penny's murder. He'd headed to the hotel because he'd panicked, because it was an escape plan, but he didn't seem to have much of an idea of what he was going to do once he got there. What arrangements did he have in place for the days that were to come? If I'd never turned up, what then?

When I'd asked him in the hotel room, he'd just shrugged.

'I don't know,' he'd admitted quietly. 'I thought about it a lot when I first found that message.'

*Go to the police and you're dead.*

'But not after that?'

'No. I thought the hotel would be a good place to go

first if Marek ever came after me, to lie low until I figured out my next move . . .' He'd faded out.

Like so many of the people I found, he'd thought a lot about running, about the act itself, but nothing of what came after.

As Waterloo station came into view, I looked back over my shoulder at the two men trailing me, eyes still down, shoulders slumped, grey under the pale rinse of the street lights. All the remorse and the guilt had drained the colour from Howson; all the frustration and distress had done the same to Richard. The two of them looked like spectres. Directionless. Lonely.

Adrift.

We came to a stop in the shadows of an escalator in the eastern corner of Waterloo. The first train left at 5.30 a.m. and headed to the south coast, and I told them to get on it and find somewhere to lie low for a few days. Given what Howson had told me, it seemed highly likely that Marek had figured out by now that I'd made a connection between Richard Kite and the school. That meant Richard was in more immediate danger than before, because of the threat Marek posed, and because of the things he himself had found out since I'd taken the case.

'I know people in Folkestone,' Howson said.

'Perfect,' I replied. 'Head there.'

It was five o'clock on a Saturday morning, so around us the building was like a tomb: both floors, the platforms, the ticket barriers, the stores and restaurants and entrances were all totally empty.

'Call work on Monday and tell them you're sick,' I said to them both. 'I'll give you a shout when I think it's safe to come up for air.'

'I know you didn't have to help me,' Howson responded.

I looked at him. It was his guilt talking: not *I know you didn't have to help me*, but *I know I don't deserve it*. I wasn't entirely sure how to respond.

Instead I asked, 'Why did Penny do what she did?'

A frown. 'What do you mean?'

'I mean, why go down this rabbit hole at all? Why go looking into Marek? The stuff you have in that sleeve tells us that she found out he was shifting money around and using the school to do it, but why would she care about that? Why put herself in such danger? She stole a keycard from under his nose and went hunting around in that security suite, in his computer. Why?'

'Because she wanted answers.'

'Yeah, but why?'

He shrugged. 'She was a good person.'

That wasn't it. Changing her name, lying about where she came from, the self-awareness to hide what she'd found and the risk she'd taken in getting inside that security suite – I couldn't accept that it was all some moral crusade, some noble effort to expose what Marek was doing. In my experience, people prepared to go to those kinds of lengths, for a cause they had no attachment to, didn't exist outside of comic books.

This wasn't the act of some righter of society's wrongs – if it was, where was the evidence she'd done it before? Nothing I'd heard about Penny, nothing Howson had told me, suggested this was some regular sideline for her.

So the question became exactly the same as before: why? Why wade in so deep?

Did it all come back to 'Caleb', the name she'd written on the top of the printouts? Were the risks she took all down to him?

I didn't know.

But now I might have a way of finding out.

## 30

River Hill was quiet. It was early and it was the weekend, so there were no lights on in the office buildings, and no one was coming off Southwark Bridge, or heading south across the Thames in the other direction. All I had to worry about were the people getting ready to open the deli at the top of the road, and anyone living in the only residential building further along.

*Or anyone already inside the school.*

I studied the side entrance, watching from the shadows of a doorway about twenty feet down. Before he'd got on the train, Howson had told me that the side entrance was open between 5 a.m. and 10 p.m. seven days a week, and was how boarders accessed the building and, ultimately, their dormitories on the second floor. I was about to find out for sure.

At a twenty-four-hour supermarket near Waterloo, I'd bought myself a beanie. The sun was still a couple of hours away, and the temperature was just above zero, so pulling up the collar on my coat and wearing the hat as low as it could go over my face wouldn't seem odd through the eye of the CCTV camera above the door.

The camera had been positioned to give a clear view of the entrance, so there wasn't much I could do to avoid its gaze. The only thing I could do was obscure my approach. I took out my mobile phone and started to pretend to use it, dropping my head. At worst, if anyone was even watching inside, the right half of my face would be partially visible. Once I was outside the door, I kept my head low and worked fast: I ran the card through the reader, praying it wouldn't ask me for a code, and – when it didn't – I heard a series of short beeps.

Nothing else happened.

The beeps stopped. I paused for a moment, keeping my head turned away from the camera, trying to act as casually as possible. Gripping the card tighter, I went to run it through the reader a second time – but as my hand got to the machine, the door bumped away from the frame and slowly inched inwards.

I didn't move as a series of warnings went off like pops in my head. What if the beeping was an alarm? What if it was the noise of the card being rejected? What if there was some way for them to see that the card was stolen? What if someone had buzzed me in and was now lying in wait? Even as the door swung back into the corridor beyond, my feet remained fused to the flagstone steps. But then I took the next step up, into the building, carried inside by everything Howson had told me about Penny's death, all I knew about Alexander Marek and Naomi Russum – and the lies that had been told to Richard Kite.

Now out of view of the camera, I stopped.

The corridor was warm and smelled pleasant, the faint hum of a heating system audible. This time, when I swiped the card through the machine on the second door, it buzzed loudly and clicked out from its frame. I tentatively pushed at it and found myself in the middle of another corridor, this one longer. There were doors at either end as well as one facing me.

The door to my left had another reader, a Red Tree logo engraved on it, and was marked DORMITORIES. The one to my right had a traditional lock and was labelled OFFICE. The one in front of me, in the middle, had a reader and a sign saying SECURITY.

Immediately, I went for the middle door, swiping the card again. Nothing happened. I repeated the action and got the same response. I ran the card a third time and waited for a buzz, a series of beeps, any indication that I'd managed to gain access to the suite. Instead, there was no response at all. Did that mean the card was duff? Or did it mean the reader had been reset?

I made for the door into the dormitories and, when I got there, glanced over my shoulder to make sure that no one had slipped in behind me, unseen. I swiped the card through.

Nothing.

My pulse started to quicken. Why would the card work on the outside but not the inside doors? Had I walked into a trap?

I retreated quickly along the corridor, to the door that led back to the street. No one else was entering the building. Everything looked the same as before. There had been no change, but it did nothing to suppress my alarm.

Briefly, I thought about getting out, about all the reasons not to stay here, but then something familiar took hold of me: the weight of responsibility I felt to the people I helped; the lifeline they'd given me in those first years after I buried Derryn; the obligation I had to the people like Penny Beck who'd fallen along the way. It was like a carcass strapped to my back. It was a burden I couldn't ignore.

So I kept going.

Pocketing the keycard, I made an immediate beeline for the third door, the door marked OFFICE; the one with no reader, just a regular lock. I tried the handle.

It was open.

As the door inched inwards, I caught sight of my face in the brass of the plaque, the C and E of OFFICE reflecting back my expression. I looked tired, which I was. I looked disquieted and anxious, because I was both of those too. I could see beads of sweat along my hairline and two, maybe three days' beard growth in a dark strip of shadow from ear to chin to ear.

Once the door had followed its arc into the room, I could see an oak desk with legs as thick as tree trunks, and a series of shelves, each set behind frosted-glass panels that had individual locks on them. To my left were two sofas facing each other, a coffee table in between, and then another set of shelves, also locked up. It was hard to tell for sure, but behind the frosted glass it looked like ring binders were stacked side by side. Sitting on the desk was a MacBook and an in-tray, and behind both of those was a window, looking out to an Italian-style garden, bordered by high walls and lit up by a line of pale lamps.

I pushed the door shut and then made my way around to the laptop. A leather chair had been rolled in under the desk, but I didn't bother sitting, just booted up the MacBook and listened to it hum into life. As I waited, I tried to shift open the shelf panel closest to me, to see if the locks on the glass were being used or just for show. The panels shifted slightly on their runners, but they didn't slide across.

I didn't worry about the panels for now, or the ring binders inside, and instead focused my attention on the laptop. A couple of seconds later, an icon – the logo for the Red Tree – appeared. Below that was a password prompt and a tiny photograph of the laptop's owner: Alexander Marek.

But then my attention switched.

Outside the door, I could hear footsteps.

## 31

I shut the MacBook down and headed for the office door, pressing my ear to it. My blood had started running cold in my veins and, out of nowhere, I'd begun remembering something a doctor had said to me once, in the aftermath of a panic attack I'd suffered: *This job of yours might cost you your life. And maybe it won't be because you get stabbed. Maybe it'll be because you're sick.* He'd meant biologically sick. He'd meant cut down by disease or infection, by my body turning against itself, erasing me from existence cell by cell. But maybe my sickness wasn't that at all.

Maybe my sickness was obsession.

I pushed down on the handle and inched the door open. Halfway along the corridor, outside the door to the security suite, was Alexander Marek.

He was dressed in black trousers and a dark grey shirt and had his head tilted slightly, clearly listening for something: a rogue noise, a sound that didn't fit this place. At first, it was hard to tell if he'd just entered the school or if he'd been here the whole time, but then I thought of the laptop, just sitting on the desk, and realized he must already have been in the building when I arrived. There was no way he would have left the MacBook unattended otherwise.

I watched him for a second. There was something different about him now, something more intense, as if he'd expanded, grown taller. It made me realize the person he'd been the day before, the person who'd shown me to Roland Dell's office, was a lie, a fabrication. This was the real him. This felt like the man Jacob Howson had described, the one everyone was scared of.

As gently as I could, I pushed the door closed.

I moved quickly across the room to the window and checked the latches. They weren't locked, and the window was big enough to climb through, but I had no real idea where the garden led – out into the street, or back into the building.

A crackle of static from the other side of the door – a radio – and then the muted sound of footsteps. They were softer now, as if he knew where I was.

He was coming.

Shit. *Shit*.

On instinct, I reached up to the window and opened it, pushing it as far out into the darkness of the garden as it would go. Sound flowed in from the city: it was starting to wake up – traffic, voices, activity.

I glanced back over my shoulder and my gaze switched from the door to the desk.

The laptop.

A moment of hesitation halted me, gluing me to the carpet. Grab it, and he'd know for sure that someone had broken in. Don't, and I might never find out the truth.

In a split second, I thought about the consequences of taking it – *stealing* it – and the fact that the school might involve the police. I thought about what sort of person it would make me if I made off with it. It made me no better than the people who came after me, who hunted me, the men who'd broken into *my* home on cases I'd worked and who'd tried to tear my life apart in the process. But then I wondered if the police would ever get called here, if what was being hidden inside the security suite, and maybe even on the hard drive of the laptop, would raise too many questions about Marek – and reveal too many secrets.

Richard Kite, and the truth about who he was.

Penny Beck, and why she'd been killed.

Maybe things that were even worse than that.

I swept the MacBook off the desk, clutched it between my arm and chest, and climbed on to a case that boxed in a radiator. A couple of seconds later, I was in the garden, surrounded by high walls and trellising, vines snaking up them, out of ceramic pots. I saw benches at intervals, a fountain, and a patio leading back to the building. Next to the patio was an arched door marked FIRE EXIT.

I pushed the window shut, and headed towards the door. It was still cold, the air chill against my skin. Windows looked out on to the garden all the way along, but they were dark and impossible to see into, and I tried to keep my face turned away from them, in case I was being watched.

On the exit door, there was a fire bar.

I pushed it, it clicked and swung open – but the second it shifted, an alarm sounded. I looked behind me, back across the garden, to the window of the office. A silhouette formed at the glass, staring out, trying to locate me against the shadows. Pulling my beanie down as far as it would go, I headed through the exit and found myself in a narrow alleyway.

Gripping the laptop as tightly as I could, I broke into a run and headed left, away from the entrance on River

Hill. Eventually, I reached the next street along, cobbled and running at a slant. It was empty except for a couple, hand in hand, going south towards the Thames.

I headed in the other direction.

By the time I got home, it was almost seven.

I opened up the house and checked it over. The alarm was still set, the windows were all shut. I didn't expect to get back and find I'd been broken into, but I made sure all the same. I'd done my best to disguise myself from cameras at the front and rear of the school, but Marek would be poring over footage now, looking for the person who'd accessed the building illegally and made off with his laptop. He probably already knew it was me – even if he couldn't prove it – and then it became a question of what happened next. I still didn't think he'd call the police, because I had a hard time believing he'd want the attention. So he'd take care of everything himself.

In most ways I could think of, that was even worse.

I turned the Wi-Fi off, so the MacBook wasn't transmitting a location, and then packed a bag, filling it with my spare laptop, a spare mobile phone, power leads, enough clothes for a few days, fresh notebooks, and everything I'd compiled so far on Richard Kite. After that, I jumped in the shower, feeling fatigue kick in.

I hadn't slept all night; I was operating on coffee and adrenalin, and now it was starting to wear off. I rubbed hard at my eyes and put my face directly beneath the shower head, trying to force some energy back into my muscles. By the time I was dressed, I felt better.

Twenty minutes later, I was gone.

# Breath

The skies were steel grey as the Land Rover bumped down the old track. Miles out to sea, it was still possible to see evidence of the sun, a brush of red paint at the horizon, but then – the next time Penny looked up – the sun was gone, the skies had darkened even more, and night was clawing its way in.

Next to her, in the bed of the vehicle, Beth glanced at her, tear trails still visible on her cheeks. Penny looked away, not wanting to see her sister's face, to see the pain and the fear in it. But then she felt herself slowly drawn back to Beth, and – as they hit a pothole in the track, and the Land Rover rolled left to right – she let the momentum of the vehicle slide her all the way over. As they bumped against each other, Penny reached for Beth's hand and gripped it as tightly as she could.

She listened to the low rumble of the vehicle, to the sound of loose stones spitting up and pinging against the underside of the Land Rover. It almost drowned out Beth's sobs – almost, but not quite. If, two nights ago, Penny had struggled with the idea of Beth only being twelve years old – the way she talked, the way she acted – there was no struggle now. Under the rain-soaked coat that was stuck to her skin, Penny could see the small swell of Beth's breasts. She remembered the conversation they'd had only four months ago about Beth starting her period. They'd felt like adults then, women, but here, now, they were girls, not grown-ups, not explorers, or adventurers, or pioneers. More memories returned to Penny: the two of them racing down to the harbour every day, trying to see who was fastest; kicking a ball around in the park; walking to and from school, their endless, innocent conversations long forgotten, like smoke drifting away from the ashes of a gutted building. Penny had sat across from Beth in that pillbox two days ago, both of them ready to head out into the Brink.

*I was born ready,* Beth had said.

*But not for this.*

*Not for what was coming.*

The Land Rover came to an abrupt halt, rocking on its suspension briefly. Penny got on to her haunches and swivelled, looking across the vehicle's flat roof.

The Brink.

It lay in front of them, half obscured by the approaching darkness, a sea of pale grass bleached by a covering of snow. Off to her left, a little way down the slope, was the pillbox she and Beth had been to, over and over, for more than five years.

As the wind picked up, snowflakes scattered around them, and at the front of the vehicle the doors opened and two men got out. One was a guy called Anthony Jessop. Penny didn't know much about him. She'd seen him in town, smoking in the shadows of the pub. She'd seen how big Jessop was, like a wrestler, and he looked even bigger now, wrapped in a thick winter coat, his face and head partly obscured beneath a green woollen hat. The other man Penny knew. She knew him as well as almost anyone.

The other man was her stepdad, Jack.

He was tall and wiry with an uneven beard. Penny remembered asking him once, when she was still young — after her own father had disappeared and her mum had moved in with Jack — why Jack's beard didn't grow very well on one side of his face, and Jack had laughed for ages and told Penny he loved her questions.

'It's an old war injury,' he'd said to her after he'd stopped *laughing, except it was a joke — even at that age, Penny knew it was a joke — because Jack was a farmer and had never been to war. 'No, seriously, I got it fighting the Morlocks.'*

Jack *loved* The Time Machine. *He used to read it to her and Beth before bed, before they started creeping out of the house without him and her mum knowing.*

*Those days seemed like another life now.*

*'It's time.'*

*Penny glanced at Jack. He had an expression on his face that was difficult to read: he was upset, but he was rigid and uncompromising too.*

*'Both of you, out.'*

*'Jack, why are you doing—'*

*'Out.'*

*Penny turned and looked across at Beth again, cowering in the back of the Land Rover, surrounded by old cans, cloths and tools.*

*'It's okay,' Penny said to her.*

*But her words didn't match the panic in her eyes and, as Beth saw that, she started sobbing even louder and Penny felt a spike of anger, as thick as a fist in her throat. 'No,' she said, turning to Jack. 'No, we won't come out.'*

*'Get out, Pen.'*

*'No, I won't do it.'*

*Jack glanced at Jessop, clearly embarrassed.*

*'Out of the bloody back, Penny,' he said between his teeth. Penny hadn't seen Jack angry much, but he was angry now. His eyes narrowed and his chest seemed to swell as he took a step towards the Land Rover. 'Get out!'*

*'Why are you doing this?'*

*'Because you broke the rules. Now get out!'*

*Penny looked around her — over to the pillbox, just visible at the*

216

edge of the gathering dark; across the ocean of grass on both sides of the fence; to the marshland, its bogs winking in the light from the men's torches; and then back to her sister. More snowflakes swirled around their faces, blown across the headland, up the hills from the water somewhere in the distance.

Penny said to Beth, 'It's okay.'

Beth's eyes filled with fresh tears. She started shaking her head.

'Beth, listen.'

Beth didn't respond.

'Beth, listen to me.'

She still didn't respond, the tears streaming down her face.

'Beth, listen to me – now.'

Beth finally looked up.

'I'll protect you,' Penny said. 'I promise.'

But while she might have convinced Beth, she couldn't convince herself, and as the wind and the snow carried her words off into the night, Penny felt tears blur in her own eyes this time.

She turned to Jack. 'You'll pay for this.'

'Shut up.'

'Both of you,' she said, jabbing a finger at Jack and then at Jessop. Jessop hardly even moved, didn't react, just stared at Penny blankly. 'You want us?' she said. 'You'll have to come through me first.'

Penny looked back at her sister and swallowed. She sounded brave, her voice tight – but she was frightened of the men, of this place, of what was coming. Even so, when she turned back to Jack, she placed her hands at her side, bunched into fists, ready to put up whatever fight she could muster.

But something had changed.

Jessop was gone.

A sharp scream ripped through the night. Penny turned around and saw Jessop behind her, standing on the other side of the Land Rover, his arms reaching over and into the back of the vehicle. He already had hold of Beth, her legs kicking out violently.

'Get off her!' Penny yelled.

But as she moved, a hand grabbed at her ankle and she lost her balance, one foot knocking against the other. She lurched to the side and hit the hard metal of the Land Rover. In a flash, Jack had dragged her towards him, clamped her against him, and lifted her out. Penny thrashed around like an eel, unable to see her sister now, desperately trying to fight back. Beth was gone, carried off into the darkness, in the direction of the pillbox. She heard a scream, a second one — and then there was nothing.

'I fucking hate you!' Penny screamed at her stepdad.

Jack held her in a bear hug. She couldn't move and now, as they headed to the boundary, she caught a glimpse of Beth again. She'd been tied to the fence further down, her back against the wire.

'No,' Penny said, struggling again. 'No!'

Jack gripped her more tightly, positioning her under his arm like a rolled-up carpet. Rope was looped around his other shoulder. They got to the fence, about fifteen feet up from where Beth had been secured, and he dumped her on the ground. She hit the earth hard, stunned for a second, and he used the hesitation against her: he grabbed Penny's arm, forced it back against the fence and began tying it to the wire. She fought back, could even feel Jack struggling to keep control of her, but then Jessop joined them, and the two men were too strong for her.

She felt the fight go out of her, felt the emotion swell in her gut, her chest, her throat, and then she was crying properly, shivering against the fence, freezing cold, frightened. 'Beth?' she said into the wind, but couldn't hear if her sister had replied or not, could hardly even see her any more. The snow swirled across the spaces between them, out of the shadows, as Jessop headed back to the Land Rover.

Jack remained where he was.

'I told you never to come up here,' he said, his voice breaking up. 'I told you two it wasn't landmines you had to worry about out there. How could you be so stupid?' He looked at Penny and then wiped at his eyes. His skin was flushed. 'How could you bring your sister up here? She's twelve years old, Pen.'

Frost cracked like glass beneath his feet as he shifted his weight and then, with the night settled like a shroud on the headland, he got down on to his haunches – tears smeared across his cheeks – and said, 'I don't want to do this but I have to. You've got to be made an example of. Everyone needs to know about the real reason you don't come up here. You need to tell your friends at school, you hear? You need to make them understand that the landmines were just a story. There's something worse out here. Much worse. It's time everyone realized that all we've been doing is trying to protect the town.'

Penny looked behind her, through the mesh of the fence, and then Jessop returned from the Land Rover with two sleeping bags and two foil blankets. He started wrapping one blanket and one bag around Penny – tucking it in around her, under her, cocooning her in – and then trekked down the hill again and did the same to Beth. Neither of the girls fought back this time: they knew they'd need the protection from the cold.

'I'll return for you before the sun's up tomorrow,' Jack said.

Penny glanced over her shoulder again.

'I'm sorry,' he muttered.

Something moved out in the Brink; the hint of a shape in the long grass. She started trying to pull her hands free, frenzied, terrified. She tried to loosen the rope with her thumbs, to wriggle her wrists out of the binds and away from the fence. But there was no escape.

'No,' she sobbed, 'no, Jack, you can't –'

But he wasn't there any more. He was already at the Land Rover, sliding in at the wheel.

'Jack?' she said. 'Jack!'

He pulled the door shut and started up the engine, cranking the gears violently. The Land Rover jolted forward, hitting a dip in the track, and then the vehicle was accelerating forward, snow spitting up from under the wheels.

'Jack!' Penny screamed.

The car disappeared back along the track, melting into the darkness. And as the sound of it dropped away, the wind came in its place, and then a new noise followed from the other side of the fence.

It was the sound of something moving out in the Brink.

And it was getting closer.

## 32

Driving west out of London, I picked up the motorway and then exited north of Heathrow. I needed a place where no one would think to look for me, and one of the faceless airport hotels that circled the runways seemed like a good bet.

I found a dimly lit corner in a faux marble foyer and removed the MacBook I'd lifted from the Red Tree. When I opened it up, it sprang into life, the password prompt showing again, the picture of Marek too, just as in the office.

Shutting the laptop down completely, I then started it up while holding Command-R. I was hoping to bypass the security by using the MacBook's Recovery Mode. Once it was loaded, I went to Terminal and began the process of resetting the password. I then rebooted it. As the loading bar filled up, I found myself nervously tapping out a rhythm on the table beside me, then looking up to watch the faces filing through the hotel: families with brightly coloured luggage, businessmen in suits, retired couples waiting in line for a bus to the airport.

Finally, the password prompt appeared.

I put in my new password, hit Return, and hoped. It worked: the MacBook continued to load. A couple of seconds later, I was looking at desktop wallpaper of a mountain in Yosemite. There were no folders on the desktop, no documents either.

Keeping the Wi-Fi switched off for now, I clicked on

Finder, brought up an 'All My Files' window, and started to scroll down the list. It was a mix of Word and Excel documents, of JPEGs and PNGs, and then a number of applications downloaded from the web as zip files.

I soon realized that there was no offline information about anyone who worked at the school; no employment – or employee – documents of any kind on the hard drive. I'd been hoping for personal information that I could then dig into and find links to Richard Kite through, to the death of Penny Beck as well, but most of the documents that Marek held on the laptop were incredibly tedious – the kind of everyday correspondence a school might have with government departments, and with outside companies delivering things they needed. Learning tools. Updated sports equipment for the gym. Meat and fruit for the canteen. The images didn't offer anything more interesting either: they seemed predominantly to be shots of exterior work that had been done at the front of the building, or test shots from a new security system. The zip files just contained standard applications: the Office suite, Chrome, Skype.

I went to Chrome. Under History, there was a record of every site that had been visited over the past week. Beyond that, there was no browsing data at all, meaning that Marek must have deliberately wiped it clean, presumably at semi-regular intervals. It was annoying, but not fatal: even going back a week, I could see enough – not least that, over the course of the past two days, Internet activity had been focused on me and trying to dig up dirt on who I was.

I could see media headlines about cases I'd taken on that had blown up and spread, bleeding into the mainstream. I saw pages titled WAPPING PIER: POLICE INTERVIEW

INVESTIGATOR and SNATCHER TASK FORCE PLAY DOWN ROLE OF INVESTIGATOR. If I clicked on the second story, I'd find a picture of myself, bleached by a camera flash, on the steps of a police station, because I'd read that story before. I'd see me half turned and shielding my face as I came out of my house. Further down his History, there was also evidence that Marek had been on – and returned to – my website, a basic landing page that simply listed who I was and what I did, together with my contact details.

In order to go any further, to attempt to get into his Gmail account, or to explore some of the less obvious links in his History, I knew I'd have to log into the hotel's Wi-Fi. If he was watching iCloud, which he would be, he'd then instantly know where I was. If he was still at the school, that might give me an hour. If he was at my house, I probably only had thirty minutes before he came through the doors of the hotel. Or he might not even come for me as his first option: he might just start erasing the Mac-Book's contents remotely. Yet, if he was going to do that, he could have started doing it the moment I left the school. What seemed more likely was that he wanted to find out where I was before he did anything else.

I tried to work fast, connecting to the hotel's Wi-Fi before following the link to Marek's Gmail inbox. It was an instant dead end. He'd logged out properly from Gmail, presumably the last time he used it, so the username and password boxes were blanks waiting to be filled. I kept going, checking out some of the other links, most of which were irrelevant, and then came to another URL, repeated over and over, that I didn't recognize: http://rt.me.com. I selected it and discovered it was a Red Tree intranet page.

The design was deliberately dialled down: white, except for the Red Tree logo in the corner and another set of username and password tabs in the centre. This time I'd got lucky. Marek hadn't had the chance to log out properly before I'd swiped the laptop from his office.

I hit Return and the intranet loaded in another, almost identical page except this one had a line of six links running down the middle. *Preparatory School. Senior School. Fees. Notices. Contact. Staff.*

I clicked on them in order.

*Preparatory* and *Senior* led me to a system, like a grid, where parents could get an overview of what their kids were up to in lessons and out on the sports field, as well as the homework they were being set. *Fees* was where money owed to the school could be settled up: it was a secure payment page, with options for a name, card number, an expiry date and the card's verification code. *Notices* was just a list of school updates, *Contact* a single window to send an email in, and *Staff* was a white page with the school's logo in the corner, and another username and password box. Again, the computer had remembered Marek's login information. When I accessed it, I found an internal instant messaging service.

It was made up of two panes, the left one a long, thin window with a series of names in alphabetical order. It had automatically selected the first name on the list – a man called Andrew Abraham. Because of that, in the bigger, right-hand pane, there was a picture of Abraham and a tab with a small amount of personal information. He was a geography teacher.

I started checking other photos, going through them

one by one, and found Jacob Howson. Soon, I noticed something else too: in the corner of each of the staff profiles, above the photograph of the staff member, there was a green clickable button. It said: EXPORT CHAT.

I was staring at a physics teacher called Marc Davies-Peters, so used him as a guinea pig, clicking the button to see where it took me. Instantly, a .txt file began downloading to my desktop. When it was finished, I opened the file. A moment after that, I realized what I had here: it was a record of every conversation that particular member of staff had had on the club's IM. And not just who they'd chatted to and when, but the actual contents. Every message, every word, saved on to a server. It meant Marek could monitor all staff conversations.

I backed out of the profile page for Davies-Peters, inched down the list and found Naomi Russum. I found Marek too.

In his photograph, his eyes were a dark blue, the colour of a deep ocean, and he'd swept his hair back from his face, into a small ponytail, revealing a scar at the arc of his forehead. I'd put him as late thirties the first time I met him, and I could see in his face, in his skin, that I'd been right. But there was a weird disconnect between his face and eyes, as if his eyes were older, someone else's, aged by the things he'd seen and done.

Just then, the MacBook started to slow, the cursor flickering as I tried to move it in the direction of the .txt files I'd downloaded for Marek and Russum.

*Shit.*

Marek was trying to remote-erase the laptop.

Grabbing a USB stick out of my holdall, I stuck it into

the MacBook and saved both .txt files and as many of the documents and JPEGs as I could, just in case. It seemed to take an age, the load bar crawling from left to right as the computer continued to slow. At one stage, it looked like it had stopped altogether and was about to lock me out. But it didn't. The load bar jumped into life for a second time, and then shortly after that it was done.

I yanked out the stick, pocketed it, scooped up Marek's laptop and my holdall and made a beeline for the toilets. In one of the cubicles, I shut the door and started hauling the lid off the cistern.

I dumped the MacBook inside.

It made a splash as it hit the water, the toilet's float rod bending as I forced the laptop past it. Water spilled out over the top and on to the floor, but then everything settled and the MacBook stayed below the surface, at the bottom of the tank.

Replacing the lid on the cistern, I headed out to my car, got back on to the Bath Road and did a four-mile loop to the south of the airport where there was another faceless hotel. I set up in the foyer, with views of the main entrance, and transferred everything from the USB stick on to my own laptop.

After that, I opened up the .txt files.

They contained the conversations that Marek and Naomi Russum had both had on the Red Tree instant messaging service; and it turned out that they'd had a lot – and mostly with each other. Something else became pretty clear very quickly too: they really only talked about one subject.

One person.

And that was Richard Kite.

## 33

Marek's style was terse, his language deliberately opaque, and it built an even clearer picture of him. There was never going to be any confirmation on the system that he was the one who had murdered Penny Beck – his language in the IM chats was too precise – but you could almost feel people squirm when they had to talk to him.

Russum was the same.

I looked for conversations between the two of them in and around the time of Penny's death – basically any hint about why she was killed and who carried out the act. There was nothing. However, repeated in both text files was a conversation between Marek and Russum that had taken place over the course of seven consecutive weeks, starting in early March; a month and a half after Richard Kite had appeared out of nowhere in Hampshire.

> **AMarek** How did the first session go today?
> **NRussum** He doesn't remember anything.
> **AMarek** Nothing?
> **NRussum** He has one quite clear memory about a beach. He says he can remember looking out at it from a window, possibly as a kid. He remembers some sort of children's TV show as well.
> **AMarek** What else did he say about the beach?

**NRussum** Nothing.

**AMarek** And the children's TV show?

**NRussum** Same.

**AMarek** All the stuff he told the newspapers last month – that's as much as he remembers?

**NRussum** Yes.

**AMarek** If he remembers any more, I need to know.

**NRussum** Yes. You've made that perfectly clear.

It was obvious that Russum had accessed the messenger from her place of work, or her home, somewhere other than the school, otherwise they'd surely have had the conversation in person. It was also obvious why she might prefer to do that. She didn't like him. She didn't want to be in the same room as him.

Other things stood out too. She was reluctant, seemed not to like being asked to keep an eye on Richard or the idea of lying to him; and, from Marek's side, there was clearly a concern, not just that Richard would remember his past, but that he might remember more about the beach and the TV show. Why was Marek so worried about those things coming back to Richard?

Where did they lead?

The only thing that really made sense in terms of the intro to the TV show was if it was local programming – a regional news show, or something specific to an area of the country – because, that way, it would help investigators to narrow down their search. But I'd already trawled a database of local TV news intros, including stills of title cards, and when I did it again now I got the same result: nothing that matched Richard's description of the TV mast.

Their next conversation was a few days later. It became apparent that Russum had just finished another session and was immediately reporting back.

> **NRussum** No change.
>
> **AMarek** No new memories?
>
> **NRussum** No.
>
> **AMarek** Did you put him under?
>
> **NRussum** It isn't an anaesthetic.
>
> **AMarek** So did you?
>
> **NRussum** Yes.
>
> **AMarek** And?
>
> **NRussum** It was unsuccessful.
>
> **AMarek** Meaning what?
>
> **NRussum** Meaning, he didn't respond.
>
> **AMarek** You do realize what's at stake here for you, don't you?

I paused, eyes on that final line.

What did it mean? What *was* at stake for Russum if she didn't do what Marek asked of her? Could it be something as coarse as her life?

I kept reading.

> **NRussum** Why are you making me do this?
>
> **AMarek** You don't need to worry about it.
>
> **NRussum** Why do I keep having to show him a picture of Corrine Wilson?
>
> **AMarek** It doesn't matter.
>
> **NRussum** I want to know why.
>
> **AMarek** IT DOESN'T MATTER. All you need to know is he represents a risk to us.

**NRussum** But what sort of risk?

**AMarek** He's dangerous.

**NRussum** That seems unlikely.

**AMarek** You don't know anything about him.

**NRussum** He doesn't seem dangerous to me.

**AMarek** I don't fucking care what you think. You got a shitload of money so you could go away and start that clinic of yours. Unless you want me to take that money back, you're going to stop asking questions and do exactly what I ask.

There it was: the reason Marek had been able to move Naomi Russum into place. He'd helped get her business off the ground. She was in debt to him. If he called in his investment, the Aldgate Clinic went down the toilet and all that she'd worked for, all the prestige, the plaudits, the acclaim, would be gone in a flash. She didn't know what Marek's real interest in Richard Kite was, just as I didn't yet, but she must have realized that, if Marek was involved, it wasn't going to be anything good. But he had her in a noose, so she chose not to ask any more questions.

He turned the screw again a few weeks later.

**AMarek** What happened today?

**NRussum** This is immoral. I hate it.

**AMarek** That wasn't the question I asked.

**NRussum** He has no idea what's going on.

**AMarek** Just do your job, Naomi.

**NRussum** You're not the one that has to face him every week.

And then, several weeks later, a bomb dropped:

**NRussum** I'm doing what you asked. I hope you're happy.

**AMarek** I am. It's for the best.

**NRussum** Is it?

**AMarek** Yes.

**NRussum** Then why do I feel like shit?

**AMarek** How far did you go?

**NRussum** I put him under and started discussing the TV intro he remembers. But it will take time. It has to be done gradually and carefully. We could be talking months. We could be talking years. We also talked about the beach. I suggested it might be a river with a city on the other side.

I could barely even process what I was reading.

Russum had looked me in the face and lied about how many times she'd used hypnosis on Richard. She'd told me she'd used it twice, both times right at the beginning, citing it as ineffective – but from the transcript, it was clear that she had still been using it almost three months after he first started seeing her. It was clear she was going to *keep* on using it too.

But that was far from the worst thing she'd done.

I thought of the phone conversation I'd had with Reverend Parsons about Richard's memories; about that one incongruous period when Richard remembered the beach differently. *He said the sea wasn't sea at all, but a river,* Parsons had told me, *and on the other side of the river was a city. He said he could picture big buildings, and long roads, and cars, and traffic.* The new memory had lasted a few days, a week, little more than that. Yet it had added to the sense of confusion, unbalanced Richard, made him doubt even the small fragments of recall he still had. And the reason he was so confused, why he couldn't seem to pin down his exact memories of the beach and the TV intro, why whole new ideas like the city were suddenly coming out of nowhere, was because, during sessions with Russum, the rug was constantly being pulled out from under him.

Established ideas vanished, or were altered; new ideas were added. She was eating away at the anchors he still had, the pillars of his past.

She was planting false memories in his head.

# 34

*What was a memory and what was a lie?*

I took a moment, anger humming beneath my skin.

Russum had talked about the dangers that hypnosis – in the hands of an amateur – could pose for the patient: the wrong line of questioning, an ungainly delivery, even a stray word. She was no amateur, quite the opposite, which only made her more irresponsible. Even if she'd made it clear to Marek that she hadn't wanted to go down this route, that it went against everything she believed in, even if she knew – deep down – that there was no way Richard was dangerous, she'd done it anyway.

And the consequences of what she was doing were huge. It might be the reason I wasn't able to find a trace of the TV show intro anywhere, or why the beach he'd looked out at as a kid was proving so hard to locate or identify – because tiny, important details were being altered or added while he was under hypnosis. For all I knew, he may have recalled new, significant details in the time since he was found; he may have sat down with Russum and told her about them. But if he had, they were lost now, buried or destroyed by Russum, before new, bogus ones were passed to her, like some stage direction, by Marek.

What seemed indisputable was that a secret – or some knowledge of what it might be – was buried inside

Richard Kite's head. Doctors, the police, the media, Reverend Parsons, me – we'd tried to lever his memories to the surface. We'd tried to pull them into the light in order to give him his life back. But Marek was busy manipulating Russum – blackmailing her – into making sure that never happened. Ultimately, he wanted Richard's recollection narrowed because what lay dormant behind his eyes was big enough to bring Marek down.

I read on, deeper into the IM transcript. After a while, a thought came back to me, one I'd had a couple of times already: *If he's such a threat, why hasn't Marek just taken care of Richard like he took care of Penny Beck?* With Richard dead, there was no danger of him compromising them; no danger of him remembering details about his past, about who Marek was and what he'd done. Why even go to the trouble of trying to manipulate his memories through hypnosis?

Because Richard was known, and he had a support network. He had people looking out for him who wouldn't stay quiet if he just got up one day and disappeared – unlike Howson had after Penny vanished. He had Parsons and the charity Starting Again on his side. He'd been all over the newspapers and Internet in the southern counties for those first few months, and although the coverage had died down, journalists would still know who he was and be interested in big new twists in his story. Couple that with the fact that the police investigation into his case, although stalled, was still active, and it got complicated for Marek. When Penny disappeared, she did so in relative anonymity; if Richard went the same way, red flags would go up at Hampshire Police and in the media.

That was why Marek had got Russum involved, why he'd manoeuvred her, and why he threatened her if she didn't do what he asked.

I called Richard's mobile.

He picked up after four rings. In the background, I could hear the hum of traffic. He said that he and Howson had got to Folkestone and were on their way to a place that Howson's friends owned. I told him to keep me updated, and then started pressing him again: on the things that Naomi Russum had been talking about in their meetings, on what he recalled of the hypnosis used on him, and about whether he ever remembered coming into contact with the school, or the people that worked there.

'I'm sorry,' he said. 'I just don't remember.'

He sounded dispirited, beaten down, even more so than usual. It was getting harder to know what to say to him, and not only because his history was so limited. I knew for sure now that there were things orbiting his life that were off kilter, secrets about Marek that were buried in the spaces that Richard had once existed in. But that was the problem. There was no clarity on where anyone or anything fitted into Richard's life, because there was no clarity on his past at all.

'You remember, back at the hotel, I asked you if you'd ever come across a guy called Alexander Marek?' I said to him.

'Yes,' he said. 'Yes, I think so.'

I spelled the surname out for him, and then described Marek to him, his physical appearance, trying desperately to jog something in the blackness of his memory. 'That name or description definitely doesn't sound familiar to you?'

'Marek,' Richard responded. 'Do you know where he might be from?'

I hadn't mentioned that Marek might be foreign. His accent was so slight, it was hard to even pick up on, and I'd become more interested in what he was doing with Naomi Russum. But now I realized my mistake. Richard was smart. I should have used that.

'I think he might be Czech,' I said. 'He's got a faint accent.'

'Oh, right,' he replied. 'Okay.'

It was a slightly odd response.

'Richard?'

'Sorry. I mean, I *know* I don't recognize his name,' he said, his voice laced with a familiar mix of confusion and frustration, 'but the physical description, the thing about him having an accent, it reminds me of this . . .'

'This what?' I asked.

'Maybe it's nothing,' he said, 'but there was this guy.'

'What guy?'

'I don't know if it's even . . .' His voice trailed off again. I tried not to hurry him, even though I wanted to.

'Richard?'

'Yes. Sorry.'

'What was it you were going to tell me?'

'It's probably nothing,' he said, 'but . . . I don't know, I've just remembered this guy who came to talk to me at the caravan at the start of the year.'

I stopped. 'What guy?'

'It was back in February time, I think.'

'Who was the guy, Richard?'

236

'He said he was an investigator.'

'A cop?'

'He didn't say "cop". Just investigator.'

I could feel myself tense. The phone suddenly started humming in my hand. I had another call waiting.

'Just give me a sec,' I said to Richard, and then checked the number.

It was blocked.

It could have been Ewan Tasker. He generally called from a secure line. Or it could have been one of my other sources, retained from my newspaper days, who needed to stay anonymous for obvious reasons. But it wasn't any of them. Deep down, I knew exactly who it was.

'Just hold the line a second, Richard.'

I switched to the blocked number. Even before I'd said anything, before I'd really had the chance to, a voice said, 'I know where you are.'

*Marek.*

'I know you're at Heathrow,' he said, and in the background of the call I could hear voices, conversation, vehicles, bland music. *Was he at the hotel where I dumped his laptop?* 'I know you're still here somewhere.'

I didn't say anything.

'I'm right, aren't I? You're still here.'

I looked out to the hotel foyer, at the faces that surrounded me, paranoid now that he'd already figured me out; that this was some game he was playing.

*That he was here, watching me.*

'Are you trying to find a flight out of here?' he said.

I moved from face to face, looking for his.

'It doesn't matter if you do or you don't.'

I couldn't see him.

'It doesn't matter, because I'll find you. And when I find you, I'll rip —'

I hung up on him.

# 35

I told Richard I would call him back, dumped everything into the holdall and headed out to my car. Marek had had enough time to geolocate his MacBook to the airport, so if he was in the area it was too much of a risk to stay put. I headed back into London, towards Chiswick. Fifteen minutes later, I was seated at the back of a Starbucks on the high street, my back to the wall and in full view of the door, with Richard on the line again.

'This investigator who came to see you,' I said, 'what did he want?'

'He was looking for a missing woman.'

'A missing woman? Who was she?'

'I don't know.'

'But you remember this guy having an accent?'

'Yes,' Richard said. 'It was very soft, but I could still hear it.'

*Marek.* It had to be him.

'Why didn't you mention this to me before?' I asked.

'I don't know. It never made sense until now.' He paused, seemed to be struggling to articulate his thoughts. 'I know how that sounds, but it's like it was there the whole time, flickering away in the background – I just couldn't remember it until you mentioned the way he looked, and his accent.'

I thought of Naomi Russum, of how she'd used

hypnosis on him. Was this her doing? Had she been try-ing to suppress his recollection of meeting Marek?

What else had she erased?

'Did the guy show you a picture of this missing woman?'

'Yes.'

'Had you ever seen her before?'

'No, never.'

'What about in the time since?'

'No.'

So the woman definitely wasn't Penny Beck.

I pushed on. 'You said he came to see you in February?'

'Yes.'

'Pretty soon after you were found?'

'Right.'

I made a note of it. 'What did he say his name was?'

'Uh, Jones, I think.'

'Which struck you as odd?'

'Yes, because of the accent.'

I tried to think. What was Marek doing? Who was the missing woman he was looking for? If he was trying to discover whether Richard knew anything about her, whether there was a chance that he remembered the woman at all, why not wait to funnel those questions via Russum's therapy sessions? Soon after Marek had been to see Richard at the caravan park, Russum had started the sessions; pretty soon after that, they'd begun building a rapport. So why wouldn't Marek just wait and tell *her* to raise questions about the missing woman, in the same way she'd been testing Richard's recollection of Penny

Beck? There had to be a reason that Marek chose not to wait a few weeks to use Russum, and I could only think of one: that something would look suspicious, even to a man with no memory, if Russum asked him about *this* missing woman.

'Did he say anything else about her?' I asked.

'He said they were concerned for her safety.'

*Which was probably a lie.*

'Did he say how long she'd been missing?'

'No.'

'What about her name?'

'No, nothing like that.'

'Okay. Give me a second.'

I returned to the IM transcripts, trying to see if anything in there matched what Richard was telling me.

There was one passage.

It was with someone whose username was LG and who had no bio on the intranet. *So it wasn't a school employee.* Whoever it was must have been set up on the system and given access codes by Marek. I tried doing a Google search for the IP address listed beneath the user in the logs, but just hit a series of dead ends.

I returned to the transcript.

> **AMarek** Nothing.
>
> **LG** He doesn't recognize her?
>
> **AMarek** No.
>
> **LG** Could he be faking?
>
> **AMarek** I doubt it. He has no memory. Have there been any more sightings of her?

**LG** We're still looking. We know she was here with him w/c
10 Jan and we've also got witnesses who reckon they might
have seen her in the time since.
**AMarek** Okay.
**LG** So do you want me to handle it or are you coming back
to the O?
**AMarek** I'm coming back. We'll find her.

Three things leaped out.

The woman wasn't being looked for, she was being hunted; she and Richard were seen together in the week before he turned up in Hampshire; and Marek had gone to somewhere called the O in an effort to find the woman.

What the hell was the O?

I returned to the documents and JPEGs I'd lifted from Marek's MacBook. I looked for anything I had missed that could hint at who the woman was, and why Marek came to Richard to ask him about her. I switched to a different view, so files scrolled right to left as icons, making it easier to see what each document was, what file type, and what it might contain.

'Richard?'

'Yeah, I'm still here.'

'Can you remember anything else this investigator said?'

I continued to tab through the files on the laptop.

'He didn't tell me how long she'd been missing,' he said, 'or, at least, I don't remember if he did. But he believed she was still in the area.'

I tried to interpret that: if Marek could place Richard with the woman, and if – as was claimed in the IM conversation with LG – they were seen together in the days before he turned up at the edge of Southampton Water, then it sounded like it was some sort of test. Marek was assessing him. He was first looking for signs the amnesia was a lie, and when he realized it wasn't, he was then looking for other lies that Richard might be telling. He was trying to get a read on Richard, trying to see if the woman had returned to find him in the days after he turned up; to see if she explained who she was, talked to him, reassured him, told him he could trust her. Basically, Marek was looking for signs that Richard was protecting her. But Richard wasn't lying about his amnesia, and he wasn't lying about knowing the woman. Whoever she was to him, he didn't remember her any more, and she hadn't sought him out after he was found with no memory of who he was. Marek would have quickly realized that.

'He showed you a picture of her, right?'

'Yes, that's right.'

'Can you describe the picture to me?'

'Uh . . . I think it was taken from a CCTV camera.'

'It was from a surveillance camera?'

'Yes.'

That had to be the reason. That was why Marek chose not to wait for Russum to talk to Richard about the woman in her sessions. Even in his confused state, he'd have instinctively started asking difficult questions if Russum began showing him CCTV stills of a woman. But if Marek turned up at his caravan, posing as an investigator, it looked far less suspicious.

They'd misjudged Richard, though.

The woman in the picture, the slight twang of Marek's

accent, the fact that the photograph was taken from a security camera; Marek had thought those details would vanish over time, just another glut of information that Russum would help to remove and that would quickly become lost in Richard's search for answers. But he hadn't forgotten.

'Where did the camera seem to be?' I asked.

'I'm not sure.'

'On a street? Inside a building?'

'Inside a building, I think.'

'A shop? An office?'

He paused for a moment. 'It looked like a hotel.'

'A hotel foyer?'

'No. It was more like a corridor.'

'There were rooms on both sides?'

'Yes.'

I rubbed a hand against my forehead. *A hotel corridor. But which hotel?*

'Do you remember anything else about it?' I asked.

I heard him take a long breath and, in the silence that followed, I began to tab through the files again, slowly. Word documents. PDFs. JPEGs of timesheets and invoices. After a while, they all began blurring into one.

'No,' Richard said finally. 'That's all I've got.'

'I need you to be sure.'

'I'm pretty sure.'

I tried again. 'Just think really hard about it for a sec—'

But then I stopped.

Another JPEG had appeared in the file viewer.

'David?'

'Wait a minute,' I said.

I double-clicked on the JPEG, opening it up, and as it loaded I dragged the laptop closer to me. I'd seen the picture before, the first time I'd gone through the MacBook, but it hadn't seemed important then. Marek had hundreds of JPEGs on his hard drive, a lot of them taken from cameras inside the Red Tree; angled shots of rooms that were hard to get a sense of. I'd assumed they were test shots, stills taken from a newly installed security system to make sure it was working.

And maybe they were.

But this one wasn't.

It was a shot of a corridor with doors on either side, just as Richard Kite had described. A patterned carpet. Paintings on the walls. At the very top of the shot, almost out of view, a woman was walking away from the lens, looking over her shoulder, as if worried she was being followed. She was blonde, dressed in black, and had a dark backpack over her shoulders.

'David?' Richard said again.

'Yeah, I'm here. I think I might've found her.'

'The woman?'

'Yeah. I'm going to message a picture to your phone.'

I took a shot of the screen and sent it across to him. Thirty seconds later, I heard a soft beep in the background of the call as the picture arrived.

'That's it,' he said.

'That's the picture he showed you?'

'Yes.'

I zoomed in on the woman's face.

The closer I got, the more pixelated it became, so I backed out again and tried to get a sense of the rest of it.

Doors. Decor. The way she was looking over her shoulder. Something was odd about the shot but I couldn't put my finger on it.

*What aren't I seeing?*

'Who do you think she is?' Richard asked.

I studied the woman again.

'I don't know,' I said, but then – for the first time – I switched my attention to the filename of the picture, and it was like the ground shifted beneath my feet.

I looked up, away from the screen, recalling something that Jacob Howson had told me: Penny was born an only child, but she'd had a stepsister. I looked at the woman in the picture again, and then at the name of the file.

The file was called 'Beth'.

## 36

*Beth*. Penny Beck's stepsister.

I tried to make connections, tried to think about the reasons they had fallen out, whether it was relevant to Richard Kite or to how the two sisters had known him. I tried to think why – over fourteen months after the murder of her sister, and a week before Richard lost his memory – Beth was seen with him in a hotel. What were they doing in that hotel? Where had Beth gone afterwards? Had Marek eventually tracked her down?

I ended the call and then did a quick search for women with the name Beth, Bethan or Bethany who had been reported missing. I couldn't find anything. Instead, I got a mix of women on social media accounts, LinkedIn profiles and YouTube videos who clearly weren't her. I went through them just in case, didn't find anything, and spent a moment trying to imagine what her invisibility might mean. That she was alive? That she had fled Marek? Or that she was dead and, like Penny's, her death had been disguised?

I returned my attention to the photograph.

She must have been in her late twenties, although it was hard to be sure due to the quality of the CCTV footage. The colour was rinsed out: reds were pale pinks, blacks were grey, white was cream. There was still something about the construction of the shot that bugged me, some aspect of it, but I couldn't decide what it was.

Doors were visible on either side of the corridor, odds on the left, evens on the right, and each one had a set of brass numbers: eighty through to ninety-two on one side, and seventy-nine to ninety-three on the other. Beth was in the top left of the frame, only a few feet from the door marked eighty, but she didn't look like she'd come out of it or was about to go in; she looked like she was passing by it, making her way along the corridor. The way she was glancing over her shoulder, her expression, even the way she was dressed, in black with a rucksack, seemed to play into the idea of someone lying low; someone who'd come to do a job, to carry out a task.

According to the timecode information in one of the bottom corners, the shot was taken at 2.09 in the morning on Friday 15 January. That was five days before Richard was found in Hampshire. If, as Marek seemed to be suggesting in his IM conversation with LG, Beth and Richard were seen together in the week commencing 10 January, that meant they may have been in and around the hotel for as long as five days, maybe even over a week, before Richard turned up on the edge of the river. So what were they were doing together? And where was the hotel?

Based on Marek's message, I did a search for hotels called 'the O' and only found one, in Vancouver. Somehow it seemed unlikely that it was the hotel in the photograph of Beth. In that, the paintings on the wall appeared to be famous British landmarks; although it was harder to make them out the further down the corridor you went, in the frames closest to the camera I could see the London Eye, in silhouette, and what looked like the Houses of Parliament on the opposite wall.

Did that mean the hotel was in London?

I went back to the web and searched for city hotels beginning with O, but there were too many results. Apart from the paintings, there was nothing else in the shot that might give away the location of the building. I zoomed in a little and began scrolling from painting to painting, and then from door to door, hoping there might be a logo somewhere, a hint as to which hotel chain this was, but the only thing I could find was what looked like some sort of flower icon above the locks. It was hard to be entirely sure, though, and the longer I stared, the more I started to think that it might not be a flower at all.

I zoomed out and looked at the picture again, at the woman frozen in the top corner, and then at the timecode squeezed into the bottom right. It was two-tiered: the date and time were on the top line, and beneath that was a second line.

This one was more difficult to understand.

5106596|4|79/93

I could guess at the last part: 79 to 99 were the rooms the camera covered. In theory, 4 could have been the floor, or maybe a particular section of the hotel, but I had no idea what 5106596 represented. It could have been some sort of identifier, perhaps the serial number of the camera itself.

Leaning closer, I switched my attention from the time-code to the decor, then to the carpet – a swirling pattern of ropes and knots, with some sort of coat of arms – and finally to the woman, and as I did I felt a tiny, imperceptible shift, a sense that I'd connected something together but hadn't grasped what it was yet. I gazed at the screen, fingers hovering over the trackpad of the laptop, eyes going back and forth between the different elements of the shot.

*What have I seen?*

I looked out at the coffee shop I was in – checking for faces that looked familiar or seemed to be paying me too much attention – and then I felt myself being drawn back to the laptop, to the picture, the construction of it, to the sense I'd had, all the way through, that there was something slightly off about it.

On-screen, the shot of Beth was still up, zoomed in by twenty per cent, her face slightly fuzzy. I returned it to its default size, then magnified the carpet. I realized the coat of arms I'd spotted had some sort of figure inside it. He was bearded and bare-chested and holding a galleon in the palm of his hand. I zoomed in on the nearest door to the camera, studying the flower-like shape that was engraved above its lock. Except it wasn't a flower, I knew that now.

It was a trident.

The figure in the coat of arms was Poseidon. I couldn't view the corridor as clearly as I would have liked because of the low lighting, but something else made sense now too: the rope pattern in the carpet wasn't just a random sequence of shapes, it was nautical knots – bowlines and figure of eights.

As I looked at Beth again, I realized everything was marginally off. That was what I'd been seeing but not been able to place. The shot wasn't straight. It was tilted, maybe only by two or three per cent, but it was tilted all the same. At first, I thought it might be because the camera itself had been bolted to the wall at something less than a perfect right angle, or that its bracket might be loose, or that it had been knocked off centre somehow.

But it wasn't any of those things.

A web search later, I discovered that the seven-digit number in the timecode, 5106596, was an International Maritime Organization reference – and that was when I knew for sure that it wasn't the camera that was at an angle, it was the corridor itself.

This wasn't a hotel.

It was a ship.

## 37

I couldn't rip my eyes away from the picture now.

Marek had said that Beth and Richard had been spotted together in the week leading up to Richard being found – so if she'd been on the ship, he had too. But why? What were they even doing on-board? Where had the ship been going?

I tried to think laterally.

The first thing I had to do was figure out what the name of the ship was. It didn't take me long. Using the IMO number, I discovered it was a cruise liner, registered in Southampton, called the *Olympia Britannia*. That explained why the corridor looked so much like a hotel and why its walls were adorned with iconic British landmarks like the London Eye.

Could Richard have worked on the ship?

It didn't feel like an absurd leap to make, and when I picked up my notebook and flicked back through the things I'd found out about him over the past week, I was reminded of something: the traces of calcium hypochlorite that were found on his hands.

The tests the forensic technicians had carried out were inconclusive, but what they *could* confirm was that the chemical was found in polishes and waxes, in solvents, oils and hydraulic fluids. Those were all things he could have come into contact with while working on a ship. Or it could have been something else entirely: calcium hypochlorite was also used to disinfect swimming pools. If that was the reason, if the chemical ended up on Richard's hands because he'd come into frequent contact with chlorinated water, that didn't discount the idea of him being aboard a ship – in fact, it played into it. A cruise liner would have had a swimming pool.

It turned out the *Olympia Britannia* had two of them.

The ship was operated by a travel company called Deep Atlantic, and on its website, I found photographs and videos mirroring the decor that I'd seen on the surveillance shot. The bleached colours, the fuzz, the softness of detail that I'd seen through the lens of the CCTV camera were all gone, replaced by pin-sharp, low-angled shots of interior corridors. I saw the trident logo, clearly embedded above the lock mechanisms on the doors; the royal blue of the carpets, the Poseidon crest, the ropes and knots; and then there were the pictures of British scenes – not just London but Stonehenge, Canterbury, Edinburgh, the Highlands.

Something about it didn't quite add up, though: if he was an employee, if people had worked with him and knew him, why hadn't anyone come forward after he was found? Even if, as was likely, they hadn't read about him in local British newspapers, was it really possible that not a single person noticed that he suddenly wasn't on-board any more?

And that was the thing I couldn't reconcile about this whole case: no one seemed to know Richard or have even come into contact with him. No one had come forward in the months after he was found to tell the authorities who he was and what had happened. What about people that went to school with him, or had lived in his street or in his town? What about others he must have worked and socialized with at some point?

I returned to the laptop.

It was still on the Deep Atlantic website, on the page that listed all of the information on the *Olympia* – its size, facilities, prices, routes. If Richard and Beth weren't aboard the ship as employees, and they weren't there as holidaymakers – which seemed equally unlikely – then I could only think of one other scenario.

They were stowaways.

But even that didn't make much sense. If they had sneaked on-board the ship, it was presumably while it was docked in Southampton. So why was Richard found only six miles from the port? The CCTV still of Beth was taken five days before he was discovered, but Marek seemed to suggest she was seen with Richard on the boat beforehand – so did that mean that the *Olympia* had just sat in Southampton docks for over a week? I studied the schedules and routes that the cruise liner operated and it seemed improbable. It was on the move the whole time, tracing the same course on repeat: Madeira, down the west coast of Africa towards Cape Town, across the Atlantic to Buenos Aires, north along the Brazilian shoreline, into the Caribbean, and on to the US. The final journey was from New York back to Southampton, and the cruise came in two different versions: a shorter, fifty-day trip, which eschewed stops in West Africa and Brazil, or an eighty-day version which included them. From what I could see, the ship wasn't ever docked in Southampton for longer than three days at a time.

Yet there was something to it – not necessarily to the idea of him being a stowaway, but of him making an escape. I pushed the laptop aside and went back to my notebook, flipping through the pages, trying to snag on something that I hadn't thought of. Eventually I stopped on a page with a familiar question at the top.

*Why doesn't anyone remember Richard?*

It was the same question I'd just been asking myself. Except, this time, something had changed. Something felt different. I looked harder at my notes, reading back what I'd written, trying to decide what it was – and then I realized that it wasn't something I'd read in my notes but something I'd read on the Internet. Something on the *Olympia* website.

*The boat's schedule.*

I felt a rush of blood, an almost dizzying sense of finally seeing the answer – and the sounds and movement of the coffee shop faded to nothing.

*I've been looking in the wrong place.*

My gaze fixed on the cruise's schedule again, on the nine days it took the *Olympia* to cross the South Atlantic from Cape Town all the way to Buenos Aires. I saw everything so plainly now it was like mist clearing from a window: Richard *had* stowed away on the *Olympia* – but he hadn't boarded the ship in Southampton.

He'd been travelling *to* Southampton.

Now I understood why I'd never been able to find the TV show that he was describing – because it wasn't ever broadcast in the UK. I understood why Penny had told Howson it always rained where she came from, why Richard had said the beach he remembered looked so

British, overcast and dreary, and yet he hadn't been able to find a trace of it. Penny had said she was from a town called Sophia, but Howson had never been able to find a place with that name anywhere on a UK map. Neither had I. I'd just assumed that Penny had lied to him. But Penny hadn't lied. Sophia existed – it just wasn't up north.

I looked at the *Olympia*'s schedule again, at the place where it made a single, two-day stop-off halfway across the South Atlantic.

The Empress Islands.

That was where all of them were from. Richard Kite. Penny. Beth. That was where the offshore bank accounts were that Marek had funnelled money into. That was why he'd asked me if I was at Heathrow, trying to find a flight.

Because that was where the secrets were buried.

A British territory, seven thousand miles away.

# Sisters

*News spread fast around Sophia. It was only about seven square miles, so people tended to find things out quickly. They heard about the two girls being taken up to the Brink. They heard about why they'd had to be punished, why they'd been left up there most of the night.*

*When the kids at school saw Penny walking around town in the weeks after, and attempted to coax details out of her, she just shrugged them off. Because of that, because she refused to talk about it, her friends gradually began drifting away, one by one, unable to maintain a middle ground where they were defending Penny to other kids while not being entirely sure of what they were talking about. After that, the distance created a kind of prism through which the other kids — including her friends — would view Penny: they were fascinated by her, seeing her refusal to talk about it as some kind of terrible trauma; but they were also scared by the idea that it was true.*

*It wasn't bombs up there.*

*It was something else.*

*Penny could see it for the circus it was, so retreated even further, not talking to people at all. She'd often be spotted alone in the town, or further out, on the concrete benches outside the lido. The benches had views of the sea and she'd sit there, even through the merciless South Atlantic winter, and watch as the ships drifted in and out. Once a week, on the day the planes arrived, she'd walk further along the coast to the airport — a small terminal building and a single* runway – and see all the people boarding planes back to Buenos Aires and Cape Town.

It wasn't the existence she'd dreamed of or wished for, but Penny could see the bigger picture: she just needed to keep her head down, to accept her new reality, and once she got her GCSE results she could plan her escape. The government on the island didn't have the facilities to teach A levels, much less degrees, so they funded kids who wanted to go on to further education; even better, all the colleges and universities they had partnerships with were in the UK. Penny had always felt reticent about leaving her mum here, of putting such a huge distance between them in order to continue studying, but she could barely look at Jack now. She could hardly even stomach being under the same roof as him, and at the end of every day she became more certain that it was what she wanted. She was leaving Sophia and wasn't ever coming back, and though she would miss her mum, though she would never get answers about her father, about where he had gone and what had happened to him, escape was the only real option. She'd get to the UK, set herself up somewhere and wait for Beth to join her.

Except, slowly, she started to realize that was never going to happen.

Beth didn't handle the aftermath as well. She liked the attention to start with, fed on the popularity she gained from her night at the Brink, but then the popularity turned to jealousy and fear, and the kids at school became more brutish and began taunting her, bullying her. Some days, the sisters were the most popular kids in class, almost revered, their status elevated by secrecy and gossip. Other days, they were treated as contaminants, disease-carriers to be avoided.

Because of that, Beth began to rebel. She played up in class and at home, went out all the time, got paralytically drunk at thirteen and was found the next day in an alleyway behind the supermarket.

Jack and Fiona grounded her, and grounded her again, and again, but after a while it stopped making any difference. Penny tried to talk to her, to use some of the closeness they'd thrived on growing up, the love they'd had for one another, but Beth was riled and resentful – at her father, at the way she was being treated at school, at Penny for making them go beyond the Brink in the first place, at the things that had happened to them up there, at anyone on the island who even looked at her the wrong way.

She was scared too, Penny could see that, scared that she might be taken up into the hills again and tied to the fence like last time, but she'd buried it all behind her anger. She took to applying too much make-up, layering on the black eyeliner, the mascara, until it was like her eyes were set in dark holes. Penny saw through that too: Beth's eyes were always what gave her away. If she concealed them, if she made them harder to read, no one would see how frightened she was.

Penny tried to talk to Beth over and over again, but Beth would either glaze over or walk away. A couple of years after the events of that night at the Brink, Penny tried one final time. Beth had been grounded again for staying out past her 8 p.m. curfew, and Penny's mum and Jack were at an assembly meeting in the town hall and had left Penny in charge. She came downstairs to find the back door open, rain hammering hard against the porch roof, and Beth smoking under a panel of ridged plastic where Jack kept his tools.

Penny went outside, to the steps of the porch. The two sisters turned to each other, said nothing and looked out into the night. From their garden, they could see the lights of the harbour at Blake Point.

'What are you doing, Beth?' Penny asked.

Beth eyed Penny. Then she shrugged and took another long drag on her cigarette. 'What does it look like I'm doing?'

'I'm not talking about the cigarette.'

Beth glanced at Penny again. Her mascara had run slightly, moving in a vague diagonal away from her left eye. It looked like a long line of stitches. Penny wondered if Beth had been crying or whether it was the rain that had done it, and after a while she started to think it might actually be tears. It was almost two years to the day that they'd been driven up to the Brink and left there. Beth would pretend she'd forgotten, that it made no difference to her, but she was like Penny.

She would never forget.

'Beth, listen to me —'

'I don't want a lecture.'

'I'm not going to lecture you.'

'I don't want any advice either.'

'You've got to keep your head down, Bethany.'

Beth paused for a second. Penny rarely, if ever, used her sister's full name — and when she did, it was because she was desperate for Beth to listen to her.

But Beth just shook her head.

'Beth —'

'I said I didn't want any advice.'

'I'm leaving in three months,' Penny said. 'Once I get my results, I'm leaving. If you keep your head down for the next two years, if you get your results too, you can leave as well. I'll be set up in the UK by then, and you can come over and we —'

'What's the point?'

Penny frowned. 'The point?'

'In listening to you. I mean, last time I listened to you, I got tied to a fucking fence.' She glanced at Penny, taking another drag on her cigarette. 'The worst thing I ever did in my whole life was listen to your advice, you know that?'

Penny tried not to show how much that hurt, but she didn't do a very good job of it. Beth, watching her, seemed emboldened by the fact that she'd inflicted a wound. She straightened, took a step towards Penny, gesturing with the two fingers she was holding the cigarette between, and said, 'You know something else?'

'Beth, please. Don't be like this.'

'You stand there and ask me what I'm doing, like I've got some responsibility to you, as if what you think even matters to me. But we're not even related, Penny.'

'Beth –'

'We're not even related. You got no right telling me anything. You dragged me up there' – she pointed in the other direction from the harbour, across the roof to where the hills were – 'when I was twelve years old, and look what you did to me. This life. This shit that's filling my head the whole time. I wake up in the middle of the night, sweating through the fucking sheets, because of what we saw up there. And you know what? I try to think rationally, I try to tell myself we didn't see what we saw, but we both know it was real. And who can I talk to about it, huh? Dad? You?'

She smirked, shook her head again.

'Do me a favour. How can I talk to either of you? He's the one that drove us up there and dumped us. His own kid. And you . . . you were the one that put us in the back of that Land Rover in the first place. If I hadn't followed you up there all those times, if we'd just done what we were supposed to and stayed away, I'd be getting off the island in a couple of years. I'd be sleeping like a baby every night and passing my exams and I'd be getting my grant and jetting off to the UK to some sixth-form college, to university; I'd be getting a job and I'd never have to come back to this shithole again. But I'm not doing that, am I, Pen? I'm getting pissed up every night because I'm trying to forget what we saw up there. I'm trying to forget the

261

sound of it breathing. I can hear it every time I close my eyes. And some days that makes me a rock star, and everyone's my best pal, and all the boys want to get in my knickers. And other days I get treated like a fucking leper. Brink girl, Brink girl, Brink girl, all the time. They whisper it behind my back as I walk home from school. I can't concentrate on anything. I'm looking over my shoulder the whole time. And you know why I'm like this, Pen? Because you made me like this. It's your fault.'

Penny felt like her throat was closing up.

'You ruined my life.'

'Beth,' Penny said, tears in her eyes, 'I never meant to –'

'I hate you.'

Suddenly, it was like the sound fell out of the night. There was no rain any more, no wind, no distant sounds from the harbour.

It was just those three words.

Beth's gaze lingered on Penny – a flash of emotion, there and gone again – and then she threw her cigarette out into the rain, the embers dying instantly in the dark, and – without looking up – brushed past Penny and went inside the house.

# PART THREE

# Extract from *No Ordinary Route: The Hidden Corners of Britain* by Andrew Reece

The Empress Islands cover an area half the size of Wales, but their two largest – Victoria Island, on which you'll find the capital, St George; and Cabot Island, where Sophia and the harbour at Blake Point are located – are, combined, only fractionally larger than the city of Cardiff. St George is relatively modern and the heart of the tax haven's banking industry, while Sophia is less pristine – in fact, really quite ugly in places – and home to a lot of the farming and fishing community. Separated from St George by the Wallace Strait and the imposing Mount Strathyde, Sophia's location on its western flank also exposes the town to the full brunt of the South Atlantic, and that hard rain and constant biting wind has resulted in an average summer high in the town of just 8°C, making it significantly colder than the capital. Despite those differences, the archipelago's 7,500 people do all have one thing in common: the same, slightly odd 'Empress accent', which linguists say has its origins in the first British settlers, who arrived here in 1766 and were a mix of farmers from south-west England and gentrified landowners.

It's actually hard to underline just how extreme the islands' isolation is. They are 2,461 miles from Buenos Aires and 1,903 miles from Cape Town, which makes it a four-day boat trip or around five hours on a plane, from either city, on the weekly charter flights. Wired Internet is, for the most part, slow, to the point where it becomes too frustrating to use; there's no 3G (although there are, apparently, plans to address this by the end of 2014); and the few TV channels that *do* exist come from the British Forces Broadcasting Service, which usually transmits to military personnel stationed abroad. There's never been any programming made on the islands themselves, with one exception: *Kids' Hour*, a magazine-style children's TV show that ran between 1985 and 1997. Its distinctive 'TV mast' intro became well known to the children of the islands, but eventually it proved too expensive to create.

In my time on the islands, it became clear that most tourists didn't stay long enough to see the full picture. They'd come in from South America or Africa on two-day 'eco-tours', heading out to the breeding grounds to watch elephant seals and rockhopper penguins and fin, humpback and sperm whales. They'd watch terns and thrushes and albatrosses in huge colonies on the eastern islands, and whip past sheep, reindeer and guanaco farms on the way from the airport. They'd coo over the rose gardens in the towns (famously, the Empress Islands have no native mammals, trees, or flora like roses, so everything has been introduced), they'd have their photographs taken outside the non-working red telephone boxes, they'd buy Union Jack flags and have tea served up in William and Kate mugs, and then they'd pack into minibuses bound for the airport terminal or head back on tender boats to where their cruise ships are anchored a mile off the coast.

For an afternoon, a day, even two, this picture-postcard slice of old-world Britannia is fine. But after three days things start to take on a different perspective. It's like a camera very slowly pulling into focus and, on the fourth day here, the fifth, the sixth, you start to feel claustrophobic.

You start to feel like you're trapped.

Now imagine what it's like living here.

# 38

The *Olympia* left Cape Town three days later.

After flying in, I spent a day killing time, revisiting places I'd come to know during my years here as a journalist. I got up early and went for a long run, along the edge of Camps Bay Beach – the sky cloudless and perfectly blue, the sand as white as chalk – and then into Clifton, where Derryn and I had once lived in a third-floor apartment. From the road, I could still see the roof garden, the part of the flat she'd chosen to spend the most time in as she'd tended to its plants. When we moved in, the flowers, even the cactuses, were all dying; by the time we left it was beautiful, so full of colour and life the landlord paid us back our last three months' rent.

Later, I found a restaurant just off Kloof Road, in the foothills of Lion's Head, and looked out at the mountains and the sea from under the shade of a baobab tree. I ate bobotie and drank Castle lager and leafed through a book I'd picked up at Heathrow called *No Ordinary Route*. It looked like a travel guide and started out like one, but then it mutated into something else, a work of gonzo journalism or something close to it, as a writer toured the furthest outposts of the British mainland, as well as some of its most remote overseas territories. I used it to try and understand more about the Empress Islands, about Sophia, about a community that existed as an image of

Britain thousands of miles away from its coastline. And then late in the afternoon, I went back to my hotel – slightly unsettled by some of what I'd read in the book, unsettled too by the idea of being pursued, of Marek guessing where I was headed.

After the sun went down, I sat and had a meal at a restaurant in Victoria Wharf, out on its terrace, and called Annabel. We talked about her day, about Olivia, about the weather back home in Devon, about their dog, and I sought solace in the small, seemingly trivial details of my daughter's life. They didn't seem trivial now, the night before I got on a ship and headed out into the ocean with no clue what was awaiting me; in fact, they seemed more important than ever given everything I'd learned about Richard Kite.

When I was done, I went back to my room and returned to the copy of *No Ordinary Route*, underlining passages and zeroing in on the author's account of Sophia. I sat on my balcony in shorts and a T-shirt, looking out at the sea. When I checked the weather forecast for the Empress Islands, it couldn't have been more different from the weather in South Africa: a high of six degrees and an overnight low of minus two. Over the course of the next three days, it was set to get colder.

The day I was due to arrive, there was snow coming.

I hoped it wasn't some kind of portent.

The boat had twelve decks and my cabin was all the way down, on the second. It was an inside room – a cabin with no view – but it was the best I could do at such short notice and on the kind of budget Richard Kite had.

Once I was aboard, I unpacked enough clothes for the next few days and left the rest in a suitcase in the cupboard. I returned to the sun deck in enough time to see Cape Town vanishing into the distance, a blur of white against the backdrop of green-grey mountains, and then I started walking the ship, its decks, staying alert for any signs of a tail or faces that I recognized.

The ship was immense, a maze of endless corridors, so it took me a while to find the place – on deck four – where Beth had been captured on CCTV. Once I did, I stopped to take in the frames on the walls, seeing them up close for the first time, and then the carpet, with its pattern and image of Poseidon lifting a boat from the water. I stood in the exact spot she had, trying to figure out why she had been in this part of the boat, but there was no compelling reason that I could see for her to have chosen this corridor over others. I walked the seven accommodation decks, bow to stern, to get a sense of them, of differences or things that looked and felt out of place, but the more I walked, the more they began to merge into one, eventually becoming just a bland parade of infinite doors, different only in the numbers on them.

I got the lift all the way up to the top, to the sports deck, which was about half the length of the others and contained a tennis court, a driving range and a bar. From there, I worked my way down again, first to the sun deck, then to the lido deck, then past the accommodation to the very bottom of the boat, where the restaurants, nightclubs and entertainment areas were. Quietly, without drawing too much attention to myself, I started asking around among the crew, using a picture of Richard Kite and a cropped-in CCTV still of Beth. I came away with nothing. No one knew them, no one had seen them on-board. Two hours in, if any of the staff showed an interest in who Richard and Beth were and why I was looking for them, I started giving them a vague version of the truth, to see where it took us, but it wasn't long before those conversations petered out as well. Over the course of almost four hours, I got nowhere.

I was conscious that Marek could have been messaging someone on the ship, that the person known as LG might work here and be able to feed back to him what I was doing and the kinds of questions I was asking. If that happened, unless he was already on-board, there was nothing Marek could personally do about it until we docked at the Empress Islands in four days' time. But I didn't know who LG was, or what kind of threat they posed in Marek's absence, and because I didn't know them or if they were even on-board, or what they looked like and might do here, I felt on edge the whole time, unable to relax, conscious of every question I asked and decision I made.

That night, I had dinner in a Chinese restaurant on the bottom deck – in a booth at the back so I could face out at the crowds – and began cycling through the images of the case: Richard Kite, Penny Beck, Beth, screen dumps I'd saved from the Red Tree instant messenger, pictures I'd taken in Naomi Russum's office, the collage Richard had made – from fragments of magazines – in an effort to remember the beach he'd looked out at as a child. I'd called him again before I flew out to Cape Town, quizzing him about the *Olympia*, about Beth, and spoke briefly to Howson as well to make sure they were somewhere safe.

He said they were in a place on the edge of Folkestone. When Richard came back on the line, he asked me about Beth, for more details about her, and whether I'd managed to find any other, better pictures of her.

'Why?' I asked. 'Do you feel like you might know her?'

'I don't remember ever meeting her, no.'

But that wasn't the question I'd asked.

He seemed to know it too, because he said, 'It might be something about the ship that's set me off, or you saying I come from those islands, but I've just got this . . .' He paused. 'You remember how I said food is like a connector for me? As in, I always knew I'd like bananas, even before I ever tried them?'

'Yeah, I remember.'

'It's like that.'

'You have a strong feeling about something?'

'Yes,' he said. 'I'm just not sure why or what about.'

When I returned to my cabin, I lay in the darkness, the air con humming, listening to the soft noises of the ship. I had no idea what time I finally fell asleep, but the sun was already up, and as I dropped off I could hear people passing in the corridor and heading towards the lifts, talking about what they were going to have for breakfast. After that, I dreamed.

It started with me boarding a ship.

It finished with me lost in a labyrinth.

## 39

I woke at 11 a.m. and turned on the television. There was a static picture detailing the day's weather, which looked pretty good until late afternoon when it slowly began to change. The sun disappeared and cloud moved in, getting greyer as day gave way to night. By tomorrow, as the boat followed the curve of the earth out into the Atlantic, further and further south, the temperature began to drop fast.

I got up, showered and headed down for something to eat. The restaurant crew were different from the day before, a separate shift, so I asked around again about Richard and Beth, but got the same response, just from different faces.

After I was done, I took the lift back up to the lido deck. It was hot and bright, the two swimming pools full, the bar in between packed too, but I managed to find a stool on the end of the counter, just about in the shade, and ordered a beer. As I waited, I set my notepad and my copy of *No Ordinary Route* down beside me, thinking about the process and practicalities of getting on-board the ship and how Richard had managed to stay so well hidden in the days and weeks after.

Judging by what I'd experienced at Cape Town, the security measures before boarding the boat weren't as stringent as at an airport, but they were still pretty robust:

passport checks, X-ray machines, metal detectors, random pat-downs. If you wanted access, you had to pass through a passenger holding area, and if Richard didn't have a passport on him, which I'd always assumed was the case – and would certainly play into the idea of him being a stowaway – then I could only see a couple of ways he could have got on without raising any alarms: either he was pretending to be a member of the crew – a waiter, or a lifeguard, or maintenance – or he made out he'd been ashore and was returning, and was already a passenger on the ship. That way he wouldn't have to check in any luggage or show a passport, and he wouldn't have to steal a uniform. It did mean, however, that he'd have to obtain one of the ship's ID cards, which were issued to passengers who wanted to go ashore when the boat was anchored.

There was a possible third option too: that Beth had managed to get him on-board somehow. But they still would have had to jump through the same hoops and, ultimately, all options represented big risks. If I didn't exactly know the how, I was starting to get a feel for the why. This felt like a getaway, like the two of them were trying to break free of something on the islands; maybe for the same reason that had got Penny Beck killed half a world away.

I looked up from some scribbles I'd made in the margins of the travel book and felt the heat of the sun on my skin. The noise had begun to build even more, without me even really noticing: people on loungers, getting into the pools, in jacuzzis dotted at their corners, or ordering drinks at the bar along from me. I shuffled a little further into the shade, the smell of suncream and salt in the air, and returned to Richard Kite. The more I thought about it, the more I started to see that the cleanest route back to who he was, to the secret locked in his head, might actually be through Penny. At this point, I knew more about her than I knew about Richard, and the fact that it was her stepsister that was seen with him in the week before he turned up made the connection more compelling.

I'd made a list of the five things that Jacob Howson had found out about Penny during the year they'd dated. The first, that she was from a town called Sophia, I'd already figured out. The rest I started to look at, one at a time.

*Her father became a sheep farmer.*

He worked in London in 'some boring office job' until shortly after Penny was born in 1984, when he moved the family to the Empress Islands. In *No Ordinary Route*, it described a drive by the Empress Islands government, during the seventies and early eighties, to encourage British farmers to emigrate by paying big subsidies and relocation costs. The agricultural industry – at the time, one of the three mainstays of the economy alongside fishing and banking – was in decline, and there was a lack of experience in the next generation of native islanders. If Penny's father had been a part of that, and it looked that way, it suggested he must have had some prior knowledge of farming before his switch to a desk job.

*When she was three, he went missing.*

She never saw him again. I didn't have any evidence that his case impacted directly on that of Richard Kite, or even Penny's murder twenty-something years later, but I couldn't get on board with the idea that it was an unimportant footnote either. Maybe it was a residual sense of something just being off, an instinct I'd built up over years and years as I'd worked more and more missing persons cases.

*Her mum remarried a man called Jack.*

It was difficult to make any kind of judgement on whether that mattered until I was off the boat at Sophia and asking around in the town.

*She had a stepsister called Beth.*

I knew this already. I even knew what she looked like and could put her in a definite place at a definite point in time at the start of the year. What I wasn't so clear on was what Howson had told me next. *They had a big falling-out.* About what? Was the falling-out even relevant? I returned my attention to the CCTV shot of Beth, to her face, to the way she was looking back over her shoulder. *Who are you?* I traced the outline of her with my finger. *How did you know Richard Kite?* With no answers, the sounds of the deck crept in again, settling around me: music, people laughing at the bar, kids screaming with delight in the pools.

'Another beer, *señor*?'

I looked up at the barman, a guy in his thirties with a badge that had GAEL MENDOZA on it and a Mexican flag. His hand was poised at my empty beer bottle.

'Sure,' I said. 'Why not?'

He smiled. 'You're on vacation.'

*Not exactly,* but I returned the smile anyway. He dropped the empty into a bin and grabbed a second bottle from a fridge behind him. As he set it down he gestured to my copy of *No Ordinary Route*. I'd left it open, midway through the chapter on the Empress Islands, a map on the right-hand page.

'You doing the day trip to the islands?' he asked.

I looked at him more closely this time. The answer was no, I wasn't doing a day trip. I was planning to get off the boat and find somewhere to stay. I was going to watch the *Olympia* sail off into the distance without me, and – in the days after that, once I'd found out the truth about Richard Kite – I was going to catch one of the weekly flights back to either Cape Town or Buenos Aires.

I wondered if he knew that already.

I wondered if he was working with Marek.

'Yeah,' I said. 'I'm thinking about it.'

'The wildlife is amazing.'

'That's what I hear.'

'Whales, seals, penguins. I went on my day off a few years back to see the southern right whales, because you only find them in this part of the world. I love whales. I love animals. I watch all the documentaries. Attenborough, man, he's the king. Anyway, I went back again in March with one of the girls who works down in the Athena. She's from the islands, so she gave me a nice tour.'

He smiled again, but it was hard to tell whether *nice tour* meant an actual trip around the islands with the woman, or an hour in the back of a car on some remote headland. Either way, it didn't really matter that much.

'What's Athena?' I asked.

'It's the coffee lounge on deck eight.'

I finished my beer and headed down there.

# 40

The woman's name was Annie. She was thin and in her twenties with short red-brown hair, clipped into place, and a line of freckles running from one eye to the other over the bridge of her nose. As I arrived at the Athena coffee lounge, a large room of about a hundred tables segregated by zigzagging glass-panelled walls, I spotted her on the far side of it, wiping down a table littered with pastry crumbs.

'Annie?'

She looked up and broke into a smile. But then she must have realized I'd addressed her by name without looking at her name badge, and the smile faded just a little as she asked, 'Can I help you, sir?'

'My name's David Raker,' I said, handing her a business card. She took it from me and, as she did, I noticed an Empress Islands flag on the badge, next to her full name, Annie Arnold-Yunk. The flag was blue with a Union Jack in the top left and a coat of arms to the right. The coat of arms featured Lady Justice holding a set of scales and, on a ribbon underneath, the Latin phrase *hic situs est*. This is the place.

'I was just talking to Gael upstairs,' I said, 'and he mentioned that you're originally from the Empress Islands.' I gestured to the flag. 'I'm interested in finding out some more about Sophia. Do you think we could have a chat?'

She seemed thrown. 'I'm not actually from Sophia,' she said and, as soon as she spoke, I could hear the same accent as Richard Kite's, the same unique mix of dialects. The *a* of Sophia came out as a hard *er*.

I held up the book. 'All I've got at the moment is what's written inside here, so any local knowledge would be a big help.'

Relaxing a little, she said, 'Oh, okay.'

She asked if I could wait until she was on break, and at 2 p.m. I met her at the front of the coffee lounge and then followed her outside. There was some shade and a few empty sun loungers further down the deck. Once we were seated, she removed a pack of nicotine gum from the breast pocket of her blouse, popped a piece in her mouth and pointed to the copy of *No Ordinary Route* perched on the lounger beside me.

'Is that the one where he says Sophia's a shithole?'

I smiled. 'Have you read it, then?'

She shook her head and started turning the pack of gum in her hands. 'I just remember there being a review in the *Empress Express* – what, like three years back?'

It would have been more like five, as the book was published in 2011.

'I don't imagine the book went down very well.'

She smirked. 'Some people reckon that, if you get seen with a copy of that by the police in Sophia, they'll confiscate it.'

'What if you get seen with it somewhere else?'

She shrugged. 'I'm from a place called Cardigan, way out east. I hated growing up there. It's one of the smaller islands. St George, Sophia, Blake Point, they're on Victoria

279

and Cabot, to the west. On Cardigan, there was never anything to do, you had to get in a boat to go to school, to the shops, to anywhere half decent. I'm twenty-nine, and until I was sixteen I didn't even know what satellite TV was. We had one channel. That was it. And it was all prerecorded shows, and the programmes were always two weeks out of date, because that's how long it took to ship the cassettes over from the UK.' She chewed for a while. 'But, as boring as my childhood was, and as tiny and uninteresting as Cardigan is, even *we* used to make jokes about Sophia.'

'What did you used to say?'

'Everyone called it "Sophucking Cold".'

'So, did it deserve the nickname?'

'It's just a strange place,' she said, rolling the gum across her tongue. 'It's the yin to St George's yang. Or maybe Mr Hyde to its Dr Jekyll. I mean, it sits on the wrong side of the mountain for a start, so it gets all the really shitty weather from the west. That's where a lot of wind comes in from, and the town just sits there, right in the middle of it. Blake Point, where the harbour is, is – what? – eight miles south of it, but there's hardly any houses there, just a few cottages, so most of the people in the fishing industry live in Sophia. That's the other thing about it. It *looks* like a fishing town, but not in a good way. It's not St Ives or Cape Cod or something. It's deprived and run-down. It stinks, literally. You've got a few farmers there too, but not much else in the way of industry. All the more upmarket stuff, the banking, the government buildings, the one decent clothes shop we've got on the islands, the big library, the DVD rental place, they're in St

George. They get pretty crappy weather there too — everywhere in the islands does; I mean, we're closer to the Antarctic than we are to South America or Africa – but, because St George is on the "right" side of the mountain, it's just never as cold, miserable or depressing.'

'Did you ever meet anyone from Sophia?'

'In my entire life? Yeah, of course. I didn't have any friends from there, though, if that's what you mean. That always seemed the strangest thing about the islands to me. We never had that sense of community, of togetherness, even though there are only seven and a half thousand of us. We've never been like the Falklands. We're bigger than they are, spread over a wider area, so I guess that doesn't help. But they had the war too, which I think kind of brought them together in a bizarre sort of way, whereas we're just a bunch of communities scattered across hundreds of miles.'

She checked her watch.

'You okay for time, Annie?'

'I've got about another ten minutes.'

I removed some pictures of Richard Kite and Penny Beck, and handed them across. She took them from me, examined them.

'Do you recognize either of those people?'

'No,' she said, shaking her head. 'Who are they?'

'I think they might have come from Sophia.'

'No, I don't recognize them.' She handed the photographs back as I brought the image of Beth up on my phone. But before I got the chance to show her, she said, 'It wasn't just that, though.'

I looked up. 'Wasn't just what?'

'Sophia.' She eyed me. 'It wasn't just that it was a lot colder, or that it stank.'

'What do you mean?'

'I mean' – she pointed to the copy of *No Ordinary Route* – 'I haven't read it but, from what I heard, the things he says in there aren't that wide of the mark.'

'In what respect?'

'He talks about Sophia having a secret, right?'

'He said he initially made it as a joke.'

'Initially. Exactly.'

I studied her. 'Are you saying you agree with him?'

'I'm saying you hear rumours.'

'About what?'

She stopped chewing for a moment. Seagulls squawked in the sky above us, following the ship as it carved across the Atlantic. We were a day and a half out of Cape Town, heading south-west across the ocean, and the sun was still hot. But, even with the heat pressing at us, even under a perfect, cloudless sky, I noticed goosebumps on Annie's skin.

'I don't know,' she said, 'it sounds crazy even saying it aloud, but we just used to hear rumours about the things that went on there. Weird things. Like, body parts being found up on the Mount Strathyde hiking trails. Bones. That sort of thing.'

I watched her. 'Did it ever get reported?'

'I'm not sure. That's the thing. The main police station is in St George, but there's a smaller one in Sophia. Like, four or five police officers. They would have dealt with it.' She looked out at the sea. 'What I mean is, if there was something going on, and the town wanted to keep it a secret, I guess the Sophia police could do that, right?'

'I don't know,' I said. 'I don't know enough about the place.'

'Well, they could. They definitely could.'

'So is that what you *think* happened?'

She shrugged again.

'But you believed the rumours?'

'There were just a lot of them, that's all, and whenever someone from Sophia told you about what they'd heard it was always along the same lines. Weird things up on the hiking trails, especially around the bogs. People disappearing. Landmines – that was the other thing. They had to build this big fence up there to stop people wandering out to the marshland.'

I remembered something being written about that in the book, about the inconsistent stories given by the residents of Sophia for why the fence was put up. I tried to think whether any of this was related to Richard Kite, to Penny Beck, to Beth, to Marek, to anything I'd found out, but the only thing that even vaguely fitted was what Annie said about people disappearing.

Penny's dad had disappeared.

I let it go for now, but one picture it did paint was of a community cut off, not just from the rest of the world, but even from its nearest neighbours. That could breed all sorts of things: paranoia, suspicion, rumour, fear.

'Point is, a lot of people said it wasn't just landmines.'

I'd been writing down what she'd been telling me, but now I stopped, pen poised above the notebook.

'In fact, some people said there weren't any landmines up there at all.'

'So why build the fence?'

She stared at me.

'Annie?'

I thought she wasn't going to respond for a second time, but then – almost inaudibly – she said, 'To keep it away from the town.'

I frowned. 'It?'

She shrugged.

'What do you mean, "it"?'

'I mean . . .' She trailed off, shaking her head, and didn't speak again for a long time. 'There were just rumours that there might be something out there.'

'"Something"?'

'Yeah.'

'What do you mean, "something"?'

'You know what I mean. Don't make me say it.' She paused, looking at me hard. But I was going to make her say it, because I didn't think for a second that she actually believed it. 'A monster,' she added quietly.

'Are you serious?'

'I don't know,' she said, shaking her head. 'That's just what people from Sophia used to say.'

It was an impossible idea to swallow. Much easier to process was the idea that it was a story built on whispers, massaged and developed inside the bubble of a town that existed right at the edge of the earth.

'I'm going to have to go,' she said.

'Okay, can I just quickly show you this?'

'Sure.'

I turned my phone to her and brought the image of Beth up on the screen. 'What about her?' I said, making sure she could see it. 'Does she seem familiar?'

'Is that taken on-board the ship?'

'Yeah, it is.'

I didn't say anything else, not about Beth, or when the picture was taken. I didn't want to colour anything that was coming. Annie leaned forward, pinch-zoomed in on the photograph, and then shuffled forward on the lounger, her teeth moving as she chewed.

'Does she work on the *Olympia*?' Annie asked.

'No, I don't think so.'

She began frowning.

'Are you sure she doesn't work here?'

'Pretty sure. Why?'

'Her clothes.'

I turned the phone around and looked at the image of Beth, at the clothes she had on. I must have looked at them a hundred times. She was all in black: top, trousers, shoes. But for the first time I noticed something else: one leg had a faint motif on it, grey and pale. I thought it had just been a random pattern, maybe a logo. But it wasn't either of those. It was a series of very thin, interlocked ropes and knots.

*A uniform.*

'That's what housekeeping wear,' Annie said.

# 41

As I exited the lift on the fourth deck, I felt again like I was trapped in some sort of loop: an echo, a movie on repeat. It wasn't just the relentless, identical doors in both directions, it was the ceaseless hum of the boat's engines as well, the only real reminder that this wasn't a hotel, or a mall, or a city, but a moving vessel in the middle of a colossal ocean. Or maybe what was getting to me wasn't either of those things but the embers of what Annie had described: body parts, a fence built to keep people out, and the town that couldn't get its story straight.

I tried to shake off the feeling as I moved through the empty corridor, heading in the direction Beth had been going when she was captured on CCTV.

Each deck had its own launderette and – on an earlier walk-through of the ship – I'd noticed that each launderette had a STAFF ONLY door adjacent to it. I found the one on deck four ajar. Through the gap, I spotted shelves full of towels, bed sheets and blankets, a mounted storage cupboard with soap and shampoo in it, and a woman in her fifties stacking toilet rolls into a wheeled cart. I waited for her to come out.

'Excuse me.'

The woman stopped as she emerged, the clipboard she'd been reading – attached by a thin cord of string – swinging back against the hard plastic of her cart. She smiled, blinked.

Straight away, without her saying anything, I knew she didn't speak much English. She was Senegalese and her name was Léna.

'Bonjour, Léna.'

She smiled a little. 'Bonjour.'

I got out my phone, went to the picture of Beth, zoomed in on her until the timecoding was no longer visible, and then tried to continue in the best French I could muster. 'My name is David. I'm a sort of policeman.' I held up the phone to her. 'Have you ever seen this woman?'

She leaned in, squinting a little, and then fiddled in her pockets for a pair of glasses. Sliding them on to her nose, she came forward again, eyes magnified.

'No,' she said.

'You don't know her?'

'No, I don't.' She took off her glasses and returned them to her pocket. 'Michael might know. He's in there.' She pointed towards the staff door behind me.

'Who's Michael?'

'He's in charge.'

'The boss?'

'Yes,' she said, smiling again. 'The boss.'

'Okay. Thank you, Léna.'

I watched her go and then knocked on the door a couple of times. When I got no response, I knocked again. Still nothing. I pushed the door further open.

The room was hot, the walls specked with moisture, and there were metal shelving units everywhere. When I took a few steps in, I could see past the initial ones and out into a space in the middle where there was a large table full of bed linen and towels, some folded and ironed, others scrunched into balls. Against the rear wall, partly disguised by the shelving units, was a skyline of industrial-sized washer-dryers rumbling at a low volume. I couldn't see anyone.

'Hello?'

The shelves created a mini network of different routes, and because each unit was stacked top to bottom, it was hard to see through them, or much further than the next turn in the towers of sheets and linen. 'Hello?' I said again, and then a third time when my voice seemed to get lost in the growl of the machines.

'Michael?'

Pretty certain that there was no one in here, I continued moving, past the centre table and out along another passageway created by the shelves, in the direction of the dryers. Their spin cycles went in minute-long phases, loud for sixty seconds, and then silent for a moment as the drum changed direction. It created a weird, eerie sound: a succession of thundering hums interspersed with frequent pauses, like hundreds of songs playing on a record player, all skipping at different times.

When I reached them – stacked two high all the way along the back wall; the noise louder than ever close up – I saw a door to my left marked MANAGER.

'Michael?'

Inside, I could see more shelves, this time loaded with bottles of bleach, bathroom cleaner and detergent. There was a desk with a computer on it and a pile of ring binders stacked against the far wall. I pushed at the door and, even above the low rumble of the dryers, I could hear the hinges whine as it fanned back and bumped against the wall.

The office was empty.

I stepped into the room and looked it over, waking the computer from its slumber. It was password protected. I went through the drawers of the desk to see if I could find an employee list, any sort of record from the past nine months, but there was nothing like that and somehow I wasn't convinced that Beth had actually worked in house-keeping, even if she'd had the uniform.

I took in the rest of the room.

If she hadn't worked here officially, then she'd been using the uniform to blend in, or to gain access to some-where. *Somewhere like here.* The CCTV camera had caught her on this deck, in uniform, heading in this direction – but what would she want with the laundry room?

I returned to the doorway and looked out at the shelv-ing units, and then faced in to the office again.

That was when I spotted the air vent.

It was low down on the wall, about an inch off the floor. One of its screws was loose, almost falling out of its hous-ing, as if it had been repeatedly unscrewed and reattached. There was something else too: fingerprint marks around the fascia plate, like hands had been pressed against the wall in order to lever it off.

I dropped to my knees in front of it and, using the end of a paperclip from the desk, slowly undid the corner screws. The plate fell away and landed with a clatter. Set-ting it aside, I got down further, looking into the hole. It was only about six inches high and all I could see at first was a bed of dust and a mesh of silky cobwebs.

But I quickly realized that wasn't everything.

*There's some sort of object in there.*

I grabbed my phone from my pocket, clicked the torch

on and placed a hand flat to the floor. Lowering the side of my face almost to the lino, I shone the light inside the air vent. Something immediately reflected back at me.

A red plastic carrier bag.

It had been pushed back as far into the vent as it was possible to get, so I had to work to get it out again, not because I couldn't reach it, but because the air vent was awkward: narrow and close to the ground. Eventually, I managed to snare my fingers on the handle of the bag and, after a couple of failed attempts, dragged it all the way out. As soon as I had it under the light, I saw what was inside.

A housekeeping uniform.

On the hems of the trousers there was a white frill of sea salt, crusted and hard; elsewhere, there were specks of dirt, food stains. But the carrier bag didn't just contain a uniform. When I pulled out the clothing, more things came with it.

They scattered across the floor around me.

A credit-card-sized ID, given to the ship's passengers when the boat was docked somewhere and they wanted to go ashore. It was scratched, the plastic coating peeling away at its corners. There was some US money as well, secured with a blue elastic band. When I snapped it off, I counted two hundred dollars. There were packets of food too: chocolate bars and dried fruit, pots of yoghurt and takeaway sandwiches, their expiry dates now passed. And then there were two photographs, both old. My stomach dropped as I looked at them.

Because now I knew for sure.

The bag had belonged to Beth.

# 42

The two photographs lay at my knees like offerings.

One was of the stepsisters. It was faded, wrinkled, the oldest picture I'd seen of Penny yet. The girls were still young, Penny thirteen or fourteen, Beth a couple of years her junior. They were in a bedroom, had their arms around each other, and were smiling broadly for the camera. I studied the picture, trying to look for clues in it, but there was nothing to find. It was just a lovely picture: happy, warm, genuine.

I shifted my attention to the other photograph.

This one was different.

It was even older, taken – at a guess – in the 1980s. In the centre of the picture was a man in his forties, dressed in a pastel jacket, a T-shirt, denims and a pair of penny loafers. He had an untidy mop of blond hair, a dark moustache, and was smiling, holding up a can of beer to whoever was taking the picture. If I didn't know the photograph was thirty years old from the outfit, I knew it from the brand of beer – Hofmeister – and in the slow deterioration of the photograph itself: its blanched colours, its grease spots, the fingerprints at its edges, as if it had been handled over and over and over again. There was a pinprick-sized hole in each corner as well, where it had clearly been tacked to a wall.

There was something familiar about the man, and

yet – as I studied him – I felt certain I hadn't come across him during the case. My gaze lingered on him, the noise of the dryers still rumbling in the room next to me, and then I switched back to the shot of Penny and Beth.

Everything shifted into focus.

I swapped between the two pictures, between the man on his own and the girls in the bedroom, and then flipped the photos over to check their reverse.

There was writing on both.

A different pen had been used – one blue, one black – but it was the same hand. I recognized the style instantly: the slight slope of the letters, the curve of the *s*, the lack of a dot on the *i*. I'd seen it over and over in the notes that Howson had shown me, in the things that had been left behind, hidden in books and taped to the underside of drawers in their home. The handwriting belonged to Penny. These photos had been hers. She must have left them behind after she headed to the UK, and then Beth had taken possession of them.

On the picture of the sisters, Penny had written, *I never meant to hurt us*. On the photo of the man, there was no message. There was a name.

*Caleb.*

Instantly, I reverted back to that hotel room with Howson, to when he'd talked about Penny, about her murder, about the reasons she may have been targeted, about all the things of hers he'd managed to find. She'd discovered that Marek had been funnelling money through the Red Tree between 2000 and 2003, she'd got hold of the financial documents to prove it, and she'd written down a name on one of the pages: Caleb.

But that wasn't why the man felt familiar to me.

It wasn't his name. It wasn't the connection I'd now made between him and the financial documents that had been stolen from the security suite. It was the fact that he looked exactly like Penny.

She was his daughter.

I looked at Caleb Beck, at his daughter, trying to get my thoughts straight, then I looked at the bag Beth had stowed in the air vent. The items had belonged to her, I was sure of that, but the moment I wondered why she'd never come back for them – why they'd been left here, why the food in the bag was past its expiry date – the answer came to me.

*Marek.*

He'd found her.

I felt nauseous as I remembered the conversation he'd had on the Red Tree IM. He'd said that he'd locate Beth, and that was exactly what he'd done. Wherever it was he tracked her to in the end – whether it was somewhere in the UK, or back in the Empress Islands, at one of the other ports on the *Olympia*'s route, or here on the boat – he'd got to her.

He'd got to her like he got to Penny.

As I glanced at the photo of the two sisters again, I felt something shiver through my blood: rage, and then sorrow, and then the impotence of knowing I couldn't do a single thing to help them. What made it worse was what was written on the back, the message from Penny to Beth, the confirmation of their argument, the falling-out that Howson had described to me. Had they both gone to their graves like that? I hoped not. The pain of loving and losing someone always faded in time. The pain of regret, of things you never got the chance to make right, didn't. It stayed on you like a scar.

I switched my attention back to Caleb Beck again, to the man who'd vanished from Penny's life when she was barely old enough to talk. As I looked at the picture, as I felt more and more certain that this definitely *was* Penny's dad – it was in the eyes, in the slant of the nose, in the jawline – an idea lodged, sour, like blood at the back of my mouth.

*The money.*

If Penny had been correct, if she'd trailed things accurately in the months before she was killed, Caleb Beck was tied to Marek's money somehow. So had he been the recipient of it back then? Was he still alive somewhere? Nothing about that made sense to me. If he was, if he was knowingly involved with Marek, it meant he surely must have known about Penny's murder too. I'd worked a lot of cases, both as an investigator and a journalist; I'd seen the terrible things people were capable of, been shaken by them and knocked off balance. But, the truth was, it was rare to see parents murdering their kids in cold blood – and not over money, and not because their child was digging around in their finances.

The more I thought about it, the more absurd the idea became, the more it started to morph into something malignant: another sleight of hand from Marek, another twisting of the facts, another ruthless act of self-interest. From there, it didn't feel like much of a stretch to suggest that the money could have been Caleb Beck's – and Marek was the one who stole it from him.

'You're not supposed to be in here.'

I looked up from the items on the floor.

Someone was back inside the laundry room.

# 43

I turned on my knees and looked out through the door. I couldn't see very far, just along the row of shelves directly outside.

'I said, you're not supposed to be in here.'

I thought someone was talking to me, but there was no one in sight, no evidence I'd been spotted. Even so, I decided it was time to go. I took cameraphone shots of everything I'd pulled out of the bag, put it back as quickly as I could, reset the fascia plate against the wall and clambered to my feet.

I peered out.

This time, I could see a woman, olive-skinned and long-haired, right in the centre of the room, her back to me. She was standing at the table, folding bed sheets. I headed left, tracing the circumference of the space, trying to remain behind the walls of towels, duvets and pillow-cases stacked on the shelves. At the door, still out of sight of the woman, I pulled at the handle and checked outside.

It looked clear.

Slipping through the gap, I exited the laundry room, back into the silence of the corridor, and headed to the lifts, getting the first one up to the lido deck. It was mid-afternoon and, as the forecast that morning had predicted, the weather had begun to change. It was cloudier, marginally cooler, but no one seemed to care. It was still crowded – at the pools, at the bar, at the outdoor restaurant.

I retreated to the other end, following a half-mile running track that looped around the deck. The throngs of people were hard to avoid, but I found an empty bench at the stern that looked out over the V-shaped wake the ship was carving into the ocean. Everything was so huge, the ship so colossal, that by the time I sat down again it was even more overcast. A wind had picked up too. Surrounded by nothing but endless horizon, I started cycling through the shots I'd taken in the laundry room. The uniform. The money. The expired food. The photographs.

'David Raker?'

I looked up.

A bear of a man in his late thirties, shaven-headed and blue-eyed, looked down at me. He was standing a foot away, too close for it to be comfortable.

I glanced at his name badge.

*Larry Grobb.*

The flag next to his name said he was from the US.

He was dressed casually in a pair of denims and a golf shirt, but it wasn't much of a disguise. I could see he was security a mile off. When he realized I wasn't going to make a run for it, he sat down on the bench beside me. I put my phone away, trying to work out where this was about to go, but then I realized something: Larry Grobb. *LG.*

'I'm Larry,' he said. 'From security.'

He glanced at me, like he was trying to get a read on me, and then returned to his previous position, staring straight ahead at the stern.

'People tell me you've been asking questions. That you're some sort of detective.' He was deliberately dialling down his voice. 'Is that true?'

'I don't think you need me to answer that, do you?'

He looked at me sideways; said nothing.

'I mean, Marek has already told you who I am.'

A flicker of a smile on his face. 'People on this ship, David, they're either here to enjoy a vacation, to relax and have a good time, or they work here. And you buzzing around like this, it makes everyone feel jumpy. It makes them think something's going on when it isn't. Crew get suspicious when serious-looking men start asking them questions, and the passengers get worried too.' He shifted on the bench, turning towards me, the slats groaning. 'That isn't a great mix.'

I continued to look at him.

'The silent treatment, huh?'

'What do you want?'

Grobb shot me a humourless smile. 'She's dead.'

I stared at him.

'Beth.' He shrugged. 'If that's who you came looking for, you're about nine months too late. He took care of her back in January.'

It was hard to tell whether or not there was regret in his voice. He uncrossed his arms and I saw a tattoo peek out from under the sleeve of his shirt: the bottom half of an American eagle, set inside a triangle, with the word AIR-BORNE underneath it.

*Ex-army.*

'Here's what we're gonna do,' he said. His expression was as hard as concrete now. 'We're gonna stand up, and you're gonna come with me.'

'Why would I do that?'

'Because you're either going to do it willingly, with your dignity intact. Or I'm gonna slap some cuffs on you in front of all these people and drag you to the elevators like a dog.'

He looked out at the crowds and – when I followed his gaze – I could see three other members of the security team, dressed like Grobb, approaching us, all from a different part of the boat. When I looked over my shoulder, there was a fourth, a man even bigger than Grobb, following the path of the running track, his eyes on me.

'So how's this gonna go, David?'

Some of the tourists had started to look at us now, drawn away from their conversations by the sight of the security team closing in on me. I tried to think of an escape plan, a way out of this, but I was on a ship in the middle of the ocean, and I was surrounded by five men who would find me eventually, even if I made a run for it.

'Very sensible,' he said, as if I'd given him his answer, and then clamped a hand around my arm and hauled me to my feet.

Once I was standing, he let go again.

'Follow me.'

# 44

They took me to a security door on the bottom deck, near the restaurants. It was unmarked, and on the other side was a corridor with plain grey metal walls and three further doors. An office, behind a panel of glass, was at the end.

The security team who'd trailed Grobb and me all the way down passed us and headed to the office, joining two others. One was eating, the other was flicking through a newspaper. The rest of the desks were empty, except for one at the back where a giant teddy bear was seated at a computer with a sign around its neck that said MANAGER.

'Here,' Grobb said and, after running his card through a reader on the wall, pushed at the first door on our right. It was an interview room: a couple of chairs, a table moulded to the wall, and a slim CCTV camera on a bracket in the top corner on the far side. There was no view and no windows; at this level, we were beneath the surface of the ocean. 'Go on in and sit down,' he said.

He gave me a sudden shove and, as I stumbled into the room, he slammed the door shut behind me.

There was no handle on the inside of the door, and nothing on the frame to grab hold of. The room was warm too: if the air conditioning was on, it hadn't been turned up. I got out my phone and checked for a signal, but it had died about a mile out of Cape Town, so I went to the table and sat down. The longer I sat, the more the panic started to build in me. I got up again and went to the door, knocking on it. It was just a dull thump, nothing more, like a sound that had come a great distance. I did it again, much harder, but no one responded.

I glanced at the camera on the other side of the room, its gaze fixed on me, a tiny pinprick of red light to the side of the lens. They were watching. They could see me trying the door. They could see everything. As I stared at the camera again, a warning blared behind my eyes – in my bones, in my blood.

I returned to the table, seating myself, trying to come up with something. I could feel sweat along the arc of my forehead, just below my hairline. I could feel it tracing the ridge of my spine. It wasn't panic now, it was heat. I'd been wrong about the air conditioning: it hadn't been turned down, it had been switched off entirely. The room was like an oven.

'David?'

It was Grobb, his voice muzzled by the door. I jumped to my feet and went across to it, thumping hard with the side of my fist.

'Are you listening to me, David?'

'What do you think?'

'I'd get comfortable if I was you.'

'What the hell's going on?'

'What does it look like?'

'It looks like you're not coming back in.'

'That's correct.'

Another protracted silence from the other side of the door. I looked back across my shoulder at the CCTV camera, its unblinking black eye focused on me.

'What's going on, Grobb?'

'Just sit tight.'

'Why?'

'You're gonna be in there for a while.'

'*Why?*'

'You'll find out when the time's right.'

# 45

Evening became night, and night became morning.

I checked my watch often to start with, counting minutes, but then – as morning became afternoon, and then afternoon turned to evening again – I stopped doing it as much, and I started to drift. Gradually, I fell into sleep, sitting up in the chair and leaning forward at the table, head resting against my arms.

I dreamed the same thing as the first night on the boat, of being stuck in a maze lined with doors, and when I woke I'd sweated through my clothes and felt disorientated, dazed, and uncertain of where I was. When I sat up and recovered a little composure, everything quickly moved back into focus.

After that, I tried to collect my thoughts and come up with a plan, but it was 8 p.m. and I'd been twenty-eight hours without water, and my head was banging hard. I turned in the seat, looked up at the camera and motioned for them to bring me a drink, but I doubted they would run the risk of it. If they opened the door, they gave me a chance – even if it was a small one.

More hours passed and my headache became worse.

I tried to close my eyes, tried to sleep it off at the table, but eventually my back hurt from being bent over. Instead, in the early hours of the morning, I got up and walked around, doing circles of the room like a convict released into a prison yard. I counted, trying to give myself something to do, something to zero in on, seeing how many times I could loop the room, but then I started to lose focus again and the numbers fell away, and after a while I just walked the circles in silence. It soon became afternoon again, then evening, then night.

I checked my phone for a signal, willing it to return, but we were in the middle of the South Atlantic, still a day away from the Empress Islands, and there wasn't even a flicker. Worse, my battery was almost out. The phone was just an extension of my notebook now, a dormant piece of plastic where ideas and outlines and photographs were stored. I powered it down.

I had nothing.

No way out.


I must have been asleep because, by the time I realized what was happening, the door had been opened and closed and a bottle of water lay on the floor. It was a quarter full.

Pushing back from the table – my head still pounding – I hurried across the room, grabbed the water and sank it in two gulps, feeling the water travel from throat to stomach. It was lukewarm but I didn't care. I drank it so quickly, some of it spilled on to my face, my hands, on to my T-shirt and across my chest. Once I was done, I felt out of breath, my clothes damp, the heat of the room forgotten just briefly. But then it returned again, like a furnace.

It was 12 a.m. I closed my eyes, trying to think. That meant we would be at the Empress Islands in about seven hours' time. Was that what they were waiting for? Was that why I was being kept in here?

*Click.*

The door opened a fraction and Grobb appeared. He fixed his gaze on me immediately, as if he'd only just been watching me on camera and knew exactly where I was in the room.

'Stay seated,' he said.

When I did as he asked, he opened the door further and I could see out into the corridor beyond the width of his frame. It looked like the night lights were on, the space a mix of pale cream lamps and thick shadow. After a beat, Grobb stepped back out of sight, and two other people replaced him.

One was Alexander Marek.

The other was Roland Dell.

# 46

It took me a second to process; seeing the headmaster of the Red Tree here, so out of context, was impossible to grasp at first. But then Roland Dell came in, his gaze taking in the room, and it all fell into place.

He was dressed in a suit jacket and jeans with a white shirt, unbuttoned at the neck, his hair slicked back, his beard thicker than when I'd seen him at the school. He looked tired, as if he hadn't slept, but he was still handsome, athletic, young for a man of forty-eight, his bright blue eyes reflecting back the bloom of the strip lights above us. There was something else too, humming just below the surface, a look in his eyes that immediately set me on edge, and I realized the school headmaster, the amiable, talented academic, was just a role to him. It was a part of who he was, but not the real part. It was a skin he pulled on.

He stood staring at me, Marek behind him, at his shoulder, almost in deference – a servant waiting to be summoned – and the truth about their dynamic revealed itself. All I'd laid at Marek's feet, I should have been pinning on Dell: Marek was just a fixer for him, someone who got things done as quietly and efficiently as possible.

Dell was the architect.

I glanced at Marek. His eyes were blue as well, but nowhere near as bright as Dell's, and they didn't handle the light the same way: they seemed to sink, like a wreck dropping to the bottom of the ocean. With his hair scraped into a ponytail, I was able to see the same scar as before, a mark tracing the line of his head. He wasn't physically intimidating but he was dangerous. They both were.

It was like a scent they gave off.

Marek pushed the door shut and, once it was closed, Dell finally moved. I could hear the air conditioning kicking into life as he glanced at the camera in the corner of the room, almost glaring at it. I watched the red light wink a couple of times and then vanish altogether.

They didn't want any of this on tape.

Dell pulled a chair out and sat down opposite me, placing both hands flat to the table. He tilted his head slightly, examining me, maybe looking for signs of fear. Inside, every muscle in my body was screaming with panic, every nerve was firing, every corner of my skull seemed to be aching – but I managed to keep a lid on all of it. I didn't break eye contact with him until he turned and looked back at Marek, who was standing in the same place, his arms behind him.

'I'd forgotten just how far away this fucking place is.' He swivelled around to face me again, smiling. 'You've been travelling – what? – four days and you're *still* going. It's a pain in the arse to get to, plus the weather's shite and the towns are all dumps. I mean, everyone goes on about St George being modern, but modern compared to what? The Middle Ages?'

He smirked, eyeing me.

'But I can tell you this.' He leaned forward over the table, his hands still flat to it, pretending that he was imparting some ancient secret. 'A tax haven being so far away from everywhere, that has its advantages too. It's not as sexy as the Cayman Islands – there's no palm trees, or rum and Cokes on the beach after work – so there aren't any investigators or journalists looking to justify a "business trip" to the Empress Islands. Everyone just forgets it's here, and do you know what that means? It means you can do things down here you can't do elsewhere.'

'I know,' I said. 'I saw your finances.'

The smile faltered, but he didn't let it derail him. 'That's what I figured. I mean, why else go to the Empress Islands, right?' As soon as he said *right*, I heard it: the accent. He'd hidden it from me at the school but he didn't have to hide it now.

He was from the islands too.

'Yes,' he said, seeing me make the connection. 'My father was a diplomat. I was born in Bermuda, but he got offered the governor's job on the islands and we moved down here when I was young.' He paused, smiled again. '*Thanks*, Dad.'

'So *you* were the one passing money through the Red Tree?'

He shrugged. 'When was the last time you heard about the taxman digging around in a school, David? I mean, it happens, but not very often. A school's a good place to hide things.'

As soon as he said that, something else clicked into place: the date that the money first started appearing in the Red Tree accounts was September 2000.

The same month Dell became headmaster.

'Let me ask you something,' he said, his eyes fixed on

me. 'Why do you think they gave me the job of headmaster at the age of thirty-two?'

Again, he'd jumped ahead of me; seen where my thoughts were focused.

'I mean, I've proven myself in the time since, and I enjoy it there. But a school like that, so prestigious, so much class, so many mega-rich parents and narrow-minded governors sitting in judgement – why would *they* give the biggest job in the school to a history teacher who'd only been there five years and had only been a teacher for nine?'

'Because you paid them off.'

He pointed at me. 'There are no flies on you. See, what I learned early on in my life is that being wealthy doesn't make you *less* interested in money. In fact, the opposite. It only feeds your obsession.'

'So you didn't pay it all into offshore accounts then? You kept some of the money back for the governors – and for yourself.'

'I did. My share never went through the school.'

'Your "share"?'

'A figure of speech,' he said, but he was lying.

'So if you never put your "share" through the school, who do the three accounts in the Empress Islands belong to?'

He didn't respond this time.

'Did you steal all of that money from Caleb Beck?'

Dell forced a smile, as if I was so wide of the mark it barely deserved an answer. But there was a moment, a flicker of something, when I'd accused him of stealing the cash. So was that what Penny had followed a trail back to, and what had got her killed: realizing that Dell had taken her father's money?

'Did you murder Caleb Beck?' I said.

Dell just looked at me.

'What about Penny?'

Nothing.

I knew I was on to something. Dell was having to concentrate, to force himself not to show any hint of surprise or anger or alarm, and while the movements in his face were all minor, they were there: fractional adjustments that said everything.

'That was why Penny told everyone her name was Corrine Wilson,' I said, as more of the puzzle came together. 'You had no idea who she was, did you? She arrived at the school, not because she wanted to teach – or, not *just* for that reason. She joined the Red Tree because she wanted to look into you, into what happened to her father. She suspected you were involved in Caleb Beck going missing.'

I paused. Jacob Howson had told me that Penny had worked hard to subdue her accent but, occasionally, he would hear it slip.

It was because she'd been trying to hide it from Dell.

So was that what ended up getting her killed? Not Marek finding out she'd stolen information from the security suite, been through his computer and taken a keycard – but a minor lapse in her accent in front of Roland Dell?

He started shaking his head, dropping his eyes away from me, as if he realized he'd become too transparent. 'You're an idiot, you know that?' He leaned back in his chair. 'You must be able to see that none of this matters. What you think I did, what I really did, it's ephemera.'

'Is that what you call it?'

He held his hands out flat, palms up, in a *you tell me* gesture.

'If it's just ephemera,' I said, 'why are you here?'

'That's actually a very good question,' he said, and glanced back over his shoulder at Marek. 'How long did it take us to get here? Twenty-two hours?'

'Twenty-one,' Marek replied.

It was the first thing he'd said.

'Twenty-one hours,' Dell repeated. 'Ten and a half to Cape Town, three on the ground, a five-hour flight on a Gulfstream from there to the airport on the Empress Islands, *another* hour's layover there, and then an hour and a half to fly two hundred and fifty miles out into the South Atlantic ocean – in the middle of the night – to land on a tiny cruise-ship helipad in the pissing rain.'

Dell brought his hands back, lacing them together on the table in front of him. 'Even when your money can buy you luxury,' he continued, 'you know, first-class flights and private jets and all of that, it still makes for a hell of a journey. So, like I said, it's a good question. Why even bother?' He looked at me, eyes boring into mine, an odd slope to his mouth; I couldn't tell if he was disgusted by the sight of me, or amused by my situation. 'See, the reason I'm so successful is because I always know what's going on in my school and in my life. I know each little part: who's who, what's what, what's working well, what isn't. Some see that as a negative – micro-management. I call it pragmatic.' He waved a finger between me and him. 'Take this as an example. A lot of people, they would have just sent Alexander down here by himself. I mean, let's be honest, that would have been a hell of a lot easier than this Jules Verne crap I've had to pull, and ultimately he would have got the job done, one way or another.'

I glanced at Marek. He hadn't move an inch the entire time he'd been standing. Same position, same stance, his hands together behind him, at the base of his spine.

'And yet, here I am.'

When I returned my gaze to Dell, the mock joviality had disappeared and in its stead was a blackness; the man beneath the man.

'I've got some questions. That's one reason I came.'

His eyes were drilling into me again.

'The other is a lot more straightforward,' he said. 'I think it's important to look people in the face and see if they're lying to you before you cut them up and dump them in the ocean.'

# 47

Instantly, the air chilled.

'What do you know about Penny?' Dell said.

I watched him: there was a moment, as he said her real name aloud, when his eyes showed something softer. A sadness, or a regret; a burst of light. But then, whatever it had been, it was gone again and his expression became a blank.

'I think you killed her,' I said.

'How do you even know she's dead?'

'Because her body was dumped on that railway line.'

'That's quite a leap, considering that she's not even registered as a missing person.'

I smiled, but there was no humour in it.

He frowned. 'Do I amuse you?'

I gestured to Marek. 'I think he killed her – for you.'

He watched me for a while, then picked a hair off his jacket and changed position on the seat. He was telling me he was in control, that this entire conversation was being conducted at his pace and on his terms.

'So who put those ideas in your head?' he asked.

'They're not ideas.'

'Was it Jacob Howson?'

Again, he watched me for confirmation. This was a fact-finding mission and a firefighting exercise: half a cold-blooded execution, half an act of survival.

'Was it Howson?' he said again.

I stared back, giving him absolutely nothing, and then I closed my eyes; my head was starting to thump again. In the darkness, I tried to shift ahead of Dell to my next move, a way to escape. How was I going to get out of here? *Come on, think of something.*

But I couldn't. I had nothing. My head was just static and, when I opened my eyes again, Dell was leaning forward, staring at me.

'You struggling?' he said. A smile skirted the edges of his lips as if he glimpsed some sort of advantage – an access point, a way to get at me. 'That's why I told them not to give you anything. A couple of days without food and just a few mouthfuls of lukewarm water, that starts to affect your ability to function. You've got a crashing headache, your muscles ache, you're trying to think straight but all you can *really* think about is getting something to eat and drink.' He leaned away from me again, the chair creaking as he settled. 'You might as well be honest with me, because nothing about this is loaded in your favour. The guys in security, they're not coming back for you. They're not interested in what goes on in here. They'll be out on shift until we're done, until we've got what we want from you, and then Alexander will message them and they'll return to their desks and they'll find no trace of us, and no trace of you. That's just how it works. You can't affect that, because all of them are on my payroll.'

They'd probably been that way since Beth was caught on camera. Marek had come to the ship to get rid of her, and Dell had paid the security team to help. I pushed my anger down. The less he thought I knew, the better.

'Who told you about Penny?' he said again.

I looked at him blankly.

'Was it Howson?'

'I don't know who that is.'

'Bullshit.'

I shrugged.

'Where is he?'

'I just told you,' I said, 'I don't know who –'

'You're lying. You're hiding him and Richard some-where.'

'I'm not hiding anyone.'

'It was Howson who told you.'

'Told me about what?'

He smirked. 'You know I'll find that little fucker, don't you?'

I shrugged again, as if it made no difference to me, but inside I was frantically thinking how I might go about getting hold of Howson. I needed to warn him to stay hidden, or even better to move on somewhere else. But then I looked around the room and reality kicked in. How was I going to do that? How was I going to get out of here? I glanced from Dell to Marek.

Maybe I wasn't. Maybe this was the end.

Dell pushed again: 'Admit it was Howson and we're done.'

'I don't know who you're talking about.'

'It was Howson, wasn't it?'

'No.'

'What did Penny pass on to him?'

'I don't know who this Hows–'

'*Bullshit!*'

Dell smashed the flat of his hand on to the table. The whole thing moved, the legs shifting, the surface vibrating. He stood, straightening his jacket, and turned to Marek. They looked at one another, and then Dell swivelled on his heel, his face burning red with rage.

'You broke into my school,' he said, pointing at me. 'You broke in and you stole that laptop from me. I always knew it was you, you piece of shit.'

I'd wiped all expression from my face.

'We've been through your laptop,' he went on. 'We found it in your cabin. There's nothing on there that we can't deal with, and everything else is in your head.' He buttoned up his jacket. 'We can contain that easily enough too, because pretty soon your head isn't going to be attached to your body.'

I tried not to show him that his words had got to me.

'But this Penny stuff,' he said, 'it's a problem.'

He brushed himself down.

'Whatever Howson has in his possession – that's a problem too.'

He went to the door and swiped a card across a reader fixed to the wall. The door buzzed. Pulling it open, he moved into the gap, looked both ways along the corridor, and then brought back a water bottle.

I looked at the bottle, fixed on it, felt my muscles tense and my throat constrict. It had been refrigerated, tears of condensation running down it.

'You know, some things you regret,' Dell said, bringing me back to him, his voice almost like a whisper. 'Penny.' He stopped at her name; a brief flicker of pain. 'That was hard.'

'So you *did* kill her?'

'She was smart,' was all he said.

It was almost as if he'd genuinely liked her. Howson had said the same thing about Marek; that he'd had a soft spot for Penny, which was how she was able to manoeuvre him. Maybe Marek was drawn to Penny through lust, a physical attraction, but I didn't get that sense from Dell. It was like whatever he felt for her was based on something much more deep-seated – and that had only made her betrayal even worse in his eyes. Could he have known her back in Sophia? It was possible, but if that was true, why hadn't Dell recognized Penny when she turned up at the school, pretending to be Corrine Wilson?

'She was a liar and a fraud,' he said, picking at the label on the water bottle, 'but I wouldn't have chosen that end for her.'

His expression endured for a moment, and then he snapped out of it and it was like it had never been there.

'You, though,' he said, using the neck of the bottle as a pointer, 'you, I couldn't give a shit about. I'll leave this ship in ten minutes and I'll never spend a second thinking about you. If you'd told me how it was you came to know so much about Penny, the next hour could have gone a lot easier for you. But now it won't. And Howson? I'll track him down, and I might have to finally take care of Richard too, depending on what you've told him. They're going to suffer badly, David. And the only person to blame is yourself. I gave you your chance. Remember that.'

He chucked the water bottle at me.

It hit the wall just to my right. I watched it all the way,

turned as it landed, and as I heard Dell leave the room, I scooped it up off the floor, parched, desperate.

And then I realized something.

Marek had moved.

My brain barely had time to catch up, my system skewed by dehydration, by the sweat in my eyes, by the prickle of fear that had coated my skin like sea salt – and, by then, he was right beside me and it was too late. I suddenly understood why he'd stayed there, in the same spot, with his hands behind his back: he'd been hiding a thin metal truncheon about the length of a forearm.

'You should have talked,' he said.

And then he swung it into my ribs.

# 48

Pain flashed through my chest. I rocked back on my chair, and the whole thing went from under me, my entire weight propelled towards the wall. I hit it hard, sliding down it, into the corner of the room.

I was in shock, dazed, my body on fire.

By the time I'd gathered myself, I realized Marek was directly over me, his feet planted either side of my legs.

I managed to get a forearm up to protect my face, but the impact just deflected the pain. It screamed through the joints of my arm – wrist, elbow, into my shoulder – and, when I tried to shuffle away, he cracked the metal rod against my knuckles. I cried out, the sound so ineffective inside the room that it disappeared the moment it left my mouth.

Another blow to my ribs. One more to my forearm.

Hands, body, forearm, over and over.

And then, finally, he got me across the back of the neck and, as the impact sent a ripple through my throat, I hit the floor. This time, I really did black out.

When I came to, Marek was at the door.

I watched for a moment, everything sideways with my face planted on the ground, pain throbbing in my hands and arms and ribs. I twisted myself, right and left, trying to see if he'd broken anything, but it just felt like cuts and bruising. The baton was simply a way to soften me up. He was breaking me down, weakening me, so that I couldn't fight back – because whatever was coming next would be worse.

Except something had changed.

Marek pulled the door all the way open.

At first, he only opened it a sliver, looking through the gap, and as I hauled myself up on to my backside and shuffled against the wall, I wondered if he was talking to someone. But I couldn't hear any words and, a few seconds later, he glanced back over his shoulder at me, making sure I wasn't going to make any quick moves, and then looked both ways and stepped out.

The door remained open.

I stayed there, uncertain whether this was a trick or not – but Marek didn't reappear. All I could see was a shadowy rectangle of corridor.

After thirty seconds, I pushed away from the wall and got to my feet. Still there was nothing. I came around the table, aching, a little unsteady, angling my head so I could see further beyond the door.

*It's a trap. It's got to be.*

The corridor was so dimly lit and the interview room so bright that, at first, it was hard to adjust to the contrast. I could hardly even make out the surface of the walls, the grey of the ceiling. But I could feel something: cold air. It purred out of a grille outside and wafted into the interview room. It felt good against my skin, and for a moment I was mesmerized by it: the sheen of sweat on my face, my arms, frozen instantly; the fever of my head and the heat of the bruises cooled. I slowly let my eyes adjust to the corridor.

Marek was standing about a foot away from the wall, mostly concealed by the shadows. The truncheon was on the floor next to him. I tried to imagine what game he was playing, and what might happen if I stepped beyond the boundaries of the room.

'What's going on?' I said.

He didn't respond at first. But then a shudder seemed to cut through him, as if he was wired to a socket. He blinked, and said through his teeth, 'You just messed up big time.'

I frowned. 'What are you talking about?'

I looked around the interview room, at the camera and then down at the one bottle of water I'd drunk from, discarded on the floor. *You just messed up big time.* Did he mean the water? Had they put something in it? I didn't feel ill. I didn't feel sick. If it wasn't the water, what was it?

Marek had come forward a couple of inches in the meantime, his frame at the edge of the light, where one of the lamps cut a livid glow across him. I looked him up and down, trying to figure out what had changed, but my head was banging so hard now, I was finding it difficult to focus. I could feel it echoing all the way down to my throat, across my shoulders, vibrating in my bruises. I couldn't figure out what was going on, what this was, what I lost by heading to the door and exiting the room immediately. There had to be a catch.

But then I noticed something else.

In the corridor, behind Marek, there was something white. I fixed on it, trying to see it more clearly. It was like a fish breaking the surface of the ocean, there and gone again. When I glanced at him, he just looked back, but there was something in his face, a confirmation.

*You're not seeing things.*

I took a couple more steps forward, only a foot from the cusp of the room, and stopped again. I could see all the way to the right now, to the office. The security staff were all gone, just as Dell had promised. Off to the left, the door back out to the restaurants was shut.

But there was something on the floor in front of it.

I tried to work out what it was, and where it had come from, and then my attention was drawn up. There was a hollow in the ceiling.

An open air vent.

The thing on the floor was its cover.

I looked at the sliver of white in the darkness behind Marek, and then it started to become more than just a sliver: it was the white of a sleeve, the straps of a back-pack, and then a hand, and then a gun.

The gun was pointed at Marek's head.

'Are you okay?' a voice said.

And from behind him a face finally emerged: blonde hair cut short; green eyes flashing in the half-light; dirt smeared across one of the cheeks; bruises in a chain along her arm. Cuts. War wounds. The scars of survival.

It was Beth.

# 49

She told Marek to go to the office.

In the shadows of the corridor, he looked almost twice Beth's size and, for a second, he didn't move, as if he was testing her, as if he was telling her he could bulldoze her, overpower her, turn the tables instantly. But he didn't. He started walking instead. I watched him, his eyes flicking to me and then away again, and saw the truncheon he'd been holding discarded on the floor, ten feet from him.

He could also see what I saw in Beth. She was small, thin and sinewy, no more than five two or five three, but there was something about her: a presence, a fierceness, an air of having already survived much worse than this, physically and emotionally. As she shoved the gun into Marek's back, both he and I understood why he was doing as she asked: there was no hesitation in her, and neither of us doubted she would fire the gun, not even for a second.

I stayed where I was as they moved – the two of them passing in and out of the lamps stationed along the corridor's walls – and then I headed in the opposite direction. As Marek shuffled into the office, as Beth told him to go to the other side of it and sit down, I opened the door and looked out at the restaurants. It was after 1 a.m. now, and they were mostly empty. From where I was, I had a clear view of two of them, one French, one an American-style diner, and I knew there were two more off to the right, out of sight beyond a red and white striped awning on the front of the diner. Some people were still milling around the entrances, near banks of sofas in the atrium, in a series of shops off to the left, but most passengers had left for the night.

I looked for any sign of the security team close by, but they weren't here and neither was Dell. It had been ten minutes since he'd left. If he was heading back to the helipad and leaving Marek here to finish things off, he'd probably be about to leave. I doubted if he would expect Marek to fail.

That gave Beth and me some breathing room.

I closed the door and watched as Beth ripped phones from their sockets in the office, taking the leads with her, a walkie-talkie too, so Marek couldn't communicate with anyone. After that, she locked him in. She tossed the key away and it pinged against the floor and landed in the shadows. But she knew the office would only hold him for as long as he remained in our sight. Once we were gone, either the security team would come back, or he'd smash his way through the glass.

Beth turned to me and put the gun in the band of her trousers. Half submerged in the dusty light of the corridor, I saw her eyes shift quickly: back to the office from which Marek looked out at us, to the hallway in which we stood, to the interview-room door, and then to the air vent she'd used to access the corridor. It was survival instinct kicking in. It was a detailed knowledge of the ship, a mechanical sense of which things were right, which things were out of place, which fitted, which didn't. When she was done, she came down the corridor towards me, her movements quick and focused.

'Are you okay?' she said.

'I haven't eaten for two and a half days, but otherwise . . .'

She nodded.

'Thank you,' I said.

She nodded again. The white of her right eye was stained red, a splintered patchwork of blood vessels tracking the border of her iris. Her skin was pale, specked in dirt and the tiny prickles of a rash, and while she was plain, in many ways unremarkable, that was exactly how I imagined she'd succeeded: because of her size and the way she looked, she was constantly underestimated – and it was only when you were this close to her, when you saw the look on her face, that you started to get it. She was compact. She was resilient. She was sharp as hell.

Again, her gaze switched from one end of the corridor to the other. It wasn't the sort of sense you developed for a place off the back of only a fortnight, or three weeks, even the time that passengers would spend on-board when the ship was at sea for eighty days. She didn't know this place because she'd spent a few weeks hiding out with Richard Kite back in January.

She knew it because she'd made it her home.

'How long have you been here?' I asked.

'Since December.'

She replied so matter-of-factly it almost hid the enormity of what she was saying.

*Eleven months.*

The boat had a continual changeover of passengers and crew, so its make-up altered all the time. It made it a perfect hiding place. It was rare that the staff would remain on-board for all eighty days – and, if she was in the uniform she'd stolen, the passengers were unlikely to take much notice of her – so that meant a rolling quota of four thousand people. It was a crowd big enough to hide in. If she was clever, which she clearly was, she could exist without ever being looked at.

I turned my attention to the gun in her belt. 'Where did you get that from?'

'I stole it.'

'From security?'

'From their safe.'

'How did you get into their safe?'

'By putting in the code.'

I thought about her using the vents, about how she might watch people from them, hear things, see things like security codes.

'And me?' I said.

'What about you?'

'How did you even know I was on-board?'

She shrugged. 'Because I saw you.'

I was about to ask her when – but then it came to me. Back in the laundry room on the second day, after I'd found the carrier bag in the vent, one of the housekeeping staff had returned. They'd said, *You're not supposed to be in here.* To start with, I thought they'd been speaking to me, but then I'd made my way out and been approached by Larry Grobb, and I'd never stopped to consider it again. I'd never had the chance to. If I had, I'd have realized the woman from housekeeping hadn't been speaking to me.

She'd been speaking to Beth.

'You came back to the laundry room,' I said.

'Yes.'

'And you saw me in there, with your things.'

'Yes. After that, I followed you. I wanted to see who you were. I watched Grobb approach you, and then I watched them take you down to the interview room, and then I waited for you – except you never came out.'

'Why?' I said. 'Why come and get me like you did?'

'Because I think you can help me.'

'How did you even know you could trust me? Coming here, doing this, it's such a huge risk for someone you don't know.'

'I heard them talking about you,' she said, eyes starting to shift again, back and forth along the corridor, hanging on Marek for a time. 'After I saw them take you down to security, I got up into the air vents. They called you dangerous. They said you were asking questions about me.'

'I was.'

'Why? What do you want with me?'

'I'm trying to help someone you may have known.'

She eyed me but didn't say anything.

'He thinks his name is Richard,' I said, 'but he's lost his memory and doesn't know if that's actually what he's called.'

Except, a moment later, I knew that really *was* his name. She reacted, a breath escaping her lips, as if she'd been holding it in, and there was a flicker of emotion in her eyes – a flash, a crack in the mask.

'Richard,' she said, almost to herself.

And that was when I knew something else: she hadn't just known him.

She'd loved him.

# 50

We sat across from each other on the floor of the corridor. I was starting to cool now, my body stiffening as the adrenalin died and the bruising began to flower.

Opposite me, Beth watched Marek, his expression the same as it had been since she'd first locked him in the room: impassive, almost indifferent. At one point, he ran a hand down the back of his head, following the line of his ponytail, but mostly he remained absolutely still, watching us both, obviously trying to understand what we were talking about.

Beth brought her backpack around in front of her, unzipped it, reached in and removed some water. As I took it, thanking her, she handed me a chocolate bar, a packet of dried fruit, some crisps, a sandwich in a packet, and then looked to her left, her features in profile, as if searching the shadows for something else. I watched her as I ate, the two of us silent, and then when I was almost done with the food and she'd turned back to face me, I said, 'How did you end up here, Beth?'

She wiped dirt away from her face, the cuts on her skin like cracks in an old oil painting.

'I don't know where to start,' she replied.

'Just start with Richard.'

She rubbed a finger over her eye; nodded. 'How's he doing?'

'He's doing okay.'

'I read online that he has no memory.'

She said it so softly, so quietly, it was hard for me to hear her above the noise of the air conditioning.

'He only remembers a couple of things. Looking out at a beach as a kid, at some sort of coastline – I'm assuming somewhere near Sophia.' I waited, but I didn't get the sense that, even having known Richard Kite, she knew where the beach might be. 'And he remembers the intro sequence to a TV show. I read in a book that it might be called *Kids' Hour.*'

She smiled. *'Kids' Hour.'*

'You know it?'

'Yes. Everyone in town used to watch it after school. We didn't have many channels growing up – we didn't have much of anything, really – so you took what you could get. They used to have this cartoon in the middle of the show, this dragon who was supposed to be huge and fierce but was actually always frightened. My sister and I, we loved that bit – it always made us laugh.'

'Your sister is Penny, right?'

'Yes.' She looked at me. 'Did you know her?'

Her accent was coming through strongly now.

'No,' I said. 'I've heard about her, though.'

'How?'

'I spoke to her boyfriend in London.'

'She had a boyfriend?'

'She didn't tell you that?'

Beth seemed to shrink. She brought her knees to her chest, looped her arms around them. 'No,' she said distantly, eyes fixed on a space between us. 'She left Sophia when she was sixteen and never came back.'

'You never heard from her after that?'

'My stepmum would sometimes, an email or a phone call. But Fiona died about five years back – she had cancer – and after that I never knew what Penny was up to, because she and I had stopped speaking, and I . . .' She came to a halt. 'I said some things to Pen that I just . . . I wish . . .' She stopped again. 'I just wish I'd never said them, that's all. She was my sister. I know we weren't blood, but in all the ways that mattered she was my sister. And after she disappeared, it was the first time that it ever hit me: I was never going to get . . . to get the . . . the . . .'

She faded out, the rest written on her face.

*The chance to say I'm sorry.*

Beth dropped her head, pressing a thumb and finger to her eyes, and it took her a long time to recover, before it felt right to gently steer us back to Richard Kite.

'What was Richard's surname?' I asked.

'Presley.'

*Richard Presley.*

I wasn't sure what I'd been expecting – perhaps after waiting so long for an answer, no name would feel right.

'Do you know if his parents are still around?'

'His dad is.'

'But not his mum?'

'She's around – or, at least, she was before I left the islands – but she had a stroke. She can't talk. She can't really communicate at all.'

'What are their names?'

'His dad's called William. Bill. Bill Presley.'

'And his mum?'

'Carla.'

I got out my notebook, a pen clipped to one of the inside pages, and wrote their names down. 'Did he have any brothers or sisters?'

'No.'

*So it was just the three of them.*

'Did you know his parents well?'

She nodded. 'His dad used to be friendly with mine.'

'What's your dad's name?'

'Jack Kilburn.'

I realized I hadn't known Beth's full name until now.

'How come your dad and Bill Presley were friendly?'

'My dad's a farmer, but he also chairs the town council. Rich's dad was on the committee for a long time too. They got to know each other through that.'

'Is Richard's dad also a farmer?'

'No,' she said. 'He's a superintendent.'

'In the police?'

She nodded. 'He runs the station in Sophia.'

I stopped, pen poised, and thought of something Annie had said to me out on the deck when I'd interviewed her: *If there was something going on, and the town wanted to keep it a secret, I guess the Sophia police could do that, right?* She'd been talking about body parts being found up in the hills around the town, about whatever existed beyond the fence. I didn't believe there was some monster hunting people in the foothills of Mount Strathyde any more than I believed there were vampires or unicorns waiting for me at the docks. But it was getting hard to deny that there was *something* going on in Sophia.

'I don't think Penny disappeared.'

I looked up at Beth. 'What?'

'Penny. I don't think she disappeared.'

'What do you think happened to her?'

'I think she was killed.'

I tried not to show my surprise.

'Why would someone kill her?' I asked.

I knew why, and I knew that Beth was right, but I needed to be delicate. If she didn't know the full extent of what had happened to her sister, telling her was going to feel like a shotgun blast. She swallowed, shifted against the wall, the noise of the air con like a swarm of flies as she gathered herself.

'I told her I hated her.'

Beth's voice roused me from my thoughts again.

'I told her I hated her,' she repeated. 'Fifteen, sixteen years ago, I don't know. I try to forget when it was and what I said, I try so hard to do that, but the trouble is, I can't. I can't forget what I said. I remember that night so clearly. I was such a bitch to her. In my teens, I just went totally off the rails and, by the time I realized what I was doing, what I'd done, she was on the other side of the world.'

I wondered how this was relevant, how it connected back to what Beth may or may not have known about her stepsister being murdered, but I didn't try to redirect her for now.

'Didn't you ever think about going to the UK yourself?'

'It was all I ever thought about growing up, but I messed up at school. My exam results were a joke. I failed everything, across the board, because I was too busy getting pissed and sleeping around. I ended up working at a petrol station on the road between Sophia and St George. The only way to get off the islands is to go on to sixth form college and university, and you need funding for that, and you only get funding if you get good results. I guess I could have tried to apply for a job in the UK somewhere – but who's going to offer someone like me a job? I had no qualifications. I had nothing anyone would want.' A sad smile skirted the corner of her lips. 'Irony is, back when I was in junior school, everyone used to say I was destined for the top. "You can be anything you want to be, Beth." Now look at me. Look at what I've made of my life.'

Her voice faltered on the last few words. I waited for her, using the opportunity to take a long drink from the bottle of water she'd given me. It was hard to take my eyes off her, though: her expression was neutral and difficult to read, which was exactly what it needed to be in order for her to survive. But there were other moments too, little flashes where I glimpsed the person hidden beneath the armour: wounded, repentant, frightened.

'In my early twenties,' she said eventually, and I had to shift closer to her in order to hear her, 'I settled down a bit, but it was too late by then. The damage was done and I was stuck in that bloody town. I moved from the petrol station to one of the boatyards in Blake Point. It was run by a bunch of fishermen who my dad vaguely knew, and they had this kind of sideline, this tourist business, where they ferried people out to the eastern islands, to the breeding grounds.'

She stopped and, again, something moved in her eyes.

'Richard worked in the boatyard,' she said. 'That was where I first started talking to him properly, where I basically got to know him.' She stopped again briefly, almost looked hurt. 'That was where everything began.'

## 51

'He didn't actually go out on the boats,' she said, 'although he was a good sailor. He just fixed the trawlers. He was quiet, but we used to chat when he was having lunch, and after a while we started going for walks after work. That was what you did in that worthless town. There was nothing else to do. No coffee shops. No restaurants. No cinema.'

Her gaze came back to me.

'Like I said, our families sort of knew each other – or, at least, our dads did – so I'd seen him around. I knew *of* him, even if I didn't know much about him. If I'm honest, I didn't fancy him much to start with, but he kind of grew on me. He was strange. Even though he fixed boats, even though he was so good with his hands, he spoke like an academic: all he'd talk about were books he'd read – he loved science fiction and history, and he'd go to the library when copies of the UK newspapers came in. They were about three weeks out of date by then, but he still read them cover to cover.'

This was the Richard I'd got to know: quiet, articulate, schooled. I remembered the way he'd talked to me about sports and politics as we'd driven out to Coldwell Point, the way he tried so hard to recall details of his life for me, the books he loved to read, the intelligence and perception he showed. For a smart guy, it must have been torture: all the things he'd learned, all the stuff he'd soaked up in his lunch hours, after work, in the library, and he couldn't grasp hold of any of it.

'After a while, we used to drive out of town in his car,' Beth said, 'this old Ford he had, and we'd cross the bridge into St George and head north to this big abandoned whaling station. It's quiet out there.' She looked at me and shrugged. 'Sometimes when we drove there, I used to joke with him and tell him to keep going, that we should escape and get as far away from Sophia as it was possible to get. But the weird thing is, for a long time, he never wanted that.'

'Why not?'

'He always said he didn't mind it there. He liked working with boats; he said he couldn't survive in a big city, that he wouldn't even know what to do with himself there. To start with, I thought the isolation appealed to him, not because he was antisocial or didn't like being around people, but it was kind of . . .' She stopped, grimaced a little, as if she couldn't find the right words. 'It was kind of reflective of him as a person.'

'But that wasn't the real reason he stayed on the islands?'

'No. The real reason was that he was scared of what would happen if he left.'

I looked at her. 'Scared?'

'Things happened to us on the islands.'

She looked at me like she wasn't sure whether to trust me with whatever she was going to say next. But in the silence I'd already skipped ahead of her, making the connection to the conversation I'd had with Annie, on the second day at sea.

'Are you talking about what's beyond the fence?'

A flash of surprise in her face.

'This "monster"?'

She eyed me with suspicion. 'Yes.'

'There are no such things as monsters, Beth. Not like the ones you're talking about.'

'I don't care,' she said. 'I don't care how impossible you think it is, it's a fact: there *was* something out in the Brink.'

I studied her. 'The Brink?'

She wouldn't look at me.

'Beth?'

'It's an area they fenced off in the hills,' she said quietly.

I remembered Annie saying the same thing, about some marshland that was fenced off on one of the hiking trails. I'd read something about it in *No Ordinary Route* too. But it didn't matter how many times it got repeated, the idea of a monster running around didn't make a lick of sense, even if some of the islanders – including smart ones like Beth – had bought into it.

'So are you saying Richard knew about this monster too?'

'Everyone in Sophia knew about it.'

'Everyone believed it?'

'I don't know if everyone believed it, because sometimes you need to see something with your own eyes before you can believe it. But everyone knew you didn't go out there. Some still believed it was because of the landmines. Others, I told them what had happened to Penny and me, or they heard about it from someone else. They knew the real reason.'

'This monster?'

Another flash of anger. 'What's out there, beyond the

fence, that's the reason I fell out with Penny,' she said, her voice harder now. 'After they left us up there, I started wetting the bed again. Wetting the bed at *twelve*. I couldn't cope with what I'd seen up there, I couldn't –'

'Slow down, slow down. You were *left* up there?'

'Yes.' She swallowed. 'For five hours. At night.'

'Why?'

'We broke the rules. We got over the fence.'

'On to the other side of it?'

'Yes.'

'And what happened?'

'There was something out there.'

'You saw it?'

A pause. 'Enough of it.'

'What did it look like?'

'I don't know,' she said, 'it was a blur. I was running for my life at the time. But someone saw us up there that night – saw us on the other side of the fence – and that was how Dad found out.'

'So you were punished?'

'They told us we had to see for ourselves why people weren't allowed up there. They made an example of us. Dad was crying when he left us there; kept telling us he was sorry. But he said it was the only way we'd understand – and everyone in town would understand – why we didn't go beyond the fence.'

I stared at her, uncertain what to say.

'Don't look at me like that,' she said. 'Don't look at me like I'm crazy. I know what I saw. I know what I heard out there. When they tied us to the fence, I could feel its *breath* on my neck. I could hear it breathing in my fucking ears.'

I held up a hand, trying to calm her down.

'So Richard saw this monster as well?'

'Yes.' She paused. 'But not only that.'

'What do you mean?'

'I mean, he got over the fence, just like Penny and I did. Not at the same time as us – it was after us – but he got punished in exactly the same way that we did. When I realized we were the same, when we first started talking about what we'd seen and heard out there, that was when I really *did* start falling for him. It was the first time, after Penny left, that I found someone who actually understood me. Except the difference was, Penny and I, we went over at night. He went over during the day.' She sniffed, looked at her hands. 'That was the reason he was so scared about leaving the islands.'

I studied her, trying to work out what she meant.

'Are you saying he found something *else* out there?'

'Yes.'

'As well as this . . . monster?'

'Yes.'

'What did he find?'

She looked away again, the first glimmer of tears in her eyes.

'Someone who'd been gone a very long time,' she said quietly.

# The Tarn

*The old whaling station lay at the northern tip of Victoria Island, five miles from St George. It was at the end of a narrow, winding two-track road that snaked a path down a steep hillside called the Bluff. Most of the people who drove out this far just stayed at the top, where there was a small bed of concrete – a makeshift car park – and a viewing platform, which some of the tourists were brought to. On clear days, you could see right the way across the spine of the islands: west towards Sophia; east towards the breeding grounds and bird colonies.*

*Beth Kilburn and Richard Presley went all the way to the bottom.*

*The station was made up of seven different buildings, a mix of power plants, warehouses and dormitories, and there were three gigantic whale-oil tanks as well, each thirty feet across by forty feet high. Everything was broken, decayed, brutalized by the ferocious winds that ripped in off the South Atlantic. There was so much rust – on chimneys, on walls that had been torn clean open, on the roofs that had fallen in – that it was like the entire place had been blanketed in a layer of orange dust.*

*They parked on the edge of the sea, to the left of the buildings, where there was a small loading area full of abandoned machinery too corroded to identify. When Richard turned off the engine, the rumble of the vehicle was instantly replaced by the scream of the wind, by the flapping of corrugated-iron sheets on some of the buildings against their fixings. They could hear doors whipping open and slamming* shut, groans and chimes from loose components in the empty processing plants. Through the windscreen, trawlers lay beached, welded to the slipways by oxidation and sea salt, their hulls speckled red with rust, and pearlescent with limpets.

'This place gives me the creeps,' Beth said.

Richard smiled and grabbed her hand, and they sat there in silence for a moment, the light dying in the sky as afternoon gave way to evening.

'How come you don't talk much about your sister?' he said.

Beth turned to face him, surprised by the question.

'Where did that suddenly come from?'

He glanced at her and then outside again. Beside them, breaking from the ground, almost clawing out of it, were the remnants of harpoons and old whale bones.

'I'm sorry,' he said.

'You don't have to be sorry.'

'It's none of my business.'

'Of course it's your business,' Beth replied, and squeezed his hand.

'I just wondered about her, that was all.'

'What do you want to know?'

'She lives in London, right?'

'Right.'

'Do you ever talk to her?'

Beth gave a weary sigh. 'No,' she said finally. 'We don't talk any more.'

'When was the last time you talked to her?'

'When she left fifteen years ago.'

They sat in silence for a moment, listening to the wind, and then Richard said, 'When you went up to the Brink, you went with Penny, right?'

'Yes. We always went up there together.'

'And you went over the fence?'

Beth watched him for a moment. 'I've already told you all this.'

'I know. I know you did.'

'Is everything okay, Rich?'

He let go of her hand and put both of his on the steering wheel, looking out through the windscreen. It was gradually steaming up, their breath and the cold of the evening creating an opaque cloud across the middle of the glass.

'What happened to Penny's dad?' he said quietly.

'Her dad?'

He looked at Beth. 'Caleb Beck. I heard he disappeared.'

'Yes. In 1987, when Penny was three.' Beth frowned. 'Why?'

'Did they ever find any trace of him?'

'No,' she said finally. 'Never.' The frown was now etched into Beth's face, like concrete that had set. 'Rich?' she said. 'Why are you asking me these questions?'

'It was just . . . I just . . .'

He stopped.

'Rich?'

'See, you and Penny, you were the first,' he said, his eyes not on Beth, but on a patch he'd wiped clear on the window. 'You were the first kids in the town to go over the fence. I didn't know you then, not really, but this town's small, the school was small, and I heard about what happened, and I saw the way that people treated you. I heard the things the other kids would say. It was just fear. I think they were frightened by what you did, maybe jealous of how brave you both were, but mostly I think they were scared of having to face the same things as you. They didn't want to be left up there with that . . . that . . .' He paused, cleared his throat, unable to form the words. 'That thing.'

As the wind carved in again, battering the hollow buildings of the whaling station, Beth tried to work out where this was going.

'I was like you,' he said. 'I was never really taken in by the stories. I mean, if there are landmines out there, why have we never heard them go off? There are sheep wandering all over those hills. They should be setting them off all the time. But I wasn't taken in by the idea that there was some monster up there either. I didn't believe in monsters.'

Beth squeezed Richard's hand again.

'What's going on, Rich?'

'I went up there because of you,' he said. 'People talked about the Brink, and I didn't believe them, but when you and Penny came back, and I saw the look in your eyes, I thought, "The only way I'm going to find out the truth about what's going on up there is by going myself." So that's what I did. I went up myself. But what I never told you was that I did it differently from you and Penny: I didn't go up late evening or at night. I went up in the middle of the day.'

Beth shuffled closer. 'Did you see something else?'

'On the other side of the fence, it starts to gradually slope down. You would have seen that, even in the dark. There's all this marshland, these huge bogs; there's walls of scree from Mount Strathyde. The slope, it eventually goes all the way down to the sea, but it must be three or four miles across. It's vast.' He stopped, watching the wheels of an overturned tractor spin. 'I walked for an hour and nothing happened. There was no monster. There was nothing out there at all. I walked all the way down, almost to the sea, and then I came back up again. On the way up, I went a different route, staying parallel to the fence, but a couple of miles across from it.'

'What did you see?' Beth asked again.

Richard didn't answer straight away. He looked at her, something moving in his eyes, and placed a hand to his head, his beanie shifting, some of his red hair escaping.

'Do you know what a tarn is?' he said.

'Yes, it's a mountain lake.'

'Right.' He nodded. 'Right. Out in the Brink, if you head towards Mount Strathyde rather than towards the sea, you eventually get to this tarn. It's hidden away, about halfway up. It's walled in on all sides by peaks, and there's only one way in and one way out of it, up a thin scree path. But, once you're inside, it's like being in this huge coliseum of hills. It's stunning.'

'What's that got to do with Penny?'

He glanced at her, running his fingers – cut, bruised, oil-stained – across his mouth, as if he wasn't sure how to express himself – or maybe didn't want to.

'There's a cabin there,' he said.

'A cabin?'

'A wooden cabin. It's on the far side; the opposite side to the way in and out. When I saw it, I started heading up the scree path, towards the tarn. I was going to walk around the lake, get closer to the cabin and see who it belonged to. But at the top of the path, as it opened out, my foot caught on something and I fell over.'

The wind ripped in again.

'I fell over a length of tripwire,' Richard said.

'Tripwire?'

'As soon as I touched it, I set something off.'

Outside, things crashed and snapped and moaned.

'There was this series of short, fast clicks. Click, click, click. Click, click, click. I could hear them coming from somewhere close by, so I looked around and I found a box – like, a receiver – hidden among some rocks. It was flashing red, on and off.'

They stared at each other.

'So what did you do?' Beth asked.

'I ran.'

'Back to the fence?'

'Yes.' He spoke quietly, his gaze fixed on the sea. 'But I only made it about thirty feet when I lost my footing on the scree. I was so scared. I was running so fast. I fell over, into some of the rocks, and there was this kind of ravine at the edge. It fell away about six or seven feet into a stream. I saw them down there.'

'Saw what?'

He paused. 'There was a telescope there. And an anorak.'

'A telescope?'

'Yes. Like people use for stargazing. But it had been there a long time. It was covered in mud and moss. So was the anorak. That was orange and really old, filthy, rotten. It clung to the rocks at the edge of the stream. Even if I'd been able to get down, I don't think I could have peeled it off without it disintegrating. So I just left them both there, got up on my feet again, and ran.' He faded out, the emotion starting to tremor in his throat. 'Maybe fifteen minutes after that, maybe more, I heard the noise.'

'The noise?'

'The noise,' Richard repeated, and this time she got it. The noise. The noise that she and Penny had heard the night they'd gone over the fence.

The noise the monster made.

'It seemed to be coming from the direction of the fence,' he said, 'but I didn't know where else to go. I didn't know how else to get home. So I just ran. I ran so fast for the fence I could barely even breathe.'

They both stared at each other.

'I never really put it together until I met you, Beth; until you showed me those pictures of you and Penny as kids. Do you remember that?'

'Yeah. That was a few months back.'

'Right. You remember there was a picture of Penny in there?'

343

'Which one?'

'She was with her dad. On his knee.'

'I remember the picture, yeah. So what?'

There was a lull filled by doors fanning open and smashing shut again; by machinery tinkling and clanging; by the creak of the whale-oil tanks as they shifted gently against their scaffolding.

'Rich?'

Finally, he ripped his gaze away from the windscreen. 'In the photograph you showed me, Penny's dad was wearing the same anorak.'

'What?'

'The anorak I saw, it belonged to Penny's dad.'

'Are you . . .' She stopped. 'Are you sure?'

But then she remembered the anorak in the picture: it was orange.

'When I got back to the fence,' Richard was saying, his fingers clinging tightly to Beth's, 'they were waiting for me. My dad. Your dad. As soon as they could see me, they told me to hurry, to run as fast as I could, and once I got there, they helped me climb over, and I thought I was safe.' One of his eyes began to well up. He wiped at it with the back of his hand, but more tears began to form. 'But I wasn't safe. As soon as they got me on to the right side of the fence, my dad picked me up and slammed me against his car, and he said, "What the fuck did you think you were doing?" He was so angry. "You know not to go out into the Brink. You know how dangerous it is. You heard about those girls. You could have been killed." They punished me like they punished you. They brought me back to the fence that night and left me there, and it . . . it was . . .' He sniffed. 'It was there.'

Beth squeezed his hand.

He took a moment, trying to quell his emotions. 'It came all the way up to the fence.' He cleared his throat. 'I saw it in the shadows, out of the corner of my eye. I heard it. I thought I could feel its breath on the back of my neck. But you know what the weird thing was?'

'What?'

'When Dad came to pick me up the next morning, it looked like he'd been crying. He untied me from the fence and hugged me, and he told me he loved me.'

'He didn't ever do that normally?'

'No, it's not that.'

'Then what?'

'You said Jack did the same when he came back to get you and Penny. It wasn't the hug – it was what else Dad said to me. He took me straight from there all the way out here.' Richard pointed to the whaling station. 'That was the first time I ever came here: when I was sixteen. He brought me all the way out here because it's as far away from Sophia as it's possible to get, and he turned to me, and he had tears in his eyes, and he said, "How far around the tarn did you get?"'

Beth leaned back a little.

'He started telling me about Penny. He said that she was going to the UK when she was sixteen, but they weren't worried because even if she told anyone over there about the monster, who would believe her? But he said I was different. He said I'd been further into the Brink than anyone else had ever been, and now people on the islands were concerned about me. He meant I'd seen more than just the monster. And that was when it got weird. He started saying to me, "Don't leave the island. If you up and leave now, they'll think you're running. So you need to stay and you need to keep quiet about the tarn. If you don't, I might not be able to protect you."'

'Protect you?' Beth said. 'Why would he need to protect you?'

Richard didn't respond straight away, his fingers tightening around Beth's as if he were slipping and trying to hold on. 'I don't know,' he said eventually, 'but I looked at the tears in my dad's eyes, and it was like I could see something else — the real reason he was crying.' He faded out.

Rain flecked against the windscreen.

'It was like he thought the worst was still to come for me.'

## 52

Beyond the noise of the air conditioning, we both tried to process Beth's recollection of the conversation she'd had with Richard Kite – *Richard Presley* – at the whaling station. 'It's something about that cabin,' she said, looking at me. 'It's hiding a secret; and our dads, they both know what it is.'

'What about the monster?' I asked her.

She frowned. 'What about it?'

'You still think it's real?'

'We've already been over this.'

'They laid tripwire across the entrance to the tarn.'

'So?'

'So doesn't that suggest to you that Bill Presley, your dad, whoever else – they're doing anything they can to stop people from getting up to that cabin?'

'The monster isn't made up.'

'It's a story they invented to keep people out.'

'It isn't.'

'Beth, think about what you're say–'

'Don't tell me to think about what I'm *saying*!' she fired back, and then stopped, realizing she'd allowed her voice to get too loud. 'You weren't there.'

'Did you actually see it?'

'*Yes.* How many fucking times do I have to tell you?'

'No, I meant, clearly. Did you see it there, in front of

347

you, in the full glare of torchlight? Or did you only catch glimpses?' I stopped, watching her. 'Have you ever thought about the reasons why your dad might tie you to that fence with your back to it, rather than tie you to it so you could see out into the Brink?'

She didn't reply.

'If he wanted to prove the monster was real, why not let you see it?'

Her head dropped to her chest. I didn't blame her for believing in it – for still believing in it, even after Richard had told her about the tarn and the cabin – because, that night at the Brink, she'd been a frightened, confused child in a place where rumours and lies had found a breeding ground. Afterwards, no one had tried to convince her otherwise; in fact, the opposite: plenty of others in the town slowly began to believe the same thing. But there was no monster.

Or, at least, not one from any fairy tale.

As delicately as I could, I leaned into her and said, 'You told me Richard was too scared to leave the islands because of the warning his dad had given him – so what changed his mind?'

She eyed me for a moment, still pissed off.

'Rich found something,' she said eventually.

'What?'

'This was last December,' she said. 'He was having trouble sleeping, so he went downstairs to make some tea and found his dad out cold at the kitchen table. He was drunk. Rich said his dad was drinking more and more. Every night he was passing out like that.'

It sounded like Bill Presley was on a downward spiral – but from what?

'His dad had left his laptop open,' Beth said. 'There was an application on it. An instant messenger.'

*The Red Tree IM*. It had to be.

'Who had Richard's dad been speaking to?'

'Roland Dell.'

I gripped the water bottle tighter.

'He was one of the men who came to see you earlier,' she said.

'I know. I've met him before. What were they talking about?'

'Penny.'

She almost whispered the name, as if it were too painful to voice. I remembered what she'd said to me earlier: *I don't think Penny disappeared. I think she was killed.* I'd been uncertain then if she was guessing, or basing her opinion on some piece of information she hadn't told me about. I realized now it was the latter. She was well aware of what had happened to her sister – because Richard had told her.

*He'd seen the truth on his dad's laptop.*

'Rich's dad must have been typing drunk. He kept saying they would go to hell for what they did. That's what he wrote: *We'll go to hell for what we did.* When Rich leaned over him and started scrolling through the conversation, to try and find out more, he discovered they'd been talking about Penny . . .'

'They mentioned her by name?'

'No, they used her initials. PB. They talked about how she'd been missing since 2014. But Dell said it like Penny wasn't missing, but something worse.'

I tried to join the dots.

349

I thought of Penny's father, of how Caleb Beck had been linked, by Penny, to the money that Dell had passed through the school. *We'll go to hell for what we did*. Penny's father was dead, that much seemed obvious – the question now was how much Dell, Bill Presley and Jack Kilburn knew about it. Whatever the truth, if Presley was involved, the corruption was endemic in Sophia and spread all the way to the police.

'Have you ever met Dell?'

She shook her head. 'Not personally, no.'

'But you know of him?'

'My dad knows him.'

'How?'

'Dad, Bill Presley, Roland Dell, a guy called Anthony Jessop – they all grew up on the islands together in the seventies and eighties. Dell wasn't born there, though – he just moved to the islands when his old man became governor. I don't know much more than that.'

With that, something else fell into place: why Dell seemed so conflicted about Penny's murder. *I wouldn't have chosen that end for her*, he'd told me. She was the stepdaughter of a man he'd grown up with. Dell would have moved to the UK in 1984, the year Penny had been born. He wouldn't have known what she looked like as a grown woman, which was how she'd managed to turn the tables on him and convince him she was called Corrine Wilson. It was how she'd been able to dig around in Dell's life and find a connection back to her father.

'There was this rumour about Rich's dad.'

I tuned back in. 'About Bill Presley?'

'Yes. But Rich wasn't the one that told me.'

'Who told you?'

'I don't know. I can't remember. But people talk. That's all they do in Sophia: they talk.'

'So what was the rumour?'

'This was from way back, when I was still a baby, so I don't know if it's true or not, but there were these rumours about Dell and Bill Presley. Basically, Dell moved to London when he was sixteen, and would then come back for summer holidays because his father was still governor. Anyway, apparently, when Dell came back at the end of his first year of university, Bill Presley was seen in town early one morning, in the back alley behind the pub. He was just sitting there, on the ground, crying. Like, *really* crying. Most people just assumed he'd spent the whole evening there; that he was still drunk from the night before. I mean, it might have been summer back in the UK but it was winter on the islands, and in the middle of winter the sun doesn't come up until 9 a.m., so it was dark and quite hard to see him. But apparently it wouldn't have been outside the realms of possibility for Bill Presley, even in his twenties, to be so pissed he hadn't made it home.' She took a moment, looking up at me. 'But some people said he wasn't drunk at all. They said Bill Presley never even went *into* the pub the evening before; that no one had seen him for the whole night. In fact, one of Bill's neighbours supposedly saw him leaving his house at six that morning. He'd been crying then as well – and not only that. There was blood on his coat.'

'Blood?'

'On his sleeves.'

I tried to process that, to put it together. Dell had

returned to the islands in his summer holidays. At some point around then, Bill Presley had been spotted, in tears, with blood on the sleeves of his coat. Presley told Dell they were all going to hell for what they did: he meant himself, Dell, Jack Kilburn and maybe this Anthony Jessop guy too. And the thing that looped it all together was something Beth had said, but didn't seem to realize the significance of.

Dell returned for the holidays after his first year of university, which would have made him nineteen at the time. It meant he'd returned to Sophia in 1987.

The same year Penny's dad went missing.

## 53

'Penny got a job at the school in order to investigate Dell, right?'

Beth nodded. 'I think so, yes.'

'So what do you think first made her suspect him?'

'Penny's dad and Roland Dell's dad used to be friendly,' she said. 'You can find all these pictures of them together at social events if you go back and look at old issues of the *Empress Express*. So maybe it was that.'

I watched her. 'Or maybe it wasn't?'

'Maybe it was something I told her,' she said. 'When I was really young, my dad got drunk once and started telling me that Caleb Beck had been rich. I told Pen about it, but she didn't believe me. I guess we didn't think much more about it after that because it never seemed like Fiona had been left anything by Penny's dad. We never lived in a big house, never had nice cars or foreign holidays, not in the entire time I was growing up. But then, a few months before Pen left the islands for good, Dad suddenly bought himself this brand-new Land Rover. Like, *brand new*.'

'How did he say he could afford it?'

'He said he'd come into a bit of money.'

It made sense straight away.

Beth had said this happened a few months before Penny left the islands, which would have been August or September 2000. In September 2000, Dell used the Red

Tree to funnel money into three accounts in the Empress Islands. What if one of the accounts was Jack Kilburn's? What if the other two had belonged to Bill Presley and Anthony Jessop? The four men had grown up together – could they have stolen Caleb Beck's money together? What if they'd killed him for it?

'So Penny didn't trust your dad?'

'I think she stopped trusting him the night he left us up there at the fence; and I think, the older she got, the more she wanted to know what had happened to her own dad.' She shrugged. 'I don't know for sure. Maybe it doesn't even matter now. But I wouldn't be surprised if she started looking into Dad's accounts and, sometime down the line, when she'd already been in the UK for a while, she finally found a connection to Roland Dell.'

*A connection that got her killed.*

Across the corridor from me, Beth moved position against the wall, the glow from one of the night lights cutting across her, painting one side of her face a pale grey. As I watched her, I turned and looked at Marek. He'd hardly moved.

'The morning after he found that IM conversation on his dad's laptop, Rich came to see me,' she said quietly. 'He told me everything. He told me about Penny.' Beth stopped, sniffed. She had a hand across her mouth, as if she were trying to hold her head up, and it softened the sound of her words. 'He said he'd been to the library,' she went on, 'using the Internet there to look for stories about Penny. Anything he could find about her disappearance.'

Now I understood why Richard was being shown photos of Penny in his sessions with Naomi Russum. In the days after he and Beth fled the islands, Bill Presley, Jack Kilburn and Anthony Jessop – with Dell pulling the strings from London – must have found out about Richard being at the library that morning. It wouldn't have taken much to discover what he was looking at: his searches for Penny would have been in the Internet history. That was when they realized they had a problem. They must have thought Richard had found out the truth: that Penny was silenced for something she found out about Caleb Beck; that she'd caught a glimpse of why her dad had disappeared, entombed deep in the islands' past. The irony was, at that stage, Richard hadn't known as much as they thought, but – with Beth in tow, with her tenacity – he would soon find out.

But there was something more disturbing: Jack Kilburn's involvement in Penny's murder. He'd pretty much brought her up. Fiona had died in 2011, but there was nothing to suggest that – before and after her mum passed on; and that night at the Brink aside – Kilburn hadn't been anything less than a loving stepfather to Penny, even if she'd grown wary of him. Yet he'd sanctioned her death – or, at least, accepted it as inevitable and necessary – and watched from afar as Marek killed a woman every bit as much of a daughter to him as Beth. How could any parent do that?

'Rich didn't find any stories with Penny's name in it,' Beth said, bringing me back into the moment, 'but he told me about this woman who was murdered in London, and left on a railway line.'

*The same story I'd found.*

I watched Beth as her eyes filled up.

'They cut out her tattoo so no one would know it was her – didn't they?'

There was no way to make it any easier for her.

'Yes,' I said. 'I'm so sorry, Beth.'

She swallowed and looked away, into the dark of the corridor. I heard her sniffing, saw her wiping her eyes, and then her face came back to me and it had changed: it was streaked with tears, but it was fierce.

'We talked about going to the police in St George,' she said, her words sharper, 'because Rich's dad ran the station at Sophia, so we couldn't go there. But Bill Presley knew the guys in St George too. And seven thousand miles from anyone else who could make a difference, who might be able to help us, it didn't seem we had any choice.'

'You stowed away on the *Olympia*.'

She wiped her eyes and it left a trail at the side of her face. 'It wasn't like we could just walk off the islands. We're surrounded by miles of sea. Plus, the people at Blake Point, at the harbour there, and the people in the airport down the road, they either knew us or they'd recognize us. So I came up with the idea of using the ship.'

'How did you get on-board?'

'I managed to work out the *Olympia*'s schedule from the documents they had at the yard. They kept a lot of paperwork because we organized day trips for the passengers who came ashore. It basically worked on five separate rotations: one eighty-day trip, one fifty-day, one eighty, one fifty, one eighty. That added up to three hundred and forty days, and they spent the other twenty-five in dry dock for maintenance. It meant the boat came to the Empress Islands five times a year, and – when I looked at the timetable – I could see that the next opportunity for us was only a week away. So Rich spent the time gathering up all our supplies, and our clothes, and I spent the time getting the rest of it.'

'The rest of it?'

'Our uniforms and IDs.'

'You pretended you worked on the boat?'

'No.' She shook her head. 'We didn't need to. A couple of the guys at the yard had been cleared by the security team on the *Olympia* because they'd been providing day trips for passengers for years. The ship always arrived early in the morning at Blake Point and anchored for the night, so they gave the guys these ID cards that let them come on to the boat first thing and hard-sell the trips to passengers directly. The IDs didn't have photographs on them, but when you ran them through the scanner at the ship's security check-in, it showed the name of the person they belonged to. So on the second day the boat was anchored, in the afternoon, when the men from the yard had taken groups out to see the whales, we took a tender across to the *Olympia*. I pretended one of the guys had left a ledger on-board the day before and he'd asked me to come and get it, and because we passed through the crew entrance, because we turned up in T-shirts with the yard's logo on, name badges, clipboards full of paperwork, because we kept them talking, they never paid attention to the bags we were carrying, and never looked at their screens. They never saw that the name on my ID was male.' She stopped, took a breath. 'It was weird. We'd spent the week before so nervous about it, about what would happen if we got caught. We went over and over what we were going to say, thinking up scenarios, throwing questions at one another. I barely slept at all. But, in the end, we just breezed right through.'

'Where did you hide out?'

'Some nights, we just stayed in the restaurant and night-club area because there were always people around and no one would look at us twice. The next day, we'd catch up on our sleep during daylight hours – at the pools, or on the sofas in the coffee lounge. Other nights, when it was warmer, we slept outside on sun loungers. After a while, I managed to swipe a housekeeping uniform and, when no one was around, I'd put it on and go to the laundry. I'd use the rotas to see what rooms were being used at what time. A few nights, we managed to find unoccupied rooms to sleep in.'

It was why she'd been wearing the uniform when she was captured on CCTV: eventually, the laundry would become a place for her to store things – food and supplies – but back then it was the place where the rota was, where they could find out which rooms were free.

'It went on like that for weeks,' she continued. 'We sailed up through South America, the Caribbean, and we never had any problems. We knew we were going to get off at Southampton, so we just had to sit tight.' She stopped. The stir of a memory; a flicker of unease. 'But then we docked at New York.'

'What happened there?'

'We started thinking that we'd made it. I mean, we were six days from the UK. We pretty much *had* made it. But as we were leaving port, I left Rich upstairs on the sun deck and went to get us a coffee, and I found this guy in there, asking the staff questions. I stood there in the queue, waiting for our drinks, when he started moving along the queue towards me. He was showing a whole bunch of photographs – and they were all of me and Rich.'

A whole bunch, not just one. Dell must have drafted Marek in after Presley, Kilburn and Jessop had failed to find Beth and Richard anywhere on the islands; and then, shortly after boarding the *Olympia*, Marek – with Larry Grobb's help – would have been through the CCTV feeds on the ship and found evidence of Beth and Richard everywhere.

'The man asking questions was him,' Beth said.

She was looking at Marek.

'What happened after that?'

'I backed out, slowly as I could, trying not to come to anyone's attention, and I ran up to the top deck and grabbed Rich. We were so scared. We'd spent the entire three weeks it had taken to come up from the islands being lulled into this false sense of security. We'd got cosy. We didn't have any back-up plans because we'd started to think we weren't going to need one.' She stopped, shaking her head, her eyes moving from Marek back to me. 'I didn't know the ship then like I know it now. Now, I've got all my things divided up: pieces of my life in different places; stuff I'll need in case an emergency hits; safe places for things I care about.' She paused, a tremor in her throat. *Things she cared about.* I knew she meant the picture I'd found in the laundry of Penny and her as kids. 'Back then, though, we had no idea how to stay hidden.'

'So where did you go?'

'For the next six days, we just kept moving. We went to

the cinema and sat there in the dark at the back, watching the same films over and over again. I mean, I must have seen *North by Northwest* about seventy times. We hid out in the toilets, in the laundry, in the corners of restaurants and bars, and when the nightclubs opened, we went in there. We took turns to keep lookout. We changed as often as we could, so we didn't get seen in the same outfits all the time, and we used the swimming pool as our bath. We'd wake before the sun was up and go to the pool, trying to keep clean, trying to act normal, because I figured anything *ab*normal would mean people noticed us. If we stank, if we were unclean or acting weirdly, they'd remember us.'

When he was found, Richard had traces of calcium hypochlorite on his hands – chlorine powder – and I'd already made the connection between that and the swimming pools on the ship. But now I was seeing the full extent of the story: the two of them, him and Beth, washing themselves in the pool every day.

'That carried on pretty much all the way into Southampton harbour,' she said. 'We saw the British coastline for the first time at four in the morning, and the boat was due to dock at half five. That time of the day, there weren't a lot of people around, but even so we played it safe. We thought it would be better if we headed back to the cinema and hid out in there. If he was still on the lookout for us, he'd probably assume that we were going to head upstairs.'

But she knew Marek better now. So did I.

He wouldn't have assumed that at all.

'He was waiting for us,' she said. 'The cinema had

become a good hiding place. You could be anonymous in there.' Her words fell away: six days of anonymity were rendered worthless the moment he found them. 'He had access to the cameras on the ship, and we were conscious of that from the moment he started showing our pictures around – we kept a low profile, stayed out of view, kept on the move. But that cinema, it became a minor routine without us even thinking about it. We felt safe in there, so it was one of the few places we'd gone to more than once or twice.' A pained expression gripped her face. 'The moment we saw him, we ran – we both just *ran* – but then, somehow, we got separated. I don't know when it happened but suddenly Rich wasn't there any more.'

'What did you do?'

'I went back to try and find him.'

She blinked a couple of times, her eyes on a space between us where I'd left the remnants of the food she'd given me: empty wrappers, a half-finished packet of crisps, crumbs spilling out.

'I couldn't find him on the deck we'd been on, so I moved up,' she said. 'I kept moving up, floor by floor, going to the places we'd hidden out in, the places that *I* would have returned to if *I'd* been him. Finally, I got to the lido deck. It was quiet. It was still very early. I worked my way from one end to the other, looking around the pools, the changing rooms, the toilets, and then I found them. They were both below me.'

'Below you?'

'They'd got on to this narrow balcony in the corner of deck eight.' She stopped and her smile was so bereft it seemed to draw the light from the corridor. 'Rich had obviously got down there and hidden, but the thing with Rich was that he wasn't devious enough for stuff like that. Everything we'd done in the lead-up to that moment, all the hiding we'd done over the course of three weeks, I'd driven all of it. His brain, it just wasn't wired that way: deceit, secrets – those things didn't come naturally to him. He thought that the balcony was the best place to hide – but what it ended up doing was boxing him in. He was trapped.'

Very softly, almost sighing the words into existence, she said, 'He grabbed Rich. They struggled and then Rich slipped over. It had been raining, so there were these patches of water everywhere, and when Rich lost his footing, when he went down, he hit the railings with the side of his face. He hit it so hard I heard it, even above the sounds of the ship. He hit the railings and then, a second later, he hit the floor and then I could see blood on his cheek.'

*It was how Richard had got his injuries.*

'Did the impact knock Richard unconscious?'

'No. He tried to stand, but kind of staggered sideways, and' – she glanced at Marek – 'he stepped back from Rich, as if he knew it was all over.' Beth's words fell away, her hand open at her side like she was trying to stop her boyfriend from going over the edge. 'I don't think he expected Rich to go overboard. But it all happened so fast. Rich brushed against the railings and lost his balance, and when he reached out for the railings again, his hand went over the side. And then, before I knew it, the rest of him had followed. I can see it so clearly. He was there, and then he wasn't. It was like I blinked and he stopped existing. I didn't hear a sound when he hit the water. He didn't scream. There was nothing. He was just gone.'

The sounds of the corridor seemed to die around us.

'I didn't find out that he was alive until much later. He was always a really good swimmer, so it must have been instinct kicking in when he hit the water. Like, this will to survive, this automatic mechanism or whatever. That must have been what got him to shore before he finally blacked out. I sneaked on to the computers on the lower deck a few weeks after that, and I was amazed when I read about him online. I couldn't believe it.'

'A few weeks later? So you never tried to leave at Southampton?'

'No.' Her open hand slowly closed into a fist. 'I knew I couldn't leave the boat at Southampton. I knew Marek would be waiting for me. If he'd used the cameras to find us, that meant he had the security team in his pocket — and that meant he'd put people at the exits. I knew I was trapped.'

'So you stayed on-board the whole time?'

'Yes. That was how I discovered places like that.' She looked up at the open air vent. 'After a while, a few weeks, a month, I think they believed that I'd somehow got off the ship at a port and they stopped looking for me on-board. But, by then, I didn't know where to go or what to do. I was scared.'

'You didn't think about going to see Richard?'

'He had no memory — what would have been the point? He was the "Lost Man" by then.' She smiled for a moment, but it was a distortion of one, meagre and heartbroken. 'You know what the really strange thing was? I had no

363

idea that he'd lost his memory until I read about it on the Internet. But there *was* this moment, before he went over the railings, when he kind of turned in my direction, almost looked up at me, and his eyes . . .' She stopped. 'I know there's no way I could *see* the memory loss, that it could never be visible on his body. But I swear to you, after he hit his head, his eyes changed. It was like they belonged to someone else. My Rich was gone.'

I stared at her for a moment, trying to understand everything I'd heard, to put it into some sort of order, and – after a while – both of us seemed to become aware of something. We looked at each other, and then out along the corridor to the office.

Marek was gone.

## 54

We'd taken our eye off him for what seemed like no time at all.

But it had been enough.

Beth yanked the gun from her belt, held it up in front of her and started to move. I followed. The closer we edged to the glass, the more I felt the tension kick in. There was no sign of him between the desks in the office. We could see under a few, through those to others, and he wasn't beneath any of them.

So where the hell was he?

It would have taken him time and effort to pick the locks on the door, if he even had any picks in the first place; and if he'd somehow come out of the office, we'd have seen him. The movement would have registered in our peripheral vision.

Beth made a beeline for the key she'd thrown away. It took her a couple of seconds and then she located it, bringing it back to the door.

I told her to stop.

The key was already in the lock, her fingers over the handle. She turned to look at me, a mixture of frustration and confusion on her face, and then I gestured to a tall, thin metal cabinet in the office, right at the back of the room. Next to it was the teddy bear, the MANAGER sign strung around its neck.

*In there*, I mouthed, pointing to the cabinet.

Its doors were slightly ajar.

Beth nodded, grabbed the handle and opened up the office. An air-conditioning unit just above the metal cabinet was pumping air downwards, making its doors move faintly in the breeze. It was hard to see all the way inside, but it didn't look like there were shelves in there, and if there weren't shelves, it was roomy enough for someone to hide in.

Yet I stopped at the door to the office.

Something didn't feel right.

Beth glanced at me once, then moved ahead, her arms in a V at the front of her body, the gun absolutely still. I saw how confident she was with the weapon, and imagined – as the daughter of a farmer – she'd grown up around them. I was the son of a farmer and I'd done the same, although my experience with real firearms, rather than air rifles and pellet guns, had come in the time since, in moments like this, on cases like this, with men like Marek.

I held up a hand, trying to get her attention, but she was already gone, two or three feet ahead of me, working her way through a route laid out by the desks.

I'd never been in the office before and Beth had only been in to rip the phones out of the walls, nothing else. After she'd locked Marek in, she'd thrown the key away. I was too far away at the time, at the opposite end of the corridor, checking out the restaurants, the passengers beyond the security suite; Beth would have been focused on the phones and then on Marek himself, on making certain he couldn't get out.

*Not on what was above him.*

I looked up.

The ceiling – a series of eighteen square panels – was being replaced, and three of the panels were missing. Above the ones that had been taken out, in the cavity, I could see insulation, covered in shiny black plastic, and rows of white iron joists. I had a second to glance at the desk directly beside me, a footprint visible on the top, and then I saw him: he was on one of the joists, shrouded in shadow, ready to jump.

*Shit.*

He landed on top of me.

We crashed into the nearest desk. A computer went tumbling off the side, smashing against the floor, and as Marek's full weight pounded against me, it was like every breath of air left my body. Shock forked up my chest, stomach to throat, and then I felt an explosion behind my eyes. White spots. Blurring. Noise.

So much noise.

I tried to focus and, as I did, I realized that I couldn't feel Marek at all. He was gone, somewhere else, and I was hanging off the edge of the desk, bruises burning everywhere.

*Where had he gone?*

I tried to stand up, slightly dazed, unsure in which direction I was supposed to be facing, which direction he would come at me from, so I looked to where Beth had been.

The blood froze in my veins.

She was standing opposite me, the gun still up in front of her. Her arms were tremoring.

There were tears on her cheeks.

I realized then that the noise I'd heard as Marek landed on me wasn't in my head; it hadn't been a reaction to his body slamming against mine, or to the migraine I couldn't shift; it hadn't been dehydration or surprise.

It had been a gunshot.

In between us, Marek lay on his side, half slumped against the desk. His hand was clutching a wound at the bottom of his throat, blood spilling out between his fingers and running down his shirt. His eyes juddered, tried to shift to me, but he couldn't move them.

Slowly, his hand began to slip away.

His body slid sideways.

By the time he hit the floor, he was dead.

# 55

After a while, she started to calm down.

'You saved my life,' I said gently, but I wasn't sure if it really helped or not. I touched a hand to her arm, wary of making her uncomfortable. 'We need to get rid of him before the security team return. Are you able to help me?'

She hesitated for a moment, then nodded.

'Okay,' I said. 'I need you to go and get something.'

I told her what we needed, and she climbed back up into the vents. After she was gone, I filled a bucket full of water and started to scrub away the evidence of what had happened, cleaning up blood and dirt and debris.

Fifteen minutes later, Beth returned through the door of the security suite, wheeling a housekeeping cart. Together, we loaded Marek into it. It was awkward, difficult work, and — even knowing the sort of man he was, the things he'd done; even feeling like this kind of ending was everything he deserved — I felt guilt I couldn't quite suppress. As we folded him into the cart, compressing him enough that he fitted, Beth and I looked at each other and I saw her thoughts so clearly they might as well have been written on the wall behind her: *This is what Marek did to Penny.* He took her body and he squeezed it into an unnatural space, somewhere dark and narrow where he hoped it would never be discovered.

She became tearful again and this time I left her alone,

checking over the office once more, making sure I hadn't missed anything. I went into the interview room too, cleared any mess I'd left, and wiped down the surfaces – the doors, the desk, the chair. I spent some time with Marek's mobile phone, which was connected to the security team's Wi-Fi network, going through his inbox and emails, but there was only one message that caught my attention: it was from Roland Dell, received an hour ago, telling Marek that he was back on the Empress Islands and just about to take off on the Gulfstream. He said he would send the Gulfstream back for Marek once he'd landed in Cape Town and, after that, would be catching the 6.30 p.m. flight to Heathrow.

When Marek didn't turn up at the airport north of Sophia, and Dell's people there let him know, Dell would start to get a whiff that something was up. Whether he found out while he was still on the ground in Cape Town, or he found out once he was back in London, either way he would find out. But I couldn't worry about that for now. Instead, I pocketed the phone and waited for Beth to regain her poise again, even as the impact of what had happened remained bludgeoned across her face.

I dressed in a security outfit, Beth used a housekeeping uniform, and we left through the main door. She walked ahead of me as I pushed the trolley, eyes everywhere, focusing on the corners and corridors of a boat she'd come to know so well. I watched her survival instinct kick in as the adrenalin overrode any memories of what had gone before, and that carried us for a while. But then, in the silence of the elevator, we relaxed for a moment, and I saw a reflection of myself in the mirror and didn't like what looked back: this man who had cold-bloodedly loaded a human being into a cart; this man who was about to dump a body in the sea so no one would ever find it. When I glanced at Beth, I saw her wrestling with the same thoughts, her expression haunted.

We emerged on to the fourth accommodation deck, the place where I'd found the carrier bag in the laundry room, and Beth directed us down to the stern of the ship where she said there was a balcony, a kind of viewing gallery, that no one ever realized was there. She was right: a set of double doors led out to an empty terrace with some chairs at either end, none of which was overlooked by cabins.

I stared out across the dark ocean. The sun was coming up somewhere behind the clouds, and there was the merest hint of daylight, but mostly the morning was ashen and achromatic, and there was so much rain in the air, running in lines down the windows behind me, that it was hard to see much further than a mile out. We were still a couple of hours from Blake Point, but we were closer to the South Pole now than to Africa.

'What's the matter?' Beth said.

She sounded afraid, so I told her nothing was wrong even as the guilt still wrenched at me, and while she kept watch, I unloaded Marek. When his body flopped out on to the floor, I looked into the glaze of his eyes, wondered again if I would ever find peace in what we were doing, and then hauled him across the floor to the railings. I lifted him up, feeling the strain in my back, my legs, in the bruises on my arms and ribs; and after I pushed him over and threw his phone in after him, I looked down into the sea, into its churn, the waves forming and swelling and flattening out, and saw Marek vanish into the darkness of the ocean.

'I can't go back there,' Beth said quietly.

We were sitting inside my cabin. It had been ransacked. My laptop had been smashed to bits, notes that I'd left had either been ripped up or taken, and my clothes were strewn everywhere. But I still had my phone and the notebook I'd been carrying on me. Grobb and the security team hadn't bothered taking the phone because, in the belly of the boat with no signal and no Wi-Fi connection, it was a worthless lump of plastic. The notebook was the same: it represented no threat to anyone while I'd been locked in the room. Once Marek had finished with me and I was dead, he would have taken both and gone through them.

'I can't go back to the islands,' Beth said again. 'I can't go back there. When I left that place, I left it for good. I'd rather spend my days living in an air vent, eating leftovers from people's tables, than ever set foot in that town again.'

'It's not safe on the ship now.'

'It's not safe in Sophia either. They'll kill us both. They'll make you suffer.' She looked at the closet, at the door, back to me. 'Penny was as much of a daughter to my dad as I was, and they murdered her. I don't know how much he knew about it, but he knew about it. They left her body on that railway track, chunks of her skin cut out of her. I don't know why, or what she found out about Dad, about Bill Presley, about Roland Dell and what they did, but I'm telling you this: if they killed her to stop her from talking, you'd better believe they'd do the same to us.'

372

She was right. Beth didn't know what lay at the edge of the tarn in that cabin, but she knew her sister was killed for what she'd found out about Caleb Beck. She knew Penny's father had disappeared the same year Roland Dell came back to the islands on his summer break. She knew Dell had grown up with her dad, Bill Presley and Anthony Jessop. She already knew too much.

We both did.

A little while later, the sound of the ship like a low groan beyond the walls, she started pulling up the sleeve of her top. It took me a moment to work out what she was doing. She shoved it past her elbow and kept going, and then, finally, I saw it: the same tattoo Richard Kite had on his arm. The same one Penny had, that all three of them had.

*A silhouette of a bird in flight.*

'Penny got this tattooed on her arm a couple of months before she left,' Beth said. 'She was only sixteen at the time, but we had a guy on the islands who would do it for cash and never ask too many questions. I always wondered why. Why this image. We weren't really talking then, so I never asked her what it was, or what it meant, or why she'd got it done. But then I found out a few years later that it's a silhouette of an Arctic tern. Do you know what's special about them?'

'No,' I said.

'They've got the longest migration in the animal kingdom. They fly further than any other animal to get where they need to go.' She paused, looking down at her own version of the tattoo. 'So that's why me and Rich got one before we left. We were all migrating. We were all trying to leave this place.'

We sat there for a while, neither of us saying anything, both of us thinking about the tattoo, the reasons for getting it, and the ways in which the next three hours, twelve hours, a day, two days, were going to work. Whatever happened, though, we'd both made our positions clear: Beth was staying on the boat and would have to return to hiding until this was all over; and I was going ashore and needed a plan where I wasn't going to get stopped, spotted – or worse.

Because I'd travelled seven thousand miles.

And now I wasn't going back without the truth.

# PART FOUR

PART FOUR

# Extract from *No Ordinary Route: The Hidden Corners of Britain* by Andrew Reece

A weird thing happens a month after I get back to the UK. I have dinner with my old friend, the journalist and broadcaster Tomas Cassell – the man who'd basically kick-started my interest in the Empress Islands in the first place, and whose father had once been a pilot stationed at the now-defunct RAF base there – and he tells me he's mentioned the trip I made to some colleagues of his from a Spanish production company. One of the crew is from Argentina.

'He says you should look into Selina Torres,' Tomas tells me.

'Who?'

'Selina Torres.'

'I've never heard of her.'

'Exactly,' Tomas says. 'That's the point.'

Intrigued, I get him to set up a meeting with his Argentinian friend, a cameraman called Juan Cota. As we sit down a few days later, Juan hands me what looks like a police interview transcript and says, 'She was a friend of a

377

friend. Her case was quite famous for a while, but only in Argentina.'

I read the transcript.

OFFICER: When was the last time you saw your sister?

EMILIO TORRES: Two weeks ago. Thursday 16 July.

OFFICER: Did she seem okay?

EMILIO TORRES: Yes. She said she had to make a trip, but that it was only a short one. Two, three days, no more.

OFFICER: Was this a work trip?

EMILIO TORRES: Yes.

OFFICER: What does Selina do for a living?

EMILIO TORRES: She's an air hostess.

OFFICER: For which airline?

EMILIO TORRES: I don't know.

OFFICER: You don't know?

EMILIO TORRES: She never talks about her work. I've never seen her in uniform. I ask her what airline she works for, what routes she flies, and she doesn't want to talk about it.

OFFICER: Why would she do that?

EMILIO TORRES: Because I don't think she's really an air hostess.

'Rumour is,' Juan says, 'she went to the Empress Islands.'

Here's the truth: I never do look into Selina Torres, not properly. I try for a while, but then I start to hit dead ends and other things crop up - other paying jobs - and I kind of forget about her. So I don't know if Selina Torres went to the Empress Islands and disappeared there. I don't know if it's just another rumour birthed in an isolated community at the edge of the earth.

But put it this way: after everything I experienced there, especially in towns like Sophia, somehow it wouldn't surprise me.

# 56

In the rain, the islands were like ghosts.

They seemed to drift in the early morning light, there and gone again, the lights at the harbour blinking in and out of existence. I sat at one of the windows in the tender, an enclosed catamaran that doubled up as a lifeboat, and watched through a swipe I'd made in the condensation. Around me, some did the same, others talked among themselves. There were a few bursts of laughter, a hum of conversation, but mostly there was just the sound of the engine and the weather.

There were about eighty people on the boat. Almost all of them would be heading straight out of Blake Point to the breeding grounds, picking up organized tours that would take them to the whales, seals and penguins; to huge colonies of birds gathered in the clefts and ridges of the eastern islands. I looked around the boat, wondering if I was going to be the only one who wasn't doing that, whether it might raise suspicions, and then I returned my gaze to the harbour. The closer we got, the more I could see of what awaited: other, smaller boats tied to the jetty, bobbing on the waves; and then a group of men in red oilskins, beacons against the grey of the rain, waiting for us to arrive.

*Or maybe just waiting for me.*

It was just after 8 a.m. and, inside the hour, a Gulfstream

jet with Roland Dell on-board would be coming into Cape Town. Once it had landed and refuelled, he'd send it back to the islands to collect Alexander Marek. He'd probably also call Marek from the ground in South Africa to make sure everything went to plan. When he got no response from him, when none of the security team he'd paid off could find Marek anywhere on the ship, that would set the wheels in motion. Dell would guess that I was still alive, and he'd then get back in touch with his people on the island. And it seemed certain that those people were Bill Presley, Jack Kilburn and Anthony Jessop, because they were the ones that knew what he was hiding. I thought about whether I should have sent a message to Dell on Marek's phone before I'd tossed it into the sea – *everything's taken care of*, or *it's done*, or *it's been sorted*; something to try and buy myself time, or – even better – dupe Dell entirely. But it was too late now, and I wasn't convinced he'd have fallen for it anyway. I probably had ninety minutes, two hours at the most, before Presley, Kilburn and Jessop were put on alert, so it meant no one at the harbour would be waiting for me yet.

But despite that, as I returned my attention to the figures standing at the jetty, it didn't really settle my nerves.

Blake Point was built around a tiny curved bay: a few warehouses and workshops were off to the left, compacted into an area full of slipways and seaweed-strewn harbour walls; clustered to the right were a row of six fishermen's cottages, painted different colours, but salt-blanched and tired. There was a small patch of grass with a seven-foot stone recreation of Big Ben in the middle, some benches too, but as the rain swelled like the folds of a curtain, everything receded into the pallor of the day.

As we all started to file off, I kept my head down while taking in the faces that awaited. None of them looked familiar as we were directed down the jetty to a wooden prefab building with TOURS written on one of its windows. As most of the passengers began to head inside, I kept going: the jetty connected to a small stretch of road running the length of the harbour and, directly behind the cottages, I found a taxi rank. There was only one car, a mud-spattered Citroën estate, and when I approached, the driver's eyes followed me all the way to the back door of the vehicle, as if he couldn't quite believe he was getting a fare.

'How you doing, pal?' he said, as I got in. He was late forties, completely grey on top with a beard that was going the same way. 'Where can I take you?'

'Sophia,' I said.

We headed away from the harbour, following a two-lane road that slowly climbed its way into the mist which obscured Sophia from view. The higher we went, the thicker it got, but occasionally I could see dots of light up ahead, fluttering in and out of existence. Once or twice, something else became visible too: the hills above the town and the ridges of Mount Strathyde.

Mostly, though, I just watched fields passing on my left and right, endless squares on repeat, some empty, some filled with sheep. Two miles from Sophia, I saw reindeer for the first time, and then guanaco, their long necks poking out over the top of a line of bushes. In *No Ordinary Route*, I remembered reading that there were no native mammals on the islands; everything had been introduced. People could own dogs, but had to apply for a permit, and there were no cats as they posed a threat to the indigenous bird population. I knew all of those things made the islands different from the UK, but as I watched the farmland and pasture go by in a blur of green, it was hard to separate the two: I was seven thousand miles away, but from the windows of the taxi, I could easily have been at home.

At the edges of Sophia, things gradually started to change. There were no trees on the islands, other than the ones that had been planted, so the buildings were all constructed from imported timber and finished in tin. Red and green metal roofs were everywhere, scattered in asymmetrical lines, the layout of the town formless and difficult to get a handle on.

The place seemed like a maze, its narrow streets filled with clapboard walls and sash windows, with enclosed porches and metal picket fences. It could have been pretty – maybe was once, a long time ago – and it put me in mind of the villages close to where I'd grown up in south Devon: their tight corners, their tricky passing spaces, the way they climbed and descended and almost never ran flat. But the villages of my childhood had been picturesque, neat and elegant, and here the buildings looked grubby, stained, the windows opaque with all the grime and salt and dust that blew in from the ocean and off the mountain. In the middle of the town, the shops and the only pub were run-down. Paint was peeling, wood was blanched, metal rusting. I saw a community centre beyond the pub and an unattractive utilitarian school building. Everywhere was deserted.

'Here we are, then,' the taxi driver said.

He pulled up outside a supermarket called Empress Stores. In its window I could see Mount Strathyde reflected, a towering presence over the town, its crest like the vertebrae of some sleeping leviathan.

'You sure you want to be dropped off here? I mean, I'm from St George, so I'm biased, but it's a lot more fun than Sophia.' He smiled, but then the smile disappeared as he looked out at the high street. I watched him, his eyes skirting the buildings. 'It's just, not many people come here. Certainly not mainlanders like you.'

I looked along the row of the shops, to the streets and alleys that coiled off the empty high street in intricate zigzags; I glanced at the hills beyond the town, to the peaks of Strathyde again, to the trails marked along its flanks like wounds.

I thought of Beth, and of Penny.

I thought of Richard.

'It's fine,' I said.

*This is exactly where I need to be.*

## 57

The driver directed me to a bed and breakfast a couple of streets away, run by a couple in their sixties. It was on a narrow, sloping road, with views south across the town. The accommodation was small and old-fashioned – floral duvet sets; vinyl wallpaper; furniture that creaked even when it wasn't being used – but it was clean. I didn't plan to be here longer than I needed to.

There was no television and no Wi-Fi, but I had a signal on my phone and the 3G worked, if slowly, so I went hunting for Bill Presley, Jack Kilburn and Anthony Jessop. Jessop was the hardest of the three to find anything on, but Bill Presley I found almost instantly.

His photograph was on the Royal Empress Islands Police Force website, in a gallery listing staff. The force had twenty serving police officers – thirteen constables, two sergeants, two inspectors, two superintendents and a chief constable. There was a superintendent each at the St George and Sophia stations, of which Presley was one, and – because both towns, though on different islands, were central in terms of the archipelago's geography – St George looked after the eastern islands, and the Sophia police had responsibility for those to the west of it.

Even so, Sophia was a much smaller station and a much smaller force. Its building was located about a quarter of a mile from the bed and breakfast, inside a converted sheep-shearing shed. It was north of me, so I couldn't see it from my window, but there was a photo of it online and it looked like it would be hard to miss: built on the same slope that the B&B was on, it was perched on big, trunk-sized stilts, parking bays below it, and made from bright blue corrugated-metal sheets.

I studied Presley's picture.

There wasn't much of Richard in his face, except maybe a hint in the eyes and around the mouth, and the same hair colour. But Presley had started to lose his, a circle of it vanishing from the top of his skull, so what remained took on the appearance of a red halo. Elsewhere, though, he and his son shared more similarities: they were built the same way – trim, in good shape – and they had the same slight flaw in one of their front teeth, a canine that grew crookedly.

I saved the picture and started on Jack Kilburn. According to Beth, he ran the town council, so I used that as a jumping-off point. But while I managed to source some articles from the *Empress Express*, all of which carried his name – reports of council meetings, of motions that had been carried – there were no pictures of him. When I tried to recalibrate the search and went looking for him as a farmer, I got nothing; when I used Beth as the foundation for another search, thinking Kilburn may have featured in stories about her going missing from the islands, quoted as a concerned parent, there was nothing. The whole thing seemed to have been missed by the paper, or was maybe never brought to their attention in the first place.

In the end, I only found one thing: a small obituary in the *Express*.

b. 20 April 1959, d. 13 November 2011

Fiona Kilburn, who died yesterday after a short battle with cancer, aged fifty-two, was a well-known figure in <u>Sophia</u>, thanks in part to her work in raising money for the <u>Empress Hospital</u> extension. Not a native islander – she emigrated from <u>London</u> with her family in October 1984 – she nevertheless embraced life here and, indeed, found herself written into the pages of its history – though perhaps not for the happiest of reasons – when her first husband, Caleb Beck, the <u>Cabot Island</u> farmer, disappeared in July 1987. Although Beck was never located and was eventually declared dead, Fiona found happiness again in January 1993 when she married another local farmer – and current Sophia town council chairman – <u>Jack Kilburn</u>. She is survived by Jack, her daughter Penny, who lives and works in the UK, and her stepdaughter Beth.

Everything that was underlined in the article led to a page full of related stories. I clicked on Jack Kilburn, but all I found were articles I'd already seen, and realized I was going around in circles. I was also beginning to flag. I'd been up since the early hours of the morning and hadn't slept properly for the best part of three days. I still had a headache. It felt like every inch of my chest, back and arms was bruised. I wanted to make the best use of the time available to me, but I knew if I wasn't functioning properly, if I could barely stay awake, I'd make mistakes.

So I closed my eyes.

I expected to sleep for a couple of hours, but when I woke it was after 4 p.m. and I realized I'd wasted most of the day. Frustrated with myself, I grabbed my coat and headed out.

It was still three hours from sunset, but because of the rain and mist the light had already begun dying in the sky. Much of the town was lit, not by street lights, because there weren't any, but by the glow of windows and doorways. I'd been hoping to find somewhere to eat, but all the shops were closing for the day or already shut, there were no restaurants, and I discovered that the pub didn't serve food. A couple of times, I saw people fall into line behind me, or their eyes fix on me from across the street, and I became worried that I was being followed or watched, so rather than get lost in the labyrinthine streets, I found my way back to the pub again and went inside.

It was like a wormhole to the seventies, a mix of dark wood and geometric patterns. Everything smelled musty, the furniture retaining the scent of cigarette smoke and spilled beer. At the bar, a few men were perched on stools, their backs to me as they leaned over their pints, but apart from them and a guy wiping down glasses, it was quiet.

'Can I help you?' the guy behind the bar said.

I asked for a bottle of beer and some peanuts. A few pairs of eyes pinged to me at the sound of my accent. The one on the stool nearest to me, a man in his fifties with a hard, weather-beaten face and straggles of black hair snaking out from under a woollen beanie, said, 'So you over from the motherland then?'

'Yeah, that's right.'

'Doing what?'

I eyed him, and then glanced beyond to the other guys at the counter. None of them was looking at us but they were all listening.

The barman brought my beer over.

'I'm here to see the wildlife,' I said.

## 58

When I got back to the bed and breakfast, Mrs Smart, the woman who ran it, was already setting the table for the next morning. Evidently, it was just me: one table at a bay window.

'Would you mind if I asked you a question?' I said.

She was small but sprightly, her eyes bright, her hair tightly curled. 'Yes, of course you can, son,' she replied, and set all the cutlery down on top of the table.

'Do you know a guy called Anthony Jessop?'

She shook her head. 'No.'

'What about Jack Kilburn?'

She looked at me, her expression neutral, obviously waiting to see where I went next.

'I think he runs the town council here,' I added.

She sniffed, cleared her throat.

'What's he got to do with anything?' she said.

I couldn't quite get the measure of her. Her words made it sound like she didn't like him, or perhaps had an opinion on him, but her face remained blank.

'I was just curious about him.'

'Right.'

She hadn't swallowed the lie.

'So do you know him?'

'I know *of* him,' she said.

'Any idea where he lives?'

She shook her head, still watching me. 'I don't get involved in things like the town council. Me and Harold, we keep ourselves to ourselves.'

I nodded, looking at the solitary table, and changed tack.

'What do you make of the stories?' I said to her, gesturing to the back of the house where the rear windows looked up the slope, towards the mountain.

She frowned. 'Stories?'

'About what exists up there.'

Her expression cemented.

'I wouldn't go asking questions like that, son.'

'No?'

'What I mean is, don't go asking questions like that *out there*.' She nodded through the window to the town, its gathering blackness perforated by only a few tiny dewdrops of internal light. 'This place has got a way of swallowing you up if you do.'

She scooped up the cutlery and then stopped, staring out of the dark windows at the front of the house: they'd become hard to see out of, but would have been easy to see into.

'Follow me,' she said, and we headed into the hallway, where she put the cutlery down on an oak dresser wedged in under the staircase, and checked that we were out of range of the bay windows. 'Look, here's what I know, okay? Before we started running this place, my Harold, he used to be the coroner here. I mean, he wasn't *qualified* as a coroner – he's just a GP – but when someone died, Harold would often be the first person to look at the body.'

She stepped closer, literally looking over her shoulder this time.

'He won't like me mentioning this,' she said, her eyes still on the door that connected the front part of the house to the annex in which they both lived, 'but one time, he said he overheard Jack Kilburn and Bill Presley talking at the morgue.'

'About what?'

'About someone called Selina Torres.'

I paused. *Selina Torres*. She was mentioned in *No Ordinary Route*.

'I've read about her,' I said.

'Yeah? Well, whatever you've read, I doubt it's the truth.'

'Miranda?'

It was her husband, calling from the annex.

'Do you know where my reading glasses are?'

'Coming!' she said.

She leaned in to me, putting a hand on my arm.

'Harold doesn't talk about it because he says the walls in this town have ears. But if you want to know who Kilburn and Presley *really* are, I reckon you have to look into what happened to Selina Torres.'

# 59

I returned to my room, unable to persuade Mrs Smart to expand any further. Her husband had come in from the annex to see where she was, and she'd beamed an immediate goodnight to me – as if we'd had no conversation at all – and then shooed her husband back through the door, telling him to be more careful with his glasses.

I didn't get far using my phone either. The connection was painfully slow, which didn't help, but there were hundreds of women called Selina Torres, hundreds more by the time I combined search results from English- and Spanish-language sites, and I couldn't find an immediate connection between any of them and either the islands or the four men on my radar.

When I finally called it a night, I looked out of the windows, across the absolute black of the fields between the B&B and Blake Point, and spotted the *Olympia*. In the dark, it seemed so far away it was like it was on another planet: the vague hint of cabin lights winking on and off; rows of bulbs at the railings like pinpricks puncturing the night; a tiny wash of alabaster where the outer decks were all illuminated. By tomorrow afternoon it would be gone, Beth along with it.

Then I really would be alone.

By the morning it had stopped raining, but a thick fog had rolled in, sitting like a ceiling above the town and shielding the entire mountain from view. I'd thought the night before about heading up into the hiking trails first thing and seeing if I could find the tarn and the cabin, but I needed better weather. It was dangerous to be on a mountain in fog, more dangerous when I had no real idea where I was going. It wasn't like I could ask the local population for a map, either. So, for now, I went to breakfast, which was served by Mrs Smart as if our conversation of the night before had never happened, and then headed out.

The streets were mostly quiet, except for tin roofs popping and shifting in the wind, but it was bitterly cold, and, as I walked, I saw flutters of snow in the air. The police station was about a ten-minute walk away, in a small cul-de-sac all by itself, with an additional car park opposite and an empty field full of patchy grass at the end. Two men in uniform were standing out front smoking, laughing about something, but when I got close to the stairs, they stopped and just watched me.

Inside, the reception area was small. Cut into a dividing wall was a sliding glass panel on a timber countertop; behind the glass was a uniformed officer.

He pulled the panel aside. 'Yes, pal?'

'I'm looking for Superintendent Presley.'

The problem I was always going to face here was that my accent gave me away the moment I opened my mouth. He came forward a little further on the stool he was on, elbows pressed to the counter, and said, 'Why's that then?'

'It's a personal matter.'

His eyes narrowed, and he made no effort to disguise the fact that he was looking me up and down, presumably trying to figure out if he recognized me, or if we'd ever met.

*Or if I was the man he'd been warned about.*

Finally, he said, 'Superintendent Presley called in sick.'

'Really?' I eyed him. 'Nothing serious, I hope.'

He shrugged. 'Just a cold, I think.'

I thanked him and headed back down the slopes to the high street, watching for signs of a tail. Stopping outside the supermarket, I could see that there was a girl inside – sixteen or seventeen – serving at the till. There was a manager too, a burly guy in a fawn shirt and white butcher's apron, unloading boxes. I counted two customers at the counter, talking to each other

As soon as they left, I headed in.

I couldn't see the manager now, but could hear him: there was the clatter of things being moved – reordered, stacked – coming through from the back.

'Morning,' I said to the girl serving.

'Hello,' she replied. 'How are you?'

There was a warmth to her greeting that I hadn't expected, and hadn't yet experienced in Sophia. Maybe that optimism was something that got ground out of you the longer you remained here.

I struck up a conversation with her, trying to keep my voice down so the guy out the back wouldn't hear, and told her I'd popped up from the ship to have a look around. I thought about Presley, Kilburn and Jessop. They'd definitely know by now that Alexander Marek had failed, so was that the reason Presley had called in sick? If they knew I was here, what were they waiting for?

*Maybe it's time to draw them out.*

'I'm actually here to see some friends,' I said.

'Oh, really?' she replied. 'Who?'

'Bill Presley, Jack Kilburn and Anthony Jessop.'

Her face brightened. 'Cool.'

'You know them?'

'I know Bill. My mum used to work as a secretary at the police station.' She paused. 'You know Bill is in charge of the police, right?'

'I do, yeah.'

'He's really nice.'

I nodded enthusiastically. 'He's a great guy.'

'So you're meeting up with him while you're here?'

'Well, that's the thing,' I said, and started fiddling around for my notebook. I pretended to check its pages. 'He gave me his address – but I think I might have written it down wrong because I can't actually find it.'

'Oh.'

'And I don't have his number.'

The girl frowned. 'I'm pretty sure he's out near the library.'

'Actually,' I said, 'that rings a bell. He said he was out that way.'

She broke into a smile.

'What about the other two guys I mentioned?'

'Did you say one of them was called Jessop?'

'Anthony Jessop, yeah.'

'I haven't heard of him – but I know Mr Kilburn. He comes in here a few times a week. He's really nice too. I'm not sure where he lives, though. Brian will know,' she said, pointing towards the door at the back of the store.

'It's fine,' I said, thanking her again and heading out.

It was time to pay Bill Presley a visit.

# 60

It took me a while to find Presley's home.

The library turned out to be three Portakabins in a gravel car park on the edge of town. It was unattractive but had stellar views: to the south, I could see the *Olympia* anchored half a mile out into the ocean; to the north, the sweep of Mount Strathyde; to the west, the rest of Sophia, built into its slopes; to the east, hundreds of islands and the suspension bridge that connected Sophia to St George.

The further out of town I got, the more the houses started to spread out, and Presley's was in a cluster of three others. Despite the extra land out here, the design remained the same: red metal roofs, timber walls, sash windows, picket fences. On the side of his house, he'd built a car port, the roof made from more tin, the supporting beams from bicycle tyres, stacked on top of each other. It looked untidy and makeshift, which kind of summed up the house itself.

Out the front, *Presley* was written on an American-style mailbox.

On the walk across, I'd thought about how to approach Presley, about what sort of threat he might pose to me, but I kept coming back to what Beth had said on the ship: the account she gave me of how Richard had come down one night and found his father drunk and unconscious at the kitchen table, fresh from an IM conversation with Roland Dell. I remembered what he'd said to Dell.

*We'll go to hell for what we did.*

That didn't suggest someone whose thinking was straight. It didn't point towards a man as cold-blooded as Roland Dell, who could easily bury the events of the past. If Presley wasn't a weak link, it seemed he was teetering on the edge, his conscience struggling to cope. The more I thought about it, the more it felt like Bill Presley might be my way in.

That didn't negate the threat he posed, though, and I wouldn't necessarily have chosen to go to his place of work and then knock on his front door. But I was banking on two things: he'd grown weak under the weight of his secret; and he loved his son, above all else.

I tapped on the door.

A Toyota Land Cruiser was in the port and I could see part of the front room: an electric fire, a mantelpiece with some photos on it, a television on a wicker table in the corner. When I knocked a second time and got no answer, I took a step back and peered further into the house. Some sofas. An oak dining table. A big, grey-blue armchair beside the fire.

In the armchair was a woman in her fifties, looking right at me.

I'd never seen her before in my life, but I knew instantly it was Carla Presley: if Bill Presley had only carried faint facial hints of his son, Carla was the opposite. It was like looking at Richard, or a feminized version of him. The shape of the jaw, the nose, the bone structure – it was all the same. I inched to my left so she came into clearer view through the glass, trying to reassure her that I wasn't a threat, but the only thing that followed my movements were her eyes.

That was when I remembered what Beth had told me. *She'd had a stroke.*

For the first time, I saw that the left-hand side of her face had sunk a little. Not much, but enough: around the lips, above and below the line of the mouth. In every other part of her body, she was totally motionless. I wasn't sure how much or how little she could move, but her hands were linked together in the lap of her pleated skirt, her feet parallel to one another on the carpet, and her head was back, perched against the top of the chair. She had long brown hair, untied, which cascaded past her shoulders.

'Mrs Presley?' I said through the glass, and stepped closer.

I dug around in my pocket for a business card, not because I thought she'd be able to see it from where she was, but because I was waiting for any reaction from elsewhere in the house; a response to the sound of my voice. I listened for creaks, looked for movement in the kitchen or hallway – but there was nothing.

Could Bill Presley be hiding and listening?

'I'm not sure if you can see this,' I said, pressing the business card to the window, 'but my name's David Raker. I'm an investigator from the UK.' I checked the living room again. 'I'm here to talk to you about your son, Richard.'

Something moved in her eyes.

'May I come in, Mrs Presley?'

I waited. Slowly, her right hand lifted an inch from her lap, her fingers shaking, and she pointed in the vague direction of the front door. It had been a fractional movement, nothing more than that, but it seemed like she was straining every sinew to do it.

'I'm coming in, okay?' I said, and opened the door.

Warm air rolled out like a wave. I wiped my feet on a mat inside the door and pushed it shut. Ahead of me was the hallway, a staircase to the right, with a stairlift built into it. I paused there for a moment, out of sight of Carla Presley, listening again for sounds from upstairs. But the house was silent except for the soft tick of a clock and the hum of the electric fire in the living room.

She watched me enter, her body able to turn only slightly, her eyes doing most of the work. I removed my coat and laid it across a nearby chair and then perched myself on the edge of one of the sofas, just across from where she was. I looked from her to the mantelpiece, where photos were lined up in frames. They all had Richard in them: him as a young boy; him as a teenager with his parents; him, alone, in his twenties.

'Thank you for letting me in, Mrs Presley.'

She swallowed, blinked.

'Is Mr Presley home today?'

A minor shake of the head.

'He's out?'

A partial nod of the head. *Yes.*

'Is he at work?'

She blinked. *Yes.*

Except he wasn't. So it meant he'd lied to his wife and lied to the people at the station. The question was why. Had he gone to find the other men?

Were they coming for me?

I returned my attention to Carla, realizing that this was already a dead end. But then, as we locked eyes again, I felt a stab of sadness and a moment of guilt: she didn't know where her son was, or what had happened to him. After he was found, no one on the islands had come forward to claim him as one of their own, which suggested the news about him hadn't made it home – or, if it had, it was covered up by people like Kilburn and Jessop before it could spread any further. The saddest thing was that Presley was likely involved too, erasing his son's life from the record down here. Perhaps when Presley told Dell they were going to hell for what they'd done, he wasn't only talking about Penny, or the ghosts they might have left up at the tarn. Maybe he was also talking about the way he'd treated his son.

Glancing at the photographs of Richard and his father on the mantelpiece, I said, 'As I was saying, I'm an investigator from London.'

Her eyes stayed on me.

'I don't know whether you know this, but your son Richard is in the UK.' I paused, watching her for a reaction again. She started shaking her head.

'You had no idea he was there?'

Another small shake of the head.

'You know nothing about what happened to him?'

*No.*

'You just thought he'd disappeared?'

*Yes.*

I got out my notebook. I didn't need reminding about the case, I just needed time to think about the best approach.

'Richard came to me nearly two weeks ago to ask for my help. At some point, he had an accident and hit his head. He's fine,' I said, holding a hand up, trying to reassure her, 'except . . .' I stopped. Except he wasn't fine at all.

A hint of a frown. *Except what?*

'I'm afraid he's lost his memory.'

She seemed to flinch.

'He has a condition called "dissociative amnesia". He has no knowledge of who he is or where he came from. He doesn't remember you or your husband.'

*No.*

She tried to shake her head in disbelief.

'I'm sorry to have to tell you that.'

Her eyes filled with tears.

'I'm sorry,' I said again, filling the silence now.

She swallowed again and tears broke from her eyes. Nothing else moved, just them. As saliva gathered at the corner of her mouth, I could see the frustration in her eyes, could see her twitch with the irritation of it, her muscle memory trying to connect her fingers to her face. Her hand came up off her lap again, but it only got as far as her stomach. The effort was too much. Instead, she had to sit there, staring at me, as more tears escaped from her eyes and the saliva bubbled at the corner of her lips.

'I was hoping to maybe speak to your husband,' I said to her gently, 'but if he's at work, I can find him there.' I shuffled forward on the sofa, uncomfortable at the idea of her husband lying to her, and troubled by having to pump her for information. 'I was also hoping to speak to Jack Kilburn.'

It was hard to tell if she'd even heard me.

'Mrs Presley? Do you know a man called Jack Kilburn?'

She was looking down into her lap, but appeared to nod.

'You know him?'

*Yes.*

'Do you know where he lives?'

As soon as I asked the question, I thought: *How the hell is she going to tell me even if she does?* But then she slowly lifted her head and directed her eyes up, towards the mantelpiece. I followed her line of vision and, for the first time, saw some papers tucked behind one of the pictures of Richard, her and Bill Presley.

Getting up, I lifted the papers out and saw that they were the minutes of a council meeting that Bill Presley had attended. They ran to six pages and there was nothing of any real interest – except for the last page. There, Kilburn – as chairman – had listed his details.

It included his home address.

I made a note of it, folded the papers back together and slipped them in behind the picture frame again. When I turned back to Carla Presley, the guilt snapped at me a second time: she was staring at me, silent, unmoved, tear tracks like ribbons against her face. There was more saliva, and I could tell now that it really bothered her; that she was embarrassed by it and frustrated she couldn't wipe it away.

'Is there something I can get for you?' I asked her.

She blinked. *Yes.*

'Tissues? Something like that?'

*Yes.*

'Are they in here?'

*No.*

'Upstairs?'

*No.*

'In the kitchen?'

*Yes.*

'They're in the kitchen?'

*Yes.*

'Okay, just bear with me.'

I got up, headed into the hallway and took a left towards the kitchen. On the wall beneath the staircase there were more photos of the three of them, the pictures packed into a thin, black iron frame, shaped like a tree. I paused briefly, looking at shots of Richard Presley, of Carla before she suffered her stroke, and of Bill, hugging Richard while in uniform.

The kitchen was small and old-fashioned, a table pushed up against one wall, dishes piled up in the sink, the microwave showing evidence of past meals. It seemed to paint a picture of a man struggling to cope, not just with his own conscience or with his job, but with the rigours of looking after an incapacitated wife.

I couldn't see the tissues anywhere obvious and, as I started going through the drawers, I saw another door, half hidden in the corner of the room. I assumed it was a pantry or a utility room, but when I opened it up, I was wrong.

It was Bill Presley's office.

# 61

A steel cabinet had been left partially open. There was a laptop on the desk and a mess of paperwork, and books had been piled up on the floor at the far side of the room. There was no bookcase to hold them, no real furniture of any kind except for the cabinet, the desk, and an unmade sofa bed in the corner, its cushions sunken and worn. There was a crumpled blanket on the sofa and an empty bottle of whisky on the edge of the desk. Presley had slept here last night.

I looked at the bottle again.

Maybe he slept here every night.

I quietly pulled out the drawers of the cabinet. They contained police files; work he must have brought home with him. At a glance, they were uninteresting: minor disputes over property boundaries, petty burglary; scuffles and fights outside the only pub in town; punch-ups after affairs had been outed; men and women, though mostly men, found collapsed and unconscious in the middle of the high street at one in the morning. For the majority, drunkenness appeared to be a by-product of living in a place where there were no cafés, no restaurants, no cinemas, one pub, few shops, and no decent Internet connection or TV stations. But I didn't imagine that was why Bill Presley got drunk. I glanced at the sofa and the whisky bottle again.

I imagined he got drunk for other reasons.

Looking at the laptop, I considered switching it on, but I'd been gone a minute already and was conscious of raising alarms with Carla, so I returned to the living room instead. I told her I hadn't been able to find tissues, and asked if she wanted me to look upstairs. She nodded.

I headed up.

There were two bedrooms. By the looks of things, Richard's had been left pretty much exactly as it was the day he took the ship out of Blake Point with Beth. His shelves were full of machine parts, things he'd half fixed, model boats he'd built, an archaic mid-2000s PC with a tower on the floor, and tons of books. There were encyclopaedias, reference texts, novels, and I realized half the books in Bill Presley's office weren't actually his, but Richard's. It reinforced everything I'd seen of him myself back in the UK.

I took a quick look at the bedroom belonging to Bill and Carla, saw that only one side of the bed had been slept in, then crept downstairs again. I moved silently along the hall, out of sight of the living room, and returned to the office.

Sliding in at the desk, I tried the laptop.

It hummed faintly into life, making the Windows Vista start-up sound. As I waited, I started going through the drawers of the desk. In the third one down, I found something: a red card folder, buried under some notepads.

On the computer screen, a password prompt flashed up, so I switched the laptop off, pushed it aside and laid the folder down on the desk. The corners of something were already escaping from inside.

*Newspaper cuttings.*

Except they weren't cuttings of stories, but cuttings of headlines, all taken from the *Empress Express*. One was a front page – I could still see part of the masthead – but most appeared to be articles confined to the interior. On the back of each one, in biro, Presley had written the date on it.

I put them in chronological order.

The first was from April 1992.

### DOG FINDS LEG BONE ON STRATHYDE HIKING TRAIL

The next was from a few months later, in June, and featured a picture. It was fuzzy, smudged from being kept in the folder, and discoloured.

### STRATHYDE FENCE REINFORCED
Tests confirm leg bone doesn't belong to missing Sophia resident Caleb Beck.

The accompanying picture was of three men, each wearing mud- and oil-stained clothes. On two of them I could make out knives, in sheaths, at their belts, but a lot of other detail had become lost because of ink smears. A caption read:

The fence was reinforced by its original construction team. *Left to right*: Bill Presley, Jack Kilburn, Anthony Jessop.

I leaned in closer to the picture.

If I hadn't already seen Presley in the shots dotted

around his living room, and from the picture of him in uniform I'd found on the web, I'd have struggled even to recognize him. He still had a full head of hair back then, and a moustache which wrapped around his lip and followed parallel lines to his chin.

I turned to the other two.

With nothing on which to base my knowledge of them, they were just a vague black and white blur. I could tell they were both big – tall and brawny – and that they had light hair and beards, but those things might not even be relevant now. They'd still be tall – but they might be fat, bald and clean-shaven.

The last cutting was from November 1997, ten years after the disappearance of Caleb Beck.

**BUENOS AIRES POLICE ASK FOR HELP AS COLD CASE
TEAM SEARCH FOR MISSING WOMAN**

*Selina Torres.* It had to be.

Going to my phone, I brought up the browser, headed to Google Argentina and put in a fresh search for Torres, this time adding *Buenos Aires* and *policía* tags.

Finally, I got something.

The story was too old to have been digitized in its entirety on the web, but I found a scan of a half-page from *La Nación*, an Argentine newspaper, uploaded to a list feature about weird disappearances. Underneath, there was a summary of the story but my Spanish was rudimentary at best, so I copied and pasted it into a translation program. The results weren't perfect, but they were good enough to understand.

Argentine stewardess Torres was last seen at the Ezeiza International Airport in Buenos Aires in July 1987. Her credit card showed coffee that she bought and a bottle of perfume, but detectives could not at the time find out for themselves which airline she worked and, in fact, began to suspect that she did not work for an airline at all, even though it was a story that she told her family. Airport cameras showed her walking to a gate with flights to Empress Islands, but immigration record and surveillance footage indicate she never made it there. On the tenth anniversary of her disappearance, a team of cold cases of the Metropolitan Police of Buenos Aires joined the Royal Police of the Empress Islands to try to discover what happened to Torres, but found never a trace of her.

Even with the imperfect translation, I could see right through it. The question wasn't how Torres failed to materialize on the Empress Islands, it was why she vanished once she'd got here. Because I was certain she had got here, even if all the evidence of her doing so had mysteriously become lost, misplaced or erased. The clue was in the date she went missing: July 1987. The same month Caleb Beck vanished. The same month Roland Dell came back to the islands for his summer holidays. The same month Bill Presley was spotted outside the pub, with blood on his sleeves.

I checked my watch.

I'd already been gone five minutes. If I was gone any longer, Carla Presley would start to get suspicious. Grabbing my phone, I took camera shots of all the cuttings, placed them back into the folder and then returned it to the desk as I'd found it. On the way, I had another quick look through the kitchen drawers, couldn't find the tissues, so went to the downstairs bathroom instead and ripped off some toilet roll. When I got back to the living room, Carla was watching me, her gaze following me like she knew something was up.

*I was meant to have come from upstairs.*

I held up the tissue, trying to pretend that everything was normal, unsure whether to hand her the paper or offer to help her to use it. Except I could hardly look at her now, the guilt welling in the pit of my stomach. All the good work I'd tried to do for her son, the obsession that had brought me to the other side of the world, and none of it seemed to matter in this moment: she knew — we both knew — that I'd been searching her house, taking advantage of her infirmity.

I looked at her. 'I'm sorry, Carla.'

I meant it, meant every word of it, but she just stared at me, unmoved as if by choice this time, not by disability.

'When this is over,' I said, 'I hope you'll understand why.'

She blinked, tears filling her eyes again.

I tried to smile at her, but it wouldn't form properly, so instead I got up, placed the tissue in her hand, and then left her alone in the silence of her house.

# 62

Kilburn lived five miles out of town, on a farm in the middle of nowhere. There was no public transport on the islands, so the only way I was going to get there – unless I fancied a long walk in the freezing cold – was by taking a taxi or hiring a car.

Neither was a great option. A taxi meant relying on someone else to pick me up and drop me off, and – in terms of disguising any approach – didn't offer a lot of subtlety. Hiring a car made more sense from that point of view, and was less conspicuous, but was no more practical: the only rental place was in St George, and that was twelve miles away.

Until I figured out the best plan of attack, I decided to focus on finding out more about the stories I'd discovered in Presley's office, and headed back down the slope to the library. The gravel crunched underfoot as I crossed the car park to the Portakabins, which turned out to be the perfect alarm call: at the windows, I saw metallic blinds part, a pair of eyes watching me. A moment later, the blinds pinged back into place.

The Portakabins were joined together, the middle one connected at either end to the others, the structure forming a vague semicircle. The entrance was up a pair of rusting metal stairs and, when I pulled the door open, warm air rushed at me. I thought of Carla Presley again, of feeling the same switch in temperature as I opened the door to her place – and then I remembered how she'd looked at me.

*The way she knew I was lying to her.*

I pushed the guilt down, burying it with all the grief I'd tried to suppress over the years, the regrets, the fear, and looked left and right. The interior was small and dated, like an extended mobile library. Old, heavy-duty carpets had begun to wear through, the cream walls were marked by fingerprints, and there were scratches and cracks where the building had begun to deteriorate with age. Stand-alone electric heaters had been placed all the way down to where a computer sat in an alcove, and, in the quiet that greeted me, I could hear its soft, insect-like buzz.

'Good morning.'

I followed the voice.

Further down, on the same side as the entrance, a woman in her forties stood behind a desk, both hands flat to the top, smiling at me. She seemed stiff, a little cautious, and it instantly put me on edge.

'Morning,' I said, pulling the door shut.

I checked the library again; there was no one else here. I glanced out of the nearest window to the sloping road that took me back into Sophia. There was no one out there either.

'Can I help you with something?' the woman said.

'I'm doing some research,' I said. 'I'm up from the ship for the morning.'

'I see,' was all she said.

I looked towards the computer at the far end. Above it, printed out and taped to the wall, was a piece of paper that said: FAST INTERNET AVAILABLE HERE. Even if the definition of *fast* was likely to be different from back home, it was still going to be quicker than dealing with a lethargic, inconsistent 3G signal, and I wouldn't have to read everything off a four-and-a-half-inch screen.

'Could I use your computer?'

She made a face.

'If you're wanting to use the Internet on it,' she said, 'I'm afraid that we're having some problems at the moment. Something to do with' – she waved a hand airily around her head – 'the servers, or the exchange, or something like that. I'm not sure that I really understand any of it.'

'Is there anywhere else that has a computer?'

'In Sophia?'

She looked at me like I was asking where I could find the Holy Grail. As I studied her reaction, I couldn't quite decide if she was telling me the truth or playing me, so I just thanked her and headed back outside.

The cold hit me like a wall. There was still snow in the air too, drifting delicately across me, blown in off the mountain. I looked up, in the direction of Strathyde, and saw that the fog was beginning to clear, the ragged edge of a peak showing through the cloud as if a hole had been punched in a roof. In a couple of hours I was hoping it would be gone, and then I'd take the trail up to the tarn and see what lay there for myself.

'You the guy that's looking for Kilburn and Presley?'

Off to the side of me, a man was sitting on a pile of concrete breezeblocks sewn through with weeds and grass. He was dressed in a thick black coat, collar up, a blue beanie pulled down over his ears. Silver-grey stubble lined the lower half of his jaw, his skin etched with years and weather. In his right hand, a cigarette smoked gently; his left was pressed against his knee, supporting his weight. He looked in his fifties and was big, maybe six two and sixteen stone, but the expression in his face betrayed his size: he was on edge – jumpy, scared.

'Are you him or aren't you?' he said.

'I'm just a tourist,' I replied, 'up from the *Olymp–*'

'Don't fuck around with me, okay?'

He got to his feet, taking a quick drag on his cigarette, then tossed it out across the gravel. It died instantly in the cold.

'Just . . .' He stopped, teeth pressed together. He leaned in closer to me and I could smell the sourness of him: tobacco, old alcohol, sweat, fear. 'You made a mistake going in there.' He meant the library. 'That's Kilburn's sister that runs it.'

He looked out across the car park, towards the Portakabin door, and then gestured for me to follow him. I hesitated for a moment and then went after him. We moved beyond the edge of the Portakabin to where the gravel dropped away, into a steep bank. A muddy trail was marked into it, thousands of footsteps embedded like fossils. The bank led down to a side street, lined with red tin roofs. It was another route leading back to the centre of town, with one big difference: the woman inside the library wouldn't be able to see it.

The man glanced at his watch, then out along the street, as if thinking.

'You know where the lido is?' he said.

'I know it's out of town.'

'Head east from the main street, out on Reynolds Road. Just keeping going. You won't miss it.' He looked at his watch again. 'It's almost midday. Meet me there at 1 p.m. It's still too cold for anyone to be there, so we'll hav–'

'Wait a second, wait a second.'

He fizzed with frustration, his fists balling. '*What?*'

'I'm not meeting you anywhere until you tell me who you are.'

'Fine,' he said, checking his watch, and then the road. The panic was like an earthquake tremoring through his body. 'What do you want to know?'

'Your name would be a good start.'

'Fine,' he said again. 'My name's Jessop. Anthony Jessop.'

# 63

I looked at him. 'You're Anthony Jessop?'

'Yeah,' he said, his fingers nervously drumming out a beat against the palms of his hands. 'Have you heard of me?'

'I saw you mentioned in a newspaper story.'

He eyed me for a second – and then it seemed to click. 'You mean, when we went up into the hills?'

I nodded.

'That got reported back in the UK?'

'No,' I said. 'It got reported in the *Express*.'

He frowned. 'So you've been to St George?'

'What?'

'To the newspaper archive there?'

'Yes,' I lied, just to move the conversation on. 'How did you find me?'

He looked up and down the street and leaned closer. 'One of my best friends works in the supermarket,' he whispered, as if even saying it aloud put him in danger. 'The checkout girl he's got in there told him you'd been in. She said you were asking about Bill Presley.'

'I was asking about you and Jack Kilburn too.'

'Yeah, well, she doesn't know me. She knows Bill.'

'So, have you been following me around?'

'Look, are you going to meet me or not?'

'I'm not meeting you anywhere until I know what's going on.'

He swallowed, more frantic than ever: whatever best-laid plans he'd had were already starting to fracture. He'd expected to be in a position of authority, of power, able to call the shots.

'Anthony?'

He held up a hand, looked like he was gathering himself.

'I was a mainlander like you,' he said, 'but I hated my life back in Wigan, so in 1985 I came over here. I liked this place to start with: the quiet, the solitude.' He glanced left and right. We were still alone in the street. 'But the quiet, the solitude, if you're not wired up right, you can lose your mind in it.'

I watched him. 'Is that what happened to you?'

'I know things about Kilburn and Presley,' he said quickly, wiping snowflakes away from his cheeks. 'I know things about a guy called Roland Dell too. You heard of him?'

'Yes.'

He looked past me, over my shoulder, and he was close enough to me now that, in the green of his eyes, I could see the reflection of Mount Strathyde. Partly consumed by cloud, it looked thinner – a jagged silhouette, like a knife blade scything out of the earth.

'I know what they did,' he said. 'Dell, Presley, Kilburn.'

'What they did?'

'Up in the Brink. At the tarn, there.'

I studied him. 'What do you mean, you know?'

'I mean, I *know*,' he said through his teeth. 'I know what they did up there in 1987.' He shifted closer to me, his lips only inches from my ear, as if scared to say it. 'I know what they did, because I was there.'

# 64

The lido was at the absolute periphery of the town, where there were no homes and buildings, just a single, two-lane road travelling west to east, and an endless blanket of grassland stretching from the foothills of the mountain to the edges of the sea. Occasionally, through the mist and snow flurries, I could glimpse the suspension bridge connecting this island to the next, but there was no sign of any other life out here, which was presumably why Jessop chose it.

As the town thinned, protection from the wind went with it, and the cold became unrelentingly brutal. I could feel it rip at my skin like nails, and putting up my hood and pulling a scarf over my face seemed to make no difference at all.

When I finally got there, I found a circular building on a plateau. I'd seen it described as a mix between a castle and a UFO, and neither was far off: it was hulking and squat, a kind of brutalist auditorium, with small, slit-like windows embedded in huge blocks of yellow-grey concrete. Around the entrance and frilled along the top were art deco flourishes – zigzags, sunburst motifs, curves, chevrons – and, when I passed through an unmanned turnstile at the front, and into the lido itself, I found an open-air foyer with a small roof. The pool sat in a depression ahead of me, surrounded by grass and old benches. Changing rooms were off to my left, and an Empress Islands flag on the roof whipped and snapped in the wind.

Snowflakes swirled and eddied as I headed back to the turnstile to see if Jessop was approaching. The road into Sophia remained empty.

I stood there for a moment, thinking.

There were no hiding places here, apart from the changing rooms, so I wasn't worried about being surprised – but I still felt on edge. I knew nothing about Anthony Jessop, other than he'd been there the night Penny and Beth were taken up to the fence, so I had no idea if I could genuinely trust him.

He could have been coming out here to kill me.

I got out my phone, saw it was almost five past one, and then went to my address book. I needed to let someone know where I was, but more importantly, I needed to let Richard know his real surname and the name of his parents.

Just in case I never came home.

He picked up straight away. 'Hello?'

'Richard, it's me.'

'Hey, David.'

He sounded relaxed, which was good. It meant he and Howson were still okay. I'd messaged Richard a couple of times since leaving the ship and he'd told me he was fine, but it was more reassuring hearing it in his voice than reading it in a text. As he talked to me about how he'd been researching the Empress Islands, trying to see if he could jog a memory of some kind, I looked again for Jessop. This time, in the distance, I could see a vehicle coming through the mist and snow.

'Richard, listen to me. Have you got a pen there?'

'Yeah, hold on.'

I heard him put down the phone and as the line went quiet, I looked back out at the road. The car was about a minute away. I could see a silhouette at the wheel. It looked like Jessop – big, broad – but it was hard to be sure. There was no sign of anyone else in the car, in the passenger seat or in the back. I scanned the fields either side, the road, the town in the distance.

He didn't appear to have brought anybody else.

*But that doesn't mean they aren't coming.*

'Okay,' Richard said, coming back on to the line.

'I haven't got a lot of time, but I need to let you know a couple of things quickly. Are you listening?'

'Yes.'

'Your surname is Presley.'

Silence on the line.

'Richard?'

'Presley?'

'Yes. Your mum and dad's names are Carla and Bill. I've met your mum. She's . . .' *She's what?* 'She's not very well.'

'What do you mean?'

'She had a stroke a few years back.'

I looked out along the road. Jessop was closer than ever and I realized – as much as it pained me to do it – I needed to move the conversation on.

'Richard, I'm sorry to have to rush this, but I need to ask you something else. Have you ever heard of anyone called Anthony Jessop?'

I wasn't sure if he was paying attention.

'Richard?'

'Sorry?'

He sounded groggy, confused.

'Have you ever heard of a man called Anthony Jessop?'

'No,' he said. 'No, I don't think so.'

'Okay, well, write this down. That's the name of the guy I'm meeting now. Anthony Jessop. He's originally from Wigan. Early fifties, been on the islands since 1985. I don't know much more about him.' I stopped, watching Jessop, his car – a metal-grey Land Rover Defender – spitting up mud and slush. 'That's what worries me.'

'What do you mean?'

'I mean, I'm meeting him in a second.'

'Oh.'

'If you don't hear from me again, you need to make sure that all of that information gets into the hands of a man called Ewan Tasker.' I read out Tasker's mobile number. 'Is that clear?'

'Are you okay, David?'

'Is that clear, Richard?'

The Land Rover was pulling in. I started to move away from the turnstile, back out on to the grass that surrounded the pool.

'Richard, is that clear?'

'Yes.' He sounded hesitant. 'Don't you think you can trust him?'

'I don't think I can trust anyone here.'

'Where are you?'

'I'm in a lido, a mile and a half outside of Sophia.'

'Can't you call the police?'

*Your dad* is *the police.*

'No,' I said. 'The cops are in on it.'

Silence on the line.

'I've got to go,' I said. 'Thanks, Richard.'

I hung up before he could say anything else, before he could attempt to try and talk me out of meeting Jessop.

It was too late in any case.

Jessop appeared at the turnstile. He flipped down his hood and came through the gate, its squeak breaking the hush of the lido. When he saw me, he seemed to relax, his shoulders inching down, as if he'd been holding his breath. He looked out at the pool again, at the changing rooms, and I realized he was doing to me exactly the same as I'd done to him: checking for back-up, for traps, for dangers.

'I didn't know if you'd show,' he said.

'Why did you bring me out here, Anthony?'

He looked confused. 'You wanted answers.'

'Yeah, but why give them to me?'

We watched each other.

Finally, he said, 'Kilburn runs the town, and Presley runs the police. Who's going to call them out?' He shook his head. 'No one. Same with Dell. He pumps a lot of money into Sophia. It might not look like it, but he does. This place' – he waved an arm at the lido, at the pool, its surface rippling in the wind – 'he basically put up the money to keep it open.' His eyes shifted to the entrance. He had the look of a man who was way past paranoid. 'If you came all the way here, I'm thinking it's for the truth, right?'

'Right.'

Jessop wiped some snow from his face.

'Then I guess we'd better start with Caleb Beck.'

## 65

We were sitting at either end of a stone bench, partially sheltered beneath the roof at the lido's entrance. Jessop suddenly seemed smaller, hunched, his elbows against his knees as he leaned forward. His hood was up, but its fur-lined rim had inched out beyond the edge of the concrete canopy, his hands, his feet as well. Snow gently landed around him, melting against his jacket.

'How much do you know about Beck?' he said.

'Assume I don't know anything.'

He looked across at me, breath forming in front of his face. It was hard to tell whether he didn't like my tone or was just frustrated at having to go back to the beginning, but he nodded, dropped his eyes to the ground again, and said, 'He was a mainlander too. Came over from London in 1984 as part of the same drive that brought me here. The promise of a better life. Sea, beaches, wildlife. Lots of land – as much as you could afford, basically. Reloca-tion all covered, subsidies, generous financial terms.' Jessop shrugged. 'I mean, what was there not to like?'

He kneaded his hands together.

'Thing is, Caleb Beck was already doing well,' Jessop said. 'He was rich. Not mega-rich, but rich enough. I moved over a year after him and used to chat to him in the pub a couple of times a week – at that stage, I was just trying to get to know people on the island. He didn't talk much about his life in the motherland, other than he'd grown up on a farm, gone to London and got an office job, and then – sometime after Penny was born – he started to realize he missed farming, and that he wanted out of the city. Some of the guys said he was in banking – that that was how he'd got all his money – but he never talked about it, and I never asked. It had to be something like that, though. Most of us, when we came here, we were in smallholdings, these starter kits with a hundred acres. He bagged himself eighteen hundred acres right off the bat. This whole chunk of Strathyde was his too. We used to joke that every single sheep on the mountain belonged to him. But it wasn't really a joke.'

'So Beck was murdered for his money?'

Jessop looked at me.

I could see he was surprised, could see from his face that if I wasn't exactly right, I was close enough. 'Is that what happened?' I said. 'Dell got a whiff of Beck's wealth, just like all the rest of you did – and Dell killed him for it?'

'Yes,' Jessop said, so quietly I almost couldn't hear him. He looked at me and swallowed, then again, the guilt like ash in his mouth.

I thought about the money, about the trail that had led Penny to her death. It started with Jack Kilburn buying himself a new Land Rover in 2000, when the cash first started coming across from Dell in the UK. A light had gone on in Penny's head, a memory of a conversation she'd had with Beth as kids, about how her family had been wealthy – except Fiona never had any money. None of them had growing up. So Penny, already mistrusting

Kilburn, started looking into her stepfather's finances, and from there she eventually ended up in the security suite at the Red Tree, thousands of miles away, in front of all the proof she needed. The only question was why Dell had waited so long to start shifting the money. Beck disappeared in 1987, his money was stolen then too, but it didn't start moving until 2000.

But then I remembered what else had happened in 2000: Dell had become headmaster of the Red Tree by paying off the school governors.

'So after Caleb Beck was killed,' I said, thinking it through aloud, 'Dell hid his part in Beck's murder, he hid the fact that he'd got his hands on Beck's money, and he sat on the cash. And after thirteen years, when he finally thought the coast was clear, and everyone had forgotten, he finally started to spend it. Is that about right?'

He nodded. 'Yeah.'

'And you were a part of this?'

He shrugged.

'So where's Beck's body buried?'

This time he looked at me. 'You don't know?'

'Is he out in the Brink?' I said.

He didn't move, didn't react at all, until snowflakes sprayed across the space between us, whirled and fanned by another blast of wind, and he was forced to wipe them from his eyes. He turned, looking out across the pool, out to the coliseum of concrete that encased us. I couldn't see his face any more.

'What do you know about the Brink?' he said.

'Enough.'

He cleared his throat, as if about to speak, but stopped himself.

'So is he buried out there?' I repeated.

He said something I couldn't hear.

'What?'

'No.'

'Speak up, Anthony.'

'I said no.'

'So where's his body buried?'

He didn't reply.

'Anthony, where's Caleb Beck's body buried? Is it at the cabin?'

He seemed to flinch, as if jolted.

'The cabin?' he said softly, eyes still on the pool.

This time, I got no sense that he was deliberately holding back on me. Instead, he looked reluctant to answer; worried about doing so. And the longer I looked at him, the more I started to think it might not be deceit, but mistrust, a disinclination to hand me everything on a plate just in case he needed something to use in return. A chip to bargain with.

'You ever heard of Selina Torres?' he asked.

The change of direction threw me.

I came forward on the bench and said, 'What?' I'd heard him, I just wanted him to face me. I wanted the chance to look him in the eyes, to get a read on him.

'Have you?' he said, and finally turned to me.

His eyes carried something else now. I couldn't decide what it was, couldn't even decide if it was something I could use or something I should be concerned about.

'Torres,' I said. 'Yeah, I've heard the name.'

He looked out across the lido again. Directly above his hood, over the roof of the building, I could see most of Mount Strathyde. I remembered all the stories I'd been told and, as I watched Jessop in the silence of this old building, my nerves fired.

*Something isn't right about this.*

'Torres was an Argie,' Jessop was saying. 'This air hostess from Buenos Aires who flew across in July 1987.'

'Did she?'

Jessop frowned.

'I read that she never arrived.'

He smirked. 'You believe that?'

'No, not really.'

'She arrived all right,' Jessop said.

'You just made it look like she hadn't.'

'Right.'

'You and who else?'

'Kilburn, Presley. Dell too. He was the one that paid the hush money before he pissed off back to London. That was when he first got hold of Beck's cash and, in a place like this, a little cash goes a long way. It can buy you all sorts of things. You can get people to look the other way at passport control; maybe they don't log your arrival in their computers. You can get them to organize a power cut on one of the surveillance cameras so it doesn't show you entering the terminal. You can get them to keep their mouths shut when a bunch of Argie coppers call up, asking questions about a missing woman – and then you can do it all over again ten years later when they reopen it as a cold case.'

'What's Selina Torres got to do with Beck?'

'What's she got to do with him?' He swivelled his head towards me, his body still, and ran a hand across his stubble. 'Everything.'

'Which means what?'

'Which means we killed Beck. And then, because we killed him, we didn't have any choice: we had to kill her too.'

# 66

Beck and Torres were murdered on the same night.

Instantly, my thoughts caught on something else: the leg bone found in the hills by the dog and its owner in 1992, five years later. It had belonged to a woman.

*It had belonged to Torres.*

I remembered other things: how her brother didn't think Torres had been an air hostess, that she'd been lying to him; about a moment in my conversation with Annie on the *Olympia*, when she'd talked about the reaction to *No Ordinary Route* in Sophia. *Some people reckon that, if you get seen with a copy of that by the police in Sophia, they'll confiscate it.* She'd said it was down to the weirdness of the town, its intolerance and insularity. But it wasn't really that: Bill Presley was running the police, Jack Kilburn was running the town – and they didn't want anyone to look into who Selina Torres was.

'Why did they both have to end up dead?' I said.

Jessop's head dropped, his chin against his chest. I couldn't see his face at all now, could hardly hear him. The only thing I could see was his hands, cupped together in front of him like he was about to drop to his knees in prayer.

'Anthony?'

Jessop glanced at me. 'What else do you know?'

It felt like the third or fourth time he'd asked me a

variation on that same question. But before I could say anything, my phone burst into life.

To start with, it didn't even register that it might be mine, but then Jessop looked from me to my pocket, as if this might be a trap, some ruse to corner him, and I started to feel it buzzing gently against my leg. I held up a hand to him, telling him to calm down, and when I got out the phone, I saw a UK number.

Richard's mobile.

I decided to ignore it for now, pocketing the phone again, and turned my attention back to Jessop. The wind whipped across us.

'Tell me more about Selina Torres,' I said.

Jessop didn't appear to have heard me.

'Why did she come to the islands?'

My phone started buzzing again.

*Damn it.*

I grabbed my phone from my pocket and looked at the display. It was Richard again. I glanced at Jessop, who was looking from the phone to me.

'Let me just deal with this,' I said, and pushed Answer.

The line hummed and buzzed.

'David?' Richard said.

'Can I call you back?'

'Uh, well, I think you need to hear this.'

I glanced at Jessop. He lowered the hood on his coat, his beanie quickly dotting with snow, and turned away from me, his eyes on the ground. He was completely still, as if thinking. But he wasn't thinking. He was concentrating. He was listening to my side of the conversation.

'What is it?' I said into the phone.

'I found out something about this Jessop guy.'

Any anger, any frustration I felt at Richard interrupting me, instantly died. I glanced at Jessop again. He was in exactly the same position as before.

'What do you mean?'

'Jacob let me use his laptop.'

'Okay. So what's up?'

'I wanted to find out who you were meeting.'

I looked at Jessop.

This time, he was looking back at me.

'Did you find something?' I said, trying to keep my voice even.

'Yes,' Richard said.

The wind ripped in again.

'I found out that Anthony Jessop's been dead for ten years.'

# 67

The man sitting next to me shifted on the bench.

He could sense something was up.

Richard continued to talk at me, telling me about how he'd found stories about Jessop online: an archived page from the *Wigan Evening Post* about how Jessop had opened a farming supplies store in 2001 after returning to the UK from the Empress Islands; an obituary for him in the same newspaper when he died of liver failure five years later. My mind spun back to the photograph of the three men in the *Express*. I'd recognized Presley, but only because I already knew what he looked like: his shape, his key features. The other two, Kilburn and Jessop, had been blurs, disguised by the poor-quality shot and the smudged ink of the newspaper page.

*Kilburn.*

I had no idea what *he* looked like.

'Hang up the phone.'

As he spoke, something curdled in my guts. His expression was different, his voice harder. At his belt was a holster with a gun in it, his coat hitched up above it now, resting on it.

I looked from the gun to him.

'David?'

I could hear Richard's voice: small, tinny, distant.

'David, are you there?'

'Hang up the phone,' Kilburn said again.

I ended the call and powered off the mobile.

Silence.

He hadn't reached for the gun, had hardly changed position at all, his body still weighted forward as if he were frozen midway to getting up. For a moment he said nothing, the lull filled by the whine of the wind as it funnelled through the doorways of the lido. Snowflakes crackled against the nylon of our jackets. There was, for the briefest of moments, a bird call – far off, as if it had travelled here as an echo – and then he finally did move: he popped the clasp from his holster, slid out the gun and gripped it hard, his knuckles red from the cold. I watched the gun, not him, even as he kept it pointed towards the ground.

'You were supposed to be dead,' he muttered quietly, almost as if he were talking to himself, his eyes on the grass in front of us. 'Everything was supposed to have been taken care of, and now look.'

His gaze switched from the grass to the weapon.

'Now look at what I'm having to do.'

I tried to stay calm.

He turned the gun in his hand, looking along the line of the weapon, all the way from the hammer to the muzzle. I kept my body absolutely still but used my eyes to scan the lido, looking for ways out, an escape plan, a survival strategy. If I did nothing, he was going to put a bullet in me. I could make a leap for him – we were only five feet apart, at either end of the bench – but he already had the gun out, his finger on the trigger. It was too risky.

He glanced at me and smiled, but it was one that looked

serious, pained. 'Having to scramble around and do this,' he said, 'acting, lying, bullshit. I hate it. I had no idea if you knew what I looked like, but once you swallowed the Jessop stuff, I realized you didn't and I could use it to get you all the way out here with the promise of the truth.' Another smile, even more distressed than the last. 'The truth. Whatever the fuck that means in this place.'

I looked again for a way out.

Doorways. Entrances. Gaps.

When I turned back to him, he was wiping snow from his face, blinking it free of his eyelashes. 'I could tell you were getting suspicious,' he said. 'You were starting to twig, thinking, "Why's this guy constantly asking me how much *I* know about Beck and Torres and the money? He's supposed to be telling *me*."'

He was right: after the third or fourth time of him asking me what I knew, how many details I'd managed to gather myself, and the way he withdrew into his shell the longer we talked, it had begun to seem as if, rather than simply being interested, being curious, he had been actively mining me for information.

'So,' he said, 'I need to know who else you've told.'

He was doing exactly the same thing as Dell had done on the boat: he was trying to see who else I'd spoken to; how far the damage had spread.

'Who else have you told about us?' he said again, waiting for an answer that never came. After a while, he glanced at the phone, still in my hand. 'The person on the line – who was that? They know, don't they? I could see your face when you took that call. So there's whoever you spoke to. That's one. Who else is there?'

The wind picked up again, the surface of the pool flickering, the concrete walls of the lido making a heavy moan.

'Who else?' Kilburn repeated, his voice thickening.

*I need something to fight back with.*

'Who *else*?'

He clenched his teeth, his chin pinched, his jaw tightening, and raised the gun for the first time, extending it out in front of him. The muzzle stopped a foot from my face. I tried not to show my fear, but my heart was so loud in my ears, it was like a noise from inside the lido itself.

'Who else?'

*I need to knock him off balance.*

'I know where Beth is,' I said.

'What?' He leaned into me. 'What did you say?'

'I know where Beth is.'

Confusion, then anger, then uncertainty: he dropped the gun away slightly, so he could see my face, read me, try to see the truth in my expression.

'Beth,' he said, repeating her name.

'I know where she is.'

'Where?'

'She can't forgive you, Jack.'

He frowned.

'She can't forgive you for what happened to Penny.'

An aftershock passed through him. He blinked and I could see him struggling to retain control of himself. I'd sandbagged him. I'd changed the entire direction of the conversation.

The gun dropped a fraction more.

'Beth,' he said quietly. 'You know where my Beth is?'

I hadn't wanted to use her as some sort of bait, but it

was his daughter. He'd betrayed her, lied to her, looked the other way as Penny, the girl he'd brought up as his own, was murdered. I didn't know the whole story, not yet, but I could see enough already: he carried the weight of Penny's death in him, a burden on his heart; and he missed Beth so much it was eating him from the inside out. Fiona was gone. Beth was too. All he had, all he went home to, was this: what he'd done, the choices he'd made.

'Where is she?' he said.

'She found out what you did –'

'*Where is she?*' he screamed. He shoved the gun towards me again, further than before, so close I could see oil at the muzzle and scratches along the barrel.

But he wasn't going to shoot.

'If you tell me what happened up in the hills in 1987, I'll tell you where Beth is.' I tilted my head slightly, looking along the side of the gun at him. 'That's a promise.'

'A promise?'

'Yeah.'

'Your promises aren't worth shit to me.'

He spat the words out, but there was no venom in them. They were just words, just sounds his mouth was forming.

'Tell me what happened, Jack.'

'You expect me to trust you?' he said.

'No. But I'm not lying to you.'

'How do I know?'

'Because I'm not,' I said with absolute conviction. He studied me, his eyes skirting mine, the lines of my face, looking for evidence I was a fraud – but the more he looked, the less he saw. I wasn't lying.

His whole body seemed to hollow out.

'Jack?'

He kept the gun directed at my face, but the rest of him seemed to evaporate, like tendrils of smoke vanishing into the darkness.

'Did all of this start with the plan to take Caleb Beck's money?'

'There wasn't any *plan* to take the money,' he said. 'There was no plan at all. We were just having fun. We never thought to take the money until after.'

'Until after what?'

He glanced at me but didn't reply.

'After what, Jack? After you killed Caleb Beck and Selina Torres?'

'You can't even imagine.'

Four words that seemed to slice through the air – through the snow, and the wind, and the moans and creaks of the building. He swallowed and looked at me, and then the gun did drop, his hand falling against the bench.

'You can't even imagine how bad it got up there.'

# 68

The temperature seemed to drop and it had nothing to do with the weather.

Kilburn looked down into his lap, saying nothing. I watched snow build up on the curve of his back, on his legs, some of it melting into his coat and trousers, some of it forming into tiny patches, crystalline and delicate, like polished jewels.

'We were all mates, I guess,' he said finally, his voice barely a murmur now. 'Me, Roland, Bill Presley, Jessop. We were different ages, but we got to know each other and just started hanging out. Roland was four years younger than me, and Bill had seven years on him – but it never seemed like it.'

'What do you mean?'

'Just that, Roland wasn't like other kids I knew. He didn't feel anything for anyone. Or if he did, it was because he thought they could give him something he needed, or could use. He was smart – so smart – but as cold-blooded as a fucking snake.' A glance in my direction. 'None of us saw it in our teens or our twenties. I mean, kids don't notice that sort of thing, do they? We only saw it as we got older. Some of the things Roland would say to people, the way he treated them, it started to register. He was – what would you call it?'

Kilburn looked at me again, trying to find the word.

He shrugged and said, 'I don't know . . . dispassionate, I guess. I think he got it from his father. Old Man Dell was a diplomat, this miserable bastard who was governor of the islands in the eighties. He should have been rich, the job he had, but he wasn't. Rumour was, the old man was in shitloads of debt. I think that's why Roland ended up taking that money from Caleb Beck – because he didn't want to be like his father.'

He'd gained control of himself again, his eyes fixed on the ground, the tails of his anorak flapping slightly in the wind.

'Beck didn't trust the bank on the island,' he said.

I eyed him. 'So he kept his money at home?'

Kilburn nodded. 'He hid it under his floorboards in six holdalls. Fiona never knew about it.'

'How much?'

'Three hundred and fifty grand.'

Kilburn shifted his body and, in his eyes, I saw that same flicker of conscience, a tacit acknowledgement of his crimes.

'Roland organized everything,' he said. 'That was what he was good at. He hid the money, or he sat on it, or he did whatever the hell he did to make sure that no one followed a trail back to us, and then thirteen years later, we finally withdrew the cash from accounts he'd set up for us at the banks here.'

But something wasn't right. The more I thought about it, the more I was starting to think that Dell had lied about that too. In fact, I doubted if Kilburn, Presley and Jessop even realized how much money they'd taken from Caleb Beck that day. They'd handed the holdalls over to

Dell and trusted him to divvy out their share once the coast was clear. He eventually did, giving them four thousand pounds each, every month, for twenty-nine months – but that was three hundred and forty-eight thousand. That was pretty much *all* of the money, and there was no way that Dell was ever going to walk away without taking his fair share. He'd want at least the same amount as the others. In reality, he'd probably want the majority of it. That meant Beck could have had at least twice that much in the holdalls.

I thought about telling Kilburn but stopped myself: he was talking now, doing it willingly, and I didn't want to derail that.

'There were a lot of times in those thirteen years,' he said, 'a hell of a lot of times when I'd look at Fiona, or I'd look at the girls, and I'd think, "What the fuck have I done?" I often thought about picking up the phone to Roland in London and saying, "Forget the money. I don't want it any more. I can't live with what we've done. I married Fiona knowing what we did to her husband." But I didn't. I loved Fiona and I guess, deep down, I wanted the money. But I also knew Roland would turn on me if I didn't keep my trap shut.' He stopped and I heard him swallow, as if the next words wouldn't form in his throat. 'There was this small part of me, this part I always hated, that was kind of relieved when Fiona passed away. I mean, I missed her so much – *so* much – but, at night sometimes, in the quiet, I'd think to myself, "I don't have to look her in the face any more and pretend I don't know where her husband went." Eighteen years we were married – and I lied to her about what happened to Caleb the entire time.'

'What *did* happen to him?'

He winced, and then finally rocked back on the bench, the snow falling away in a gentle avalanche.

'Roland's old man was friendly with Caleb Beck,' he said, 'and Roland heard the two of them chatting one night at the house. Beck started telling Roland's dad that – way up on his land, way up in the hills on Strathyde – there was this tarn. It technically belonged to Beck, but he was thinking of opening it up to the public. Beck had all these grand ideas about getting foreign visitors in – he said it would be good for the economy. A lot of the mainlanders were like that. They arrived here thinking they were going to revolutionize the way of life down here. I mean, all that bullshit I fed you earlier about *me* being a mainlander, that was Jessop's story, not mine. I was born and bred here, lived here all my life, it's just I worked hard at not picking up the local accent. But Jessop, Beck, even Fiona – they were all different. Different mindset.' The mention of his wife put a hitch in his voice. 'Fiona pretty much built the new wing on the hospital here. She may not have laid a brick, but she raised the money. That's not what people do a lot of here. That's a mainlander thing.'

He was straying off course, but I didn't press him.

Slowly, this was heading somewhere.

*Somewhere bad.*

'The moment she came to the islands, I liked her,' he said, his thoughts still snared on Fiona, his wife, on the ways he'd betrayed her over the course of nearly two decades, the way he'd done the same to Penny and Beth. 'She was five years older than me. I married young, Fiona was married to Caleb and they had Penny – I knew nothing was going to happen. But it didn't stop me liking Fi. I got hitched in '85, and it took me about six months to realize I'd made a big mistake. Sheila, my first wife, she was nuts, on my case the entire time we were together. Literally the only good thing I remember from three years with her is her handing me my daughter in the delivery room.'

*Beth.*

Kilburn cleared his throat, went to speak, and then stopped. He looked up from his lap, out across the lido. 'She was beautiful,' he said, so softly it was like the words had been carried in with the snow. He raised his trigger finger, away from the gun, straightening it. 'I can still feel her on my skin; the way her entire hand went around the top half of this finger. I remember she made these noises when she breathed, these little squeaks; she made them all night the first night.'

His eyes began to fill.

He turned to me, wiping the tears away with his spare hand, but they kept forging new routes and pathways across the redness of his cheeks. 'Please tell me where she is,' he said, and raised the gun off the bench. He waved it vaguely in my direction, the muzzle passing across my face.

It was so hard watching him. Whatever he'd done, whatever terrible crimes he'd carried out, whatever he'd concealed and submerged in his past, in this moment he wasn't any of that.

He was just a father.

'You were telling me about the tarn,' I said.

It was difficult to pretend he hadn't got to me, or that the things he'd said about Beth didn't resonate, but I kept focused on something he'd told me earlier.

*You can't even imagine how bad it got up there.*

He was a father, but he was a murderer too.

He'd said there was no plan to take Caleb Beck's money; that the decision to do that came later. *After.*

He glanced at me. 'Like I said, Roland told us that he'd overheard Caleb Beck telling Old Man Dell about this tarn; he said he heard Beck talking about a cabin on the edge of it.' He ran his tongue around his mouth, like there was something caustic on his teeth. 'He said it was an old hunting lodge; some place that hadn't been used for decades. Beck talked about it being too far into the hills to be of any real use to him – and Roland being Roland, that got him thinking.'

'About what?'

'About how *he* could use it.'

'Use it for what?'

'We were just kids, really.'

I frowned. 'What are you talking about?'

'That's all we were,' he said, like he hadn't heard me, 'just kids. Roland had just turned nineteen at the time. He'd left to go to sixth-form college in London three years before that, but he'd come back for the summer holidays, and – that year – the first thing he said was that we should all go up to the cabin one night.'

'To do what?'

He sniffed. 'I was twenty-two, Bill was twenty-six. I know I was married, I know Beth had just turned one; I know Bill was the same, married with a son – Richard was, what, four by then? That's just what happened here. You married young, had kids of your own, got on with life. But that didn't make us mature. I was a husband, a dad – same as Bill was – but I had no idea about the world. Roland had found out more in three years abroad than I'd found out in twenty-two years on the islands.'

'What did you go up to the cabin to do?' I repeated.

As he drew a long breath, I realized how cold it was. I could feel it right the way down into my bones, in the collagen, in the calcium, like an arthritic ache.

Kilburn looked at me. 'Roland's dad was a serial shagger. I mean, the way he told it to us, if that had been my old man carrying on like that, doing that to my mum, I'd have ripped his balls off. Roland, though, he thought it was great. He *admired* his dad. And his dad, he was clever, sneaky, because he knew this was a small community, that tongues would wag, so he never screwed anyone from the islands. Not ever. He went out on business trips. That was how he found Torres.'

Things snapped into focus.

'Dell's father used to fly her in from Argentina,' I said. Kilburn nodded.

'Was she a prostitute?'

He shrugged. 'She got paid, if that's what you mean.'

'And Dell flew her in that night in 1987?'

'He went through his dad's contact book and found the phone number for Torres. She wasn't keen on the idea of coming over to start with, especially because Roland told her to keep it a secret from Old Man Dell, but then Roland promised her a shitload of money and she changed her mind. Like I said to you earlier, we were kids, really. No experience of the world. Getting a go on some hot Argentinian woman, playing poker, drinking beer, smoking weed until we blacked out, doing it all up in the mountains

444

where no one would ever find out, where no one in the town would ever know – why *wouldn't* we do it?'

'Was Torres killed up in the cabin?'

'Near it,' he said.

'Why?'

'Because of Caleb Beck.' He shook his head. 'Fucking Beck. He wasn't supposed to be anywhere near us that night. We went up to the cabin *because* no one ever went there.' He stopped again, a thin smile edging his lips. 'Beck liked the stars.'

'What?'

He waved a finger towards the sky. 'He was a stargazer. Turned out he'd found a spot about half a mile from the tarn where he used to take his telescope a couple of times a week.'

*His telescope.*

I remembered the story Beth had told me: how Richard had stumbled across a telescope and an orange anorak in a ravine near the tarn; how they'd been there so long they were covered in mud and moss. The telescope had been Beck's too.

'I read about it after,' Kilburn continued. 'I read about how we're one of the best places in the world to see stars. In the middle of the ocean, hardly any light pollution. You can see the Andromeda galaxy, clear as a bell. You can see for two million light years –'

'So Beck discovered you were all in the cabin?'

'Yes.'

'And he came to see what was going on?'

'Yes.'

He must have dropped everything to go and investigate,

thinking he would only be gone a short time. Instead, his telescope and anorak had never been retrieved; they'd ended up in the ravine, perhaps blown there shortly after by the wind and rain, and no one had ever found them until Richard went out into the Brink that day.

'So you *killed* him because he came to the cabin?'

Kilburn had become distant.

'Jack?'

'It got out of control,' he said.

'Out of control how?'

His attention was fixed on the space beyond us, the walls of the lido, the ugly concrete, the grass banks leading down to the pool.

But then I realized something.

Somewhere beyond the snow and the wind and the groan of the building, I could hear a new noise. I'd been so engrossed in the conversation, so absorbed, I hadn't noticed it.

It was an engine, idling.

*A car.*

As I twigged it, Kilburn did too, and he instantly gripped the gun tighter. We both turned on the bench and looked at the entrance, towards the direction from which the noise had travelled. As we did, the turnstile creaked into action.

Someone was entering the lido.

## 69

For a moment, Kilburn disguised the gun he was holding, pulling it in towards his body. But then a woman emerged from the turnstile and I saw him relax again.

It was the librarian.

She was swamped in a thick windbreaker, strands of hair escaping from inside the hood, breath balled in front of her face. Coming a little way in, to the edge of the covered foyer, she looked from me to Kilburn, neither surprised that we were here, nor that Kilburn was armed, and I remembered what Kilburn had said to me earlier, when he'd still been pretending to be Anthony Jessop.

*You made a mistake going into the library.*

*That's Kilburn's sister that runs it.*

He'd told me plenty of lies today. He'd lied about who he was. Maybe he'd lied about the night at the cabin and what had happened there. But he wasn't lying about this. She *was* his sister. I could see a physical similarity between them now. I could see her lack of surprise that he was armed, and the ease with which he stood – the gun at his side – expecting her to tell him why she was here.

'They found her,' she said.

'What?'

'They found her,' his sister repeated.

He glanced at me. 'Where is she?'

'Grobb's got her.'

My stomach dropped.

They were talking about Beth.

'She's on-board the boat?' Kilburn said, disbelief in his face.

'Yeah.'

He glanced at me. 'How long's she been hiding there?'

I wasn't sure if he was asking me or his sister, but she came forward a step, the toes of her boots flattening the grass, and replied: 'I don't know. Grobb didn't say. He just said they found an air vent near their office that hadn't been reattached properly, and they went looking and found her in there.'

'Does Roland know?'

'I'm not sure. I don't think so – not yet.'

He didn't want Dell to know.

He didn't want a repeat of what had happened to Penny.

The wind suddenly cut across us hard. Kilburn rocked gently against its power, then swivelled to face me, the tears still evident on his cheeks. But his eyes – scorched from being rubbed – showed none of the emotion of before. I'd been able to keep him talking, to keep the story going, on the promise of revealing where Beth was. In truth, I'd been uncertain whether I would, ultimately, not because I didn't believe he loved his daughter, but because it would put her in danger. If Kilburn knew, Dell would find out.

But now it didn't matter either way.

'Where's the ship now?' he said, looking at me, but talking to his sister. His expression had steeled.

'It left an hour ago.'

My bargaining chip had gone and so had the ship. I

had nothing to use and nowhere to go. I was seven thousand miles from home, totally alone, with no way out. I glanced beyond him, looking again at the curved concrete boundaries of the lido hemming us in like prison walls. I flicked a look left, to where the changing rooms were, and then back to the entrance where Kilburn's sister was standing.

Kilburn smiled. 'Bit late to run for it now.'

The smile broadened and he let out a long breath of air. Most of it was drawn from relief, from knowing he was back in control, that his daughter was safe, that he would be seeing her again soon. Whatever he'd done in his life, whatever the whole truth about that night at the cabin, Kilburn wasn't a sadist. He didn't lie, injure and kill because any of it appealed to him. He did it because he was protecting himself, purely and simply.

'Get on the phone to Barry Sargent at the airport,' he said to his sister, still watching me, still holding the pistol at his side, 'and tell him I need a pilot to take me to the ship. Tell him I'll be there' – he checked his watch – 'in thirty minutes.'

*After he's taken care of me.*

His sister looked at me. She seemed uncomfortable with the idea of what was coming, of the subtext hidden behind her brother's demand. I tried to stare her down, to appeal to her somehow, to get her to talk him back, but she ripped her gaze from me and headed for the turnstile.

'Jack,' I said. 'You don't need to do this.'

'So is this what you were going to tell me?' he said, shoving the gun at me. 'Or were you just stringing me along?'

I shook my head. 'No.'

The turnstile squeaked again as Kilburn's sister moved back through. He didn't look at her once, just kept his eyes focused on me, but I did: I followed her as she emerged on to the other side, fleeing the lido; watching as she glanced over her shoulder at me, once, twice, before finally vanishing from view.

'Were you going to tell me?'

I turned to him.

'Yes,' I lied. 'Beth wouldn't want this.'

'How would *you* know what she wants?'

'I spoke to her on the ship.'

'*So?*'

'So this violence is what drove her away in the first pl—'

He smashed the gun across my face.

I was on the floor, dazed, before I'd even realized what was going on. I could feel snow against one side of my face, blood leaking from a cut above my eye on the other, and Kilburn was standing over me, leaning forward, screaming at me, 'Don't talk to me about my *daughter*! You'll never know what it's been like for me!'

I'd brought my arms up to my face to protect myself, expecting the gun to go off, steeling myself for a punch, a kick, praying his finger didn't slip against the trigger. I could hear my heart in my ears, feel a thump behind my eyes. I took my arms away again and watched him level the weapon at me.

'Jack, *please.*'

My voice wavered.

'Jack, you don't have to —'

'Shut up.'

'You don't have to do this.'

'*Shut up.*'

He leaned down and pressed the gun against my head, rolling me on to my back. I listened to Kilburn's sister driving away, the engine disappearing against the moan of the wind, and then it was just the wind, and the snow, and us.

'If you're going to do it, Jack,' I said to Kilburn, 'then do it.'

I closed my eyes.

In the darkness, I thought of Richard Presley, a man who'd survived, knowing nothing about himself, on the other side of the world; and now here I was, about to die for knowing too much, seven thousand miles from home.

'What the fuck are you doing here?'

I opened my eyes again.

Kilburn was looking beyond me. I shifted, propping myself up on to an elbow, and again felt the warmth of blood at my face.

'We've betrayed our kids.' Another voice, the words slurred.

I twisted and looked over to the changing rooms.

The voice belonged to Bill Presley.

# 70

Presley stood about three feet away, still in his police uniform. Across the front of his black windbreaker were the letters REIP, in white, the badge of the Royal Empress Islands Police on his breast. He was holding a shotgun, the stock against his shoulder, and aiming it at Kilburn, but he seemed to sway as he stood. The smell of booze carried across to us on the wind.

Kilburn shook his head, his own gun still at his side. 'How long have you been hiding?' Kilburn took a step forward, looking past Presley to the changing rooms. He made a show of sniffing the air. 'Do they serve whisky in there now?'

Presley didn't respond.

Kilburn shook his head again, looking down at me and back up to Presley. 'Bill, you're drunk at two in the afternoon, so why don't you let me handle this?'

'You know when it changed?'

Kilburn sighed. 'What?'

'You know when all of this changed?'

'What the fuck are you talking about?'

'What we did up there,' Presley said, nodding sideways at the hills, at the folds and clefts of Mount Strathyde, 'it was survival to start with. You and me, we weren't as clever as Roland, so it took me a while to catch on.' He wasn't fully drunk, but his words were soft, the edges of them doughy and flat. 'The fence and the lies and the bullshit; the money we took – waiting thirteen years for Roland to hand out our share to us like the good little boys we were; at his beck and call when the Argie police came here asking questions. It was all survival.'

'You're rambling,' Kilburn said.

'No,' Presley shot back, shaking his head. He glanced at me. 'No. We were trying to survive for a long time, trying not to get sent to prison for what we did, and I swallowed it and I accepted it, we both did, because that's what Roland said was for the best.' He adjusted both hands at the shotgun. 'But you know when it all changed, Jack? You know when it suddenly hit me? The full weight of what we'd done, all the things we'd covered up, the misery we'd brought to other people, the families they had – you know when I saw it clearly for the first time?'

Kilburn looked at me again, but something was different. He'd worked out where this was going. He knew where Presley was headed.

'Penny,' Presley said.

Her name made Kilburn jolt.

'When Roland told us she was dead, *why* she was dead, when he told us that Kraut, or Pole, or whatever the fuck Marek is, dumped her body on that railway line, shoving her into those sleepers like she wasn't worth a damn thing, you just accepted it. This girl you'd brought up as your own, you just accepted –'

'I didn't accept it.'

'So what did you do about it? Huh?' Presley waited for an answer. When he didn't get one, he said, 'It's been two years, Jack. She's been gone two years.'

'I mourn her every day.'

'*Do* you? You never signed off on her murder, I'll give you that much. But you went along with it after. You're as culpable as that prick who put her there on that line. And that was the moment when I saw everything clearly.' He glanced at me again, and this time he addressed me: 'When Roland told us about you, I thought, "Good. Let him come."' He stopped for a second. '"Let him come."'

'Put the gun down, Bill,' Kilburn said.

'I'm glad my boy's got no memory,' he said in reply, his voice starting to break. 'He doesn't remember me. He doesn't remember the things he found out about us. He doesn't know who we are and what we did, the lives we ruined.'

'Bill,' Kilburn said again.

I watched Presley's eyes shift to Kilburn's gun.

'Why would Beth ever want to see you again, Jack?'

Kilburn's eyes flashed. 'She's my daughter.'

'No.'

'I'm her father.'

'No,' Presley said again.

He took a step closer to Kilburn.

'You stopped being her father two years ago. You stopped being her father when you allowed Roland to get away with what he did. Beth's better off without you, Jack. Richard's better off without me. You and I, we betrayed our children.'

They watched each other for a second.

The wind blew; the snow surged and swelled.

And then the silence was shattered by a gunshot.

## 71

Birds scattered from the roof of the lido, taking off into the sky.

I got up on to my feet, still woozy, my trousers damp from the grass, my face burning along the ridges of my cheekbone. I used the sleeve of my coat to wipe away the blood, and looked at Presley. He was standing between the bench Kilburn and I had been sitting on and the changing rooms, his shotgun at his side.

He was sobbing.

I turned to Kilburn. He lay on the slant of the grass as it dropped away to the swimming pool, eyes staring up into the granite of the sky. As the snow fell around us, it began forming in patches on his body, on the toes of his upturned boots, in the folds of his coat, in the cleft at his throat. Blood spread out either side of him, like a pair of red wings, the embers of his life finding a path through the grass, artery-like, filling microscopic chasms and voids.

I looked back at Presley.

He was crying harder, waves of it coming up from his chest, bending him almost double. The shotgun became a walking stick, the barrel of the weapon in the ground supporting his weight as he leaned into it. When he lifted his other hand to his face, swabbing tears away; his fingers wiping at his nose, I noticed that something was poking out of his pocket: the corner of a colour photograph.

I took a step closer, conscious that he was armed and loaded on whisky, but he didn't move, didn't even react, and as I took a second step towards him, I saw more of the photo. It had been on the mantelpiece in his house that morning. It was him and Richard, arms around each other's shoulders, in a different time.

*A different life.*

I noticed something else too.

Matted to his hands was earth and what looked like rose petals. I thought of Jacob Howson then, of how he'd brought flowers to the railway line, to a grave site on the opposite side of the world.

And now here I was in another.

For a while, I'd thought it was going to be mine as Kilburn had pressed the gun to my head, but it was his. I looked at him, his body splayed across the ground, and again I felt a moment of remorse for him, despite what he'd done.

'Here.'

I turned back to Presley.

He was looking at me, tears running into his beard. In front of him, he was holding something out, pinched between his fingers.

It was a key.

'Is that for the cabin?' I said.

He nodded, sniffed.

'What will I find up there?'

He didn't seem to have heard me.

'Bill?' I said, using his first name as a way to try and get his attention. He looked up at me. 'Bill, what will I find up there?'

I saw more earth on his hands, forming little brown crescents beneath his fingernails. It was on his jacket, along the bottom fringes of it, at his knees.

'If it isn't you,' he said, looking past the key he was still holding out to me, 'it'll be someone else.' He paused, his lips parting slightly. At his gum, I could see the slightly skewed front tooth he shared with his son. Beneath his beanie, a hint of thin red hair poked out. 'You, the Argies, there'll be others too. You'll just come and come because the thing is, no secret can stay hidden. You think you've buried yours somewhere far up into the hills, you think you've put them behind a fence, behind a thing that scares the shit out of everyone, but they don't stay up there.' He threw the key to me. 'As long as human beings have a conscience, secrets will never stay hidden.'

I glanced at the key.

'He had the most beautiful soul.'

I looked at Presley again.

'Richard,' he said. 'He was a beautiful kid. He used to read all these books, one after the other. He'd know so much about everything. I'd listen to him over dinner, or when we went out fishing or kicking a ball around, and every time was like the new, best moment of my life. When you look at your kid, and you realize they're so much better than you'll ever be, even in your best moment, it's like . . .' Presley ground to a halt, unable to form the words, tears running down his face. He wiped them away and smiled, but it was a smile that was hard to watch. It was like sunshine after a bomb – it lit him up, but the devastation was done.

'Tell Richard I love him.'

'Bill, wait a second –'

'Just tell him I love him.'

He raised the shotgun at me.

'And tell him that beach he can remember – just to forget about it.'

I frowned. 'What?'

'I read online that he can remember looking out at a beach as a kid. I read that they think it might have been where he grew up.' He shook his head. 'It isn't. He didn't grow up by the beach. Just tell him I'm sorry, okay? Just tell him to forget it.'

'What are you talking about?'

'I want you to leave now.'

I stared at him.

'You have the key,' he said. 'Now leave.'

'You don't have to do this.'

But he was already shaking his head.

'This is exactly what I have to do.'

I walked into a wall of wind, following the half-mile road back towards Sophia. In the distance, smudged by snow and sea mist, I could see the lights at Blake Point. The *Olympia* was gone. The islands were cut off from the world again.

I was marooned here.

After a few minutes, I looked back over my shoulder at the lido, sitting like a blister on the edge of the plateau. I heard birds somewhere close by – and then they stopped, and the wind dropped away.

A single gunshot rang out.

# 72

The hiking trails were all scree, grey veins worming their way up the side of the mountain. As I climbed in the direction of the Brink, the snow eased off, thinning out, but the wind got stronger, drawn to the mounds and drops of Strathyde.

It was freezing cold and hard on the body: at points, I was leaning forward almost at forty-five degrees, the wind hammering against me, blowing the hood off my head, its noise like a dog whistle against my eardrums. Everything hurt: the bruise on my face, the ones on my hands, on my arms, on my ribs. I paused at one stage and, through the gauze of the snowfall, thought I could see an actual road somewhere in the distance, its shape gouged out of the hills. I remembered how Beth had talked about Kilburn coming up in a vehicle and leaving her and Penny at the fence. But the road looked difficult to negotiate, full of hairpin turns, and even if I'd had a car I wasn't convinced it would have been safer. The snow wasn't thick but it was thick enough, and up here the roads wouldn't be gritted.

Twenty minutes after that, the landscape changed.

It seemed to come out of nowhere, the mountain cleaving in two. I glanced back, estimating that I was about eight hundred feet up, and looked ahead of me again. The trail petered out about thirty feet in front of me, and was replaced by two distinct halves. On the right, Strathyde continued its ascent, just without a defined path, rising another two thousand feet to its peak. On the left, there was a kind of plain, a flat shelf of land that, as I got closer, I could see gradually sloped away. It was wide, too wide to properly get a sense of in the weather – but I knew immediately where I was.

*Somewhere near the Brink.*

I kept going, leaving the last of the scree and crossing into grass. Initially it was shorter, less dense, but it soon thickened, condensing into chunks, the ground becoming softer, the snow struggling to settle because of how moist it was. In front of me, though, flakes still whirled and dipped, massaged by the wind, and a faint mist began to land, gripping the outline of the mountain. I could see far enough ahead to know where I was going, but at eight hundred feet above the town, hardly any of Sophia was visible any more.

I walked on a little further, then stopped.

For the first time, I could see the fence.

It was six feet tall and ran all the way across the marshland, right to left. It was hard to gauge for how far, or how many wire-mesh fence panels must have been put up, but it was more than enough. I tried following it for a while to see if there was any break in it, tracing the downward cant of the hill, but I couldn't see any gaps, no breaches at all, and then I spotted something else.

The pillbox.

Feeling a flutter of unease, I walked to the fence and looked through the wire at the size and scale of the Brink; into the ring of mist that had bedded in, to snow that moved and whirled and constantly changed shape.

460

I'd been to places like this before, to buildings that carried the weight of their past, to patches of land whose history was burned into their soil. I'd never believed in ghosts – not the sort that rattled chains and made noises in the attic – but I believed a place could retain a sense of the things that had happened in it, like a residue that never dried out. And this was one of them.

I could see it, feel it.

I laced my fingers through the mesh, found a hole with the toe of my boot and started to haul myself up. At the top, a leg on either side of the line, I looked out into the long grass again, everything moving in the wind – swaying, altering – and I felt a hesitation. Somewhere deeper down, a part of me argued against the idea of going beyond the fence at all. The feeling became stronger the longer I chewed on it, a magnetic pull wanting to drag me back to safety.

I pushed the doubt away, swung my leg over and climbed down the other side. When my feet hit the ground, I felt them sink into the wetness of the peat bog, the long grass whipping against my legs in the wind.

I turned and looked left down the slant of the mountainside, and then right, higher up, in the direction of the place that Richard had described to Beth: the tarn, the cabin, what I hoped would be the truth. I couldn't see anything, no landmarks at all except for the looming shadow of Strathyde, its crags lean and emaciated.

Again, I felt a moment of indecision.

But then I started across the Brink.

## 73

Everywhere I looked, the Brink moved, its grass dipping and lurching as the wind rolled across the mountainside. I followed a vague trail, trampled out of the bogs, that seemed to follow the slant of the hill, but the further up I went, the more disorientating it seemed to become. It was like the whole place was mobile, changing and evolving, and even when it calmed in the lulls between gusts, it didn't settle completely: snow flecked against my face; the ground squelched and shifted, as if it were about to slide out from under me; grass seemed to reach up – swiping at my hands, grabbing them.

It was mid-afternoon and some of the light had already disappeared, but it wasn't the grey skies that were recolouring the plain, or the sunset that lay in wait, it was a mist. It wasn't thick, in fact the opposite: I could see in all directions for at least two hundred feet. But it clung to the edges of the mountain like a gossamer sheet that had snared on some peg further up, and – beyond its limits – there were only shadows, traces of things, vague shapes that formed and dissolved, and it wasn't long before I felt even more discomfited.

*Just keep going.*

I looked at my watch, saw it was almost four, and then looked again what seemed like twenty minutes later – except barely any time had passed, only five or six minutes.

The marshland was drying out now, the peat dragging less and less at my heels. When Richard had talked to Beth about it, he'd described the lake being ringed by peaks, the arena in a coliseum of crests and summits.

I couldn't see anything like that.

A vague sense of panic started to grip. I didn't know where the hell I was or how far I'd gone, and the absurdity of coming up here without a map, without the right equipment or supplies, hit home. I'd been focused on the cabin, on finding answers. Now all of that felt secondary: as the wind cut through me, everywhere looked exactly the same.

Something moved.

It was right on the periphery of my vision, so far off to my left that I had to turn my entire body forty-five degrees. I looked down the pitch of the hill, south of me. There was no sign of the fence or the pillbox, although I knew both were somewhere in that direction. Between me and the ring of the mist nothing had changed: it was just mounds of tussock grass and streaks of peat, like puddles of oil sprayed across the earth.

I watched, waited.

Nothing.

I began moving again, glancing over my shoulder, then again, my heart starting to beat faster, a vibration that had nothing to do with the exertion of the climb. I looked behind me again and then again, each time scanning the mist, watching it form and re-form, as if it were maturing and growing. I picked up the pace like I was being pursued, but there was nothing behind me, just my own uncertainties and the echoes of the stories I'd heard about the Brink.

And then the landscape changed.

It happened dramatically, suddenly, the steady slant becoming sharper, a huge wall of rock climbing out of the ground in front of me. The closer I got, the more I realized it was the slopes of another ridge, formed out of Strathyde like a growth, and that the slope – its clefts, crevices and folds – was part of a wider range, sweeping off into the mist. A second after that, it clicked: it was an amphitheatre.

Partially hidden in shadow, I saw a natural passageway ahead of me, a ragged oval carved out of the face of the hill, like a tunnel without any roof.

Beyond that, there was a hint of water; a shimmer.

*The tarn.*

I quickened my pace. From my position it appeared shallow, an immense puddle, smooth except for the snow-flakes dusting it – but I knew it was deep. It had that sense about it, an indefinable aura, its surface reflecting back the crown of peaks surrounding it, each one a different size and shape but every one a giant. I made it halfway when something seemed to change – the ground, the air itself.

Out of nowhere, a sound tore across the hillside.

It caught me so much by surprise I stumbled, the noise loud enough that I could feel it tremble through the earth. But I knew what it was.

The noise Penny and Beth had heard; Richard too.

*The call of whatever was out here.*

As it came to an end, the echoes of it seemed to hang in the thickness of the air. It was like the cry of an animal that had been distorted; one long note full of turbulence and static. It was bizarre and disconcerting, and the longer I stood there, the more exposed I began to feel. I tried to think rationally, tried to stay focused and logical, but I was so far up in the mountains and the sound felt so out of place in this moment, so alien, it was impossible not to feel unsettled by it.

I looked around me, and then quickly carried on up the slope until I had an unobstructed view of the tarn. On the opposite side of the water, a dark building came into view.

The cabin.

Then: another noise from behind me.

I looked back, down the part of the pathway I'd already walked, out at the plain I'd crossed to get here. Streaks of peat glistened. The long grass moved and the snow kept coming: it was light, fine and delicate, but as it swirled and changed direction, it gave the impression of things stirring. And then I fixed on something.

*What was that?*

*What the hell was that?*

Inside the mist, hidden in it, I glimpsed a silhouette. It was there and then gone again, like a shape standing at a window as the light snaps off. I raised a hand to my face, trying to protect my eyes from the snow, to see clearly, maybe to hear something too, but all I could see now was mist and all I could hear was my heart thumping in my ears and my breath whispering in my throat and chest.

Keeping my gaze fixed on the same spot, I started walking backwards, up the slope to the very edge of the tarn, trying to pull the memory into focus; reassemble what I'd seen of the silhouette, rebuild it in my mind's eye. I stumbled on the scree, the stones slick with mud and snow, kept going and did the same again. I was drained, on edge, the exhaustion of the trip starting to eat at me. There were no more shapes, no hints of movement.

But that didn't calm my anxiety.

I waited a while longer, unsure now of what I believed and what I didn't, and then I zeroed in on what mattered: the case, the truth, what took place here.

I started heading to the cabin.

But I didn't walk, I ran.

# 74

The closer I got, the more I could see, the building emerging from the mist like a ship sailing into existence. Small and compact, it was sixty feet back from the lake shore and constructed of dark wood, but the wood had become bleached with age, and the tin roof was so awash in moss and bird shit it was hard to see its original colour.

When I got to the steps leading up to the front veranda, the cabin creaked in the wind, the sound almost like a moan. It made me stop, and I looked back along the edge of the tarn, in the direction I'd come.

Beneath my feet, the stairs felt soft, the wood warped and rotten, bending under my weight. My first step on to the veranda seemed to send a shudder along it, as if I'd awoken something. The wind picked up and I watched the lake shiver out of its stillness, and then everything settled again: the windows, rattling in their frames, became silent; the creak of the walls faded.

There was a window next to me, its curtains pulled, but I could see hints of things inside: furniture, boxes, right angles. At the far end of the veranda was a log pile. It had collapsed, some of the logs spilling off the side, untouched on the ground for so long that grass had grown around them, enclosed them, trapped them.

At the door I removed from my pocket the key that Presley had given me. But I didn't need it. The door was stiff, difficult to manoeuvre out from the frame, but it swung back, already unlocked, whining on its hinges towards the darkness of the entrance.

I paused, my pulse rising.

Why was it already open?

Immediately, I could see three more doors, on the left, on the right and at the end. It was difficult to see into any of them from where I was, but I thought I could make out a black cast-iron stove in the back room, streaked with ash, and the outline of a table. I could hear something coming from that direction as well.

Uncertain of the noise, uncertain of what awaited me inside, I levered out the longest, thickest log I could find in the woodpile, gripped it like a baseball bat, and then headed through the door. I thought of everything I'd seen and heard until now, the stories, the silhouette in the hills, the noise.

*Concentrate.*

Floorboards groaned underfoot. The walls were panelled in dark wood, the ceiling a series of planks, lined up one after the other, like the underside of a boardwalk. I stopped at the first door, the one on my left, and peered around the frame. The room was empty except for a couple of chairs. In the room on the right, shelves were filled with tins, all decades old: food, oil, glue, nails and screws, rat poison, empty bottles. They were coated in cobwebs and everything carried the same stench of rust, a tangy scent that hung in the air and lingered in the walls.

I headed for the back room.

As I did, I heard the same noise again, more defined this time. It was like a clatter, the snap of wood hitting wood. I glanced behind me, back to the front of the cabin, snow blowing in from outside, and then arrived at the door to the last room. I saw the stove, archaic and idle, the table I'd glimpsed earlier set against one of the walls. There was other furniture too: an old red sofa, so worn and old it had become a light pink; more chairs, one still standing, one on its side, one smashed. There were shelves full of tins here too, food mostly, although none of it was new, and there was a radio, its antenna snapped, in among some canned soup.

But it wasn't any of that that caught my eye.

It was the rose petals.

They were strewn across the floor of the room in a vague trail leading all the way to the rear door. This was also unlocked like the front and was being blown back and forth in the wind. I had the key Presley had given me pinched between my thumb and finger, but I didn't need it now, so I pocketed it. I watched the back door hitting its frame, making the snapping sound I'd heard, that same clatter of wood against wood. As it did, I felt the breeze ghost past me, drawn from the back of the cabin to the front, and watched the petals scatter even further out.

As I inched towards the back veranda, my mind returned to the lido, to the moments after Bill Presley turned up. I remembered the stains at the knees of his trousers, evidence of earth, mud and grass. I remembered the dirt under his nails, as if he'd been digging in the ground. But mostly I remembered the rose petals.

They'd been stuck to his skin.

*He'd been up here before he came to the lido.*

I noticed something else too. The closer I got towards the back door, the more of them I could see: tiny holes embedded in the wall of the cabin, fanning off in a line. My eyes switched between the holes and the door, looking beyond the room to the rear of the cabin where a hillside full of long grass swept up and out of view about forty feet from the building. The glass panel in the door had fractured, cracking like ice on a pond, and as it swung back and forth in the wind, I could see mangled hints of the room reflected in it – and I realized I'd missed other holes in the walls behind me as well.

They'd all been made by bullets.

There were ten shots that I could see. There could have been more, but late afternoon was starting to give way to early evening and shadows were beginning to creep inwards. This time, as the door swung back in the wind again, I caught it and held it in place. Cold air swept past me as if the cabin were drawing breath, and I moved on to the back veranda. To the right of me, the far end, I was surprised to see another door, but my attention was quickly drawn from that to the hillside. Things moved through the long grass, flickers of white, and I realized it was more petals. They were being torn from the stems of flowers that had been left at the bottom of the veranda steps.

I thought of the mud stains on Presley's trousers, the earth matted to his knees, and then looked out across the hillside again, up, following its ascent. There was something else dotted in the grass, other flashes of colour that weren't flowers.

The back door snapped shut.

I turned automatically, watching it banging against the door frame, and when my gaze drifted into the cabin, I saw something inside the back room.

*Movement.*

I gripped the log harder and slowly began peeling the door open.

The room was still empty.

I let out a breath, my mind starting to fill with images of what I'd seen earlier – what I *thought* I'd seen – out on the slope, and then I moved inside, past old, broken furniture, past the stove, out into the hallway and down towards the front door.

It was darker in this part of the cabin now, the light fizzling out. I glanced at my watch and saw it was just before five o'clock.

I had about an hour and a half of light left.

And then I noticed something on the front steps of the house, sitting there as if placed. I took a step towards it. It was small and tubular, a C-shaped horn; a replica of the type of wind instruments that medieval huntsmen had used.

*That's it.*

That was what I'd heard out in the Brink.

'David.'

My heart hit my throat.

A voice, so close to my ear, it felt like it had come from inside my head. I turned, following the sound, but then a hand clamped on to the back of my neck, catching me off balance, and pushed me hard – face first – into the nearest wall.

Roland Dell wasn't in London.

He was here.

# 75

He pressed my face into the wall and then released his grip, backing up. I turned, ready for him, but he didn't attack. Instead, he retreated another step, pausing in the space between me and the entrance to the back room, and raised a weapon.

It was a crossbow.

The stock was bedded against his shoulder, and he was looking through the sights mounted to a bridge at the beginning of the arrow track. The bow was black, compact, no more than two feet in length, and loaded. Spare arrows were sitting below the end of the flight groove, each one streaked a luminous yellow.

He wasn't in a suit any more; he was in black trousers, a grey fleece and a black gilet. His hair was hidden beneath a beanie, his black boots still showing the evidence of snow, of having come across the slopes himself.

He'd been the shape I'd seen inside the house.

He'd drawn me out.

'I guess if you're going to get a job done properly, you just have to do it yourself,' Dell said, moving a little closer to me. Once he had, he eyed me, watching me carefully, as if I were about to launch myself at him. He looked every bit as tired as I did, a man who'd spent the past week on edge, worrying about how far I might get; a man who'd flown halfway around the world to stop me getting any further. He said, 'I wasn't going to leave Cape Town until I knew you'd been taken care of. So when I realized Alexander had failed, I sent Kilburn to find out what you knew and finish the job. Then he failed too, although I think that probably had less to do with your ability to cheat death, and more to do with Bill being an old drunk.' He sighed and shook his head. 'I stopped relying on Bill years ago and, judging by what's gone on at the back of the cabin here, I'd say that was a pretty good decision, wouldn't you?'

Did he mean the flower petals?

I kept my face neutral, making out like I knew what he was talking about.

'What is it with you?' he said. He used the crossbow as a pointer, jabbing the tip of it towards the front door, signifying the tarn, and the hills, and the mountain. 'All this effort, all these miles, and for what exactly? Just to fill in a few blanks for a guy who's better off not remembering anything anyway?'

'Is he?'

Dell shrugged, the crossbow rising and dropping at his movement. 'Well, it's not going to make him any happier.'

He wasn't playing with me this time. I looked at him, at the contours of his face, and then remembered something Presley had said to me about his son, before I'd left him at the lido. *I read online that he can remember looking out at a beach as a kid. I read that they think it might have been where he grew up. It isn't. He didn't grow up by the beach. Just tell him to forget it.*

*Just tell him I'm sorry.*

'I wish I could have just killed him.'

I tuned back in, looking at Dell.

473

'I wish I could have dealt with him like we dealt with Penny. But Richard was trickier. He had a police force on his side. He had a charity looking out for him. Local people, local media – they were interested in his story, where he came from. It would have been a circus if he suddenly vanished, or – worse – turned up dead. I'd have put myself at risk.'

'Because it's all about you.'

He smiled. 'You know what this place is?'

I didn't answer.

'It's a card trick. It's the best card trick you've ever seen in your life. It's a card trick so fucking good that it could have been invented by the Devil himself.'

I frowned, unsure what he meant.

He burst out laughing, his face partly hidden by the crossbow. 'Look at you,' he said, a derisory slant to his words. 'You look like a soldier having flashbacks. Are you confused? Frightened? Have you shit yourself?'

He took another step closer, his movements becoming more aggressive.

'How about now? Huh? I'm going to put an arrow through your eye and I'm going to bury your body out the back with the others.'

I tried to ignore the fear and focus on the idea that Dell thought I'd found something out back; something more than just petals in the grass. *The others*. He must have meant the hillside was the burial ground for Caleb Beck and Selina Torres.

*Or was it even worse than that?*

I thought of what Kilburn had said (*You can't even imagine how bad it got up there*) and of all the bullet holes in the walls, and then an image started to form, a memory filling in from earlier: standing on the back veranda here, looking out at the hillside and seeing something else – not the petals, not the flowers, but other flashes of colour in the grass. I hadn't recognized them for what they were then.

But it came together now.

They'd been crosses, hidden beneath the level of the grass. I could picture them clearly, as if I was operating on a delay: each one was two pale lengths of plywood nailed together. As the wind picked up, they'd bent in the breeze, making them harder to identify, but they'd been there. *Graves.* Presley had had earth matted to his trousers because he'd marked them out for me to find.

Worse, there had been many more than two.

I looked at Dell. 'How many?'

'How many what?'

'How many people did you bury out the back?'

He came forward, jabbing the crossbow at me, reminding me of who was in charge. I rocked back on my heels, hitting the wall hard, and dust showered me. I felt it touch my face, saw it land on my shoulders, but I didn't move. He had the crossbow poised only a couple of feet from the tip of my nose.

'They're gone,' he said.

'Not to their families they're not.'

He watched me for a moment. 'Much as I got on with Bill,' he said, 'with Jack, with Anthony, I wasn't about to make do with their sloppy seconds.'

I felt a moment of confusion again – but then I got it.

'Torres wasn't the only woman you flew over.'

He didn't respond.

'How many others?'

'I don't remember.'

'You're a liar. How many?'

Dell shrugged. 'Enough for all of us.'

'What the hell did you do up here?'

'Like I told you,' he said, 'this place is a card trick.'

The card trick was the Brink.

It was him I'd seen out there, a shape in the mist. He'd been toying with me, but that was all it had taken. The noise from the horn, the glimpse of his silhouette, it had been enough to knock me off balance, to make me question myself, so it would have been more than enough for three terrified kids. It would have been enough to sow the seed of doubt in town too: a fiction, a myth, that grew with the construction of the fence, with the whispers that it might not just be landmines up here, with the nights three kids spent tied to the fence as punishment and the details they must have let slip about it afterwards. And when the dog brought Selina Torres's leg bone back, that hadn't been part of the plan, but, ironically, it may actually have aided the lie. It was a story controlled by the most powerful men in town; a story created by them, and then disseminated in a place where rumours couldn't just disappear.

'That's the thing with stories,' he said, almost as if he knew what I'd been thinking. 'All of them, even the fictional ones, have to be built on an element of truth. And most people, they only believe what they can see with their own eyes.' He took a step back, a twitch of a smile at his mouth again; but he wasn't amused this time, he was triumphant. 'You arrived here as a non-believer, didn't you?

You were shouting down the idea of something being out here. But on that mountain, just for a moment, you had your belief shaken. And that's all it takes. In a place like this, full of insular people with simple ideas, you only need a glimpse. And the little fuckers – Richard, and Penny, and Beth – who came up here snooping around, well, we had to take it a stage further with them. They broke the rules. I admired their courage in a way, but we couldn't let it slide. I mean, Jack had had his suspicions that his girls were creeping out after dark for a while, so he and Bill followed them up there one night. That was who the girls saw at the fence. Jack was the "monster" they glimpsed as they ran for their lives. Jessop was who they heard out in the Brink the night they were left there. We tied them up so they could see and hear *just* enough for the story to grow, and then we gave the rumours a little push in the town when we needed to. And do you know how many other kids thought it might be a good idea to come up here after Richard got over the fence?'

'None.'

He nodded. 'None.'

'And you invented the story to cover up what happened here?'

'We did what was necessary.'

'To cover up the truth about all the people you shot?'

'We did what was necessary,' he said again.

'Beck turned up here, angry and wanting to know why people were on his property, and somehow it all got out of hand. Somehow it all went crazy and y–'

'Sssshhh.' He held a finger up to me, his other hand still gripping the crossbow.

Wind whispered past us, seeking out the spaces of the house, and like a sound caught in a loop the back door slammed against its frame, once, twice, three times. In the silence, I looked from Dell to the front of the house, then to the back room, trying to work out if this was another trick he was playing; another story dreamed up to unsettle me. But there was no playfulness in him this time.

He looked nervous.

A second later, I realized why: there was another noise, hidden behind the exhalation of the wind, behind the snap of the door. He'd heard it first because he was so familiar with the cabin: its tones, vibrations, the way it breathed and felt.

Now I heard it too.

It was someone softly calling my name.

# 76

It was coming from the back of the cabin.

Dell moved around me, so that he was between me and the front door, and then gestured with the crossbow that I should go ahead of him. I did as he asked, conscious that he was nervous now, alarmed, his finger readjusting on the bow. I only needed him to lose concentration for a second and he might accidentally press the trigger too hard.

'What's going on?' he whispered as he followed me.

I shook my head.

'Are you messing with me, Raker?'

I shook my head again.

I wasn't sure if he believed me or not, but I used the moment to my advantage, as I passed from one area of the cabin to the next, to take in the room, to see if anything had changed. My eyes traced the bullet holes, the petals on the floor.

Nothing looked different.

The rear door wafted open and slammed shut again, and then he prodded me in the back with the crossbow, the hard plastic of the arrow track sniping at my spine. I headed for the door, again letting my eyes do the work. I took in the sofa and the chairs and the stove and imagined what it had been like in 1987; how it had been the night Dell, Kilburn, Presley and Jessop had come here. I thought of the women Dell had flown over, paid for, employing their services because, presumably like Selina Torres, they were discreet. I didn't know what any of them looked like, what their names were, but I knew they'd never been cabin crew, they'd never had desk jobs, they weren't jetting off to far-flung places to attend meetings, even though that was what they'd told their families back in Buenos Aires. Even three decades on, their families still believed the stories. All they knew of their daughters, sisters, wives, girlfriends was that they left home in July 1987 and never came back.

*So many missing people.*

'Stop,' Dell hissed at me, and then shoved me aside, to the right of the rear door. I stumbled, hitting one of the chairs, and by the time I'd recovered and looked back at him, he was pulling open the door, the crossbow still aimed at me.

I watched his eyes scan the veranda.

It was so quiet now, I could see that he was thinking exactly the same as me. Had we actually heard anything at all? Was it *really* my name that had been called? Who would have been calling my name? He glanced at me, beckoned me over, not trusting me to stay where I was. Once I was close to him, he retreated from the door and shoved me out on to the veranda.

It was cold, getting dark.

This time I could feel the wind. It rushed through the grass, swiping at it, cresting it – and in the gaps that were created I finally saw everything properly.

The crosses.

They whipped back and forth in the breeze, drifting in

and out of view like spirits passing through walls. In among the grass, I counted two. Three. Four.

Five.

Six.

I stood there, stunned.

'You killed *six* people?'

'Shut the fuck up,' he said, shoving me forward with the palm of his hand, so that I stood at the top of the veranda steps, looking at all the crosses.

It hadn't been a murder.

It had been a massacre.

'You killed six people,' I muttered, almost to myself, the words so sour on my tongue, so surreal, I could hardly process them.

'I said shut up.'

He looked stressed, the blue of his eyes subdued in the light, their lustre lost, his fingers seared red from the cold and from holding the crossbow so hard.

I followed his gaze, out on to the hillside.

Now I was closer to it, I could see patches where the grass grew higher, more rampantly, elongated squares that seemed to have been specifically watered. But they hadn't. It was what was underneath the soil, long since decayed, that made them grow like that. They were exactly where Presley had placed the crosses.

The wind came again, blowing snow across us, and when the grass moved in time, in a sweeping arc, I thought I saw something shift further up the hillside.

Dell saw it too.

He tightened his grip on the crossbow, forced the stock in harder against his shoulder, and moved to the very edge of the veranda. I watched him, his gaze scanning the slope, panic in his eyes. He shouted, 'I can see you up there!' but his lie was carried away by the wind.

He glanced at me and then back to the hillside.

'Is this something to do with you, Raker? *Is* it?'

He sounded desperate, frightened, for the first time.

'I said, is this something to do with *you*?' he screamed again, and swivelled the crossbow around to face me. It was juddering against his arm, the anger and panic sending ripples through his body. 'What the hell is out there? Huh?'

I held up both hands. 'I don't know.'

'You're lying to me.'

I took a step further back. 'I'm not.'

'You're *lying*!'

'I don't know what it is,' I said to him, 'I swear to you I don't,' and I turned to study the hillside again, the grass, the flecks of snow, the plywood crosses, the whites of the petals as they fluttered and spread.

'Come out!' Dell screamed at the hillside.

The wind settled.

'Come out!' he said again, then again, shouting so hard his voice began to break up. He turned the crossbow and took a big step towards me. 'I'll kill him!'

He took another.

'I'll put an arrow through his head!'

He was three feet from me, maybe even less. I waited, hands in the air, trying to show him I wasn't a threat, that the danger was coming from the hillside, from whatever was hidden out in the grass. It seemed to pass from me to him, my lack of threat, reassurance that I wasn't about to try anything, because he swung the crossbow back around, directing it out at the shadows, and – his voice hoarse – started shouting into the wind again.

'I'll come up there and kill you!'

He went back to the edge of the veranda.

'I'll fucking kill you!'

He scanned the hillside, looking along the arrow track, swinging the weapon from left to right. And then he placed his foot down on to the first step.

The wood instantly snapped under his weight, so rotten, so sodden, it just collapsed beneath him. He lurched forward, trying to grip the crossbow at the same time as trying to prevent himself from toppling over.

Sensing my chance, I threw myself at him.

He didn't have time to react. I smashed into him with as much power as I could muster, putting everything behind it. His foot was ripped out of the hole he'd created and both of us crashed through the banisters on the steps.

The *ping* of an arrow releasing.

We hit the long grass of the hillside hard, me on top of him. I landed with my knees bunched at his ribs, and felt something snap inside his skin: bones breaking and bending; muscles twisting. He yelled out, his voice lost in the rush of air exploding from him, his saliva flecking against my skin. But I ignored it and scrambled to my feet. Looking for his crossbow, I spotted it three or four feet away.

I went for it, scooped it up, yanked another arrow out of its housing and loaded it into the weapon. It took me longer than I wanted it to, but any worries I had about him coming at me were soon dispelled: he remained on his back, face creased up, holding his ribs.

He tried to speak, but the noise was like a wheeze from an old engine. His ribs were broken. He looked at me, blinked. He knew it was over.

I took in the hillside.

I couldn't see anything out there, not from the angle I was at. Against the ashen haze of early evening, it was just flecks of snow and acres of grass, lying across the hillside like a carpet. Off to my right, smudged behind mist, I could see the outline of Strathyde, the peak itself, hundreds of feet further into the sky.

'Hello?' I said.

My voice sounded small in the wind, in the whisper of the grass as it went from left to right, a dance I'd seen over and over since I'd been here. I glanced at Dell, still in the same position clutching his ribs, and then back out at the hillside.

Now someone was standing about twenty feet up the slope.

They were in a coat, cocooned by its blackness. The hood was up, but I could see strands of brown hair, the hint of pale skin. As they came forward, passing through the grass, I realized it was a woman, could see it from her shape, the way she moved. She was wearing grey weatherproof trousers and dark fur-lined boots, wet and scarred.

She moved between the graves, her head down, watching where her feet went, careful not to stand on the resting place of these victims; of five women and one man who never returned home.

Finally, she came to a stop.

'I know my husband's dead.'

She'd thrown back the hood of her coat.

'So now I want to know the truth about Richard,' she said softly. 'All of it.'

Her words were eloquent and exact, no hint of a slur, no impediment, just as there was no hint of infirmity to her body. She hadn't been paralysed by a stroke.

She'd just made the world believe she had.

## 77

Carla Presley came further forward. She stopped again a few feet from me, the hillside moving around her. Inside the coat, her face was a perfect oval. I could see a hint of a slope to her mouth – minor, negligible – confirmation that she hadn't lied about having a stroke.

But it hadn't confined her to a chair.

'It happened two years ago,' she said, referring to the stroke, 'before Richard left. For the year before he disappeared, I couldn't communicate with him. I just had to watch him. He lived out on the edge of town, and he'd come home to us, to see how I was, and he'd stay with me while Bill was out working, or getting drunk at the pub, and he'd talk to me, or he'd read to me.' A flicker of a smile. 'I'm his mum, so I know I'm biased, but I was always so proud of him. I still *am* proud of him, of course. He was so gentle.'

It was an echo of what Bill Presley had said.

*He had the most beautiful soul.*

'I had absolutely no idea where Richard went,' she said.

I remembered her reaction back at the house when I told her that her son was alive and living in the UK; the shock when I revealed he had no memory. It was why I felt like I could trust her: you couldn't fake that reaction, even if you could fake the rest of it.

'I had absolutely no idea,' she said again, quieter now. 'And I had no idea that Bill was lying to me either. I couldn't have imagined that he might know the truth about where Rich went and why. He loved that boy like I did. Bill could be difficult, selfish. He was an alcoholic. He'd fly off the handle about nothing and be simmering for days. He slapped me once and spent the weeks after apologizing, over and over, getting down on bended knee asking for forgiveness; and when I didn't forgive him, he flew off the handle again and stormed out. That was who he was. He was a man who it became impossible to love. But the one thing that never wavered, even for a second, was how he felt about Rich. So the thought that he might know something, it didn't cross my mind.'

She stopped, swallowed, and I saw the echoes of the stroke once again.

'Sorry,' she said. 'My speech has mostly recovered, but sometimes words catch and I struggle to say things the way I want.'

'Would you rather sit down inside?'

She nodded.

In the cabin, I found a chair for her and then returned to check on Dell. He looked up at me as I approached, eyes streaming, hand still pressed to his ribs. I dragged him to the steps of the cabin. He cried out as we moved, the sound wet in his throat, the grass flattening and rising again as his body snaked across it.

When we got to the steps, I set him down.

He wasn't going anywhere.

I headed up the steps again, into the back room, within sight of Dell. Even if he was capable of making a move, I could see him, and I'd be on him in seconds. I sat opposite Carla, in the gathering shadow of the mountain.

'Why pretend that you never recovered?'

Her lips flattened into a kind of grimace. 'At the time Richard disappeared, I could feel myself getting stronger. Well, physically stronger. Emotionally, I was a wreck. I was so panicked for Rich, so scared he might come to harm. When search parties didn't find him or Beth anywhere on the islands, I couldn't work out why they would even *want* to leave. It didn't make sense to me. But because I couldn't move very easily, because I was still having problems with my speech, I just had to sit there and watch. I watched Bill come home every night. I heard him out on the phone in his office, talking in whispers. I realized that, although I was improving, Bill hadn't even noticed. He was so consumed. In his head, I was exactly the same as I'd been since the day of the stroke. He still treated me in the same way. He talked *at* me, not to me; he carried me around, assuming I couldn't walk, couldn't do anything for myself at all. But the weirdest thing was, he never spoke about Rich. Our boy disappeared – and all Bill ever said about him was that there was no news.'

'He didn't seem upset?'

'Not upset enough. He didn't react how he *should* have reacted. If there was no news, if he genuinely didn't know where Rich was, he should have been in pieces. But instead he was so controlled. "There's no news, but we'll find him. There's no news, but we'll find him." He just learned the words by rote. That was why I began to get suspicious.'

The cabin moaned again in the wind.

'So I kept my recovery from him,' she said, looking down into her hands. Her hood shifted against the back of her head, and some of her hair escaped, twisted coils of brown, weaved with threads of silver-grey. 'I didn't want a carer, I didn't want to be looked in on, so I showed him enough improvement that he wouldn't be afraid of leaving me alone during the day, and I just sat there and watched. I watched him, listened. I let him install emergency buttons and rails in the bathroom, the stairlift. I let him do all of that so he wouldn't be home during the day and, when he disappeared to his office in the evenings to make calls, I knew that he'd never consider that I might be listening. I mean, he didn't think I could walk unaided.'

'What did you find out?'

She looked up at me. There was a flash of guilt in her face, a concession that she'd lied, cheated and tricked her husband and now there was never going to be a chance to say sorry. But then her expression solidified, as if she realized he'd done exactly the same to her, more than her, worse than anything she'd ever done to him, and she said, 'I went through his office. I searched it top to bottom. I found those newspaper cuttings. He'd buried them deep in a drawer and I couldn't figure out why. I wanted to find out more, but our Internet connection had stopped working and it wasn't like I could head outside and walk down to the library. I mean, I could. By then, I could *easily* do that. But I would have given myself away.'

She wiped the corner of her mouth. There was no saliva there – not in the same way as there had been earlier, at her house – but she'd become used to doing it, the routine of it, and now she did it automatically.

'But you know something?' she said. 'Our Internet *hadn't* stopped working – it had been switched off. I found a couple of statements in the office that showed Bill had cancelled it in January.'

She stopped again and looked at me, and I saw all I needed to: in the time between me leaving her house and now, she'd worked out the reasons why her husband had cancelled their Internet. Because, in January, Richard had washed up on the shores of Southampton Water, and his case had been covered by the papers there. And however small the risk was of Carla guessing her son had gone to the UK and *then* her trawling every single local media outlet in Britain for any trace of him, it still represented a risk. By getting rid of the Internet at home, Bill Presley reduced that risk to zero.

'No one else in Sophia knew about Richard?'

'No. It never got reported here.'

She halted, emotion rattling in her throat again. I wasn't sure if it was the mention of Richard, the idea of him losing his memory, or the lies she'd been told by her husband.

I glanced outside at Dell. He was just watching us; listening.

'You said you overheard Bill talking in his office?'

'Yes.'

'What did you hear?'

'For a long time, it was just snatches of things. Conversations with Jack Kilburn that didn't make a lot of sense to me. I didn't think any of them could be about Rich, not for a second; I thought Bill might be having an affair, or that he was in financial trouble. I even thought he might have some terminal disease and was too frightened to tell me. I kept listening to him, kept going back to his office when he was at work or out in the evening. I tried to get into his laptop, but it was locked. I went through his cabinets but it was just old cases.'

She glanced at Dell, his arm against the steps, wheezing softly, and a look of disgust twisted her face. 'Then I saw you coming towards my house again this afternoon,' she said, 'and I thought you were returning to ask me more questions. But you went right past, as if you were heading up into the hills; and ten, fifteen minutes after that, I saw him going the same way' – she gestured to Dell – 'only he was carrying a crossbow. I knew something wasn't right.'

Her eyes switched to the hillside.

'These hills,' she went on. 'We've heard so much about them. Everyone was so scared of what lay beyond the fence. Everyone understood that it was off-limits, even grown adults like me. If we didn't believe the stories about some monster, we believed there were landmines. Whatever was up here, we knew enough to keep away.' She stopped, her gaze returning to me. 'But look at what's up here. Just more lies.'

There was a long pause.

'Bill did something terrible,' Carla said.

I nodded. There were no words to comfort her, nothing to sugar-coat the truth about what her husband, Kilburn, Jessop and Dell had done here in 1987.

'I knew Bill was involved in something bad. Eventually, I just knew it.' She wiped her mouth again, stopping for a second. 'And then I knew it for sure about a week ago, because I heard him on the phone again.'

'Saying what?'

'Saying a name. Raker,' she said. 'I heard the name Raker.'

'You knew I was coming?'

'When I heard him talk about you, what you did for a living, I hoped you were.'

She looked across at Dell, his skin a pale moon against the half-light of the early evening, and then started trying to find something in the pocket of her coat. A moment later, she brought it out: a piece of A4 paper, folded into quarters.

'Here,' she said, holding it out to me.

'What's this?'

'Bill was gone before I got up this morning.'

I took the piece of paper from her and opened it up. It was a map, hand-drawn in felt-tip pen, of the Brink, the approach to the tarn, the lake, the cabin.

'He left that for me by the side of my bed.'

Below the map, he'd drawn a top-down illustration of the cabin, the rooms all marked off, the front and back verandas drawn on, the hillside out the back represented as six coffins. Beside most of the coffins he'd written names; beside a couple he hadn't written any name at all. Those were just *Female 20–30*. I didn't know if Presley couldn't remember the women's names, or if he'd never known them in the first place, and I wasn't sure which of the two was worse. But then my eyes were drawn to something else.

An *X* was marked over one of the rooms.

'Follow me,' I said to Carla, and led her out back.

The cold hit us like a wall, fierce and brutal. I looked down at Dell – his teeth chattering, his skin pale – then out to the graves on the hillside, some of the crosses bent over permanently by the wind. Then I felt around in my pocket for the key that Presley had given me at the lido. I thought it had been for the cabin; for the front or the back door. But it wasn't.

I looked along the slats of the veranda to the door at the end.

The key was for the one room I hadn't been into.

## 78

The door inched open.

Inside, a single bed was pushed up against one wall with a faded, threadbare mattress on top and a length of rope knotted around one of the bedposts. My gaze lingered on the rope, and then I looked across at the opposite wall, maybe only four feet away from the edge of the bed, where there was a chest of drawers. I stepped further in, the smell of mould in the air, and slid out the drawers, one after another. All of them were empty.

The only other piece of furniture was a TV/VCR combo unit, perched in the corner of the room on a side table and coated in a layer of dust. There was no mains electricity in the cabin, so the unit was attached to an oil-powered generator. It sat beneath the table, covered so thickly in cobwebs it was almost impossible to see it.

I glanced over my shoulder at Carla. She was standing in the doorway, the map still clutched in her hand. Her eyes flashed as she glanced from the television to the bed, to the rope, then to the chest of drawers.

To what was on top of the drawers.

An audio cassette player and a cassette.

I picked up the cassette, saw from the spools that it was about two-thirds used, and popped the lid on the player. Glancing at Carla again, wondering what we were going to find on the tape and whether she should listen to it, I slid it in, pushed the lid down again and gently pressed the Play button.

' . . . out of hand. Just totally out of hand.'

It was Bill Presley.

He was quiet, the silence filled with the crackle of the tape, the sound of the wind, the creak of the floorboards as Carla took an instinctive step closer to me, drawn by her husband's words. I quickly realized what this was: an account of that night in 1987. How so many bullets ended up in the walls. How so many people ended up in graves on a hill. I'd been wrong earlier: I'd seen the flowers and the crosses as the last act of a guilty man's life. But that wasn't quite the last act.

'Caleb Beck turned up here,' Presley said. I heard tears in his voice; the echoes of thirty years of secrets and remorse. His words were slurred too. 'He went fucking berserk. He'd been out looking at the stars and he saw us, or heard us, and he came storming up here and through the front door.' I heard Presley swallow, go to speak, then swallow again. 'I can hear Beck, even now. His voice; what he was screaming. "What's going on here? What the hell do you all think you're doing? This is *my* property." He was right. It *was* his, and we'd destroyed the place. Desecrated it. Booze, poker chips, smashed glass, empty bottles, puke. All the women. There was piles of weed just lying in packets on the tables. Most of us were half-drunk or stoned.'

As he faded out, I looked at Carla.

She was wiping her eyes.

Presley began again: 'Roland was in one of the bedrooms with Torres. We didn't actually know most of the women's names, but we knew hers. When Beck came into the cabin, Roland heard him and came running out of the bedroom. He barely had his bloody trousers on.' Presley made a sound in his throat, a kind of *it would have been funny on any other night*. 'Beck immediately goes for the jugular. He sees Roland and he zeroes in on him, because he *knows* Roland is the ringleader, because that's the type of person Roland is, and he says, "Your dad is going to hear about this. This is disgraceful. This is unacceptable."'

Presley stopped and, on the tape, there was the distinctive *pop* of a cork. The glug of liquid filling a tumbler. The *ching* of a bottle being placed back down.

'Roland wasn't scared of many things,' Presley said, the words softened by the booze, 'but he was scared of his dad. Not physically scared of him, but scared of upsetting him. Him and his old man, they were like peas in a pod. They were the same, but they had this weird relationship – it was cold and stand-offish, and Roland was always slagging him off, telling us that his dad was useless, in tons of debt, a disaster, stupid, an idiot, a failure, all this sort of thing. Yet Roland constantly sought his dad's approval, right up until the old man died in '92. So when Beck said he would tell Old Man Dell what had gone on at the cabin, he was pushing all the right buttons. He knew that, of all the things he could threaten Roland with – and there wasn't much that could get to Roland – that was the one. Of course, what Beck *didn't* know was that Roland had fucked up on an even bigger scale: he'd discovered his old man's contact book and had been through it, he'd found Selina Torres in it and persuaded her and four of her friends to fly across; he'd promised to pay their flights, their expenses and give them two grand each. And worse than all of that was that he'd taken the entire amount from his dad's safe – basically, the last of Old Man Dell's money.'

Presley quietened; the calm before the storm.

'It all happened so fast,' he said. I heard him take a drink, and then another. He cleared his throat, the tape crackling in the gaps between words. 'Roland pulled out this gun. I don't know where the hell he got it, because Roland was no marksman, but suddenly he had it. I don't think Beck thought he would fire it, I don't think any of us did, but you could feel this ripple go across the room. The air seemed to change. Roland pointed it at Beck.'

I looked at Carla; she looked back.

'Beck tried to grab it from him.'

I turned to the tape.

'And the gun went off in Beck's face.'

As Presley spoke, his voice wobbled, breaking apart, as if he still couldn't believe what he was saying, couldn't recognize the image burned on to the back of his eyes. On the tape, I heard him move, and when he spoke again he was closer to the recorder, his voice distorted, not just by the distance between him and the device, but by what he was having to describe.

'There was screaming,' he said, his voice so small now, it was like it was coming from somewhere outside the cabin. 'There was screaming and furniture got knocked over, and the booze and the drugs went everywhere. The women went crazy and started retreating into the corners of the room. I did too. I'm not too proud to admit it.' Another drink. 'And then one of the women – I think her name was Calista – she grabbed her clothes off the sofa and made a break for the back of the cabin. At this point, Roland's in a state of shock. I just remember him looking down at the gun, holding it like he didn't recognize it or know how to use it. Beck was dead at his feet and there was blood everywhere.'

The tape whirred, hissed.

'So Jack and Anthony, they went for their guns too.'

Another drink.

'They were sons of farmers. That's who we are here: farmers and hunters and fishermen. The banking, the tourism – that's not who we are. We're on the edge of the world with nothing around us but ocean and emptiness. It's the last wilderness. We were hunters and farmers and fishermen before anything else.'

Another drink.

'Jack and Ant went for their guns, and as soon as this Calista yanks open the rear door of the cabin – *bang* – Jack puts one in her back. I don't know what he was thinking; maybe that, if one got away, everything would go to shit for us. Or maybe he *wasn't* thinking, maybe that was the whole problem, but she died there on the veranda, bleeding through the slats. The others scattered.'

Another drink. Another.

'*Bang bang*, Ant does the second and the third. *Bang bang bang*, Roland does for Torres as she comes out of the bedroom. He's putting bullets all over the walls because he's such a terrible fucking shot, but by then, him and Jack are so pumped up on adrenalin, it barely even matters. They turn to me, because the last of the women is sitting next to me, crying so hard she can barely breathe. It's like I can feel her heart coming through her chest, even though I must be a foot away from her. Jack starts to come over, and she can see what's coming, and she grabs my arm and starts to beg for her life in Spanish, and I . . . I just . . . I . . .'

There was no sound of him taking a drink this time, only the noise of him sobbing. When I turned to Carla, she was crying too, staring at the tape in silence. In the spaces behind her, I could see just the vague hint of the hillside, the night setting in. I thought about Dell, about having left him alone out there, but even if he'd somehow made a break for it, it wouldn't really matter. He'd shattered his ribs. He could barely stand or breathe. He wasn't going to get far from this graveyard.

The end was coming for him.

'I watched the light go out in her eyes,' Presley said, harder to understand now. 'They shot her there while she was still looking at me, while she was still begging for her life. I had her blood all over me, bits of her brain on my face, and that was bad enough. But it's her eyes. I wake up and see them. I go to sleep and see them. It'll be thirty years next year, and it never stops, and do you know what hurts the most?' Finally, we could hear him take another drink, swallowing hard. 'One of them was Selina. One of them was called Calista. But I couldn't even tell you what this one's name was. I never found out.'

I stepped closer to the tape as Presley drifted into silence again, the cabin moaning like it had been exorcized of the memories that had tormented it.

'But all of that,' Presley said eventually, crippled by his burden, deformed by it, 'all of that wasn't even the worst thing I did. I helped bury Beck and those women on that slope. I went with the other three down to Beck's farm-house the next day to make sure there was nothing to connect us to his disappearance. I stood by and said nothing when Roland discovered holdalls full of money – literally, hundreds and hundreds of thousands of pounds – hidden under Beck's floorboards. And I stood by and said nothing, thirteen years later, when I got my share of it. I said nothing. I said nothing while Jack moved in on Fiona, a woman who never knew about the cash we'd stolen from her husband – from *her* – and had no idea what had happened to Beck. I helped sow the seeds of rumour about the Brink. I helped create the insanity that exists in this town. But all of that isn't why I'm going to burn in hell . . .'

I waited, frozen to the spot.

'I'm so sorry, Carla.'

It wasn't what I'd expected from him. I glanced at her, her tears like a road map on her face, her frown in a deep V, and she looked back at me – confused – and said, 'What? What does he mean? What does he mean by "I'm so sorry, C–"'

'You went out at the last minute. Your sister was sick, so you stayed with her for the night in St George.'

Presley again.

'I didn't know what else to do.'

I could feel panic starting to grip me.

'I tied him up.'

Presley took another drink.

'That was the worst thing I ever did.'

He started sobbing again.

As the tape rolled on, the room filled with the sound of

Bill Presley crying, and my eyes pinged from Carla to the bed, to the rope knotted around the bedpost.

*I tied him up.*

I looked at the TV-VCR unit. It was a Sharp, built in 1985 and shipped over from the UK according to a sticker on its flank. Bending down at the generator, I brushed the cobwebs away, tiny insects fleeing the invasion, and then switched it on. It chugged, spat, and seemed like it was about to die again. But then, slowly, steadily, it began to find a rhythm and the TV unit switched itself on.

I pressed the Eject button on the VCR and, with a clunk, the slot spat out a VHS tape. On the end of the tape, facing out, was a printed label. It said: WINTER SPECIAL – JULY 1987. The tape was almost thirty years old. The unit was even older. They'd both been here the night six people were killed in the room next door.

*No*, I thought. *No, not this.*

I pushed the tape back into the player.

In the corner of the screen, a small videotape icon flashed. I glanced at Carla who had come further in, the temperature so cold now, our breath was gathering in front of our faces, even inside. Within a couple of seconds, the audio cassette tape had clicked off, Presley's sobs lost for ever, and a picture had sprung into life on the combo unit.

*Kids' Hour* started.

I watched the familiar TV mast intro, the one Richard had remembered so well even as Naomi Russum tried to chip away at his recollection of it. I felt Carla move closer as the intro finished and a presenter appeared on-screen. The sound was poor, choppy, but I could hear enough:

the presenter was saying that this was a special episode of the programme; that they were going to show a one-off thirty-minute drama, set on the Empress Islands.

*No. No, don't let it be this.*

The opening credits of the drama started rolling.

*Please don't let it be this.*

I'd never seen the film before but, as soon as the credits were finished and the first scene faded in, I began to feel nauseous. On-screen, a boy of eight or nine was walking through a kitchen. He stopped to pick a banana out of a fruit bowl on the table and then the picture crunched again, warped, reshaped.

As I watched, I remembered again what Presley had said to me at the lido: *I read online that he can remember looking out at a beach as a kid. I read that they think it might have been where he grew up. It isn't. He didn't grow up by the beach.*

*Just tell him I'm sorry.*

By the time I refocused my attention on the TV, the picture had settled again and the boy was heading towards the kitchen window. He stopped in front of it and looked out, peeling the banana. As I watched, I remembered something: Richard telling me how bananas were one of his connectors; how he'd instinctively known he would love them even before he'd ever had the chance to taste one.

On-screen, the camera moved in behind the boy, taking in the dome of his head in silhouette and the view beyond him. There was a smooth bank of grass immediately in front of the house – and then a sweep of white beach and a bay.

It was Richard's memory.

The window. The beach. The bay.

It wasn't somewhere he'd grown up: it was a drama he'd watched, over and over and over again on that night in 1987. Because Carla had gone out at the last minute when her sister became sick, and Presley hadn't known what else to do. He'd already committed to coming up to the cabin. He couldn't back out.

So he'd brought the four-year-old Richard with him.

He'd locked him in here with this VCR.

And he'd tied him to the bed so he wouldn't wander off.

## 79

The interviews took five days.

I sat in the poky confines of the converted sheep station on the slopes of Sophia and answered questions from some of the officers who'd worked under Bill Presley. Most were still in shock, unable to reconcile my descriptions of what had happened out at the cabin – on the edge of a tarn a lot of them had never been to, or even knew existed – with what they knew of the man they'd worked with.

It seemed to be broadly accepted that Presley liked a drink, but in a place where the bottom of a bottle was sometimes the only place to seek solace, it wasn't viewed as any sort of crime by the locals, and certainly wasn't an indication of a person's morality. Presley had served the police force for thirty years, he was genial and sociable and he cared for a disabled wife, and, for the first few days, that bought him some goodwill. When his name came up, people – even the officers who knew what he'd done – would continue to speak highly of him. But that gradually began to change as detectives started arriving from the UK – at the request of the Empress Islands governor in St George – to lead an independent investigation.

All three UK detectives were from the Met, and all three of them sat in the same room as me and listened to my account of what had happened during the search for Richard Presley's memories. I told them the truth, mostly, except about Marek's death. When we got on to the subject of that, I said I had no idea where he was; that the last time I saw him was when Beth and I had locked him in the office on the ship. I was certain that the Met team knew about me, my history with the police back home, the unintentional enemies I'd made there through my cases, but they never brought it up and never tried to use it as a way to attack me. The only time we hit any resistance, any major discord, was when we got on to the subject of the Brink.

The people in the town closed up about it in the days after. No one would talk about what was out there, or they denied ever hearing any rumours, or they just frowned and sat there in silence. It was hard to tell whether it was out of embarrassment, anger at having been strung along for so many years, or whether – somewhere much deeper down – the stories had become so powerful and so ingrained that a part of them still believed them.

'Did they honestly think there was some sort of monster out there?' one of the female detectives asked me.

All three of them were the same. They sat there with half-smiles on their faces, unable to quite believe that so many in the community had been taken in by the idea, and it was easy to see it from their point of view now. They'd arrived at the end, when the truth was lying in graves on a snow-streaked hillside.

But I'd arrived in the days before that, and as much as I'd tried to deny it, I'd been out on that mountain in the mist and all it took was a glimpse of something strange to shake the foundations of my belief. Like Dell had said to me, it was a card trick. It was an illusion.

It didn't have to be real, it just had to be real enough.

Between interviews, in my moments alone, at night when I'd stare up into the darkness of my tiny room at the bed and breakfast unable to sleep, I'd find it hard to think about anything except that bed in the room at the cabin. The VHS tape in the player. The rope. The four-year-old boy who was tied up, at his ankle or at his wrist, and made to watch the same programme over and over again while his father was in the next room. He must have heard the guns going off, the screams of the women as well. He must have heard the footsteps out on the veranda. But when Richard was back home, if he had chosen to say anything to his mum, to people who might listen, it would have been written off as confusion, as the wild imagination of a young boy.

On the tape, Bill Presley never talked about how Richard was in the days after, and Carla didn't remember Richard ever mentioning anything to her about his father tying him up, or the sounds of gunshots and people shouting from the room next door. At four, he was probably too young to contextualize the sounds, even if being bound to a bed would have seemed odd and upsetting, regardless of how much his father had tried to comfort him about it. It wouldn't have been the sort of thing that his dad usually did – every account I'd been given, even from Carla, was of a man who loved his son unconditionally – so it wouldn't have been a surprise if Richard had mentioned something in the days afterwards.

But he hadn't, or at least no one could say otherwise.

Anthony Jessop was long dead. Kilburn was in the morgue. Roland Dell might have remembered, and was perhaps the only person left who could, but when I asked the detectives if he ever mentioned anything about the four-year-old Richard in his interviews, they said he didn't, that he only remembered Presley bringing the kid along. After that, the police had moved on again, to other things, their interrogation of Dell focusing on bigger issues: six bodies in the hillside behind the cabin; the theft of what turned out to be nearly nine hundred thousand pounds from Caleb Beck; and the murder of Penny Beck by Alexander Marek. They wanted to know about Naomi Russum as well, because it turned out she and Dell had been in a relationship in the early 2000s, and that she'd borrowed money from Dell – money he'd stolen from Beck – to help start her clinic. She'd been reluctant to deceive Richard, that much had always been obvious, but she'd chosen to go along with Dell's lies all the same.

I understood why those things seemed bigger.

I understood how important they were.

Yet I couldn't stop thinking about a four-year-old boy being tied to a bedpost; about the memory of a beach that had become everything to his future self; about the fact that he'd believed it had been the view from his family home.

He'd looked on it as an image to cherish, to build on, to make something of; a way to regain a life he so desperately wanted to remember and be part of again. But when it came down to it, the man who'd betrayed him the most – his father – had been the only one who'd called it correctly.

Maybe it was better that he didn't remember.

And perhaps it was the exhaustion of the case, of

following it so far into the rabbit hole that I'd ended up at the edge of the world, but when I lay awake in the darkness of that room thinking about that boy, I wanted to cry for him. I wanted to cry for Penny and Beth as well, who'd been tied to a fence in the dark.

Because we'd all been those children once.

And we'd all trusted the people who loved us.

# 80

When the *Olympia* dropped anchor at Buenos Aires four days after leaving the Empress Islands, Argentinian police officers and one of the Met detectives were waiting for it. They boarded the ship and found Beth Kilburn locked in an interview room, where she'd been kept for almost the entire journey across from the islands; and they found security staff that had been on the payroll of Roland Dell since Marek had come aboard looking for Beth back in January.

Beth returned to the islands, but only for the duration of the interviews. Her promise never to return had been broken, but not for long: a week after the interviews ended, she gathered her things together and flew to Cape Town. Thirty-six hours later, she landed in the UK.

I helped her out for a while, letting her crash in my spare room, and then she found a job in a local supermarket and moved into a shared house. At some point after that, she'd got in touch with Richard, but she told me their meeting had been weird, and difficult, and uncomfortable, and she wasn't sure if they were going to see each other again. I felt sad at that, at the idea of a bond that – through no fault of their own – could never be properly repaired, and I felt even more upset as we sat and had coffee one day and Beth, totally out of nowhere, burst into tears and started telling me she missed Penny.

I gathered her hands in mine and said nothing, because anything I said would be worthless.

But then something changed.

On a bright day in December, I met Jacob Howson for a drink in a café close to the Red Tree School. We talked about his time lying low on the south coast, about how the school was under investigation, and how Roland Dell would never see daylight again, except from a prison yard. The whole time, Howson was quiet, worn down, suffering for the guilt he carried over Penny's death and his choice to remain silent.

The police had interviewed him as Penny's boyfriend and not charged him with anything, and he kept looking for reassurance that it was a good sign. But there was a haunted aspect to him, a kind of premonitory look to his eyes, that said he knew it was only a matter of time before they realized he'd withheld information.

Perhaps because of that, he told me he'd been going back over his house, dismantling furniture, looking inside books, under beds, in wardrobes, in a new attempt to see if he'd missed anything from Penny. It was guilt again, the lingering knowledge that he'd betrayed her: he wanted to feel like he was helping, and he wanted to believe that, somewhere, there was a message of forgiveness for him.

But it turned out the message wasn't for him.

'I found this,' he said, handing me a folded piece of paper.

It was a handwritten letter, dated a week before Penny went missing, her writing rushed, untidy, words crossed out, some illegible. It was as if, at the time she wrote it, she knew something bad was coming. She'd got into the security suite at the Red Tree, she'd found the truth, and now the walls were closing in.

I read the letter with a heavy heart, knowing all that had followed it, and when I got to the end of it – like those moments when I lay awake in the dark of the bed and breakfast in Sophia – I found it hard to rein in my emotions.

'Can I take this?' I asked Howson.

'Yes,' he said, seeing it had got to me. 'Yes, of course you can.'

I met Beth the next day in our usual spot, a coffee shop halfway between my house and the supermarket in which she worked, and I gave her the letter. She took it, saw it was Penny's handwriting, and immediately began to well up. And having read it countless times myself, even in the short time it was in my possession, it wasn't hard to understand why.

*Beth,*

*What we said at the end isn't important. They were just words. They never mattered to me, because I knew they weren't true, so they shouldn't matter to you. What we were then, the things that were said before I left, that wasn't us. That wasn't who we were to each other. So don't fret on them. Whatever's to come from here, you mustn't ever fret on them.*

*There was never anything to forgive because you never did anything wrong. Neither of us did.*

*We were innocent.*

*We were children.*

*So wherever I am when you read this, all you need to know is this: you were my sister, you always will be, and I'll never stop loving you.*

*Penny x*

# 81

On the day I flew home from the Empress Islands, a month before Penny's letter to Beth was unearthed, I'd spent a morning in Sophia talking to Richard Presley on the phone, trying to fill in as many other blanks as I could. He listened quietly, only offering the occasional question, and when I was done he took a long breath, as if he wasn't quite sure where to go next.

'What's it like there?' he asked.

'The Empress Islands?' I was sitting on the steps of the police station, mist clinging to the folds of the mountain once again. It was damp, cold, grey. I looked around at the tin roofs, at the knotty layout of the town, listening to the silence of the place. 'I guess it's like a Britain I don't really know,' I said.

He was quiet for a moment.

'So do you like it there?'

I thought about lying to him, telling him I did, just in case he wanted to come back and make a life for himself on the islands again. But I couldn't bring myself to do it. He'd been lied to enough.

'No,' I said eventually. 'I'm looking forward to getting home.'

During our conversation, I'd stopped short of telling him about that night in the cabin, of destroying his recollection of what he thought he'd seen from the window of his childhood home, not because I'd been afraid to – although the thought had made me anxious – but because Carla had asked me to. At some point after we came back down from the Brink, she decided that she wanted to tell him about that night herself.

She'd been there, alongside me, while her husband's confession had been playing on the tape, so she knew what had gone on; and anything she wasn't able to work out in those moments, I filled in for her in the hours that followed. Yet at no point did I feel completely at ease about it. I trusted her ability to deliver the news in the most sensitive way possible – she was his mother, after all; she knew him better than anyone else. But that was just the point: Richard Presley wasn't the same person who'd left the islands almost a year ago. He wasn't the same person she'd been a mother to for thirty-three years. He didn't know her, as far as he could remember had never met her, and because of that, I'd begun to wonder if such profound information would be better coming from someone like Reverend Parsons. Richard had built a relationship with him. He trusted Parsons. Parsons had been there for him in the months after he turned up at Southampton Water, when everyone else – all the media attention – had started to fade. In lieu of friends or a family coming forward, Parsons had become something of a father figure to Richard.

I floated the idea of using Parsons to Carla, though never pushed too hard because ultimately it wasn't my decision. But, as it turned out, it only took one phone call with Richard for Carla to start seeing the sense in it. As I watched her speaking to her son for the first time in two years, I saw her start to understand: his voice was the same, his accent, the way he spoke about things. But it wasn't the son she remembered. Not quite.

I introduced Richard to his mother on the phone, and when she said hello back, the two of them seemed uncertain where to go next. I filled in the gaps, trying to connect them to one another, and slowly the conversation began to gather momentum. Carla began telling her son what he was like as a boy, what he was like as an adult, and then she mentioned Bill Presley and stopped.

'Is my dad there too?' Richard asked.

I looked at Carla.

'No,' she said, looking back at me. Tears flashed in her eyes. 'No, he's not, sweetheart. Your dad . . .' She stopped again. 'Your dad was, um . . . He was . . . He . . .'

'He passed on,' I said.

'Oh.'

Just *oh*. He wasn't upset. He didn't know his father enough to be upset.

So that was the point at which Carla changed her mind. That was when she understood that, even if she did end up telling Richard the truth about his memories, maybe it was better if Parsons was present as well.

A month later, I set something up.

Carla flew over to the UK and I met her, Richard and Reverend Parsons at the church in Dorset. We sat in the room that Richard and I had used during our first ever conversation, and Carla told her son everything: who he was, where he came from, what he loved doing as a kid, who he'd become as an adult. She told him the truth about his father, and though I could see the conflict in her, the echo of the confession we'd heard on the audio tape, she was fair to Bill Presley.

To start with, the conversation was stilted, often awkward, and I just sat, slightly removed from the others, and listened. Parsons was the glue that bound it, redirecting it and threading it together, and I knew that it had been the correct decision to involve him. And, after a while, things began to loosen up a little. There were jokes between them, light-hearted comments, and Carla was natural and engaging when she talked about Richard's childhood.

'We used to have a Labrador called Wolf,' she told her son at one point. 'It was ironic because he was the soppiest dog ever. You used to love him.'

'Did I take him for walks?'

'All the time,' she said. 'All the time.'

Her fingers were pressed flat to the table and I could see that she wanted to touch her son's hand – but she didn't. She said, 'You had so much fun with that dog.'

'Did he sleep on my bed?'

'When we let him.' She smiled. 'You had this old Action Man – one of his arms was missing and you'd drawn a beard on him with marker pen – and you used to bury him in the garden, a different place each time, and Wolf would have to find him.' Carla smiled again, but this time there was a hint of sadness to it. 'When Wolf wasn't around, you'd make your dad find the Action Man instead. You'd literally make him get down on his hands and knees and bark, and he would do it. You'd ride around on his back, and he'd do it. He'd always do it. The two of you . . .' Her voice trailed off, and she lifted her hand off the table and wiped at an eye. 'Your father loved you, that's all,' she said softly. 'We both loved you so much.'

The emotion vibrated in her throat and it took a moment for her to gather herself, but then she did and she went on to talk more about what they used to do as a family, what Richard liked and what he didn't.

It was polite and pleasant, often quite tame.

It was respectful, and gentle, and quiet.

But, for now, for a mother trying to make sense of everything and the son she thought she'd lost, all of those things were enough.

# Acknowledgements

Writing a novel is only ever the start of the publishing process and, as always, this book would never have been possible without the brilliant team at Michael Joseph – they really are some of the most talented, most creative and plain nicest people I've ever had the pleasure to work with. Thank you to everyone there who has had a hand in bringing *I Am Missing* to life, both within MJ and across Penguin as a whole.

An extra special shout-out to my former editor, Emad Akhtar, who had been trying to persuade me for a while to write a book where the missing person wasn't physically missing but had actually suffered memory loss. It all seems a bit silly now, but back then I genuinely couldn't see how that one tiny idea would sustain an entire novel, so kept telling him no. Not only, then, am I enormously grateful to him for his persistence, but also hugely appreciative of everything he did for me during his time at Penguin, including his hard work on the first draft of *I Am Missing*.

A giant-sized thank you is also due to Maxine Hitchcock, who picked up the reins once Emad left, who delved into subsequent drafts and helped improve them immeasurably, and who has been an absolutely amazing advocate for the book ever since. Finally, thank you to Caroline Pretty, my eagle-eyed copy-editor on all eight books, and supreme unraveller of timelines that make no sense.

My agent, Camilla Wray, is officially The Best. In fact, there isn't a day that goes by when I don't feel grateful for her advice, patience, ability to deal with mid-manuscript meltdowns, and random stories about dogs and guinea pigs. She's a brilliant agent, a lovely person and a great friend. Thank you to the ladies at Darley Anderson as well, particularly Mary, Emma and Kristina in foreign rights, Sheila in film and TV, and Rosanna in the bank vault.

To Mum, Dad, Lucy and the rest of my amazing family: thank you so much for everything you do for me. To Erin, who makes me so proud, and to Sharlé, who gets to experience the whole gamut of emotions from word one to word last (and always pretends not to mind) – I couldn't do this without either of you.

And, finally, the biggest thank you of all goes out to my wonderful readers. Without your support, there would be no *I Am Missing*, no Raker books at all in fact, and I wouldn't be spending my days dreaming up new and exciting ways to make people disappear.

# Reading Group Discussion Points

1. Discuss how you think technology has changed the work of the police. Is it ultimately a help or a hindrance to finding criminals and victims?

2. Richard Kite is in some ways a victim of bureaucracy as well as of his own amnesia. Discuss the unexpected ways loss of identity could make an impact on someone.

3. The police tell Jacob Howson that 'a person has the right to disappear'. Do you agree with this?

4. Do you think the inhabitants of Sophia were foolish to believe the rumours about the Brink? Or is it human nature to fear the unknown?

5. Bill Presley tells Raker that Richard is better off not remembering his past. Is this true, and do you think it could ever be right for a parent to hide the truth from their child?

6. Which characters do you think are victims in this story, and which do you think are in control of their fates?

7. Is greed at the root of all the crimes in this story? Or are there other factors at play?

8. Are Roland, Jack, Anthony and Bill all equally guilty for what happened at the cabin? Why, or why not?

9. Discuss the role of place in this story. How do the various locations shape the characters and the action?

10. Is it dangerous to trust in the people who are closest to you? Or is this ultimately what could have saved Penny?

11. David Raker succeeds in solving the mystery, but do you think the outcome of the case is a good one for Richard?

12. How does the case affect David Raker? What parallels can you detect between his life and those of the people he works with?

Read on for an
exclusive extract from
Tim Weaver's next
David Raker novel

Coming summer 2018

# I

After it was all over, they let me watch the footage of her entering the police station. She seemed small, almost curved, as if her spine was arched or she might be in pain, and she was wearing a green raincoat and a pair of black court shoes. The quality of the surveillance film was poor, the frame rate set low, so that it made it disorientating, a series of jerky movements played out against the stillness of the station's front desk.

She paused at the entrance to start with, holding the main door ajar so that light leaked in across the tiled floor and seemed to bleach the one side of her face. The faded colours of the film didn't help, reducing blacks to greys and everything else to pastels, and even when she let the door go again and it snapped shut behind her, her features didn't quite articulate. Her gaze was a dark blob, her blonde hair appeared grey. I couldn't see anything of the slight freckling that passed from one cheek to the other, crossing the bridge of her nose; not the blue and green flash of her eyes. Under the hard glare of the camera, she may as well have been just another visitor to a police station.

A stranger, nothing else.

Once she let the door go, she headed across the room to the front desk. On the timecode in the corner I could see it was just before 8 a.m. An officer in her mid-forties was standing behind the counter, engaged in conversation with someone else, a kid in his late teens with a black eye and bloodied cheek. The woman waited patiently behind the teenager until the front desk officer told her to go and take a seat. She did so, almost reluctantly, her head down, her feet barely seeming to carry her to where there was a bank of chairs.

Ten minutes passed. The angle of the camera made it hard to see her, her head bowed, her hands knotted together in her lap, but then, after the desk officer finished with the teenager and told him to take a seat, she beckoned the woman back across to the counter. I met the desk officer when I turned up at the station in the hours after: she had short black hair flecked with grey and a scar high on her left cheek, but on the film I couldn't see the detail in either, just a vague impression of who she was.

The woman stopped at the counter.

The desk officer bent slightly, so that her head was level with the woman's and even though the film's frame rate was low and it didn't record her lip movements in real-time, I could still tell what she'd asked the woman.

*You all right, love?*

The woman didn't respond immediately. Instead, she reached into the pocket of her coat and started looking for something. It began as a slow movement, but then became more frantic when she couldn't find what she was looking for. She checked one pocket, then another, and in the third she found what she was after: a piece of paper.

As she unfolded it, she finally responded to the officer.

*Hello.*

I couldn't tell what the woman said after that, the frame rate making it all but impossible to follow the patterns of her mouth, but she shifted position and, because the camera was fixed to the wall about a foot and a half above her, I could see more of her, could see there was just a single line on the piece of paper. Under the pale rinse of the room's strip lights, her hair definitely looked blonde now, not grey, and it had been tied into a loose ponytail. Despite that, it was messy and unkempt, stray strands everywhere, at her collar, across her face, and even within the confines of the film, the way it twitched and jarred between frames, it was easy to tell that she was agitated.

Finally, her eyes met the officer's and the woman held up the piece of paper and started to talk. I could see the teenager – seated close to her – look up from his lap, as if sparked into life by what the woman was saying. They told me afterwards that the woman had been crying, that it was difficult to understand what she was talking about, that her voice, the things that she was saying, were hard to process; she was rambling, or distressed, or both. I watched the desk officer lean in towards her, a hand up in front of her, telling the woman to calm down. I watched the woman pause for a moment, her breathing – even through the surveillance footage – appearing to slow, her body swaying slightly, her shoulders moving up and down and up and down, like a piston.

She gestured to the piece of paper again.

And this time I could read her lips clearly.

*Find him.*

# 2

The call came on 28 December.

I'd spent Christmas with my daughter, Annabel, in her house in south Devon. She lived at the end of a cul-de-sac, within sight of a lake, on the edges of Buckfastleigh. Annabel was twenty-seven, her sister Olivia – who wasn't mine, but who I looked out for just the same – was twelve, and although Liv was past the point of believing that someone came down the chimney with a sackful of presents, she was still a kid, and kids always made Christmas more fun. We opened gifts, we watched old movies and played even older board games, we ate and drank and chased Annabel's dog across a Dartmoor flecked in frost, and then I curled up with them in the evenings on the sofa and realized how little I missed London. It was where I lived, where my work was, but it was also where my home stood, empty even when I was inside it. It had been that way, and felt like that, every day for eight years, ever since my wife Derryn had died.

The morning of the call, I woke early and went for a run, following the lanes to the west of the house as they gently rose towards the heart of the moors. It was cold, the trees skeletal, the hedgerows thinned out by winter, ice gathered in slim sheets – like panes of glass – on the country roads. After four miles, I hit a reservoir, a bridge crossing it from one side to the other. Close by, cows grazed in the grass, hemmed in by wire fences, and I could see a farmer and his dog, way off into the distance, the early morning light winking in the windows of a tractor. I carried on for a while longer until I reached a narrow road set upon a hill with views across a valley of green and brown fields, all perfectly stitched together. Breathless, I paused there and took in the view.

That was when my phone started ringing.

I had it strapped to my arm, the mobile mapping my route, and I awkwardly tried to release it, first from the headphones I had plugged in, then from the pouch it was secured inside. When I finally got it out, I could see it was a central London number, and guessed it would probably be someone who needed my help, somebody whose loved one had gone missing. Very briefly, I toyed with the idea of not answering it at all, of protecting my time off, this time alone with a daughter I'd only known for five years, and was still getting to know. But then reality hit. The missing were my ballast. In the time since Derryn had died, they'd been my lifeblood, the only way I could breathe properly. This break would have to end and, sooner or later, I'd have to return to London and, when I did, my work would become my anchor again.

'David Raker.'

'Mr Raker, my name's Detective Sergeant Catherine Field.'

Thrown for a moment, I tried to recall if I'd come across Field before, or if I'd ever heard anyone mention her name.

'How can I help you?'

'It's, uh, it's a bit of a weird one, really,' Field responded then paused. 'We've had someone walk into the station here at Charing Cross this morning. She seems quite confused.' Another pause. 'Or maybe she's not confused. I don't know, to be honest.'

'Okay,' I said, unsure where this was going.

'She doesn't have anything on her – no phone, no ID. The only thing she brought along with her is a scrap of paper. It's got your telephone number on it.'

I looked out at the view, my body beginning to cool down, the sweat freezing against my skin. My website was only basic, little more than an overview and a contact form, but it listed my email address and a phone number.

'I expect she found my number online,' I said.

'Maybe,' Field replied.

'You don't think that's it?'

'I, uh . . . I don't know.' Field cleared her throat, the line drifting a little. 'This woman, she's telling us that she's been missing since 2009.' She went quiet again.

'So are you saying she wants my help?'

'I'm not sure what she wants.'

'What do you mean?'

'I mean, she says she knows you.'

'Knows me how?'

Field cleared her throat for a second time.

'She says she's your wife.'

I frowned. 'My *wife*?'

'That's what she says.'

'No,' I said. 'No, my wife has been dead for eight years.'

'Since 2009,' Field replied. 'I know, I just read that online.'

I waited for her to continue, to say something else, to

tell me this was a joke at my expense, some bad taste prank. But she didn't. Instead, she said something worse.

'This woman, she says her name's Derryn Raker.'

'What?'

'Derryn Alexandra Raker.'

'No,' I said. 'No way. She's lying.'

'She told us you'd say that.'

'Because it's not Derryn. Derryn's dead.'

'Yes, well, that's the other thing she told us,' Field said, her voice even, hard to intepret or analyse. 'She says that everything you believed about her death was a lie.'

# Broken Heart

A woman drives to a beautiful headland overlooking the Devon coast. She is never seen again, and no trace of where she went can be found.

The woman's sister calls missing persons investigator David Raker. As Raker tries to find her whereabouts – fearing the worst – he learns that she was recently widowed from a reclusive film director.

It seems that, going through her husband's belongings, she found a secret so dark and shocking that it forced her to leave her entire life behind. Chasing the truth will consume Raker and place him in grave danger...

Don't miss a single case:

The *Sunday Times* bestselling
David Raker Missing Persons Series

# Chasing the Dead

*One year ago, Alex Towne's body was found.*
*One month ago, his mother saw him on the street.*
*One week ago, David Raker agreed to look for him.*
*Now he wishes he hadn't.*

Mary Towne's son, Alex, went missing six years ago.
Five years later he finally turned up – as a corpse
in a car wreck. Missing persons investigator David
Raker doesn't want the work: it's clearly a sad but
hopeless case of mistaken identity brought to him by
a woman unable to let go of her son. But haunted by
a loss of his own, Raker reluctantly agrees.

Big mistake.

For as he digs deeper, he discovers that Alex's
life was not the innocent one his mother believed.
Buried in his past are secrets that were never meant
to be found – and dark, dangerous men willing to kill
to protect them.

Soon Raker will discover that there are things far
worse than death . . .

# The Dead Tracks

Seventeen-year-old Megan Carver was an unlikely runaway. A straight-A student from a happy home, she studied hard and rarely got into trouble. Six months on, she's never been found.

Missing persons investigator David Raker knows what it's like to grieve. He knows the shadowy world of the lost too. So, when he's hired by Megan's parents to find out what happened, he recognizes their pain – but knows that the darkest secrets can be buried deep.

And Megan's secrets could cost him his life.

Because as Raker investigates her disappearance, he realizes everything is a lie. People close to her are dead. Others are too terrified to talk. And soon the conspiracy of silence leads Raker towards a forest on the edge of the city. A place with a horrifying history – which was once the hunting ground for a brutal, twisted serial killer.

A place known as the Dead Tracks. . .

# Vanished

No life is perfect. Everyone has secrets.

For millions of Londoners, the morning of
17 December is just like any other. But not for
Sam Wren. An hour after leaving home, he gets
onto a tube train – and never gets off again. No
eyewitnesses. No trace of him on security cameras.
Six months later, he's still missing.

Out of options and desperate for answers,
Sam's wife Julia hires David Raker to track him
down. Raker has made a career out of finding the
lost. He knows how they think. And, in missing
person cases, the only certainty is that everyone
has something to hide.

But in this case the secrets go deeper than
anyone imagined.

For, as Raker starts to suspect that even the police
are lying to him, someone is watching. Someone who
knows what happened on the tube that day. And, with
Raker in his sights, he'll do anything to keep Sam's
secrets to himself . . .

# Never Coming Back

A secret that will change lives forever . . .

It was supposed to be the start of a big night out. But when Emily Kane arrives at her sister Carrie's house, she finds the front door unlocked and no one inside. Dinner's cooking, the TV's on. Carrie, her husband and their two daughters are gone.

When the police draw a blank, Emily asks missing persons investigator David Raker to find them. It's clear someone doesn't want the family found.

But as he gets closer to the truth, Raker begins to uncover evidence of a sinister cover-up, spanning decades and costing countless lives. And worse, in trying to find Emily's missing family, he might just have made himself the next target ...

# Fall From Grace

## NO GOODBYE

When Leonard and Ellie Franks leave London for
retirement in secluded Dartmoor everything seems
perfect. Until their new life is shattered. One evening
Leonard heads outside to fetch firewood –
and never returns.

## NO TRACE

Nine months later, with the investigation at a
dead end, Leonard's family turn to David Raker – a
missing persons investigator. Nothing could prepare
Raker for what he uncovers.

## NOWHERE TO HIDE

At the heart of this disappearance lies a devastating
secret. And when Raker realises how deep the lies
go, it's not just him in danger – it's everyone
he cares about.

# What Remains

Colm Healy used to be one of the Met's best detectives. Until, haunted by the unsolved murders of a mother and her twin daughters, his failure to find an elusive killer left his life in ruins.

Missing persons investigator David Raker is the only friend Healy has left. As they reopen the investigation together, Raker learns the hard way how this case breeds obsession – and how an unsolvable puzzle can break even the best detective.

Their search takes them down a trail of darkness, unravelling a thread of tragedy, and forces them to sacrifice everything they have left.